The Late Child

THE
LATE
CHILD

A NOVEL

Larry
McMurtry

ORION

The right of Larry McMurtry to be identified as
the author of this work has been asserted by him
in accordance with the Copyright, Designs
and Patents Act 1988.

First published in Great Britain in 1996 by
Orion
An imprint of Orion Books Ltd
Orion House, 5 Upper St Matin's Lane
London WC2H 9EA

A CIP catalogue record for this book
is available from the British Library

ISBN 0 75280 070 1

Printed and bound in Great Britain by
Butler & Tanner Ltd, Frome and London

For Curtis

Take me back to Tulsa,
I'm too young to marry. . . .

Bob Wills

Book
One

1.

When Harmony got to the line in the letter that told her Pepper was dead, she stopped reading the letter and stuffed it in a glass. She had been home from her job at the recycling plant in north Las Vegas maybe five minutes, just long enough to drink a glass of iced tea. The sides of the glass were still wet—moisture soon began to soak through the yellow paper the letter was written on. Harmony watched this process with a little bit of hope: maybe this terrible information would just soak away and not be true.

Harmony felt like pouring more iced tea into the glass to make the soaking happen more quickly. Just yesterday she had complained to the kids at the recycling plant that she never got any interesting mail. Day after day her mailbox would be stuffed with flyers from supermarkets or department stores, informing her of big savings she could realize if she acted quickly. If something else happened to show up in her mailbox it was usually just a bill she couldn't afford to pay, or an ugly letter from a collection agency, telling her she better pay the bill anyway, even if she was down to around eight dollars in her checking account, the amount that always seemed to be there when she got worried enough to check her balance.

Now, though—if the words in the letter were true—a bill had come that she could never pay. The only feeling she had immediately was that she didn't want the letter so close to her, so she opened the screen and pitched the glass out in the yard. Her apartment was first-floor; the glass didn't break when she threw it out. It rolled up against a little green cactus and stopped. The letter was still in it, yellow as ever.

Jimmy Bangor, Harmony's boyfriend, happened to be coming into the little patio of the apartment building just when Harmony pitched the glass with the letter in it out the window. Jimmy Bangor was a man not much troubled by curiosity—he took life as it came, as he was fond of saying—but the fact that Harmony, the most stable girlfriend he had ever had, had just thrown a perfectly good glass out the window of their apartment did catch his big brown eyes. Jimmy was a parking lot attendant at Caesar's; he spent many long days squeezing himself into tiny cars that were definitely not the kind of cars high rollers drove when *they* showed up in Las Vegas.

Harmony and Jimmy had been a couple for nearly six months —Jimmy had never seen her throw a glass out the window before. It occurred to him that he might have witnessed a freak accident of some kind: the glass might have just popped out of Harmony's hand somehow, and come to rest against the little green cactus in their tiny yard. Why there was a piece of yellow paper stuffed in the glass was beyond Jimmy's ken, but he picked up the glass anyway. It didn't appear to have suffered from dropping out the window; there were no chips in the rim that he could see.

Jimmy could just make out Harmony, through the window, waving at him—he had no idea what the waving meant. He smiled at her anyway, which was easy to do: Harmony was by far the sweetest woman Jimmy Bangor had ever had to come home to.

"I don't want that glass in here, Jimmy, please put it back in the yard," Harmony said, before Jimmy even got both feet inside the apartment. Harmony's voice shook, and she wasn't smiling, which made Jimmy feel a little hurt. One thing he and Harmony had agreed on from the first was that the least a woman owed her man was a welcoming smile when he got home from work in the evening—although, since they lived in Las Vegas, men such as Jimmy

16

Bangor didn't necessarily get home from work in the evening; they were apt to get home from work at any hour of the day or night.

So far, though, Harmony had always produced a welcoming smile, and it wasn't just a "Hi, honey, how was your day?" smile, either. Harmony really *was* welcoming. She loved to see her Jimmy come through the door; only, at the moment, just as Jimmy was expecting to have his spirits lifted by the welcoming smile, Harmony didn't have the welcoming smile.

"What's wrong, honey?" Jimmy asked. The look on Harmony's face was so different from any look he had ever seen on her face before that he felt, for a moment, that he might have stepped into the wrong apartment.

It wasn't the wrong apartment, though: the seventeen-pound bass that Jimmy had caught up near Green River, Wyoming, was still there, stuffed, over the television set, claiming pride of place over several framed pictures of Harmony: one with Elvis, one with Liberace, one with Wayne Newton, even one with Mr. Sinatra. All of the pictures were taken back in the days—long-ago days, now—when Harmony had been the most beautiful showgirl in Las Vegas. To some women it might have seemed in bad taste, putting a stuffed fish right in the middle of a lot of pictures of a beautiful showgirl hobnobbing with celebrities, but Harmony had not only been nice about it, she had insisted on putting the big bass right there: after all, Jimmy was her man, he had caught the big fish; it belonged where visitors could see it and appreciate it, right away. Anyone seeing that fish would know what a fine fisherman Jimmy Bangor was.

Actually, Harmony and Jimmy didn't have that many visitors, though both of them considered themselves to be friendly people. Most of Harmony's friends in Las Vegas had either died or drifted away—quite a few went east, to try their luck, when the big new casinos began to open in Atlantic City. Some of Jimmy's old buddies had left town, too, but the reason Jimmy Bangor developed the habit of hanging out mainly with Harmony was that he had fallen in life. Once Jimmy had been head of security at the Tropicana, but he had got caught sleeping with a girl who was a little underage—five years underage, to be exact—so he had lost that job and slipped all the way down to his present level, just a parking lot attendant at Caesar's. Jimmy didn't care to socialize with too many of the people he worked with, who tended to be either kids or dopeheads. Every time one of the security men at Caesar's stepped outside to get five minutes of sun, Jimmy— if he happened to notice the security man—became a little depressed. He didn't like to be reminded of the days when he had been head of security at the Trop, and had a name that was respected all over town.

"Jimmy, I don't want that glass in the house, would you throw it back in the yard?" Harmony said, again. Keeping the glass with the yellow paper in it as far away as possible felt like her only chance.

"Why, hon? It ain't broke," Jimmy said, before he noticed that Harmony had tears in her eyes. She was not the same cheerful woman he had left only eight hours before. It occurred to Jimmy that the freak accident he had been speculating about might have occurred in Harmony's head, but before he could do more than formulate the thought Harmony snatched the glass out of his hand. This time she didn't simply roll it out the window, either. She threw the glass as hard as she could, not into the street—that might have endangered someone—but at the sidewalk, only a step or two behind Jimmy.

The glass shattered, but the paper that was in it just lay there. There was no breeze; the paper didn't even flutter, much less blow away. The tiny fragments of glass that lay on it and around it sparkled in the sunlight like diamonds.

Jimmy Bangor was dumbfounded.

"Well, it's broke now," he said, noticing that two or three tiny pieces of glass were lodged in the cuffs of his trousers. He knelt in the doorway and picked them out, as carefully as if they had been grass burrs.

Before Jimmy could even get all the glass out of his cuffs, Harmony shoved past him and began to kick at the paper. There were three sheets of yellow paper in all, and Harmony soon kicked them apart. She seemed to be trying to kick them into the air, or into the street, or into the corners of the yard.

"Don't, my God, don't, you'll cut yourself—there's glass everywhere," Jimmy said. Harmony was barefoot, of course; she always kicked off her shoes the minute she was inside the door. Now she

18

was kicking about wildly, on a sidewalk strewn with sharp fragments of glass—kicking at the three sheets of yellow paper.

"Hon, what is it?" Jimmy asked, trying to grab Harmony and pull her away from the glass. Already he could see blood on her feet. Jimmy was respectful of property, and the apartment had wall-to-wall carpet; he had an impulse to go spread some paper towels before he steered Harmony inside, but her feet were cut already, she might cut an artery or something if he didn't get her off the sidewalk quick.

"Is it PMS or what?" he asked—surely some freak accident had occurred in Harmony's head; Jimmy had no idea what the accident might involve.

"PMS—my daughter's dead!" Harmony said, stopping suddenly: out of the corner of her eye she saw the school bus round the corner; in only a second or two it would be stopping in front of the apartment, to let Eddie out. Eddie was five—he was a preschooler—and it would be a big embarrassment to him if his little friends saw his mother kicking pieces of paper around the yard and cutting her feet to pieces in the process. She couldn't be a crazed mother, even if the terrible words in the letter were true. She had to think of Eddie—if the words were true, if Pepper was dead, then Eddie was the one person left that she absolutely *had* to think about.

"Jimmy, would you just get me the broom and the dustpan, real quick?" Harmony said. "I need to sweep this glass up before Eddie gets off the bus."

Jimmy was only too glad to grab the broom and the dustpan; he immediately started sweeping up the broken glass himself. In his haste he forgot what Harmony had just said, until he looked up and saw that her cheeks were now wet with tears. Jimmy had never met Harmony's daughter, he had no idea what she was like and now he never would, because she was dead.

Just then Harmony saw the red lights flashing, as the school bus pulled up to the little gate in front of their apartment building. She dried her cheeks as best she could. She caught a brief glimpse of Eddie as he came down the steps of the school bus, but then, for a moment, all she could see of him were the golden curls on the top of his head. Eddie was just the height of the little gate that led into the yard; then, there he was, a big smile on his face as he burst through the gate and came racing toward his mother, just as he did on every normal day.

"Eddie, don't run please, there's glass on the sidewalk—somebody broke a glass," Harmony said; but Eddie didn't heed her, he loved to run into his mother's arms at the end of a day of preschool.

"Mom, I drew a lion," Eddie said, and then he gave an almost perfect *grrrrr* sound, just the sound a little lion might make, as he flung himself into his mother's arms.

Harmony hugged her son tight—really tight. Just for a moment, kneeling on the glass-strewn sidewalk, her sunny five-year-old in her arms, she was able to kid herself, to pretend that it was still a normal day.

2.

"Mom, you need a Band-Aid," Eddie said, when he saw the blood on his mother's feet. He wasn't too concerned, though. He himself often needed Band-Aids—fortunately there was a big box full of them, in the bathroom. One of his Mom's toes was allover blood, though.

"I think it might take *five* Band-Aids!" Eddie said, when he noticed that his mother was crying. "Can we still have the macaroni and cheese?"

Harmony remembered that she had promised Eddie macaroni and cheese for dinner—it was his favorite meal. Fortunately she had made it to the supermarket the day before and had plenty of macaroni and cheese. She picked Eddie up—he looked so cute, with his little bookbag that mainly had coloring books in it. Jimmy Bangor, meanwhile, was frantically trying to spread paper towels to protect the carpet when she carried Eddie in.

"Wait, hon, wait, you're bleeding," Jimmy said, but Harmony didn't wait, she went right to the kitchen and got out the macaroni and cheese. Long ago her friend Gary, a man who knew as much about life and death as anyone in Las Vegas—maybe as much as anyone, anywhere—told her that the best approach when some-

21

one close passed away was just to keep on doing normal things as normally as possible. Making macaroni and cheese was a normal thing; so was popping Eddie's favorite movie, *Benjy*, into the VCR.

"Mom, make it go fast until we come to the grizzly bear," Eddie requested; then he picked up the remote and made it go fast himself—he wanted to get to the scary part right away—the part where the wolf gets after Benjy.

"Maybe Jimmy can watch the scary part with you," Harmony suggested—Eddie definitely liked company while the scary parts were happening. She tried very hard to follow Gary's instruction to do normal things, which meant concentrating on the macaroni and cheese.

"Honey, you're bleeding all over everything, this whole carpet will have to be took up," Jimmy said. He stood by the refrigerator looking helpless, a roll of paper towels in his hand.

Harmony knew that bleeding pints of blood on the wall-to-wall wasn't too normal, but the major normal thing that still seemed within her grasp was to make Eddie the macaroni and cheese she had promised him yesterday, before the tragedy happened, or before she knew about it, at least. She felt that if she concentrated on the macaroni and cheese and made it and fed it to Eddie, as she had so many times, she might not go crazy. But she had to concentrate very hard on that one thing: feeding her son. Her feet were down there somewhere, bleeding, and the carpet was down there too, getting bled on, but Harmony couldn't direct her attention to the plight of her feet, much less the plight of the carpet. She had to get the right dishes out of the cabinet, and she had to turn the stove on.

"Hon, I'm going up to the Circle K and get some cigarettes," Jimmy said, setting the roll of paper towels on the counter by the sink.

"Need anything?" he asked, just before he went out the door.

"No, Jimmy . . . I guess not," Harmony said, glancing at him. Even before the door closed behind him she had the feeling that Jimmy Bangor was gone. The look in his eye, before he stepped through the door, had been the going-away look, a look she had seen, sooner or later, in the eyes of every man she had ever been involved with except one. At a certain moment, because of this or that, it just seemed that life with her became too much for her boyfriends to handle. One after another, year after year, they went out for bread or beer or cigarettes and never came back. How women got men to stay with them, month after month and year after year, was a mystery to Harmony. Whether it was better cooking, or tricks in bed, or proper housekeeping techniques, she had no way to know. Men seemed to like her, and certainly she liked them. But usually only a few weeks or at most a few months would go by and she would look up one day from making spaghetti, or maybe a sandwich, and there her man would be, at the door, the going-away look in his eye. She was pretty sure it had just occurred with Jimmy Bangor—maybe it was her bloody feet. Jimmy was sort of a squeamish man, even if he did like to fish.

"Do you think he'll bring Popsicles, Mom?" Eddie asked. The grizzly bear had just scared the wolf away from Benjy, which meant that he could relax his attention for a few minutes.

Harmony went to the couch and sat down beside him—she felt like being close to her son, for a little while. As for Eddie, he always liked to be close to his Mom; he immediately climbed up in her lap. After all, the really scary part of the movie was coming up: the part where, just when the black wolf almost has Benjy, Benjy tricks him and the wolf goes off the cliff and falls for a long time and never comes back. It meant the wolf was dead, Eddie believed, though you never really got to see the wolf being dead, which made Eddie worry just a little. It would have been good to see that the wolf was really dead. Then no one would have to be afraid that he would somehow make his way back up the cliff and chase Benjy again.

"Do you think Jimmy will bring Popsicles, Mom?" Eddie asked, again.

"I don't know—did you really like Jimmy?" Harmony asked. It made her feel a failure, that her little boy would always have to be losing people he really liked. But Eddie had been a little cool with Jimmy, a little reserved—maybe it wouldn't be such a heartbreaker for him, if Jimmy turned out to have hit the road, rather than just going for cigarettes.

To her surprise Eddie looked up at her with a giggly look.

"I didn't really like him but I can't tell you why, Mom," Eddie said.

That was sort of unusual—Eddie was such an open little boy:

he would even talk to her about his little penis, if he got a good feeling in it while he was wiping himself on the potty, or fooling around a little in the bathtub.

"Honey, if you didn't like Jimmy, why can't you tell me why?" Harmony asked. It took her mind off Pepper for a second: what if Jimmy had molested Eddie or something. Eddie had a giggly look on his face, though; probably he wouldn't have looked giggly if there had been some form of abuse.

"I can't because it's a bad word," Eddie said. "At school you're not supposed to say it."

"Eddie, you're right here with me, watching *Benjy*," Harmony reminded him. "What kind of bad word would mean that you didn't like Jimmy?"

"Fart!" Eddie said, before dissolving into helpless giggles.

"Oh," Harmony said.

"He farts all the time—I could smell him in my bunk bed," Eddie said.

"Oh," Harmony said again. It wasn't as bad as abuse, of course —on the other hand it sort of made her wonder a little about the level of boyfriend she had chosen to bring home. Why should her beautiful little boy have to smell her boyfriend's farts, while he was in his bunk bed trying to sleep? It wasn't a huge failure, like taking in a child molester would have been, but it didn't exactly make her a candidate for the mom honor roll, either.

"You're supposed to fart outside," Eddie reminded her. "You're *never* supposed to fart inside.

"I don't care, though, if he brings the Popsicles," Eddie added. His Mom looked like she might cry. Maybe he had said the fart word too much.

Harmony was remembering that she had been a little offended by that very problem when she first began to go out with Jimmy— or rather, when she had first sort of given up and gone to bed with him. It was during their intimate moments that Jimmy's habit of expelling wind—lots of wind, and no fragrant breeze, either—had first manifested itself. Harmony's first thought had been, Whoa, what am I getting myself into, here? But Jimmy hastened to explain that it was a digestive condition he had picked up in Asia, while in the service. He didn't want her to think it signified any lack of social graces—it was just a medical problem, really. He looked so hangdog when he discussed it that Harmony, as usual, felt sorry for the man. After that she did her optimistic best to turn off her smeller, at such moments, if Jimmy's digestive condition began to act up—and it usually did.

But then, after all, nobody was perfect. After rashly, and to be truthful, accidentally, having Eddie at age forty-two, Harmony herself had developed a female problem that probably wasn't too attractive—it may have been the reason Webb left her, a bare six months after their son was born. Webb was one of the best tow-truck drivers in Las Vegas—he had spent twenty years racing to every wreck, particularly big smashups on I-15. Webb definitely liked to be first on the scene when there was a big smashup; he was the first to admit that he was an impatient man, it didn't matter whether it was getting a burger quick at Jack-in-the-Box or break-fast or sex or what, waiting was not Webb's mode. Harmony was a little messed up after having Eddie; there had been a few com-plications. She eventually healed fine, but long before that day Webb had decided he couldn't wait, he was gone. It was rare, after that, that she could get him to take even twenty minutes' interest in Eddie, even after Eddie learned to walk and talk and was obvi-ously a wonderful little boy. Webb was just too impatient to get interested in watching children grow, even his own sons—he had three more sons around town that he also wasn't watching grow.

Why am I thinking about all this? Pepper's dead, Harmony thought: then she remembered birthday parties when Pepper was six or seven, and she remembered dance classes and taking Pepper to school—she began to swirl downward into memories that were like blows, any one of them could knock her reeling.

"Oh Eddie, I nearly forgot the macaroni and cheese," she said, kind of dumping him off her lap as she stood up.

"Mom, it's the wolf part, very soon," Eddie said. "Just watch the wolf part with me—it's too scary."

What Harmony ended up doing was turning the TV a little, so Eddie could sit on the cabinet, right where she was working, and be close to her while the scary part of the video was showing. Having him close was good for her too, otherwise some memory of Pepper might hit her and flatten her before she could finish fixing Eddie his macaroni and cheese.

She *did* fix it, too. The movie ended, with Benjy still safe—the black wolf, whether alive or dead, at least had never reappeared.

"When are we getting the pup, Mom?" Eddie asked. He had eaten a more than acceptable portion of macaroni and cheese and had been rewarded with a big scoop of chocolate chip ice cream, although bossy little Connie, who worked next to Harmony at the recycling plant, had tried her best to convince Harmony that chocolate was a bad substance that should definitely be kept out of the mouths and stomachs of little children Eddie's age. To hear Connie talk, chocolate was only a little less harmful than rat poison, but Harmony took all that with a grain of salt. Eddie loved chocolate chip ice cream and so far his skin hadn't turned green from eating it, so why not?

"Eddie, we're going to get you a nice puppy, I just don't know when," Harmony said. She opened the door and looked out, hoping she had been wrong about Jimmy—maybe he was just off having a few beers to calm his nerves—the sight of her bleeding on the carpet had probably upset him quite a bit. She still hadn't done anything about her feet, either; the carpet looked like a few chickens had been slaughtered on it, but that was the least of her worries. She was thinking that pretty soon she was going to have to call the person who had been kind enough to write and tell her about Pepper's death. She wanted a few details; well, wanted them and didn't want them, it wouldn't be such an easy call to make. Also, she would have to call Madonna, Pepper's old dance teacher, and Gary and Jessie and a few others who had known Pepper when she was a beautiful little girl, growing up in Las Vegas.

What Harmony was hoping was that Jimmy Bangor would get control of his nerves and come on home; maybe he could give it another week or two, at least. If he would only come back she would have him to hang on to, in bed, and not have to be totally alone on the night that she learned of her daughter's death. Having him there at least for one night would make up for a lot; certainly it would make up for the farts.

So, despite herself, every few minutes, Harmony would walk over and look out the door, hoping to see Jimmy coming up the sidewalk. Finally, after she had given Eddie his bath and read him his favorite Porky Pig story three times, and sat by him until he fell asleep—the falling asleep didn't take long, Eddie had had an active day at school—he counted his mother's fingers once or twice and twisted the little wedding band Ross, Pepper's father, had given Harmony twenty-five years earlier, when they married; then, Eddie's eyelids went to half-mast and, in another moment, he was sleeping like an angel.

Eddie twisting the wedding band reminded Harmony that Ross was also someone who would have to be called—she had not heard from him in more than five years. Ross was a light man and was undoubtedly at some casino somewhere, working the lights for some floor show; but what casino and what floor show was anybody's guess. Harmony would have to do some asking around, which meant that Ross would probably get a few days' grace before he had to face the fact that he didn't have a little girl anymore.

Harmony turned the light off over Eddie's bunk bed and went to the bathroom and ran water in the tub—just enough to soak the crusted blood off her feet. The fact was, her feet were kind of shredded but even so she couldn't keep her mind on them, she just soaked the worst of the blood off and went downstairs. After opening the door and looking for Jimmy and shutting it again in disappointment, Harmony thought, Why shut it if I'm going to open it again in two minutes? She left the door open and sat down outside, on the step. When she did she felt a few prickles—in his panic to keep her from bleeding on the carpet Jimmy had not done a perfect job of sweeping up the broken glass. To keep her mind off things, she gathered up a few sharp specks of glass herself and held them in her palm.

Harmony sat in her doorway till one in the morning, long past the point when she had given up on seeing Jimmy Bangor again. Jimmy was no night owl—nine-thirty was normally lights-out for him, unless it was Saturday night, when he might try to stretch his wakefulness till ten, in order to maybe attempt a sex act or something. Harmony rarely turned her TV off until one or two; years as a showgirl had accustomed her to real late hours. Besides being a farter, Jimmy had been a snorer; she had to keep the volume up a little higher than she normally would in order to hear over his snores. It was a little inconvenient, but at that it was better than what she was looking at now: no one to hold her when she started sinking. Pepper, her daughter, was not only dead, she was cremated. The person who had written the letter, a woman named

27

Laurie, had wanted to know where Harmony wanted the ashes sent—Harmony had noticed that line in the letter before she stuffed it in the iced-tea glass.

In Tulsa, where Harmony came from, dead people were usually just buried whole—she had never given any thought to what should be done once a human body was cremated and reduced to ashes. Maybe the ashes would be as fine as the little specks of sharp glass that she held in her palm for almost three hours. That such a thing as death could happen to a child she had given birth to, and arranged birthday parties for, and picked up after dance class, was too terrible. Harmony felt such a feeling of tearing and ripping inside herself that she began to squeeze the little sharp pieces of glass into her hand. She needed to feel something different from the ripping—even a cut. Jimmy wasn't coming, no one was coming, yet someone had to, she couldn't sit there on her own step and survive the tearing and ripping feeling, not much longer, not alone. Pain was coming up in her throat, it was going to become a scream or something—if it was a scream it was going to be so loud it might wake the neighbors; Eddie might hear it and be scared—sometimes Eddie had bad dreams anyway; he certainly wouldn't get the normal amount of sleep he needed if he had to be awakened by his mother screaming in the yard.

After all, it was one in the morning: Harmony didn't have the school bus coming, or the macaroni and cheese to make, or *Benjy* or the Porky Pig stories to help keep her a stable mom. She didn't even have Jimmy Bangor, snoring or farting beside her; usually he snored so loud that she couldn't hear the comics on the Comedy Channel. Now it was just her alone, on the step, with the terrible news.

Harmony jumped up—she began to shake and was about to stumble back into the house and dial the first phone number she could remember, when the gate to the yard creaked. Harmony turned in her doorway and saw Juliette coming.

"What's wrong, Harmony—what's wrong?" Juliette asked. She was way back down the sidewalk, trying to get the latch on the gate to work correctly; but she picked up some vibe out of the air—it was most unusual to see Harmony on her doorstep at one in the morning.

Juliette came hurrying up the sidewalk, still in her tux: she was a blackjack dealer at the MGM Grand, dealers were still required to wear tuxedos at the Grand. Juliette was a little chubby; sometimes she reminded Harmony of Lou Costello, whom she had met long ago, in her first days as a showgirl. Juliette was very kind; she would always make tea for Harmony and listen to her troubles if she happened to be low. Juliette herself didn't seem to have troubles—actually, there was no one in her life to cause her trouble, loneliness was probably Juliette's trouble; but, for the moment, with a scream of pain about to pour out of Harmony's throat and maybe wake her young son, Juliette in her tux was the answer to a hope she had not expected would be answered at all.

"Oh, Juliette, Pepper's dead, she's cremated," Harmony said.

"Pepper, your daughter?" Juliette asked—she had never met Pepper herself, but of course she had seen the scrapbook Harmony kept, of all Pepper's recitals and shows. Seeing even two pictures of Pepper was enough to tell anyone that she was beautiful; the camera loved her, always had.

"Pepper, your daughter?" Juliette asked, again—it was a stall, mainly. She was trying to keep her wits about her and think what to say or do next.

"Pepper, my daughter," Harmony said, noticing that her hand was bleeding from the specks of glass she had squeezed into her palm.

3.

Juliette didn't even take the time to change out of her tux; she was determined not to leave Harmony alone in her distress. In no time she had taken Harmony inside, picked the glass shards out of her hand, and disinfected the cuts.

"Harmony, first things first," Juliette said, when she saw the shredded feet. She did a much better job on Harmony's feet than Harmony had done, too—Eddie had underestimated the Band-Aids that would be required. It took eleven in all, and even then Juliette wasn't really content.

"You ought to go to the emergency room and get stitches for one or two of those cuts, but I guess it can wait," Juliette said. She covered the couch with towels, in case the Band-Aids didn't completely do their job. Then she made Harmony tea, in the largest mug she could find; she got a box of Kleenex out of the bathroom and put the box by Harmony, on the couch. Harmony wasn't really crying hard, but she was leaking, twice Juliette saw a line of tears move straight down Harmony's cheeks and puddle momentarily at the corners of her mouth. The sight of tears gathered at the corners of Harmony's mouth touched something in Juliette—she cried a little, too. The fact that she herself was childless had always pained her; it seemed a failure. Most humans managed to mate, but not her.

Now it occurred to Juliette that maybe childlessness wasn't such a terrible fate, after all; what Harmony was going through, and would keep on going through for the rest of her life, was undoubtedly a lot worse.

"Harmony, we better start making calls—we should probably inform your family first," Juliette said. She got a mug of tea for herself—the only lemon in Harmony's refrigerator was pretty runty but at least it was a lemon, and then she brought the Portaphone over to the couch and pulled up a chair for herself.

"If you'll just tell me the numbers I'll dial and then you can talk," she said.

"I guess I ought to call Gary first," Harmony said. Gary was her best friend—maybe by now he was her only real friend—and he had known Pepper all her life. Gary was sort of an honorary uncle; he had always thought Pepper was totally beautiful. It was going to break his heart when he heard that Pepper was dead.

"If I were you I'd call your family first," Juliette said.

"I know you don't like Gary, he does get bitchy at times," Harmony said, remembering that Gary and Juliette had had words one time, at a party Harmony had been attempting to give. It had been Eddie's fifth-birthday party; Eddie's birthday parties were about the only parties Harmony attempted to give. From Eddie's point of view the parties were a big success, but from Harmony's point of view things were more complicated. It was plain that Juliette wasn't crazy about calling Gary first.

"No, Gary and I made up, we're civil," Juliette said. "I just think you ought to call your family first—it would be more appropriate."

Harmony suddenly realized what Juliette meant: she meant she should call her family in Oklahoma first—her two sisters, her brother, her mother and father. *That* was the family Juliette was talking about. Juliette was from Iowa herself—of course she would know what was appropriate and what wasn't in times of grief.

"I don't see them very often—they weren't real close to Pepper," Harmony said. But then she took the Portaphone from Juliette and without thinking about it another second called her sister Neddie. Her sister's real name was Grace, but for some reason she had always been called Neddie. It had been so many months since she had called her sister that Harmony was a little surprised to find the number still in her head. Maybe it was because Neddie, who lived on a farm near Tarwater, Oklahoma, had had the same phone number all her adult life—in the same period of time Harmony had had at least thirty phone numbers.

"It's three a.m., who's calling?" Neddie asked; she was always matter-of-fact in phone conversations.

"I'm sorry, Neddie—I'm confused," Harmony said. "My feet are all cut up, and Pepper's dead."

"I'm coming, Sis," Neddie said. "Me and Pat will get ourselves to the airport and be there as soon as we can. What'd the poor child die of?"

Pat was Harmony's other sister's nickname—her real name was Hope. She worked in the bank in Tarwater and had for many years.

"Neddie, she's cremated, that's as far as I got in the letter," Harmony admitted. "The letter's out in the yard. I guess I'll try to read it in the morning."

"If she's dead, she's dead," Neddie said. "It's a tragedy for this family. Have you got a friend with you, hon?"

"Juliette's with me, you met her," Harmony said. "She hasn't even been home to take her tux off—she's here, a foot away."

"Does Eddie know?" Neddie asked.

"No, I was a coward, I didn't tell him," Harmony said. "I just made him macaroni and cheese and put him to bed. It's important that he get a good night's sleep."

"It's important that you get them feet tended to, too," Neddie said, still being matter-of-fact. "We don't need you getting blood poisoning, on top of all this."

"It was just a glass I broke, it had just come out of the dishwasher," Harmony said. Though she had not talked to her sister in a long time, she knew that Juliette had been right and that Neddie, her sister, had been exactly the right person to call. Gary might have gone into hysterics, he was prone to them, though mostly from getting his heart broken by boys he fell in love with who didn't reciprocate. In other kinds of crises Gary was pretty stable, but no one in the whole world, so far as Harmony knew, was as stable as her sister Neddie Haley. Already Harmony had begun to dread the moment when she would have to hang up.

Probably Neddie didn't have a Portaphone but Harmony had a fantasy that she did and the two of them just kept talking while Neddie gathered up Pat and got to the airport and flew to Las Vegas and arrived at Harmony's apartment. It was an absurd fantasy, she could never afford to pay for a phone call that long, and anyway Neddie was frugal and would no doubt cut her off at some point even if Portaphones did exist in Tarwater. But it was a comforting fantasy too: if she could just keep her big sister on the line indefinitely maybe the tearing, ripping feeling wouldn't split her apart so badly that she couldn't be a stable mom when Eddie woke up, expecting a waffle and clean clothes to wear to school.

"You better let me call Pat, she's wild in the head these days and there's no telling what she might say if you and her get into it," Neddie advised. It was plain that she was about ready to hang up and start making plane reservations and doing other matter-of-fact things.

"I know she thinks I'm a bad mother, she always has," Harmony said—and it was true, her sister Pat had always disapproved of almost everything she did, particularly her behavior as a mom. When Pat discovered that Harmony had let Pepper go off to New York alone, at the age of seventeen, to dance in a Broadway show, she informed Harmony immediately of her absolute disapproval.

"Pepper's a teenager, she has absolutely no business being alone in a place like New York City," Pat informed her the first time the subject came up.

"How would you know what kind of place New York is? You've never been there," Harmony replied, trying to keep calm. Pat was blunt when she was talking to Harmony—she just treated her like a little sister who couldn't possibly know much. She had hurt Harmony's feelings with her bluntness hundreds of times, over the years.

"You've never been anywhere," Harmony had informed her, at the time. "I wish you wouldn't try to tell me how to raise my daughter. She's in a Broadway show and this is a wonderful opportunity for her."

"Yeah, opportunity to become a drug addict or to get mugged or to get AIDS," Pat said. "I've seen those crack neighborhoods they have up there—they show them on TV."

33

"I'm sure Pepper doesn't live in a crack neighborhood," Harmony replied, although she had never been in New York either and was not quite as convinced as she would have liked to be that Pepper was living in a safe neighborhood. Really, she didn't know how Pepper lived, other than that she had an address on East Ninth Street. She had plenty of maternal worries herself. Gary had informed her that eight million people lived in New York City —that was too many people even to imagine, and some of them were bound to be unsavory characters. That was a phrase Jackie Bonventre had been fond of before he died—in his view unsavory characters were men who were stingy at the craps tables, ate too much garlic, and got his showgirls pregnant.

But Pat was not convinced by anything Harmony said, and she never had been. When they were teenagers in Oklahoma Pat had done nothing but try to steal Harmony's boyfriends, what few she managed to have before leaving home at age sixteen. Pat didn't stop stealing boyfriends just because her little sister left home, either—so far she had stolen three husbands from various women in the Tulsa area, and got all of them to marry her. The third one had just dropped dead on a golf course the year before. Harmony was a little surprised that Pat hadn't already got busy and stole a fourth husband.

Neddie, however, had been married all her life to Dick Haley, a farmer. Harmony had only met Dick a few times. He was a stern Baptist who refused to come to a sinful place such as Las Vegas, even though his sister-in-law lived there.

"What about Pat, is she married again yet?" Harmony asked— it was mainly a ruse to keep Neddie on the phone a few more minutes.

"She's working on it," Neddie said. "Pat wasn't meant for the maiden life."

"Neddie, her feelings might be hurt if I don't call her myself— she likes attention," Harmony reminded her sister, though Neddie lived about a mile from Pat and probably didn't need to be reminded.

"Call her if you want to, Harmony, but do it quick," Neddie said. "We got to get cracking right now."

"I'm just afraid she'll say I told you so," Harmony said. "I know she did tell me so but if she tells me she told me so right now I may go crazy—I may anyway, Neddie."

"Well, you lost a child—it's something I ain't had to suffer, thank the Lord, and neither has Pat," Neddie said. "She might suffer it yet though—and I might too. All our kids take dope. They're all just about to the point of being drug addicts."

"Drug addicts?" Harmony said. She wasn't used to thinking of people back home in Oklahoma as drug addicts—much less her sisters' children.

"Yes, and little Deenie has already been in trouble twice for forging her mother's name on checks," Neddie said. "She does it so she can buy drugs for that worthless hulk she's shacked up with."

"Good Lord, she's only about seventeen, isn't she?" Harmony asked, shocked.

"Right, her birthday was last week—you should have sent her a card, hon," Neddie said gently.

"I'm sorry—I know I'm not the best at keeping up family ties," Harmony said, ashamed of herself. Even Pat, despite being disapproving, had never failed to send Pepper and Eddie cards or little presents on their birthdays. The cards and little presents always came just on the right day, too—both Pepper and Eddie had always known that they had aunts who cared. She herself had been shamefully lax; she did mark all her nieces' and nephews' birthdays on the calendar, but then she would forget to turn the pages of the calendar, as the months went by, or forget to check it. Eventually she would always get around to mailing cards and presents— she had Deenie's card in her purse at that moment—but they always drifted in quite a few days late.

"Neddie, I'm going to call Pat myself, I just think it's better—do you think I should call Billy too?" Harmony asked.

"Billy's in jail," Neddie informed her. "He made one too many obscene calls to his old friend Mildred, so they nailed him again."

"Uh-oh," Harmony said.

"Her husband's a dead shot, too," Neddie said. "This is a small town. Married men don't take kindly to having their wives get dirty phone calls in the middle of the night."

"I thought Billy would outgrow all that," Harmony said.

"That's what we've all been hoping," Neddie said. "But Billy's fifty years old and he's still doing it."

"Can't he get counseling?" Harmony asked. It was sad to think of her only brother in jail for making obscene phone calls.

"He's done been to just about every psychiatrist in this part of Oklahoma," Neddie said. "There's got to be a woman somewhere would love Billy and keep him out of trouble, but if there is she sure ain't living in Tarwater."

"He could move out here and be a parking lot attendant," Harmony said. "I know a job that's just come open."

She heard a closet door creak, through the receiver, and knew that Neddie was packing even as she talked.

"What's that mean—did Jimmy leave?" Neddie asked.

"Jimmy left—he went out for cigarettes six hours ago and he isn't back," Harmony said. "He had the going-away look in his eye, Neddie. I guess the tragedy was just too much for him."

"What kind of worthless piece of shit would leave you on the night you got the news that your daughter was dead?" Neddie asked.

"The kind I keep falling in love with," Harmony said. Compared to Pepper's death, Jimmy's departure didn't matter all that much —still, it mattered some. Harmony began to cry so hard that she couldn't talk to Neddie anymore; she had to hang up. It was a lie that she had fallen in love with Jimmy, though; it was not that serious—he was just a man she had brought home for a few months. It was a long time since there had been a man she was serious about; she started counting back through the years, to the last man she had been in love with, but after she had counted back almost fifteen years and was still at zero, zilch, she gave up and let Juliette hand her Kleenex until she cried herself out.

"My sisters are coming, I have to call Pat," Harmony said, listlessly, when she was finally able to stop crying for a few minutes.

"Tell me the number and I'll dial," Juliette said, wondering if she should tell Harmony that Jimmy Bangor had made at least fifty passes at her in the few months he had lived next door. Would it make her feel better, knowing that she was rid of such a scumbag? Or would the knowledge that the man she had lived with for six months was a faithless asshole just make her feel worse?

"Juliette, just go change out of your tux," Harmony said. "I'll be all right for a few minutes."

"Okay. I've got some chicken salad in my fridge, would you like a little?" Juliette asked.

She decided to keep quiet about Jimmy Bangor's fifty passes; Harmony might think she had encouraged the man or something —why take a chance?

"I don't think so, would you please just hurry back?" Harmony asked—she knew Juliette needed to change out of her work clothes but at the sight of her getting ready to go next door Harmony got a bad sinking feeling—she definitely wanted Juliette to hurry back.

When Juliette left, Harmony became so befuddled that she couldn't remember who she had been supposed to call next. Gary came to mind, but there was the factor of Gary and Juliette not being on such good terms. It might not be quite the moment to call Gary. Before she could make up her mind Juliette came back through the door. She had done a really quick change, and she also had a box of Red Zinger tea in her hand.

"Have you called Pat yet?" Juliette asked.

"No, I forgot—that was a real fast change," Harmony said. She felt lucky to have a friend like Juliette, so quick in a time of crisis that she had changed out of her work clothes and come back before Harmony could even think to call her other sister.

"I hope Neddie's already called and told her—if I wake her up she might get real mad, she's got the worst temper in the family," Harmony said. It took her a moment to remember the number, but as soon as she remembered it, Juliette dialed.

4.

"I know it's a late hour—did Neddie tell you?" Harmony said, when Pat answered the phone.

"Sweetie, I'm packing," Pat said. "Neddie's coming by in fifteen minutes."

"That's good, she's not mad," Harmony said, putting her hand over the receiver for a moment—she wanted to reassure Juliette.

"I know this is real inconvenient, Pattie," she went on.

"You're telling me, I was getting married today," Pat said.

"Oh my God, Neddie didn't tell me," Harmony said.

"She didn't tell you because she didn't know," Pat said. "Neddie thinks I'm a slut anyway. I don't necessarily tell her about every little marriage I undertake.

"Besides she's jealous of me because I keep getting husbands and she's had to make do with Dick for about ninety years," her sister added. "Dick Haley's the dullest man in Oklahoma—maybe in the world. I'd be jealous of me too, if I was Neddie."

"He's loyal, though," Harmony reminded her.

"So's a dog, and dogs can at least bark," Pat said. "If Dick Haley has said anything more interesting than 'Pass the gravy' in the last thirty years I haven't been around to hear it."

"I hate it that I'm spoiling your wedding day," Harmony said—mainly she was just trying to change the subject. She didn't feel that she needed to hear Pat run down their brother-in-law just at that moment.

"Don't worry about it, sweetie," Pat said. "We had the honeymoon last week. Rog took me to Hot Springs and blew the whole honeymoon, unassisted. It's no big deal whether I marry him now or not—there's other fish in the sea."

"Why did he spoil your honeymoon?" Harmony asked—despite herself she wanted the details.

"Fizzled," Pat said. "Just my luck. The silly bastard's been dying to crawl on top of me for months and I finally let him, blah's the best word I can come up with for the result."

"Was he nervous or what?" Harmony asked. Her sister had always been liberal with details of her sex life—evidently nothing had changed.

"No, boring," Pat said. "I told him he might as well keep on crawling, if that was the best he could do."

"Pat, Pepper's cremated," Harmony said—after all Pepper's death was the reason they were talking. So what if Pat's honeymoon hadn't been so thrilling, sexually? The fact that her sister couldn't think of anything else to talk about was just another reminder of what she had always known, which was that Pat was selfish.

"Yes, and I'd like to skin whatever Yankee did it to that poor little soul," Pat said. "You're her mother—you should have been consulted about the remains."

Remains was a very bad word choice; Harmony couldn't bear to think of Pepper just being remains now, ashes. Harmony began to sob so violently that she had to hang up on Pat; even that didn't help, Juliette finally had to hold her tight for several minutes; she felt as if she might be dying herself, she must have gasped out something that scared Juliette because she got a horrified look on her face.

"Harmony, you mustn't talk like that, remember that sweet little boy upstairs," Juliette said.

"Juliette, I just got carried away for a minute—I'll never say it again," Harmony assured her—the look on Juliette's face made her feel guilty. She managed to stop crying quite so hard—of course she had to go on living, otherwise Eddie would have no mother.

"He's a wonderful little boy, Harmony—you have to go on, no matter what," Juliette said, just to be certain that Harmony got the point.

Harmony knew well enough that that was the point; she had only had a momentary lapse, she wasn't going to let Eddie down. Just when she was finally calming down to the point where Juliette didn't have to hug her quite so tightly the phone rang.

"I better get it," Juliette said.

"Maybe it's Jimmy," Harmony said—she couldn't help grasping at straws.

"Is my sister hanging in there?" Neddie asked Juliette.

"She's shaky, it has to be expected," Juliette said, handing Harmony the phone.

"You hung up on me and you hung up on Pat—I guess we're worried," Neddie said.

"I wish you'd told me it was Pat's wedding day," Harmony said —then she remembered, a beat too late, that Pat had been keeping that very fact a secret from her older sister.

"What wedding day?" Neddie asked.

"Oh, no . . . now I've done it, won't the night ever end?" Harmony asked. "I forgot it was a secret, but there's no harm done, she was thinking about breaking up with the guy anyway."

There was dead silence on the line, for several seconds: Harmony could imagine the look on Neddie's face; it was the kind of look that could easily make a selfish person like Pat shrivel up until she felt about the size of a grain of sand.

"This family gets more like the CIA every day," Neddie said, in her same, matter-of-fact voice. "Of course, if I was gonna marry Rog Blankenship I'd keep it a secret too, at least until I could arrange to divorce the son of a bitch."

The conversation just seemed to end there; whether she hung up on Neddie or Neddie hung up on her, Harmony didn't remember—she had begun to feel very tired. At that point she sort of faded for a few minutes; actually it must have been longer than a few minutes. When she opened her eyes again Gary was there, and also Jessie and Myrtle. Juliette had evidently taken the initia-

40

tive and called a few people—Harmony was relieved to see that there didn't seem to be any hostility between Gary and Juliette.

"Harmony, it's the worst thing ever, I'll never get over it," Gary said. It was obvious he had been crying a good deal, his eyes were red. As for Jessie, she was a total basket case, that was only to be expected. Jessie had never been a strong person.

"Oh, Harmony, what will we ever do without her?" Jessie said. The whole front of her dress was wet from tears. She tried to come over and hug Harmony but just wasn't up to it; her legs began to go out on her and she had to flop into a chair, she was really upset. Jessie had known Pepper since birth; Harmony was touched that she took it so hard.

Myrtle was harder to judge; she was rapidly drinking a bottle of vodka that Jimmy Bangor had left behind. After quaffing about three glasses she wobbled over and gave Harmony a hug.

"You poor thing, what killed that precious child, was it a mugger or what?" Myrtle asked.

"Myrtle, I don't even know, it's in the letter but I never got past the cremated part," Harmony said.

Then she started crying again, and so did everybody else, even Myrtle. The last time Harmony could remember Myrtle crying was when her beloved goat Maude passed away.

5.

When Eddie came downstairs for breakfast, carrying Ernie in one hand and Bert in the other, he was surprised to see his Mom and Jessie and Gary and Myrtle and Juliette all in the living room —the TV was on but nobody was watching it and it wasn't on the right channel anyway—no *Sesame Street*.

"Is it a birthday party, Mom?" Eddie asked. He had never seen so many people in their house so early in the morning. If it was a birthday party Eddie was glad, he liked them, although he knew it couldn't be *his* birthday party because his birthday came in October.

"Eddie, it's not a birthday party, your sister died, now you'll never meet her," Harmony said.

Everyone in the room took the position that the sooner she told Eddie the better; now that she *had* told him, she really didn't think it was for the better. Eddie had come downstairs looking like his confident, happy self. Sometimes it amazed Harmony that her own body had yielded up a little boy as confident and as happy as Eddie. But there he was, you couldn't doubt it, not if you were in Eddie's company for five minutes.

"She deaded?" Eddie asked—it seemed to him a better word than died.

"Yes, but your aunts are coming today," Harmony said. "Your Aunt Neddie and your Aunt Pat, they haven't seen you since you were three."

"Could I have a waffle with real maple syrup before they come?" Eddie asked. "Aunt Pat is so squeezy, I want to eat my waffle now, before she gets here."

"He doesn't understand it, he's too young, bless his little heart," Myrtle said.

"Is it okay if I change the channel?" Eddie asked, grabbing the remote. "*Sesame Street* is on."

"It's good that Eddie has a positive attitude," Gary said, wiping away some more tears. "I wish I had one."

"Are you crying because she deaded, Mom?" Eddie asked. He had never met his sister, Pepper, and had only heard her voice on the telephone, once or twice. It was too bad that she deaded, if it was going to make his mother sad, but the main things on his mind were the waffle with real maple syrup and watching as much as possible of *Sesame Street* before the school bus came to take him to school. He wanted to see Kermit and Grover and Bert and Ernie, of course, and also Oscar the Grouch, if he had time.

All the women went into the kitchen at once, to make him his waffle.

"There's four ladies in the kitchen," Eddie said to Gary. "What if they make too many waffles?"

In fact Harmony and Jessie and Myrtle and Juliette all wanted to make Eddie his waffle—it would give them something to do and help get their minds off the tragedy for a few seconds.

"Harmony, let us do it, you'll just wear yourself out," Jessie said. "You need to save your strength."

"I don't need to save it, either, Jessie," Harmony said, a little annoyed to find herself suddenly squeezed out of her own kitchen. They weren't going to let her make Eddie's waffle, though, so she opened the door and went out into the bright Nevada sunlight. The heat of the morning sun felt good—it was the first thing that had felt good since she opened the letter and read that Pepper was dead. Besides the sunlight, the only other thing that felt good was the sight of Eddie coming down the stairs, his usual cheerful self. Inside the happiness that sight gave her was a pain, though, for now her two children would never meet one another: Pepper would never know what a beautiful little brother she had, and Eddie would never meet his talented sister. Of course she was always sending Pepper pictures of Eddie, and had shown Eddie a great many pictures of Pepper; but it would never be face-to-face, brother and sister, as it should have been. Eddie and Pepper would never sit and talk, or call one another in the night if there was a crisis—the way she had just called her sisters, Neddie and Pat. Once or twice Pepper had vaguely mentioned that she might come home someday and meet Eddie, but she never found the time, one show followed another, she had to think of her career—that was something Harmony certainly understood; only now it was too late, that was that.

Outside in the sunlight Harmony remembered the day she had driven Pepper to the airport and put her on the big shiny airplane for New York. Pepper had looked so grown up, that day; she had perfect confidence in her own dancing and was certain that she was flying away to become a big star on Broadway. Still, Harmony knew that underneath Pepper's confident manner she was still a seventeen-year-old girl; she wasn't so grown up, not really. Pepper said goodbye and got on the plane and was gone. On the way back from the airport Harmony had cried so hard she had to stop at a Jack in the Box and have several cups of coffee in order to regain her composure.

Harmony reflected that if she had known the truth, that day— that she had just seen her daughter alive for the last time—all the cups of coffee in all Las Vegas would not have been enough to restore her composure. If she had had any inkling of what was to come she would have given up right then; and there would have been no Webb, no Eddie, no job at the recycling plant, no nothing.

But mainly, that day, she had just felt like a mom might feel whose child had gone away to college—Pepper had departed for the big college called New York City; she would be home for Christmas, probably, or at the worst, for summer vacation—she could not have imagined that nearly six years would pass without Pepper coming home for a visit. Harmony was soon to have Eddie inside her; she had to concentrate on having a healthy pregnancy

—after all, she was almost forty-two at the time, she might not sail through this pregnancy quite as easily as she had sailed through her pregnancy with Pepper.

While she was thinking back to that day, which she had not realized would be her last day in the company of her daughter, Jasmine Legrande came wobbling along the sidewalk—very likely she had been out drinking all night. Jasmine had once been the reigning showgirl of Las Vegas herself, from an era earlier than Harmony's—well, much earlier, really; there had hardly even been a Las Vegas at all when Jasmine reigned at the Sahara from the very day that it opened. Even Gary, who was sort of the oral historian of Las Vegas, hadn't been there the day the Sahara opened.

"Harmony, I had a bad dream, is something wrong in your life?" Jasmine asked; she was a kind old woman even if she was almost always drunk and even if she did weigh three hundred and fifty pounds. Once her days as a reigning showgirl were over Jasmine had definitely let herself go.

"Oh Jasmine, Pepper died," Harmony said—why conceal it? Everyone she knew in Las Vegas would know it soon enough, probably most of them already did know it.

To her surprise, Jasmine began to tremble, and the next thing Harmony knew, she fainted dead away and fell against the little faux picket fence in front of the apartment building. The pickets were just plywood or some other very weak wood; when Jasmine collapsed on the fence a whole section of fence collapsed with her —the apartment manager certainly wasn't going to like that, and who could blame him?

Still, the fact was Jasmine had fainted and was lying in the yard. Harmony knew she couldn't lift her, so she raced back in the house to seek help; everyone was just sitting around watching Eddie gobble his waffle when she appeared.

"Help me, please, Jasmine's fainted," Harmony said. Everyone looked completely startled except Eddie, who went calmly on eating his waffle.

"Is she deaded too, Mom?" he asked—the concept of deading had interested him ever since he watched *Benjy* the first time and had to grapple with the question of whether the black wolf was really gone forever once he fell off the cliff.

"Eddie, I hope not—I think she just got too hot or something," Harmony said.

"I'll get a cold rag," Gary said, and he did; pretty soon they were all standing over Jasmine, fanning her and trying to shade her with newspapers. Harmony couldn't quite get her mind off the destroyed fence; the manager was a Mormon who didn't like for things of an unexpected nature to happen around the apartment building.

Gary's cold rag was having a good effect, Jasmine was definitely still breathing. Harmony realized she was going to have a close call when it came to getting Eddie ready for school—when she went back inside to see about him he was flipping channels with the remote despite the fact that his fingers were sticky from the maple syrup.

"Eddie, you're getting the buttons sticky, the remote won't work if you do that," she said. "Jimmy won't be able to switch to the ball game."

"I thought you said he had gone away," Eddie reminded her. "He wasn't here for breakfast."

"You're right," Harmony said—she had forgotten that little fact. "He's not here but it's still not a good idea to get the buttons sticky on the remote."

"Did he fart himself away?" Eddie asked; he was in one of his giggly moods, which was fine with Harmony. In three minutes she had him upstairs and dressed and back down to the front step, just in time, too; the school bus pulled up ten seconds later, while Gary and Juliette and Jessie and Myrtle were still trying to get Jasmine to her feet.

"I don't need to latch the gate this morning, Mom, because the fence is down," Eddie observed, just before he gave her a kiss and raced up the steps into the school bus.

"What happened?" Eddie's friend Eli asked, seeing a crowd around a fat woman in Eddie's yard.

"Jasmine fainted and broke our fence and my sister died," Eddie said. He always tried to sit by Eli on the bus.

"I wish my sister would die, she's a dickhead," Eli remarked.

Eddie wanted to giggle, but tried to hold it in. He knew that dickhead was an even worse word than fart—if the teacher ever

46

heard Eli say a word like that Eli wouldn't get to go out at recess for many days—probably for a whole week.

Eli was eating licorice; his Mom put it in his lunch and he always got it out and ate it on the school bus on the way to school. The licorice made his teeth black.

"Did you have to smell farts last night?" Eli asked. He was interested in the fact that Eddie's mother's boyfriend farted a lot.

"No, he didn't even come home last night, I think he deaded, too," Eddie said. The last was just something pretend he thought up to impress Eli.

"Boy, you're lucky, a lot of people die at your house, it must be exciting," Eli said.

6.

Driving to the airport, later in the day, Harmony reflected that it was a little bit of a sad comment on her years in Las Vegas that she was still borrowing cars—Gary's, in this case. It was an old Mercury that had been involved in a few fender benders. After all, she had been a reigning showgirl too, for more years than Jasmine had; and yet she had never quite got far enough ahead to buy a car. Even carpooling for Pepper or picking her up at dance class had always been in borrowed cars—usually she would just borrow one at the casino, at the last minute. Once or twice she had sort of chipped in with boyfriends and owned parts of cars for a while, but, without exception, when the boyfriends left they forgot about Harmony's chipping in. They always took the cars with them.

Recently she had promised Eddie that they would get a car and a puppy soon. She knew she had to pull herself together and make good on the puppy at least. In view of the wall-to-wall carpet, getting the puppy housebroken quickly was important—the manager wasn't going to take kindly to any messy puppies, not after Jasmine smashed his fence.

After Jasmine had recovered enough to come inside and drink vodka with Myrtle, Gary took Harmony aside and reminded her that Jasmine had also lost a daughter—the daughter had been involved with a trapeze artist, but, after that, the story grew vague. Not many people left alive had been in Las Vegas when it happened.

"Even if you knew exactly what happened I wouldn't want you to tell me about it," Harmony said. "I just don't care to hear about it right now, Gary."

But it did make her feel a sadness for Jasmine—that was probably what caused her to let herself go to the extent of weighing three hundred and fifty pounds.

"I know what you're thinking," Gary said. He had known Harmony so long that much of the time he actually did know what she was thinking—at least he usually came close.

"I'm trying *not* to think, Gary," Harmony pointed out. "The fewer thoughts I have right now, the better."

"Harmony, you're not going to turn into a drunk who weighs three hundred and fifty pounds," Gary said. "This is the worst tragedy ever, but you'll survive. You have to. You have Eddie."

Well, it was the truth—and if any little boy deserved a good mom it was Eddie. For sure he deserved a mom who could afford to own a car. Right now, when he was only in kindergarten, maybe it didn't matter so much; but in a few years it would be a big embarrassment for him, that his Mom couldn't even afford a car; there probably weren't two hundred people in Las Vegas so poor they couldn't afford some kind of car. When he got big enough to go on dates—after all, that would only be another seven or eight years—lack of a car would amount to a serious problem.

"Maybe they'll make me manager of the recycling plant," Harmony said, thinking out loud. Gary got a look on his face that suggested that he didn't think being manager of a recycling plant was aiming high enough—but, from Harmony's point of view, it was sort of shooting for the stars. After all, she didn't have many skills—for most of her life her beauty had been the only skill she needed, nobody else had been chosen Miss Las Vegas Showgirl three times running.

"Gary, don't look that way. I want to make enough money to buy a car, otherwise Eddie's going to be embarrassed," Harmony said.

The truth was, the people in her house—although they were

her dearest friends—were beginning to depress her. Jasmine had passed out on the couch—her makeup was all runny.

Meanwhile, Gary had gone to the bathroom and taken several pills. Gary had never been able to stay off speed; he claimed it was working odd hours that made him need it but why he needed it didn't really matter; the fact was, Gary took a lot of speed. It made him bitchy when he was on his way up and even bitchier when he was on his way down. Pretty soon he was going to start bitching out Jessie, who had been crying continuously ever since she heard the news. If there was such a thing as a contest for continuous crying, Jessie would win hands down.

Juliette had finally worn out and gone to sleep in a chair, and Myrtle, very drunk, was sowing disorder in Harmony's kitchen. She was so drunk she couldn't tell a clean dish from a dirty dish; she took a whole dishwasherful of unwashed dishes and put them back in the cabinet on top of the perfectly clean dishes that were already there.

"Myrtle, those dishes haven't been washed, please leave them in the dishwasher," Harmony said.

"Harmony, I was washing dishes before you were born," Myrtle said. It was pointless to argue with her when she was drunk. Reason was the last thing Myrtle wanted to listen to; even when she was sober, she wasn't crazy about listening to it.

Harmony decided she couldn't stand to be at home anymore. Of course, it was several hours before her sisters would be arriving from Tulsa, but she didn't care. Several hours of sitting in the Las Vegas airport was preferable, in her view, to even one hour of watching Jessie cry or Jasmine smear her makeup or Myrtle sow disorder in her kitchen.

So she drove Gary down to the Stardust, where he worked. He was in love with a Chicano boy who was a janitor there. Gary was happy to loan Harmony his car; his new love was on his mind, not his old Mercury.

On her way to the airport, Harmony remembered Ross, Pepper's father. She knew it was up to her to start looking for Ross; Gary had said he would ask around, and maybe he would, but Gary had never thought much of Ross. He had even sort of opposed the effort Harmony made to get back with Ross, seven years earlier, when Ross was working as a light man in Reno.

50

Gary had been right about that one, her effort to hitch up with Ross again had been El Floppo, as Myrtle would say. Harmony knew before she went to Reno that Ross was involved with a young woman named Linda, who happened to be pregnant by him at the time, but she had allowed herself to be convinced that Ross's relationship with Linda was just kind of a roommate thing. Then Harmony got to Reno and found out that the relationship with Linda *wasn't* just a roommate thing—it was closer to being a mad passion; why Ross had even urged her to come to Reno she never knew. On the whole, that venture had been pretty discouraging— so discouraging that she hadn't talked to Ross a single time since she got herself back on the bus and limped back to Las Vegas. For the next year or two her self-esteem was at a low ebb, which is probably why she ended up getting pregnant by Webb.

Still, getting pregnant by Webb had produced Eddie, just as getting pregnant by Ross had produced Pepper: Harmony was not willing to think of either guy as just a total mistake.

"Harmony, never go out with a guy with sideburns like that," Gary had said, in disgust, the first time he met Webb. "Those sideburns are from another age."

It was true that Webb had biker sideburns—he had mainly been a biker until he got in the tow-truck business.

"Gary, I guess my standards are just different," Harmony said. She couldn't imagine rejecting a guy with a shy grin like Webb's just because his sideburns were a little long—that was before she knew about the impatience, of course, or any of Webb's other bad habits, such as having five or six girlfriends strung out up and down I-15, from Las Vegas to San Bernardino.

Speaking of impatience, Gary himself didn't have much room to talk; he was becoming more and more intolerant of her boyfriends, although quite a few of *his* boyfriends were really nothing to write home about.

"Your standards are the standards a doormat would have if a doormat wanted to claim it had standards," Gary said. He was on his way down from taking too much speed and was unusually bitchy—later he apologized for that remark. It *had* hurt Harmony's feelings; she didn't feel she was exactly a doormat because she tried to be accepting of things about her menfolk that maybe she wasn't too fond of, such as Jimmy's digestive condition or

Webb's impatience; after all, nobody was perfect and if you weren't willing to put up with a little imperfection in a guy, here and there, then the alternative was to have no relationship, and be alone.

Harmony had gone to see Pepper's rich husband, Mel, in the hospital in Tulsa, a few days before he died of pancreatic cancer. Mel was very weak at the time, he was on his way out and he knew it, but being weak didn't make Mel less smart. Even if Pepper and Mel hadn't actually lived together very long, before Pepper went to New York, Harmony considered that her daughter was lucky to have been married to a man who was so smart. Mel's eyes were tired when Harmony visited him the last time; she could tell that he had had about enough of the pain and the struggle. Harmony was feeling apologetic about Pepper. After all, Pepper and Mel were still married and Mel was dying, but Pepper didn't come to visit him—it seemed to her that Pepper ought to make a little more effort to be a wife in Mel's last days as a living person.

But when Harmony tried to apologize for her daughter, Mel smiled his sad little smile—it had been a sad little smile even before he got cancer of the pancreas—and shook his head.

"We choose our lovers for their flaws, you know," Mel said. "People would be bored shitless if they had to love only the good in someone they care about."

The comment took Harmony by surprise; it was not something you would expect a dying man to say—or any man to say, for that matter.

"Pepper's very very selfish," Mel said. "You know that and I know that. Yet you and I are mature people, Harmony, and we both love her deeply even though we both know she's totally selfish. She's not going to walk around the block for either of us, but I'll be thinking of her when I die, and I'll be lucky that I had someone in my life who was flawed in such a way that I could love her that much."

"I wish you wouldn't die, Mel," Harmony said. He was such a kind man, and so wise, and he had been so good to Pepper.

But, less than a week later, Mel did die—maybe it was better. At the end it was clear that he had been in too much pain, despite all the drugs they gave him. The pain still showed in his eyes.

As Harmony was trying to ease Gary's car into a parking space at the airport, she thought of Mel's remark, about loving people

52

for their flaws; she decided it was probably true. Most of the guys in her life had flaws you could drive a truck through; even so, she loved them. The one man who hadn't seemed too flawed was Didier, her first lover, a Frenchman who produced the floor show at the Tropicana—Didier had died in a suite, upstairs at the Trop, one morning while waiting for his breakfast.

Of course, Harmony had only been sixteen then; had she been older, she might have detected a few flaws in Didier; but she hadn't been older, and she remembered her time with Didier as the one perfect love of her life. It was still all she could do not to cry when she thought of him, he had been so kind.

There had been something in Didier's kindness that reminded Harmony of Mel; she wished she could remember Didier better, so she could compare the kindnesses.

In Mel's kindness, it seemed to her, there was a kind of defeat —though it wasn't that Mel wasn't cheerful. Lots of times, after Pepper left for New York, Mel would ask Harmony over for dinner; maybe they'd just have soup or a salad or something and then play rummy or some simple card game. They would tell jokes, and reminisce about Las Vegas in the old days. Mel had even known Didier, for example.

Still, Harmony thought she had at least a little intuition—there was some defeat lurking in Mel's kindness; maybe there had been defeat in Didier's kindness too; but, at sixteen, she had known nothing of the defeats that haunted men—what could she know? It was only remembering Mel's remark about loving flaws that got her thinking about it; that, and the fact that Pepper and Mel were both dead.

Harmony didn't have a confident feeling about there being a heaven; somehow the descriptions she had heard didn't ring true; but she did like to think that *something* of a person survived. She wanted to hope that Pepper and Mel would make some kind of contact in the afterlife, if there was one. Mainly she hoped it for Mel's sake. He truly loved Pepper and really, in Harmony's opinion, deserved more contact with her than he had got to have in life.

When she and Gary walked out to his car that morning, the letter about Pepper was still there in the yard. One page was over in a corner of the yard, one page had sort of curled up, and the third page was under the little cactus. Harmony was for keeping on walking at that point, but Gary noticed the letter right away.

"Is that the letter?" he asked.

"Yes, let's hurry, I don't want to be late to the airport," Harmony said.

"Harmony, it's at least five hours before your sisters will be here," Gary said.

"The plane could be early," Harmony said—it was just a dodge, and she knew it. No plane was going to be five hours early. But she was afraid there might be something in the letter that was too upsetting—reading it might cause a bomb of grief to go off inside her, disabling her permanently. The bomb might damage her so badly that she wouldn't be able to be a stable mom to Eddie—and being a stable mom was her one duty, now. Pepper was dead, there was no more to do for her, but there were years and years of waffles to make for Eddie, birthday parties to give, puppies to housebreak; someday there would be Little League, and trips to Disneyland, and thousands of meals involving macaroni and cheese and the other foods Eddie liked to eat.

Gary, though, was oblivious to her worries about the bomb of grief. He gathered up the three pages of the letter and handed them to Harmony.

"You're going to have a long wait at the airport," Gary said. "Maybe you'll feel like reading this then."

"I'll never feel like reading it, Gary," Harmony said, but she put the letter in her purse anyway. Gary seemed to think she ought to preserve it.

One thing Gary was right about was that she was going to have plenty of time on her hands once she got to the airport. It was four and a half hours until her sisters' plane came in, but Harmony felt a little relieved at the prospect of the wait. It was nice of everybody to gather around at the time of tragedy, but it also took dealing with.

At the airport, she didn't have to deal with anything. She went straight to the bar and had five Bombay martinis—probably she had not consumed five Bombay martinis in her whole thirty years in Las Vegas. She didn't feel them at all, either—the only problem was that the bartender looked familiar and actually *was* familiar;

his name was Wendell, and he had once been a boyfriend of Myrtle's.

It wasn't that Harmony didn't like Wendell. She had always liked him—but the fact that he was a bartender made the airport a little less of a neutral zone. The last time she had seen Wendell he had been working at an Exxon station on the Strip; it was a shock to see him behind the bar at the airport lounge, serving her Bombay martinis at eight-thirty in the morning.

"Harmony, that's gin you're drinking, not water," Wendell commented—he seemed a little disapproving. Probably he just didn't want her to drive, if she was drinking. It was good of Wendell to be concerned, but it didn't explain why he had stopped being a filling station attendant on the Strip and become a bartender in the airport lounge.

"Wendell, did you always want to be a bartender?" Harmony asked. She was curious about people who suddenly made big changes in their lives. The big changes that had come in her life had mostly been made from the outside; being fired from her job as a showgirl, for example, or getting pregnant by Webb.

"I went to bartending school," Wendell informed her, with some pride. "The thing was, I got tired of being greasy, and having to use that strong soap to get clean. That strong soap ain't good for the skin."

By this time Harmony's memory had begun to work a little. She remembered that Wendell had a son, and the son had died of AIDS. That Wendell had had a tragedy in his life made her feel sorry for him. Many times, in the old days, Harmony had defended Wendell against some of Myrtle's wilder charges.

"Wendell, do you remember my daughter?" Harmony asked—in those years she and Pepper had shared a duplex with Myrtle.

"Pepper, why sure I remember her," Wendell said. "Who could forget a girl that pretty?"

"She's dead," Harmony said. "I just found out. I'm here to meet my sisters."

"My Lord, don't tell me," Wendell said.

"That's why I'm drinking, but it's okay," Harmony said. "My sisters live in Oklahoma, they're both good drivers. They can drive me home."

"You're in shock, no wonder you don't feel that gin," Wendell said. "How old was she?"

"Twenty-two," Harmony said. "Nearly twenty-three."

"Well, my Lord," Wendell said. "My boy was twenty-three when he passed on."

Wendell had big, sad eyes. Harmony thought it said something good about his character that he had wanted to improve himself badly enough that he enrolled in bartending school. Not many men who were older and who had a big sorrow would keep trying to that extent.

Harmony had several more Bombay martinis—now that he knew the circumstances Wendell had stopped being disapproving. Then she realized she might not have enough money to pay for so many drinks. Fortunately she had just enough cash, but it meant she had no money to leave Wendell as a tip, though she would have liked to tip him.

"Don't worry about no tip," Wendell said, seeing her dilemma. "Couldn't we have a date sometime? I've been moony about you all these years."

That was a bolt from the blue—she had been right to feel that the airport wasn't as much of a neutral zone as she had hoped it would be.

"Wendell, you have?" she asked, sort of stunned.

"Sure, you remember how good I used to do your windshields?" he said.

Harmony was flabbergasted, she hadn't even seen Wendell in six or seven years, though now that he mentioned it, she *did* recall that he had done a very thorough job of cleaning her windshields if she happened to gas up at the Exxon where he worked.

"I know Myrtle was mean to you, maybe that's why," Harmony said.

"No, it's because you're beautiful, that's all the why there has to be," Wendell said.

All of a sudden Harmony felt drunk. She was having trouble even closing her purse, and Wendell seemed to be hovering over her, waiting for some form of answer about the date. She was regretting that she didn't have enough money just to leave him a tip, it would make things so much simpler. What made it all complicated was that it had just occurred to her that when people died there was a funeral, but Pepper was already cremated, could there be a funeral for a person who was cremated?

"Wendell, Pepper's cremated, can there still be a funeral?" Harmony asked; maybe Wendell would know—even if he didn't it might sort of deflect the question of the date.

"Sure, you can have any kind of service you want, we had a real nice one for Johnny," Wendell said.

Harmony was about to ask him if she could think about the date for a day or two, but that was just a slow way of saying no. His big sad eyes would just get sadder, and, anyway, Jimmy Bangor was gone; there was no particular reason why she shouldn't have a date with Wendell. After all, they had something in common: a dead child.

Later, Harmony couldn't exactly remember how they left it about the date; the next thing she knew, she was standing in front of a picture of herself with Mr. Sinatra—a picture made long ago. The walkways that led to the boarding lounges were lined with photographs of famous celebrities who had performed in Las Vegas. There were showgirls in quite a few of the pictures, and, down one of the walkways, there was a picture of her with Elvis, another of her with Liberace, and one of her with Mr. Sinatra—that was the one she had just happened to stop in front of. He had been a perfect gentleman and had even sent her flowers once.

The problem was, she looked like Pepper, standing there with Mr. Sinatra. All through Pepper's girlhood people were always telling Harmony how much Pepper looked like her, but Harmony could never see it. Pepper had always seemed so much more beautiful. But, looking once more at the picture of her standing with Mr. Sinatra, Harmony suddenly saw what people had been talking about. She had looked a lot like Pepper, just as beautiful, only with a good deal more bust. The woman in the picture with Mr. S. could have been Pepper, although she hadn't even been born when the picture was taken.

Mr. Sinatra was still alive, she herself was still alive, Wendell was still alive, but Pepper, her beautiful daughter, had come and gone. Pepper never would be photographed with Mr. Sinatra, though he was probably still a perfect gentleman and would probably even send Pepper flowers, too.

While Harmony stood in front of the photograph, several people stopped to ask if she was all right—it must be clear even to strangers walking by that she was pretty upset; she couldn't help it, she felt as if she were looking at her daughter, though really she was looking at herself, in a time when she was young and had not known loss.

Thinking about it gave Harmony the feeling that the bomb of grief was about to explode inside her, so she stumbled into the ladies' room and shut herself in a stall, to wait for the explosion. Instead of the bomb going off, though, she just began to feel tired. Probably it was all those Bombay martinis—she had never been able to drink huge amounts without fading out at some point.

She took the letter out of her purse—Gary was right, she would have to read it sometime, it might as well be now, while she was safe in the stall. The whole ladies' room was empty, she had finally found a neutral zone; probably when people arrived in Las Vegas they were so eager to gamble that they just rushed right to the casinos and let their bladders make the best of it—no doubt that was why the ladies' room was so empty.

Harmony unfolded the letter and got the pages in the correct order and was about to begin reading it—certainly it was written in a very clear hand—when her eyelids began to get heavy. It felt as if someone had attached little tiny weights to them; despite her efforts to focus on the letter her eyelids just kept descending. Finally she had to give up; she leaned her head against the side of the stall for a moment. Since no one was in the rest room she thought it might be permissible just to nap for a few minutes; after all, it had been a long night.

It seemed to Harmony that she had barely closed her eyes when she heard her sister Neddie say something to her sister Pat. No doubt it was a dream—Neddie and Pat lived only a mile or two from one another and talked to one another in person or on the phone ten or fifteen times a day; it was logical to dream of them having a conversation, they had them constantly.

In this dream, though, Neddie and Pat seemed to be talking about her—they were wondering what could have become of her. Of course, nothing had become of her, she had just dozed for a minute or two, in a stall in the ladies' room.

"She never has developed no sense of direction, she could be halfway to San Francisco by now—and still expecting to come to the airport any minute," Neddie said.

"I figure some man waylaid her," Pat said. "She's prone to having that happen, you have to admit."

"I wouldn't talk, if I were you," Neddie said dryly. On the whole Neddie stuck to a very dry way of speaking.

"Look at it this way, she's got a bigger pool to fish in," Pat said. "If I'd had Las Vegas to fish in, instead of Tulsa, I expect I'd have held my own in the boyfriend department."

"No, because you keep marrying them," Neddie said. "Harmony didn't make that mistake but once."

Harmony was getting a little more awake, but the dream wasn't stopping, exactly. It was almost as if Pat and Neddie were right there in the ladies' room with her, Pat in the stall to the left and Neddie in the stall to the right. Harmony glanced at her watch and almost fainted: four and one half hours had gone by since she sat down in the stall. Her sisters' plane could have landed. It wasn't a dream. Her sisters themselves were right there in the ladies' room, talking about her.

To make sure, she peeked under the partition between her stall and the stall to her right. She saw a plain brown shoe and knew she hadn't been dreaming at all, her sisters *were* in the ladies' room, in stalls on either side of her. It seemed a little peculiar that they had just gone on talking, with an innocent third party in the stall between them; but, then, Neddie and Pat weren't very formal, they tended to continue speaking their minds whatever the circumstances.

Anyway, Harmony was excited that they were there, she wanted to make her presence known before either sister accidentally said something that would create an awkwardness.

"Neddie, I'm not lost, I'm here—I've been asleep," she said. "Pat, don't say anything too mean about me."

About that time the toilets on both sides of her flushed—she wasn't too sure her sisters even heard her; if they *hadn't* heard her they might just walk off—neither of them was the type to hang around waiting very long.

She popped out, and there they were. Neddie was skinny and Pat was chubby; both were soberly dressed, as befitted the occasion.

"Poor thing, I guess you cried all night," Neddie said, taking Harmony into her arms.

"What's that red splotch on her cheek?" Pat asked, waiting her turn to hug. "Is that from going to sleep in the crapper or did some big bozo slug her?"

"I guess from going to sleep in the john," Harmony said, hugging her. Pat still wore a strong perfume.

Then Harmony realized she still had the letter from New York in her hand—the letter that had brought her the news.

"Pat, would you carry this letter?" Harmony asked, quickly handing it to her.

Pat took the letter and began reading it as they walked out of the airport. It irked Harmony a little, that Pat would just immediately start reading the letter, instead of putting it in her purse. It was just like Pat, though—she had always been nosy about family matters.

"Pat, you don't have to read it right here in the airport," Harmony said. "You could read it when we get home."

Neddie glanced at her when she said it—she could tell from Harmony's tone of voice that she was a little bit irritated with Pat for diving right into the letter.

Then, as Pat read the letter, she stopped walking along in stride with the two of them. When she finished a page she carefully put it behind the others. Her pace had definitely slowed.

"What's the matter with you, can't you keep up?" Neddie said. Just looking at Pat's face made Harmony really apprehensive. It might be that the letter contained news that was worse than any they had expected to receive.

Harmony began to wish she had never handed the letter to Pat. She wished it had blown away in the night. Pat was hardly walking at all, as she read. Then she came to a complete stop, right in the middle of the airport; she had a very sad look on her face.

"Pat, was she murdered, is that it?" Harmony asked; she suddenly couldn't bear not to know what the letter said.

Pat stood right where she was until she had read all three pages of the letter, which she then very carefully folded and put in her purse. She started to take out a compact and powder her nose, an act that was almost a reflex if she happened to have her handbag open. In this case, though, she decided to let the handbag be.

"Was she murdered, Pat?" Harmony asked, again—she knew from watching the news that crime was bad in New York City.

"No, honey," Pat said. "Pepper wasn't murdered. Pepper died of AIDS."

"Oh," Harmony said—then the bomb of grief exploded, right there in the airport. It was a quiet explosion, so far as the public knew; she didn't even scream. All she did was cry so hard that she became a little unsteady on her feet. The ten Bombay martinis probably hadn't helped any—though they had made her drunk enough that she could go to sleep in the toilet stall.

Her sisters, who held her arms, had to ask her for directions several times before she was able to guide them across the parking lot, in the bright Nevada sun, to Gary's car.

7.

When Wendell showed up at the door of the apartment, expecting to have a date with her, Harmony lay on the couch, semiconscious from having cried herself out. Neddie was reading Eddie a Bible story from a book she had bought in a religious bookshop in Tulsa. Specifically, she was reading Eddie the story of Daniel in the lion's den, when the doorbell rang.

"Get it, Pat, maybe it's Gary," Harmony said—after all, she still had his car.

Eddie liked it when his Aunt Neddie read him stories, but he was not totally convinced by the story of Daniel in the lion's den.

"Lions are supposed to be fierce," he said. Then he made his grr sound for his aunt.

"I know that—they're fierce," Neddie said.

"Then how come they didn't eat Daniel—were they wimpy lions or what?"

Pat opened the door, spoke briefly to Wendell, and shut the door again.

"It's not Gary," she informed Harmony. "It's some big clunk who says he has a date with you."

"Oh, no . . . it's Wendell," Harmony said. "He's a bartender at the airport. I got drunk this morning while I was waiting for your plane. Maybe I told him I'd have a date with him. He used to go with Myrtle."

"Well, he's here—do you want to have the date with him or don't you?" Pat asked. She had been making biscuits for Eddie and had flour on her hands.

"No, I don't, I must have said the wrong thing while I was drunk," Harmony said.

"Then would you mind if I go in your place?" Pat asked. "I kinda like his looks."

"Pat, you're making biscuits!" Harmony protested—it had never entered her mind that Pat might want to go out with Wendell.

"The biscuits are made," Pat said. "All Neddie's got to do is take them out of the oven in about ten minutes. I've already set the timer."

"You shouldn't have let her answer the door," Neddie said, in her flat way, giving Harmony a look. "Pattie, she'll take just about anybody she finds on her doorstep."

"Well, do you care or don't you?" Pat asked. "I hate to keep the man waiting—it's hot out there."

"No, you can go with him, I don't care—where was he planning to take me?" Harmony asked, feeling extremely confused. Her daughter was dead of AIDS and now her sister was itching to go out with Wendell, who had arrived expecting to have a date with her.

"Burger King, he said, but I'll see if I can't raise his sights a little," Pat said. "I feel more like Hawaiian food."

"Pat, Wendell doesn't have much money," Harmony said, remembering the days when Wendell had been a gas station attendant—sometimes he would have to go Dutch with Myrtle even if they just went to the Taco Bell.

"He'll have less before the night is over," Neddie predicted.

"What about the lions, why didn't they *eat Daniel?*" Eddie wanted to know. He hated it when stories were interrupted.

"Daniel prayed to God and God made the lions gentle," Neddie told him.

"But lions *can't* be gentle, they have to be fierce," Eddie insisted.

Pat opened the front door a crack and smiled at Wendell, who stood on the front steps as if planted. He looked a little confused.

"My sister's prostrate with grief," Pat told him. "She don't want to ruin your evening, though. How about if you and I go eat some Hawaiian food?"

Wendell had been a little frightened at the prospect of actually going out with Harmony, though he had been wanting to do just that for at least ten years. He knew she had been drunk that morning, when she made the date, and was prepared for her to inform him it had all been a mistake; but now her plump sister was proposing to take him off to eat Hawaiian food, whatever that might be. Despite being plump, the sister looked pretty in the face, too.

"Okay, don't go away, I'll just be a minute," Pat said, shutting the door in Wendell's face before he had a chance to think up an excuse.

"Pat, you could have asked him in," Harmony said. "You said yourself it was hot out."

"Why risk it, he might remember it's you he's in love with," Pat said, taking off her apron. "Seeing you in your nightgown might jog his memory or something, and then I'd have a boring evening."

At that point Harmony remembered how irritating her sister Pat could be. Supposedly she had come all the way from Oklahoma to provide a little comfort in time of grief, but now all she could think of was making Wendell buy her a Hawaiian dinner that was probably way more than he could afford.

"Pat, he's not good at conversation," Harmony said, but Pat had already raced upstairs to freshen up; two minutes later she raced back down and was out the door without a fare-thee-well.

Meanwhile, Neddie was having hard going with the Bible stories. Harmony had never told Eddie much about God, mainly because she didn't know much about God; she sort of believed in letting children figure religion out for themselves. Now Neddie was reading Eddie the story of Jonah and the whale and Eddie had the look on his face that he got when he was hearing something from an adult that he didn't believe. It was a skeptical look—if Eddie didn't believe something, he didn't believe it, even if it was from the Bible. Harmony began to feel a little guilty; probably she should have been taking him to Sunday school instead of letting him watch TV so much.

"Aunt Neddie, whales don't eat people," Eddie said immediately, when Neddie finished the Jonah story. "Whales eat plankton

64

—they're like little tiny shrimps. Whales eat millions and millions of plankton. I learned about them on the Discovery Channel."

"This story happened a long time ago, Eddie," Neddie said. "Maybe whales ate different foods in those days."

"But whales are gentle creatures," Eddie protested. He loved the Discovery Channel—it was full of information about animals he was interested in.

"People can swim right up to them and pet them in the water," he added. "They don't swallow people."

"Well, the Bible says one swallowed Jonah, but at least the story had a happy ending," Neddie said, closing the book of Bible stories. She had three grandchildren and none of them had any trouble believing that the whale had swallowed Jonah. All of her grandkids were as mean as little wildcats, whereas Eddie was a sweet, bright boy, who said "Please" and "Thank you," and who probably didn't bash his playmates, as her own grandchildren were always doing. He just happened to have a skeptical attitude toward Bible stories, which was no doubt mostly his mother's fault, for not taking him to Sunday school, not to mention letting him watch too much weird TV.

Later, after Eddie had gone to bed, Harmony wanted Neddie to read the letter from New York; she decided it was time to try and absorb a little more information about Pepper's death—how Pepper got AIDS, if anyone knew, and where her ashes were now, and what procedures needed to be followed in the next few days. She was also curious about who Laurie was, the kind of person who had written the letter. Harmony had the feeling that someday she would maybe want to go meet Laurie and try to find out what Pepper's last years had been like.

But when Neddie went upstairs to get the letter she discovered that Pat apparently still had it in her purse, and now Pat had left on a date with Wendell.

"I guess we'll just have to wait till your friend brings her home —if he does," Neddie said.

"What do you mean 'if he does'?" Harmony asked. "It's just a first date. They won't do anything on their first date, will they?"

Neddie didn't answer. She had begun to smoke more lately, and she was smoking now.

"It was me he was supposed to have the date with, not Pat,"

Harmony said. The fact that Pat had casually taken the letter off with her seemed to be just one more example of how inconsiderate her sister could be. She had not only taken the letter, she had also taken Wendell, who was Harmony's admirer, if he was anyone's.

"It wouldn't hurt you to take Eddie to Sunday school once in a while," Neddie said.

"Neddie, I never got in the habit," Harmony said, a little defensively. Mainly Eddie watched cartoons on Sunday morning, when Sunday school was happening.

"He's just five," Neddie pointed out. She didn't know why she bothered, though—Harmony was never likely to take Eddie to Sunday school. "It wouldn't hurt him to have another point of view and not just have his head totally filled with things he's learned on TV."

Harmony couldn't quite get her mind off the vexing problem of Wendell and Pat.

"You don't think she'd do anything on the first date, particularly since it was supposed to be my date, do you?" she asked—she was beginning to feel a little insecure.

"Do you know about Masters and Johnson, that couple in St. Louis?" Neddie asked. "They're doctors."

The names sounded familiar but, tired as she was, Harmony couldn't quite place them.

"Do they have a talk show?" she asked.

"No, they're them sex doctors that they send molesters to, and stuff," Neddie said.

"Oh," Harmony said. "What about them?"

"Your sister's been to see them three times," Neddie said. "They're trying to get her cured of sex addiction, but so far they ain't had much luck."

"What?" Harmony asked. Her mind had been sort of switching channels, it had just switched back to the Pepper channel; the fact that Pepper was dead just wouldn't go away, not for long—it kept returning, to weigh down her mind and her heart. She didn't understand what Neddie was getting at, when she mentioned Pat and the sex doctors in St. Louis.

"She's been there three times for sex addiction," Neddie repeated, in her flat voice.

66

"Pat's got sex addiction?" Harmony said—that was certainly a channel-switching piece of information.

"Yep," Neddie said. "It's the talk of Tarwater, and has been for years. Masters and Johnson thought they could get her calmed down, but they ain't having no luck. If you ask me, Pat's more revved up than ever."

"Oh, my God," Harmony said—it had never occurred to her that anyone could be a sex addict, much less one of her own sisters. Though, thinking back, she could imagine that maybe sex addiction was what had been wrong with Denny, a boyfriend from years ago. If anyone in her own life had been afflicted with sex addiction, it was probably Denny; he had not been interested in much of anything else, not while he had been with Harmony anyway. The reason she broke up with him was because he had had the gall to ask Pepper for a blow job, this was when Pepper was no more than sixteen. But that was just Denny, he was no prize—she had booted him right out of her life the day she found out he had made that offensive suggestion to Pepper.

"Neddie, are you sure?" she asked.

"I guess I'm sure—I drove her to St. Louis myself all three times," Neddie said. "Every man in Tarwater knows better than to go within thirty feet of Pat."

"Good Lord," Harmony said. "I wish you'd told me that before I let her go off with Wendell."

"I meant to but it's kind of hard to work sex addiction into a conversation, particularly with Eddie bouncing around," Neddie said. "He liked them biscuits, didn't he?"

Eddie liked the biscuits so much that he had eaten four, with various jams and jellies. But now all Harmony could think of was that she had sent her sister off with Wendell, never dreaming that her sister was a sex addict who had been to St. Louis three times to get help. Years back, when Wendell had been dating Myrtle, Harmony remembered that Myrtle had been trying to slow him down a little bit, sexually, on the grounds that he had a bad back that was apt to go out and cause him excruciating pain if he wasn't careful in his movements. Pat had just met Wendell and was unaware of the problem with his back—Wendell, of course, was unaware that Pat had sex addiction. What if Pat's addiction flared up and tempted Wendell into some movement that caused him to become paralyzed? It would be terrible if, after going to bartending school and struggling to improve himself, Wendell became paralyzed because her sister Pat didn't have the self-discipline to keep her hands off him.

"How do you think Pepper got AIDS, Neddie?" Harmony asked. No matter how hard she tried to distract herself with thoughts of Eddie's skepticism about religion, or Pat's bad effect on Wendell's new career, little bombs of pain kept exploding inside her, and they were all about Pepper.

"Harmony, she's at peace now, however it happened, it's over," Neddie said.

"She was my daughter, I need to know," Harmony said. "She's been gone for six years. I wish I'd gone to visit her."

"Why didn't you, hon?" Neddie asked.

"She didn't want me to—we weren't real close," Harmony admitted. "Pepper was ashamed of my clothes, or something."

"That's just daughters, mine are the same way," Neddie said. "You just have to ignore the friction and do what you think ought to be done, anyway."

"I was scared of Pepper, she was always so sure of herself," Harmony said. "I should have taken Eddie to meet his sister, though—even if I was scared."

"There's lots of things I wish I'd done that I didn't do, honey," Neddie said. "That's life. We're all scared of something."

"What are you scared of?" Harmony asked. Her sister Neddie had never seemed to be the scared type. The one time Harmony had visited Neddie and Dick on their farm, Neddie had killed three rattlesnakes in her yard in one day. Having that many rattlesnakes around would have made Harmony too scared to move, but it didn't seem to faze Neddie at all.

"I'm afraid one of my kids will die," Neddie said. It was something she had never been able to get off her mind, during all her years of motherhood—and now the very thing that she had always feared had happened to her sister Harmony. Often she had dreamed that a child of hers would be taken by one of the common afflictions: car wreck, drowning, hunting accident, fatal disease, drugs. And yet it had turned out that Harmony's gifted daughter was the only second-generation loss the family had suffered.

About all Harmony could remember about her brother-in-law, Dick Haley, was that he believed every word of the Bible to be literally true. Whether he had been a good husband to Neddie she had no way of knowing. It seemed to Harmony that it was just as well that Eddie and Dick had never met, given the fact that Eddie had his doubts about some of the Bible stories. She didn't know how Dick would react to some of the information Eddie had picked up on the Discovery Channel, even though most of it was just normal information about animal life, as far as she could tell.

"Why don't you come home with us, Sis?" Neddie asked.

"Do what?" Harmony asked. She had been wondering whether Dick and Eddie would hit it off; she had read an article in a magazine she had browsed through at the hairdresser's, an article about role models. The article made her feel a little guilty, because she definitely had not provided Eddie with much in the way of role models. Jimmy Bangor was a recent example of a boyfriend who hadn't been really bad but who also wasn't much to write home about if you were picking role models for a bright little boy like Eddie.

"Come home with us," Neddie said again. "You been out here in this desert too long, Harmony, and the glory days are over. Come home to Tarwater and let Pat help you raise your little boy."

"But Pat's a sex addict, you just said so yourself," Harmony said. Actually, the remark took her by surprise; she wanted to give herself a little time to think. With Pepper dead and her heart so weighted down, with bombs of grief exploding inside her practically all the time now, it was hard to know where she was going to find the spirit to be a good mom to Eddie. The thought of having her sister's help was so appealing and so comforting that she was a little afraid to let herself really consider it. What if Neddie had just said it without really meaning it? What if Dick Haley vetoed the notion because she had not given Eddie good training in regard to the Bible? Having her sisters to help her was almost too much to hope for, though part of her certainly wanted to hope for it.

"Oh, Pat's wild, but she's got her good points," Neddie allowed. "She's good with kids, as long as they ain't *her* kids. She's been a good aunt to my kids—they'd go to her in a crisis ten times quicker than they'd come to me."

"Eddie does like her biscuits, he ate four," Harmony said. "But he's in school here—he's got his little friends."

"Harmony, Eddie's five years old," Neddie reminded her again. "He's sociable too. He could make friends in Oklahoma."

"I guess so," Harmony said. "Eddie's just always led an urban life."

"Tulsa's urban," Neddie reminded her. "I didn't mean you'd have to live right in Tarwater—I know our schools ain't as good as the schools in town. You can live where you please, as far as that goes. I just think you need to be closer to your kinfolk, so we can help you in this time of grief."

"Oh, Neddie," Harmony said. "Why did she have to get AIDS?"

Then a big bomb of grief exploded, and all Harmony could do was cry.

8.

"**W**here's Aunt Pat?" Eddie asked the next morning, when he came bounding down the stairs. His Mom was asleep on the couch, wrapped up in an old red blanket, and his Aunt Neddie was sitting at the kitchen table, smoking and drinking coffee.

"Good question, where is your Aunt Pat?" Neddie asked.

"Maybe a dinosaur ate her?" Eddie speculated. He owned several small rubber dinosaurs himself; but he knew that real dinosaurs were very large—and, unlike whales, they didn't just eat plankton.

"Dinosaurs might even eat aunts," he told his Aunt Neddie. "Is my Mom just taking a nap?

"I'm in the mood for an omelette," Eddie added. "My teacher says eggs are fine as long as you don't eat them every day."

"Why wouldn't they be fine?" Neddie asked. "Your Uncle Dick eats three or four of them every day and he's pretty healthy."

"Bad cholesterol!" Eddie said. "You're not supposed to eat them every day. Are there any biscuits left?"

"One," Neddie said, looking in the oven. She cut the last biscuit open and buttered it for Eddie, who munched on it while she made the omelette. Now and then he went over and peeked at his mother, to see if there was any sign that she was about to wake up from her nap.

"She doesn't usually nap when it's time to get me off to school," he informed his aunt.

Harmony wasn't sleeping that deeply; she was just a little reluctant to open her eyes and face the truth, which was that her daughter was dead. Her son was alive, though—she heard his quick voice through the fog in her head. When she reached out to Eddie, she happened to catch him by the hand that held what was left of the buttery biscuit.

"Uh-oh, Mom—crumbs on the carpet," Eddie said. "Aunt Neddie's making an omelette, would you like to share?"

"No, but you're sweet to offer, honey," Harmony said, pulling Eddie up onto the couch with her, crumbs or no crumbs. He was still in his pajamas, and smelled sweet, the way he always smelled when he had just bounced out of bed.

"Aunt Pat's gone, we think a dinosaur ate her," Eddie said. "Aren't you going to work today, Mom?"

"Not today," Harmony said. "I think I'll just stay home and visit with your aunts."

"One aunt," Eddie corrected. "A brontosaurus ate Aunt Pat."

"I hope so," Harmony said. "That's better than having your Aunt Pat eat Wendell—how dare she stay out this late?"

"Ever since Pat got money she's been a law unto herself," Neddie said. "Come eat your omelette, Eddie."

"I love having my aunts here to cook, Mom," Eddie said, pouncing on his omelette. "That way you can take naps."

"It wasn't so much a nap as just going to bed too late, honey," Harmony said, sitting up. The movement made her realize that her head hurt—her stomach didn't feel in the best condition, either. Later in the evening, after Neddie had dozed off, she had had a few rum Cokes; she wanted to fog out, if possible, and not sit there feeling that she would have to be awake forever, with little bombs of regret and sadness exploding over and over in her consciousness—the little bombs seemed to rock her harder each time.

"What kind of cookies do you have for my lunch?" Eddie inquired.

"Maybe just Oreos," Harmony said, dragging herself up.

72

"I'll make his lunch, hon," Neddie said, seeing that her sister was not too steady on her feet.

"No," Harmony said. "I want to."

"Yes, because my Mom knows *exactly* how I like lunches," Eddie said. It was fine having his aunts to cook breakfast, but he preferred to have his own mother make his lunch and pack his lunchbox, even though she usually had a variety of cookies, not just Oreos.

Harmony and Neddie stood in the yard and waved at the school bus as it pulled away—through the window Eddie, sitting, as usual, with his friend Eli, waved back.

"One of my aunts didn't come home last night," Eddie informed Eli. "I think a dinosaur ate her."

"It couldn't have been, because dinosaurs are extinct," Eli said. "You know that."

"There might be just one that isn't extinct," Eddie said. "It could be over there behind that building eating my aunt. Maybe it will eat this school bus and then we'll all be deaded."

Eli didn't take the remark seriously. As usual, he was eating the licorice out of his lunch.

The school bus had barely rounded the corner when a white limo pulled up at the apartment building and stopped.

"I wonder if that's Giovanni?" Harmony said. She had briefly had an Italian boyfriend who was a limo driver—once in a great while Giovanni would cruise by, and stop in for a little visit.

It definitely wasn't Giovanni this time, though, because Pat got out of the limo and came sauntering up the sidewalk, as if being dropped off by limo at her sister's apartment in Las Vegas was the most normal thing in the world.

"Boy, they make lousy margaritas in this town," Pat said. "You'd think with all the Mexicans here they'd make better margaritas. I hope you have lots of coffee—I've got a headache that won't quit."

"Probably if you tried sleeping normal hours you wouldn't get them bad headaches," Neddie suggested.

"I'll sleep when I'm old, like you," Pat said. She appeared to be in a very cheerful mood, headache or no headache.

"What'd you do with Wendell?" Harmony asked. She still felt a little annoyed that Pat had just marched off with him.

"Wendell dulled out on me," Pat said. "That's why I started

guzzling margaritas. Listening to the ice clink is more interesting than trying to make conversation with that big lug."

"I *told* you he wasn't good at conversation," Harmony reminded her.

"You should have just said he was mute and left it at that," Pat said. "I don't know where you find these men, Harmony—or *why* you find them, either. There's livelier old boys than Wendell in pretty much any beer joint in Oklahoma."

"They may be livelier but I bet they aren't sweeter," Harmony said—she hadn't seen Wendell but once in several years, though she felt obliged to defend him against her sister's insults.

"So who popped for the limo?" Neddie inquired, once they were back inside. Pat poured coffee into a cup until the cup ran over, and then started drinking the coffee out of the saucer.

"Some high roller from Venezuela, I never gave him the time of day," Pat said. "He ain't discouraged, though—I expect I'll hear from him later."

Both Harmony and Neddie received this news skeptically.

"If you never gave him the time of day, why'd he send you home in a limo?" Neddie asked.

"Because he thinks I'll give him the time of day and put a little sugar on it, at some point," Pat said. "Why does any guy loan a lonely-looking lady his limo?"

"Pat, I'm worried about Wendell, he isn't sophisticated," Harmony said.

"That's the understatement of the year," Pat said.

"Wendell's been sweet to me ever since I've known him," Harmony said. "He used to do a real good job on my windshield, when he worked at the Exxon station. I hope you weren't rude to him, or anything.

"If I hadn't been drunk at the airport I never would have agreed to the date," she added.

"Why not, if *he's* so sweet?" Pat asked.

Harmony didn't answer. The last thing she needed to be discussing with her sister was her reasons for not dating Wendell—actually, the main reason for not dating him was that she hadn't even known he was still in town, that plus loyalty to Myrtle. Once Myrtle laid claim to a man she never really entirely relinquished the

74

claim. Myrtle had been known to reclaim boyfriends from thirty or forty years back. No doubt she would immediately try to reclaim Wendell if she thought Harmony had the least interest in him.

"I meant to read the letter last night," Harmony said. "But we couldn't find it—it must still be in your purse."

Pat opened her purse and handed Harmony the letter without comment.

"I think Harmony ought to move back to Oklahoma, what do you think?" Neddie asked Pat.

"I think she'd be bored shitless in Oklahoma, but maybe I'm wrong," Pat said, looking at Harmony in a kindly way. "It'd be good for Eddie, though—he don't need to be growing up in an environment like this."

"Pat, it's a good environment, the air's real clear," Harmony protested. "Eddie hardly ever gets a cold."

"I wasn't thinking about the air, Harmony," Pat said. "This town is about gambling and sex and drugs and staying up all night wasting money."

"The very thing your kids are into, back in Oklahoma," Neddie said, in her dry voice.

"I know, but at least we don't have a whole city of it, with twenty-four-hour roulette," Pat said. "Harmony, haven't you lived here long enough? Wouldn't you like to come home with Neddie and me and live a normal life for a while?"

"Maybe," Harmony said. "I want to read the letter before I decide."

She took the letter and started outside with it. Both sisters looked startled.

"What's wrong with just sitting on the couch and reading it?" Neddie asked.

"No, I'd rather sit in Gary's car, he's going to want it back pretty soon," Harmony said.

"You're going to sit in a car and read that letter?" Pat asked.

"Pat, it's where I feel safe—maybe it's because Gary has been such a good friend," Harmony said.

Or it might have been because she had borrowed so many cars in her years in Las Vegas that sitting in a borrowed car made her feel at home or something. Actually, the letter from the girl named

Laurie did not take a long time to read; Laurie's handwriting was quite large.

Dear Mrs. Palmer,

I regret to inform you that your daughter Pepper died last week. Some friends and I took up a collection and had Pepper cremated, as was her wish. I will be glad to send or bring you her ashes at your request.

Pepper and I had lived together for three years—it is a great loss for me, as I know it is for you.

The cause of death was AIDS. We were able to bring Pepper home about six days before the end—she died in the bed we shared so happily.

I am sorry I have to bring you this horrible news. Also, I'm sorry we haven't met. Pepper was always ambivalent about inviting you to come to our home, but I'm the same way about my mother and I love her very much. I guess girls just sometimes have trouble being friends with their mothers.

If you would ever like to come and stay with me and talk a little about Pepper's life you would be more than welcome.

I'm from California, if you don't feel up to a trip to New York perhaps someday we could meet in the west.

Pepper was the love of my life—I will miss her forever. She was a beautiful dancer and would have been a great star, had she lived.

> *Yours,*
> *Laurie Chalk*

Harmony sat in Gary's car for more than two hours, looking at the letter. Now and then she reread part of it, but mostly she just sat in the car, thinking about Pepper, thinking about Eddie, thinking about the future. Once the sun really got going it became a little too warm in the car, but Harmony rolled all the windows down and made the best of it. After an hour her sisters began to worry about her; they came out to the car to see whether she

76

was behaving rationally or not. Harmony told them she was fine. Neither of them believed it but there wasn't a great deal they could do about it, so they finally drifted back to the apartment.

For about five minutes Harmony considered the notion of stealing Gary's car and just driving away. Gary was a very understanding man; probably he would think it over and forgive her for stealing his car. Meanwhile Pat and Neddie could take Eddie home with them and raise him in a healthy rural place; he would grow up and be happy and maybe avoid the fate of his big sister: the fate of dying young. She knew she could count on her sisters to do a good job with Eddie. Even if Pat was troubled with sex addiction Neddie said she did a good job with children.

While daydreaming about stealing Gary's car and taking off, Harmony didn't develop much of a sense of what her own future might be. She thought she might just leave it to luck, her future. She would drive around America in Gary's car until the car suffered a final breakdown. Wherever that occurred, west, east, north, or south, Harmony would then live for the rest of her life. Fate would have decided the location for her. Perhaps it would be Biloxi, Mississippi, or somewhere, she had no idea how far Gary's car would make it, but at least it would make it to a place where no one knew her, a place where she would not have to conceal how guilty she felt about failing her children. Maybe some of the people she got to know would suspect that she had had a tragedy, but they would have no way of finding out what it was.

About noon, when Harmony was thinking she had better either steal the car or go inside and cool off, Neddie came out to check on her again.

"Are you ever coming in? It's hot in that car," Neddie said.

Harmony didn't answer. It *was* hot in the car, but she still felt reluctant to get out of it. As long as she was in the car she felt that she had options.

"You wasn't thinking of running away, was you?" Neddie asked. "That little boy would never get over it, if his Momma did something like that."

Harmony knew then that she had waited too long to steal the car.

"You can't run away and leave that little boy," Neddie repeated. "That would be the worst possible thing you could do."

Harmony didn't answer. How did Neddie know what the worst possible thing she could do might be? Even though Neddie was older, she couldn't know everything.

"Worse than if I became a drug addict?" she asked, in a voice that was almost a whisper.

"Yes, worse," Neddie said, without hesitation. "I was a dope addict myself, but I didn't go off and desert my kids."

"You were a dope addict?" Harmony said. "Neddie, I didn't know that."

"After Davie was born I got on them pain pills," Neddie said. "I stayed on them three years. Dick could never figure out where the egg money was going. That's where it was going, to pay for my dope."

"Oh, Neddie, was it a hard birth?" Harmony asked.

"It was hard enough, but that wasn't why I stayed on the pills," Neddie said. "I was sick of my life, so I doped out."

"Here," Harmony said, handing Neddie the letter.

Neddie got in the front seat of the hot car and unfolded the yellow sheets of paper. Neddie still moved her lips when she read; Harmony thought that was interesting. When Neddie finished the letter she folded it and handed it back to Harmony. When she did Harmony took the keys out of the ignition and gave them to Neddie.

"What do I want with these keys?" Neddie asked.

"Just give them to Gary when he comes to get his car," Harmony said. She didn't want to tell her sister that she didn't trust herself not to desert Eddie.

"Well, that's a decent letter," Neddie said. "It sounds like Pepper had a true friend in her hour of need. That's more than some people get."

"More than a true friend, Neddie," Harmony corrected. "Pepper was the love of Laurie's life. She died in the bed they were happy in—that's what the letter said."

"I can read," Neddie said. "If she was a girlfriend, so much the better, I guess."

"It says they shared it happily, that's good," Harmony said. "Pepper was the love of Laurie's life—that's a big thing to say.

"Is Dick the love of yours?" she asked, seeing that the phrase hadn't quite registered on her sister.

78

"No," Neddie said. "I like Dick and I respect him. But I was never in love with him."

"Not ever?" Harmony asked, shocked.

Harmony tried to figure out what that could possibly mean, in terms of her sister's life. She had lived with a man for more than thirty years, but had never been in love with him? Of course, she herself had frequently brought men home without being in love with them—Jimmy Bangor was a recent example—but she didn't keep them around for thirty years.

"Neddie, that's sad—isn't it?" Harmony said.

"Not everybody gets everything, Sis," Neddie said. "I was in love with Rusty, though. I guess I still am. He just won't do nothing about it."

"Who's Rusty?" Harmony asked.

"Dick's baby brother," Neddie said. "Rusty's a whole lot cuter than Dick. He's even got a sense of humor. Dick Haley wouldn't know a joke if one clobbered him."

"Where does Rusty live?" Harmony asked, trying to remember if she had ever known Rusty. So far her memory drew a blank.

"Down the road about two miles," Neddie said. "Rusty's a big help to me anyway. I go see him two or three times a day."

"So maybe he's kind of the love of your life," Harmony said.

"If he ain't then I didn't get to have no love of my life," Neddie said.

"Neddie, you're not old," Harmony said. "You could still have a love of your life."

"In Tarwater, Oklahoma?" Neddie said. "At my age?"

"Somebody could show up and surprise you," Harmony said. For some reason it had become important to her to at least keep the hope that her sister Neddie would get to have a love of her life, even if it was only her husband's brother, Rusty Haley.

"Who was the love of yours?" Neddie asked—they both saw Pat coming down the sidewalk with a pitcher in her hand, and three glasses.

"Didier, he died when I was eighteen," Harmony said, without hesitation.

"Seems like it's been kind of a long drought, in the love-of-your-life department, for both of us," Neddie said. "Let's ask Pat. She gets a new love of her life every week or so."

"Why are you two sitting in this hot car?" Pat asked, getting in the back seat. "I brought some martinis—if you're going to be hot you might as well be drunk."

"Okay, Pat, come clean," Neddie said, accepting a martini. "Who was the love of your life?"

"Mind your own business, Neddie," Pat said. "Is that what you two have been doing out here all this time? Talking about sex?"

"Nobody said a word about sex, Pat," Harmony pointed out. "You're the first person even to mention the word."

"Harmony, are you calling me a slut, or what?" Pat asked. "Get to the point. Just because I'm drunk don't mean I'll stand for much name-calling."

"Who was the love of your life, that's all we want to know," Neddie asked. "I've already confessed that Rusty Haley is mine, so who's yours?"

"Rusty's more like the lust of your life, Neddie," Pat said, unsentimentally. "If you'd gone on and had sex with him a few times, you'd have got it out of your system and figured out what a lazy piece of shit that man really is. Now you and him have put off doing the wild thing for twenty years and you think you're the love of one another's life. Oh boy."

"Quit dodging," Neddie said. "You still ain't told us about the love of *your* life, if you can remember him."

"I won't tell you because he's famous and you and Harmony would blab to the newspapers," Pat said. "He's several cuts above Rusty Haley, I can assure you of that."

"Pat, don't be mean," Harmony said, wondering why she bothered to say it.

"Famous for what?" Neddie asked. "You don't mean that old boy who got famous for trying to steal two thousand drilling bits from a warehouse in Oklahoma City, do you? Is that what you call famous?"

"No, Jesse was just a criminal, and a dumb one at that, though I will say he was good-looking and a fine dancer, too," Pat said. "But Jesse Birch don't come nowhere near being the love of my life, Neddie."

"Pat, you can tell us," Harmony assured her. "I don't even know the phone number of a newspaper and anyway we're in Nevada."

"News travels fast and far," Pat said. "I don't trust either one of you."

"I want to get some orange juice in case we drink vodka," Harmony said. She got the keys back from Neddie and they drove the two blocks to the Circle K. There Jasmine was, in the parking lot of the Circle K, crying because the bottom had dropped out of her bag of groceries. Her bottle of wine had broken when it hit the cement. Two black teenagers were skateboarding around in circles in the parking lot.

"There's Jasmine, let's find another Circle K," Pat said. "That woman depresses me."

"Pat, she's my neighbor, besides, her daughter was killed," Harmony said. She went in, bought the orange juice, and persuaded the little Asian man who was managing the Circle K to come out with a broom and dustpan and sweep up Jasmine's mess. Jasmine was so dejected by the loss of her wine that she had wandered out into the street—she was almost hit by a Dr. Pepper truck.

"Life's not for the faint-hearted," Neddie observed.

When they got back to the apartment Harmony still didn't feel like going inside, so they sat in the hot car and drank more martinis.

"What would I do if I went back to Oklahoma?" Harmony asked.

"Well, you could steal Pat's boyfriends, you're younger and prettier," Neddie said. Often, when she drank, Neddie developed a wicked tongue.

"Yeah, but she don't know as much about sex," Pat said. "Harmony was always an inhibited little thing," Pat said.

"Inhibited—I was a showgirl, Pat," Harmony protested.

"I didn't say you wasn't an exhibitionist," Pat said. "That doesn't mean you're any fun in bed."

"Pat, drop the sex stuff, we ain't addicts like you," Neddie said. "The one thing Harmony could do that would be real useful is help out with Mom and Dad."

"You got a point," Pat said. "I've about had it with Mom. It's time Harmony came home and did her part."

"It'd give Eddie a chance to get to know his grandparents, too," Neddie observed.

"Okay, I'll come," Harmony said. She wanted to get it settled in her mind. The thought of not having her sisters with her made her feel total panic.

The thought of her parents, though, just made her feel guilty. She definitely had not been a dutiful daughter—Eddie was five and had never met his grandparents; that was one example she wasn't proud of.

"I don't see how Dad stands it," Pat said. "All she does is cuss at him—it's been ten years since the poor man's been able to do anything right. I been trying to get him to get a dead bolt for his door."

"Why a dead bolt, are there thieves?" Harmony asked.

"One thief, Mom, she robs him of every cent he gets right out of his billfold. She's got it in her head that he stole a hundred thousand dollars from her when they sold that worthless piece of land over by Broken Arrow. Now every time she catches Dad with cash money on him, she steals it.

"The reason I think he ought to get the dead bolt is because she'll sneak up on him some night, thinking about that hundred thousand dollars, and beat the shit out of him with a ball bat or something."

"Pat, she wouldn't—would she?" Harmony said. It was very hard for her to imagine her mother beating her father with a ball bat, or beating him at all, for that matter.

Harmony thought of Eddie—she wondered if it would shock him to move far away to Oklahoma.

"Is Tulsa on the cable?" she asked. "Eddie's never lived anyplace that wasn't on the cable."

"What do you think we are, hicks?" Pat said. "Of course Tulsa's on the cable."

"Tarwater, too," Neddie said.

9.

About the middle of the afternoon, the three sisters began to try to do something about their hangovers. Harmony took a long hot shower and then ate three bowls of Cheerios—they were watching a rerun of *The Man from U.N.C.L.E.* at the time. Neddie swallowed some Excedrin and washed her hair in the sink. Pat lined up six pills of different kinds and mixed herself a Bloody Mary. Then she swallowed all the pills.

"Pat, are you sure it's safe to take six pills at once?" Harmony asked.

"Hangovers are mostly psychological," Pat informed her. She continued to drink Bloody Marys until long after the rerun had ended. It was just as well that it ended—Neddie was blow-drying her hair and the dryer made static on the TV.

"Everything's psychological, according to you," Neddie said. "I can do without psychology myself."

"Nobody can do without psychology, it's just your mind and your emotions mixed together," Pat informed her. "I'm the one with a B.A., not you."

"I don't mix my emotions with anything," Neddie said. "It's hard enough work just living with them separate."

"I hope Eddie won't mind leaving his little friends," Harmony said, but before her sisters could comment the doorbell rang.

Neddie was closest, so she answered the door.

"Uh-oh," she said, when she looked out.

Harmony hurried over—it was Gary, he was bleeding on the doorstep from cuts on his face and hands. Before anyone could say a word Gary staggered out in the yard and began to vomit—then he collapsed and flopped on his back.

"Oh God, are you dying, Gary?" Harmony asked; she had seen Gary with black eyes before, but she had never seen him collapsed on a patio.

"I think he's got stab wounds, I'm calling nine-one-one," Pat said.

"No, I'm not dying, forget about nine-one-one," Gary said. "I just drank too much."

Then he got to his feet, as if he were perfectly all right, and marched right into the apartment. Harmony noticed that he was dripping blood on the wall-to-wall, but so what? She had done it too. Anyway, Jimmy was the one who couldn't tolerate any threat to the wall-to-wall, and Jimmy was probably already back in Nampa, Idaho, or somewhere quite far away.

"Gary, it's more than drinking too much, you're cut," Harmony pointed out. "I think we ought to drive you to the emergency room at least."

"Somebody's been washing their hair in the sink, I can smell the shampoo," Gary said, trying to get his face under the faucet.

"It smells like it came from Wal-Mart," he added. Gary was definitely a snob about things like shampoo.

"Yep," Neddie said, looking a little bit offended.

Gary immediately realized he had hurt Neddie's feelings.

"I'm sorry, Neddie—I should be grateful I have a sink to bleed in," Gary said. "It's just that I have allergies. Some shampoos make me sneeze."

"It's all right, I ain't too proud to shop at Wal-Mart," Neddie said, still a little bit offended.

"Gary, what happened?" Harmony asked. "You're still bleeding."

"The little fuckers shoved me out of the car," Gary said. "I don't

84

know how fast we were going at the time, but we definitely weren't stopped."

"Oh," Harmony said. Quite a few of the boys Gary fell in love with were prone to criminal acts; but none, so far as she knew, had ever shoved him out of a car before.

"I still think we oughta go to the emergency room," Pat said. "You might have a concussion or a broken neck or something and not even know it."

Gary ran several gallons of water over his face and neck and began to pat himself down with a lot of paper towels. It seemed, from looking, that he was just a little skinned up. Harmony didn't notice any stab wounds.

"Why are you three girls so glum?" Gary asked. "I'm the one who got shoved out of a car."

A second later he remembered Harmony's tragedy.

"I'm sorry, Harmony," he said. "It was just a memory lapse."

Then he came over and put his arms around Harmony—Gary really was a very old friend.

"We're all hung over, and I'm moving back to Oklahoma with Neddie and Pat," Harmony said.

Gary looked shocked. "No, you can't," he said. "If you go back to Oklahoma where will I go to wash up when some dirty little boys shove me out of a moving vehicle?"

"Couldn't you at least find clean boys?" Pat asked. She had never been totally reconciled to Gary's homosexuality.

"Pat, it was a figure of speech, actually I'm very careful," Gary said. "I just don't know what I'll do without Harmony, she's my only true friend."

Sometimes Harmony had a little difficulty with Gary's homosexuality herself, the difficulty being that it meant Gary wasn't ever going to be a boyfriend. There were times when Gary was brokenhearted over some lost love when he would just sort of move in and stay with her and Eddie for weeks. That could only happen, of course, if Harmony herself happened to be without a boyfriend at the time. When it did happen she and Gary and Eddie got along just fine; Gary even cooked, sometimes, and they watched a lot of TV together and played some of the card games that Eddie knew how to play. Gary had been known to stay with them for six weeks or so, if the heartbreak was a serious one. Usually he just fell asleep on the couch watching TV, and slept there, but sometimes Harmony made him sleep on the other side of her queen bed. Once in a while Gary would come in looking so exhausted that she didn't want him sleeping on the couch; she insisted that he occupy part of her bed. Sometimes they even held hands in the night, if they happened to be chatting or something. They almost never quarreled, and if they did it was usually only for a minute or two. Gary sometimes got a little smart-mouthed about some of her habits, or a hairstyle or something. Once in a while Harmony would enjoy the fantasy that Gary had stopped being gay and wanted to marry her. Eddie loved Gary and preferred that he be there; usually Eddie was in droopy spirits for a few days when Gary left.

Gary had always been a sort of honorary uncle for Eddie— there were times when Harmony wished he could be more than honorary. If they were married it would be better for Gary, too; he would be a little less likely to get shoved out of cars. It seemed to Harmony that she and Gary had a good chance of being sweet to one another, long term, even if they lived together, but of course it wasn't going to happen, it was a fantasy.

"I doubt you'll last long without Harmony, myself," Neddie said. "You two have been friends a long time."

"I'm beginning to wish I'd picked another house to hose off in," Gary said. "You girls are *too* gloomy today."

"Don't say that, Gary," Harmony said. "I don't want you to pick another house."

"Can I just have coffee before I say something else dumb?" Gary asked.

The next thing that happened was that conversation died. Harmony sat in a rocking chair, Pat sat on the floor, Neddie lay on the couch, and Gary sat at the kitchen table.

"You don't have to sit on the floor, Pat," Harmony said.

"I don't have to do anything but breathe," Pat said—after that, not a word was uttered for nearly twenty minutes. They all just sat and stared at whatever space was in front of them. Harmony began to feel a little desperate. Neddie and Pat were her family, Gary was her lifelong best friend, and yet it was as if they were all complete strangers; it felt like just an accident that they were all in the same apartment in Las Vegas, Nevada.

"Can't somebody talk?" she asked, when she felt she couldn't stand it any longer.

"I guess times like this was the reason TV was invented," Neddie said. "When nobody has a word to say you can always turn on the TV."

"I don't know what to do," Harmony said. "I should go to my job. That's what Eddie thought, too."

"Why bother, if you're really going to move to Oklahoma," Gary said. "I don't think recycling is going to save the planet anyway."

"Gary, don't be pessimistic," Harmony said. "It *might* save the planet."

"Unless I can find a better boyfriend pretty soon I don't care whether the planet gets saved or not," Pat said.

"Pat don't care, she looks out for number one," Neddie remarked.

"Is it going to be like this if I move to Oklahoma?" Harmony asked. She had not stopped feeling desperate and, so far, the conversation had been as bad as the silence.

"Like what?" Neddie asked.

Harmony felt too tired to attempt to describe what she meant. She began to want to talk to Laurie Chalk and find out about Pepper's life, in her last years.

"Could we go to New York on the way to Oklahoma?" she asked. "I want to meet Laurie."

"I guess we could, but it's thousands of miles out of the way," Pat observed.

"If you're really going to move, why don't I give you my car— it's got a big trunk," Gary said.

"Gary, that's so generous," Harmony said. She had begun to wonder just how the move would be accomplished.

"But how will you get to your job if I take the car?" she asked. Gary had always been impulsive—he often gave things away that he soon turned out to need.

"Harmony, my car is not the only motor vehicle in Las Vegas," Gary said. It was an example of his tendency to be a little smart-mouthed: of course she knew it was not the only motor vehicle in Las Vegas.

"I just meant, what if you need it, Gary?" Harmony said. The thought of all the misunderstanding and tragedy there was in the world made her feel so low that she couldn't seem to summon any optimism at all. She even began to wonder if recycling was worth it—maybe the planet had so much tragedy on it that it didn't deserve to be saved.

"I feel like giving up," she said.

"Hon, it's just a mood," Neddie said.

"Poor thing, this death is just about too much to bear," Pat said. She sounded sympathetic for once.

"Gary, could you get me a drug?" Harmony asked.

Gary seemed startled by the request, she didn't know why. At one time or another Gary had taken every drug known to man.

"Harmony, I don't know if that's a good idea," Gary said.

"It's a great idea," Neddie said. "She's in pain. The whole point of drugs is to take away pain. Get her some dope."

"The fact is I don't have a cent," Gary admitted. "The dirty little boys robbed me before they shoved me out of the car."

"Oh, no—did they get your credit cards?" Harmony asked. Gary's boyfriends were always stealing his credit cards and running up huge bills buying stereos or clothes.

"Oh my God—that's what I was trying to remember," Gary said. "I came here mainly to use your phone—I need to cancel all my credit cards."

"Hurry, Gary, hurry," Harmony said. In her mind she could already see four or five of Gary's tough little boys in a stereo store, charging thousands of dollars that Gary would end up having to pay off. Once one of his boyfriends had charged fifteen hundred dollars' worth of kitchen equipment and taken the stuff right out on the street and traded every bit of it for drugs.

Naturally Gary couldn't remember the numbers of a single one of his credit cards—he had to sit and think for several crucial minutes before he could remember whether his Visa had expired or already been canceled. Harmony finally had to come out of her slump, in order to deal with it. Having to deal with major corporations such as Visa or American Express made Gary very shaky, even in the best of times. Pretty soon, thanks to the credit card crisis, he stopped talking about getting drugs for Harmony and started thinking about getting some for himself.

"See what I mean?" Neddie said. "He ain't gonna last a week without Sis." At the time, Harmony was on the phone with the Visa people, waiting for them to check and see whether Gary's Visa had already been canceled.

"Let's take him to Oklahoma with us—it might save his life," Pat suggested.

10.

When the idea of moving to Oklahoma was first presented to Eddie, that night after his Aunt Pat had finished reading him several stories, his immediate reaction was negative.

"No way," Eddie said firmly. "My Mom and I want to live here in Las Vegas, where my school is."

"Eddie, I'm not too sure your mother still wants to live here," Pat said. "The school is no problem. We have wonderful schools in Oklahoma."

"But you don't have *my* school," Eddie reminded her. "*My* school is here in Las Vegas, Nevada."

"Eddie, any school can be your school, once you go to it for a while," Aunt Neddie said, trying to help the discussion along. "I agree with Aunt Pat. I'm just not too sure your Momma still wants to live in Las Vegas."

"Yes, she does want to, *I'm* sure," Eddie said, annoyed that his aunts were trying to tell him what his own mother wanted.

"She wants to live in Las Vegas, Nevada," he repeated, loudly. "And I do! Forever and forever, until everybody in the world is deaded."

"Dead, not deaded," Neddie said, patiently.

"Deaded!" Eddie said, even more loudly. He hated to have his word choice corrected.

Harmony lay on the couch, listening without much interest.

"Please change the subject," she said. "I don't want to hear the *d* word tonight."

She thought Pat had chosen a bad time to bring up the move. After Eddie heard some stories he usually turned on his small TV and watched a video or two. Harmony had saved to buy Eddie the TV, and Gary had given him a VCR for his fifth birthday. Eddie had accumulated forty-eight videos already, most of them previewed. There was a shopping cart full of used videos right by the checkout counter in the supermarket. They were $4.99 apiece, a saving Harmony usually couldn't resist.

At the moment, Eddie's favorite videos were Roadrunner and the Coyote cartoons, although the coyote's stupidity annoyed Eddie at times. He had seen a program about coyotes on the Discovery Channel, a program that emphasized what smart animals coyotes were. But the coyote in the cartoons definitely wasn't smart.

"The roadrunner tricks him over and over," Eddie complained to his aunts. "It's a dumb coyote."

"Anything can be dumb, Eddie," Pat said. "I'm no rocket scientist, myself."

Eddie failed to see what that had to do with anything.

"Coyotes are supposed to be smart, not dumb," he reminded her.

"If the coyote was smart the video wouldn't be funny," Aunt Neddie said.

"It's *not* funny," Eddie said. "It's a story."

"Stories can be funny," Pat argued. "All cartoons are funny."

"Change the subject again," Harmony begged. She felt a little insane. Listening to her sisters and her son argue about cartoons made her feel like screaming, but she didn't.

"Don't talk anymore, my mother's sad," Eddie said.

Eddie walked over and lay next to his Mom, on the couch.

"Don't be sad, Mom, be happy," he said. "I have some hugs for you—do you want some?"

Harmony wanted some. Later, once Eddie was asleep, Harmony remembered his effort to reassure her. The way he had said, "I'm here," made her feel a little guilty.

"Eddie shouldn't have to comfort me, it's too big a responsibility," she said.

"He's your child, why shouldn't he comfort you?" Neddie asked. She was drinking vodka for the second night in a row.

"All he did was give you some hugs," Pat said. "What's wrong with that?"

"Pat, I don't know what's wrong with anything," Harmony said. "I guess I'm just scared Eddie will be unhappy if we move."

"The tail don't get to wag the dog, and the child oughtn't to wag the parent," Neddie said.

"He'll do fine in Oklahoma," Pat said. "Dad can take him fishing."

"Dad can still see to drive pretty good, unlike Mom," Neddie said. "Mother couldn't see a brick wall if it fell on her. She's blind as a mole."

"As a bat, you mean," Harmony said.

"No, as a mole," Neddie said. "Bat's can see a little ways, but moles can't and neither can Mom."

"I'm not sure Mom really wants to see," Pat said. "Everything she does manage to catch a glimpse of irritates the hell out of her."

"Like what?" Harmony asked—her mother had never had a very positive attitude.

"Like her friends' clothes, and the fact that Pat's children have long hair," Neddie said.

"She don't think *your* kids are no angels, either," Pat said.

"She's right," Neddie admitted.

"How does Mom get around, if she can't see?" Harmony asked.

Both sisters gave her blank looks, as if she had just asked a question an alien might ask.

"In her car, of course," Neddie said.

"Yeah, but who drives for her?" Harmony asked. In fact, even before her sisters started giving her funny looks, she had *felt* a little bit like an alien—a person who didn't quite fit on planet Earth, and never had.

"She drives for herself," Pat said.

"But I thought you said she couldn't see a wall," Harmony said.

"She can't, but it don't stop her," Neddie said. "The only thing that slows her down is that she loses her car keys every five min-

92

utes. Usually she blames it on the niggers. Mom's racist, among other things."

"I guess if I move home I could drive for her," Harmony said. "It might protect the public a little."

"Nope," both sisters said, in unison.

"Why not?" Harmony asked, feeling that she had lost track of the point of the conversation.

"Where is Gary?—I thought he went off to buy you drugs," Neddie said.

Harmony had been wondering about that herself. Gary had been gone several hours. Drugs weren't hard to locate, in Las Vegas. So where was he?

"Why can't I drive for Mom?" she asked, hoping to clear up that puzzle.

"You ain't thick-skinned enough—neither is a rhinoceros," Neddie said. "Neither is anything. Mom's critical and she don't take no prisoners."

"Even getting in the car with her would be a mistake," Pat said.

"Starting the motor would be another," Neddie said. "Mom hates to start up the car."

"Why?" Harmony asked.

"Islamic terrorism," Pat said. "She's afraid some Arab has put a bomb under her hood."

"The real reason is she hates to spend money on gas," Neddie said.

"I didn't know there were Arabs in Tarwater," Harmony said.

"Mother's view is that anything that's in the world anywhere could be in Tarwater, trying to blow her up," Neddie said.

"Mom never liked me—what if I move home and she still doesn't?" Harmony asked.

"Besides being a racist she's a sexist too," Pat said. "She only likes men. She adores Billy, even though the rascal is in jail for making obscene phone calls."

"Pat was always Dad's favorite," Harmony remarked. "Dad thought Pat hung the moon."

"I *did* hang it," Pat said, with a grin.

Neddie began to look over the furniture and count the dishes.

"I think we should just stick this stuff in a big U-Haul trailer and go," she said. "Maybe we could whip through New York and let Harmony visit with Laurie a little before we go home."

"I don't much fancy pulling a big trailer through them crack neighborhoods," Pat said. "If Harmony goes up there and meets Laurie she's going to have to deal with the fact that Pepper was gay."

"Pat, she's dead," Harmony said. "I don't care that she was gay. I just hope she had a little happiness in her life, that's all."

The next thing she knew, she was beating Pat with one of the pillows on the couch. Something broke inside her—she just jumped up and started hitting Pat with the pillow.

"Harmony, I hope you didn't break my bifocals, you knocked them off," Pat said. She was on her hands and knees, looking for her glasses. Otherwise she didn't seem to be too upset by the fact that Harmony was pounding on her with the pillow.

"Just protect your specs, Pat," Neddie advised. "She needs to get this out of her system."

Harmony was about to wear out when Gary came through the door—he had his own key, a fact he had forgotten that morning, when he was bleeding so badly.

"Oh my God, violence," Gary said.

"Shut up, Gary—you got shoved out of your own car," Harmony reminded him.

"No I didn't, because you had borrowed it," Gary said. He could be extremely reasonable, just when you didn't want him to be.

"I got shoved out of somebody else's car," he informed her.

"I was just hitting Pat with a pillow," Harmony said, dropping the pillow. Pat was still crawling around on her hands and knees, looking for her glasses. She didn't seem very upset, but Harmony was upset. What did the gayness have to do with anything? Gary himself was gay, and he had been like a father to Pepper—or at least like an uncle.

"She needed to get that out of her system," Neddie said, again. "We're a family—it don't matter if we beat on one another a little, with pillows."

"I wish I didn't have Eddie," Harmony said. "If I didn't have Eddie I could die. It would be so nice to just be dead."

Everyone looked away from her, when she said it. Harmony

knew she had said a terrible thing—somehow she had just been unable to hold it in.

"I know it's wrong to say that," she said. "I can't help it, though. It's how I feel."

Still, nobody said a word. Pat found her bifocals and got to her feet.

"The fact of the matter is, you've got Eddie," she said.

"I've wished I was dead several times, with less excuse," Neddie said.

"Yeah, life isn't for sissies," Pat said. "Gary, do you know where we can get some boxes?" Pat asked.

"I guess at a liquor store," Gary said. "Why?"

"Harmony's thinking too much," Pat said. "She's gonna lose her mind if we don't get a move on. I think we should just pack up and leave."

"You mean tomorrow?—that's awfully soon," Harmony said.

"I don't mean tomorrow, I mean tonight," Pat said. "Come on, Gary, let's hit the liquor stores. Is there an all-night U-Haul rental in this town?"

"Pat, everything's all-night—this is Las Vegas," Gary said.

"Bring some newspapers," Neddie said, as they were leaving. "We need to wrap the dishes."

11.

"Why do I have to take the dishes?" Harmony asked. "Why do I have to take my clothes? Pepper thought they were tacky anyway. Why can't I give them all to Myrtle to sell in the garage sale?"

Neddie was smoking, and methodically wrapping dishes. Pat wrapped the glassware. Gary stood in the middle of the floor, looking lost. It turned out that he *had* purchased some drugs for Harmony, but the thought of her leaving upset him so that he took them all himself.

"I've depended on you for thirty years," he said, several times. "What am I going to do when you leave? Who will take me in when some boy breaks my heart?"

"Gary, you can come," Harmony assured him. "You're welcome wherever I am—come. We'll just all pile in your car and leave."

"There are no casinos in Oklahoma," Gary reminded her. He was costume manager at the Stardust; no costume manager in Las Vegas was more respected.

"There are no floor shows, in Oklahoma," he said. "What would I do? I'd starve."

"That ain't true, there are floor shows all over Oklahoma," Pat said. "It just that they're titty-bar floor shows."

"It'd be too much of a comedown for Gary," Neddie said. "He's been in the big time all his life."

"He could take the civil service exam," Pat suggested.

Harmony was trying to adjust to the fact that within an hour or two she would be leaving Las Vegas, her home for more than thirty years. She didn't know why she was leaving—it had been her sisters' idea—but she also didn't know how she would survive if she didn't leave.

"The civil service exam?" Gary said, horrified. "Do I look like a civil servant, Pat?"

"You've always been civil to me—why not?" Pat said.

"I'd go mad being a civil servant," Gary said. "I'd do something irresponsible and they'd send me to prison."

"It was just a thought," Neddie said. "You could probably get work in the oil fields now that the price of oil is up a little."

"Harmony, this is absurd, why are you leaving me?" Gary asked.

"Gary, I said you could come," Harmony said.

The next minute they were hugging and crying.

"The sun's gonna come up and I'm going to have to tell Jessie that you left without saying goodbye," Gary said. "It's going to be a setback for Jessie."

It seemed to Harmony that Gary was trying to make her feel guilty. Everyday life was a continual setback for Jessie. If Napoleon, her toy poodle, spit up a few grams of his food, it was a setback for Jessie. If Monroe, her boyfriend, belched too loudly while they were eating at Burger King, it was a setback for Jessie.

But Pepper being dead wasn't a setback. Pepper being dead was the end.

"I have to go with my sisters, Gary," Harmony said. "Otherwise I can't stand it. I'll go crazy and not be a good mom. I'll do drugs and they'll take Eddie away from me and put him in a foster home."

"I'm sorry, go then," Gary said. "I don't want Eddie to be in a foster home—it would break his heart."

"If you want to be useful, stop ragging Harmony and start loading the trailer," Pat advised. "That high roller from Venezuela's been calling a little too often. I'd like to roar out of here before he zeros in on me."

"Pat, just say no," Harmony said. "Pretend you're Mrs. Reagan."

Three hours later Harmony was shocked to discover that every single thing she owned would fit in a U-Haul trailer. Her queen-sized bed, her couch, her clothes, Eddie's toys, the TVs, Eddie's clothes, the dishes, the pots and pans, and all the surplus macaroni and cheese in her little pantry all fit right into the U-Haul. The only thing left to load was Eddie's bunk bed—they wanted to wait until the last minute to wake Eddie and inform him that the move was in progress.

Gary turned out to have lower-back pain, so Pat and Neddie carried the mattress downstairs. In fact, Neddie and Pat loaded the whole trailer, while Gary took a nap on the floor. Harmony wandered up and down the stairs, feeling that she was probably going to go crazy anyway, unless she was very lucky.

By four A.M. every single thing was loaded in the U-Haul, except the coffee cup Neddie was drinking out of, the bottle of vodka Pat was finishing off, and some very old pills that had turned up in a box in the closet—they were remnants of old prescriptions Harmony had given up on. Gary was rummaging through the pills with a gleam in his eye, hoping to find some that would alleviate lower-back pain, heartbreak, headaches, and all the other ailments Gary suffered from. Eddie's bed had even been packed. They had eased him off onto the floor, into a cozy pallet of blankets, while they took his bed apart and carried it out.

Harmony was hoping Eddie—a sound sleeper—would sleep until they were a few miles out of Las Vegas. If he woke up in the apartment where there was nothing left but the wall-to-wall carpet, it might upset him. In fact, seeing the apartment empty upset Harmony—with nothing to occupy the eye except the dingy walls and the blood-spotted wall-to-wall, it was clear what a cheap, tacky little apartment Eddie had spent most of his life in.

"I guess I don't own very much," Harmony said, as the four of them stood in the empty living room. "I thought I surely owned more than would fit in one trailer."

"Hon, you don't even own as much as would fit in a trailer," Neddie said. "We could cram in a king-sized bed and a couple more TVs if we had them."

"Be a little more diplomatic, Neddie," Pat suggested. "Harmony's depressed."

"Making her stuff seem any more piddly than it is cannot be helpful at a time like this," Gary said, in his formal voice.

"Oh well, gang up on me," Neddie said, looking as if she might cry. She took the coffee cup and went out to the trailer.

Harmony tried to pick Eddie up as gently as she could, so he would stay asleep until she could carry him to the car, but Eddie's eyes popped open the minute she lifted him off the floor.

He grinned at his Mom, as he always did when he woke up, but then he looked around and saw that there was nothing at all in their apartment.

"Where's my stuffed animals?" he asked, in some alarm. "I hope they didn't get anthrax and die."

Everyone looked startled, as they often did at Eddie's statements.

"I don't think stuffed animals get anthrax, Eddie," Gary said.

"It's mostly cows that get anthrax," Neddie informed him.

"Well, I have a stuffed cow named Teresa," Eddie said. "I don't want Teresa to die."

"She won't, she's just moving to Oklahoma," Pat said.

"Are we going away from our home, Mom?" Eddie asked, his eyes very wide.

At the sight of his eyes, so surprised, Harmony felt guilty.

"I guess so, Eddie," Harmony said.

"Forever, Mom?" Eddie asked. "Are we leaving our home forever?"

"Oh, Eddie, I don't know," Harmony said. The way he said the word forever struck her to the heart.

Eddie sank to his knees, and put his head down on the carpet, as he sometimes did when overcome with sorrow.

"He's got a right to be sad," Neddie said, sighing. "This has always been his home."

Eddie kept his head pressed against the carpet for a while. His Aunt Pat started to run over and pick him up, but then thought better of it.

"He's got a right to be sad," Neddie said, again.

Eddie looked up, anger in his face.

"Don't say those words!" he said. "Don't say those words!"

Then he stood up, marched outside, and crawled inside the trailer. All his stuffed animals were in three or four boxes. Eddie kept looking until he found his cow, Teresa. Then he crawled into one of the boxes, holding Teresa in his arms.

Harmony, Neddie, Pat, and Gary all stood by the open door of the trailer.

"I didn't know he'd take it *this* hard," Gary said. He was appalled by the depth of Eddie's sorrow.

Eddie saw all the adults looking into the trailer. He knew they wanted him to come out, but he had no intention of coming out.

"Eddie, we have to leave," Harmony said, finally. "Come ride with us in the car."

"I want to stay with my animals," Eddie said. "They all might die of anthrax because they had to leave their home."

"Where would a kid that age get a vocabulary with 'anthrax' in it?" Pat asked.

"Discovery Channel," Gary said.

"My kids never watch that stupid channel," Pat said. "Now I'm beginning to be glad."

"Eddie, please come out, you can bring Teresa," Harmony said.

"No, I want to stay with my animals so they won't die when we leave," Eddie repeated.

"Eddie, they won't," Harmony said—but just then another bomb of grief exploded and she began to cry. Her legs grew weak; she knelt in the street and cried. Neddie couldn't calm her down; neither could Pat; neither could Gary.

Finally Gary crawled into the trailer, in order to make a desperate plea for Eddie's help.

"Eddie, this doesn't mean you're going away forever," Gary said. "It's just that your mother is too sad to stay in Las Vegas right now. Please come out and see if you can make her feel a little better."

"She didn't give me a chance to say goodbye to my friends," Eddie informed him. "She should have told me sooner. I didn't get to say goodbye to Eli and I didn't get to say goodbye to Maggie."

"I don't think she actually made up her mind to leave until tonight," Gary said. "You have to try and be a little forgiving. Your mother's been very upset since she found out that your sister died."

"Well, *I'm* very upset because I didn't get to say goodbye to Eli and Maggie," Eddie said.

100

"Eddie, you can write them letters," Gary suggested. "They'll understand that it was an emergency. They'll still be your friends."

"I hope so," Eddie said.

After a minute or two he crawled out of the box of stuffed animals, bringing Teresa with him. He walked to the back of the trailer and jumped out. Harmony was still kneeling on the pavement, crying. Eddie sat Teresa on the pavement and put his arms around his mother's neck.

"Come on, Mom," he said. "We all have to get in the car now. It's a very long way to Oklahoma. We better get started."

Gary closed the doors to the trailer. Neddie and Pat began to argue about who was the better driver. Eddie continued to hug his mother—in a while Harmony stopped crying.

"Oh Eddie, thanks for forgiving me," Harmony said. "I don't know what I'd do without my big boy."

"I'm afraid you might get anthrax," Eddie said, as he and his mother and Teresa and Gary crawled into the car.

12.

Neddie had managed to outargue Pat and won the right to drive the first leg, but then, when she got in the car, she didn't drive. Everyone in the car was in such low spirits that it seemed to paralyze her.

"It's a very long way to Oklahoma," Eddie said, clutching his cow. "I think we should go *now*."

"What's wrong with you?" Pat asked Neddie. "If you're not going to drive, let me. I'm a better driver anyway."

"It's a big deal, moving people away from where they live," Neddie said. "I was for it in this case, but now I don't know that I'm still for it. Maybe we should unload all this stuff and put it back in the apartment."

"Maybe we should," Gary said.

"No," Eddie said. "I don't want to be here anymore."

"But you *did* want to be here a minute ago," Neddie said.

"It makes my Mom too unhappy," Eddie said. "That's why I don't want to be here anymore. But I still want to get the puppy, Mom."

"We'll get the puppy, I promise," Harmony said. "We'll get it as soon as we get settled."

"I hope it's a yellow puppy," Eddie said. "Yellow is my favorite color."

"There's puppies every color of the rainbow in the Tulsa pound," Pat said. "Switch on the motor, Neddie. Let's go while we have at least one person in the mood."

"Drive down the Strip—I have memories," Harmony said.

At a stoplight between Caesar's and the Stardust, Gary suddenly leapt out.

"I can't do this," he said. "I can't live in a place without casinos. My soul would starve."

He began to cry and gave everyone in the car kisses that had tears mixed in them.

"I apologize, I apologize," Gary said; then he ran across the street and just missed getting hit by a taxi.

"I hope he explains to Jessie," Harmony said.

"It may be for the best," Pat said.

"I don't think anything's for the best except Eddie," Harmony said.

"Yeah, he might not have fit in too well in Oklahoma," Pat said. "Some people around Tulsa aren't too friendly to gays."

Once he made it to the safety of the sidewalk, Gary turned and waved. Harmony and Eddie waved, too; Eddie stuck his head as far out the window as possible so Gary would be sure to see that he was waving. Then they drove along the Strip all the way to the end. At one of the stoplights, Eddie went back to sleep, his head on his cow, Teresa. "Postcards," was the last word he said, as he faded out.

"I think he means he wants to send them to his friends, the ones he didn't get to say goodbye to," Neddie commented.

Harmony looked at the casinos as they passed them, one by one. Caesar's Palace and the Stardust, the Sahara, the Sands, Circus-Circus and the Tropicana, the MGM Grand. She had been a showgirl in every one of them, at one time or another, but now, when she looked at them with all their glittering lights, no memories came, she just felt numb.

When they were a little ways east, out of town, Harmony saw a line of buttery light ahead, on the horizon, meaning it was dawn. They were near the little road to Myrtle's duplex, where she and Pepper had lived when Pepper was a teenager, just before Harmony made her futile stab at hooking up again with Ross. The little house on the edge of the desert had been nice—she had even been able to have peacocks for a while, and the fact that Myrtle ran a permanent, three-hundred-sixty-five-day-a-year garage sale in the driveway meant that there were usually a few characters around, pawing through the stuff.

"Should I say goodbye to Myrtle, or would it upset her too much?" Harmony asked.

"I don't know about Myrtle, but it might upset *you* too much," Neddie said. "Let's keep rolling while we're rolling."

"Good advice," Pat said.

Book
Two

1.

"Do we even know where we're headed?" Neddie asked, when they were about fifteen miles out of Las Vegas. To the east the sky was lightening, but in the west it was still night. Harmony looked out the back window of the car, watching the lights of Las Vegas, bright against the dark western sky.

It had always been her magic place, Las Vegas. Now life had abruptly jerked her out of it, she had no idea why. In a way it seemed like years since the news of Pepper's death came, but in another way it only seemed like minutes. She was in a car with her son, her sisters, and all her possessions. What the future held she did not even want to try and guess. All she hoped was that she could live long enough to be an adequate mom to her son, who slept beside her, his curly head resting on his cow, Teresa.

"I guess where we go next should be Harmony's choice," Pat said, in a tone that was more subdued than her usual tone.

"Well, we ain't bound for L.A., are we?" Neddie asked. "If we ain't bound for L.A. we might as well go east and see where the road takes us."

"I vote for New York City, if Harmony feels up to it," Pat said.

"I'm in no rush to get back to Oklahoma. I'd just have to deal with my broken engagement."

"Not to mention your fucked-up kids," Neddie added.

"Yours are no better," Pat said.

"I didn't say they were," Neddie said. "Do you think we ought to call and see if any of them are in jail?"

"No, let's forget Oklahoma for a while, do you mind?" Pat said.

Harmony was getting the sense that her sisters' lives weren't too perfect, either. She also got the sense that neither of them was in a great hurry to get home. That was a little bit of a shock. She had always assumed that her sisters loved their homes.

"What about your families, don't you miss them?" she asked.

Neither sister answered.

"Neddie, what about Dick?" Harmony asked.

"Well, what about him?" Neddie said.

"He's your husband," Harmony said. "Won't he get lonely without you?"

"Dick don't have enough imagination to get lonely," Neddie said.

"I second that," Pat remarked.

"Nobody asked you, it's my husband we're talking about," Neddie said.

"It wasn't so much him as his lack of imagination we were talking about," Pat said.

"Pat, his lack of imagination *is* him," Neddie said. "That's our whole problem, in a nutshell. Maybe if I run off to New York for a while he'll show a little initiative and rustle himself up a girlfriend or something."

"Neddie, why would you want your husband to find a girlfriend?" Harmony asked.

"So he'll let me alone," Neddie said.

The thought struck Harmony suddenly that maybe her sisters' lives were even *more* depressing than her own. If so, it was a bad comment on life. It seemed to her that all three of them were nice women. Even if Pat was troubled by sex addiction, she was still a nice woman. Why were they all driving around in a car in the desert, all of them middle-aged and totally uncertain about what might happen next?

"What do *you* think is supposed to happen next, Pat?" Harmony

108

asked. One minute Neddie seemed more stable than Pat, but the next minute Pat seemed more stable than Neddie.

"Nothing's *supposed* to happen next, Harmony," Pat said. "Do you know what the word arbitrary means?"

"I think so," Harmony said.

"Well, that's how life is," Pat said. "Arbitrary."

"Christians don't believe that," Neddie said. "At least Baptists don't."

"I'm not a Baptist," Pat said. "I don't even know if I'm a Christian. Does Eddie go to Sunday school?"

"No, but he went in a synagogue once," Harmony said. "His friend Eli took him."

"Mom will be glad to hear that," Neddie said. "If I were you I'd skip that chapter when you get into how Eddie's been brought up."

"Mom's just confused on the subject, Neddie," Pat said. "She can't tell Jews from Arabs."

Harmony decided that it was going to be a little taxing, listening to her sisters bicker for as long as the trip turned out to be. It was just their way of being sisters, she knew; but that didn't mean it couldn't get on the nerves of other family members. Already it was getting on her nerves, and they weren't even out of sight of the lights of Las Vegas.

"I hope you two aren't going to fight all the way home," she said.

Both sisters looked surprised.

"Honey, we ain't fighting, we're just chatting," Neddie said.

"To me it sounds harsh," Harmony said. "Eddie's very sensitive to harshness. He likes gentle words."

"Good Lord, Harmony, do you want to raise him in a bubble?" Pat said. "There has to be a little give-and-take in this world."

"Why?" Harmony asked.

"Because if you just agree all the time, it gets boring," Pat pointed out.

"I guess that's why I've never been bored," Harmony said. "Nobody ever agreed with me about anything. It's why I never married but once."

"Now she's getting maudlin," Pat said. "Let's stop at the next bar and get a drink."

"I bet Gary wishes he'd come," Neddie said. "It would be a change from the same old routine."

"I don't want to stop until Eddie wakes up," Harmony said. "He might want a waffle—it might cheer him up."

"Kids adapt," Pat said. "Eddie won't be hard to cheer up."

"It'll help if it's a good waffle," Harmony said. "He's very particular."

"Good Lord, a waffle's a waffle," Neddie said.

"That's not how Eddie sees it," Harmony said.

2.

Eddie woke up as they were passing through Boulder City, where they found a big truck stop with a cafe attached. The cafe was called the Belt Buster.

"I used to run with truckers, they're fun when you're young," Pat said. "Let's try it."

Most of the parked trucks still had their motors running, a fact which annoyed Eddie. He insisted on taking Teresa into the restaurant.

"Stop those motors!" he said loudly, the minute he got inside the cafe. "They're making exhaust and exhaust is bad for the Earth."

Several of the truckers looked startled; they had not expected to be yelled at by a five-year-old boy while eating their ham and eggs.

"You better shut up or you'll get us stomped, Eddie," Pat said. "Some of these old boys probably don't take kindly to environmentalists anyway."

Harmony smiled at the men, to let them know she wasn't quite as strict about the planet as her son was.

When Harmony asked Eddie if he wanted a waffle he shook his

head. He was smiling, but it was his defiant smile, not his coopera-
tive smile.

"I'm sorry, but I'm on a hunger strike," he informed them all.

"A hunger strike—to protest what?" Pat asked. "You're only five,
remember?"

"A hunger strike to protest everything," Eddie said.

"To protest anthrax and everything, even AIDS," he said.

"What kind of school teaches preschoolers to go on hunger
strikes?" Neddie wanted to know.

"I don't know, do I look like I'm a member of the PTA?" Harmony said, feeling very defensive. She looked at Eddie, to gauge
her chances of coaxing him to eat at least something; she decided
her chances were small.

"Eddie, is it because we moved away from your friends?" Harmony asked.

"No, but it wasn't very nice that we did that," Eddie said. "My
friends will be sad now, and I'll be sad."

"At least you'll get a chance to see your Grandma and
Grandpa," Neddie said. "They've never even got to meet you."

"What are they like?" Eddie asked, in a slightly less defiant tone.

"Well, they're very old, for starters," Neddie said.

"Two thousand years old?" Eddie asked.

"Not quite, but nearly," Pat said.

"What TV shows do they watch?" Eddie asked.

"They don't see too clearly," Pat said. "I think they mainly listen
to the news."

"Which news?" Eddie wanted to know. "ABC or CBS or NBC
or CNN?"

"Good Lord," Neddie said. "I give up."

Harmony knew how stubborn Eddie could be when he chose to
go into a hunger strike or some other form of protest.

"Couldn't you at least have juice so you won't get dehydrated?"
she asked.

"Is that like being abducted?" Eddie inquired.

"Please don't mention abduction, it's my worst nightmare," Harmony said.

While his Aunt Pat was explaining dehydration to Eddie three
cowboys walked in and sat down at the next booth. They all had
spurs on and the spurs jingled as they walked. Eddie forgot his

protest in order to study the cowboys, two of whom were young and friendly.

"Howdy, pardner," one of the young ones said to Eddie.

Pat was also looking at the cowboys, but not at the young ones. She had her eye on a middle-aged cowboy with huge freckles on his face. He had watery blue eyes and was missing a finger on his right hand. Harmony got a little nervous—maybe Pat's sex addiction was going to flare up before they could even finish breakfast.

"How'd you lose that finger, cowboy?" Pat asked.

"Pat, it might be personal," Harmony said.

"Were you on a hunger strike?" Eddie asked the cowboy. "Did you starve until your finger fell off?"

"Whoa, that's a new one, little buddy," one of the younger cowboys said.

"I doubt Jethro even knows what a hunger strike is," the other young cowboy said.

Jethro ducked his head and looked embarrassed.

"Leave him alone, Pat—he's shy," Neddie said.

"If he's shy he might welcome a little encouragement," Pat said. She had not taken her eyes off the freckled cowboy.

"Uh," Jethro said, trying to remember what the original question had been. He was not used to being addressed by ladies; the few he knew rarely said a word to him.

"She wants to know how you lost your finger, Jeth," one of the young cowboys reminded him.

"Roping accident," Jethro said. "What I get for trying to dally."

"I'm going to do my hunger strike for a *long* time," Eddie said. "I'm going to do it until both my arms fall off."

"Oh, Eddie, please don't," Harmony said. "How could you give me hugs if your arms fall off?"

Sometimes when Eddie was annoyed with the way life was going he made up terrible fates for himself. Harmony tried not to take Eddie's made-up fates too seriously, but the problem was that Eddie was very convincing when he made up terrible fates.

"I'll give you many kisses but I won't be able to give you hugs," Eddie said.

Pat was still staring at the freckled cowboy.

"Is your name really Jethro?" she asked.

"Dallying means roping with a loose rope," one of the young

cowboys explained. "Jethro got his finger caught in the rope and it popped right off."

"I'm from Oklahoma, I know what dallying means," Pat said. "I was dallying myself, before you were even born. There's more than one way to dally, you know."

She addressed her last remark to Jethro, who looked at Pat briefly, and then directed his gaze back to his coffee cup.

Harmony thought it might be a good idea to send Laurie a postcard, to let her know they were coming. Most of the postcards in the rack by the cash register were of the Las Vegas Strip, which they had just left behind; or of the Grand Canyon, which was just up ahead. Harmony bought one of each, plus a postcard of a jackalope, a jackrabbit with deer horns on its head. Jackalope postcards seemed to be very popular. She had the feeling that she might go crazy at any moment—or, at the very least, within the next few days—if she didn't do something normal, such as buy postcards, and send them to people. She meant to send one to Gary, to let him know they had at least made it as far as Boulder City.

When she asked for change for a dollar, in order to buy stamps from the stamp machine, the old lady at the cash register began to glare at her.

"The place to buy stamps is at a post office," she said. "I can't be sitting here doling out change all day."

The old lady had pink hair.

"I just asked for one dollar's worth," Harmony said.

"It adds up, though, and the next thing you know, I'm out of quarters," the old lady said.

A fact Harmony had noticed before was that people in other parts of Nevada weren't as friendly as people were on the Strip. She bought some orange juice, and a package of Oreo cookies, in case Eddie relented on the hunger strike, later in the day.

"Where is this Grand Canyon?" Neddie asked, once they were rolling again. "Me and Dick meant to have a look at it on our honeymoon, but then the cow fell into the cistern and we never got out of Tarwater."

"It's in Arizona," Harmony said. "Ross and I meant to go there too, but we never got off."

114

"What was your excuse, lust?" Pat asked. "Or can you remember that far back?"

Harmony tried her best to remember why she and Ross had skipped their honeymoon to the Grand Canyon but her memory failed her.

"I think I had a bladder infection," she offered.

"Lust, what'd I tell you?" Pat said, directing her remark to Neddie, who was still driving.

"I don't think so, Pat," Harmony said, annoyed that her sister's sex addiction seemed to come into every conversation. Why couldn't she just give it a rest? She knew that she and Ross had been lovers at some point, otherwise Pepper would never have been born, but now that it was many years later she couldn't remember or imagine why she would even consider sleeping with Ross.

"Where did you go on *your* honeymoons, Pat?" she asked. She thought it was interesting, which place people planned to go on their honeymoons, even if most of them never made it anywhere near the place.

"Which honeymoon would you like to hear about? Cozumel was the best," Pat said. "I guess I'll never run off with that cowboy, he was too shy to look at me."

"Eat your eggs, honey, I won't harass you anymore," Pat had said to Jethro, as they were leaving.

"Harass is not a very nice word," Eddie remarked.

"Oh shut up, Eddie," Pat said. "You're gonna end up an educated fool if you're not careful."

"Keep on with your hunger strike, little buddy," one of the cowboys said. "Don't let these tough old girls wear you down."

"I'm only going to do it until my arms fall off," Eddie had said.

"I don't remember my second honeymoon too well," Pat said now. "In fact I don't remember my second husband too well."

"That's a fine comment, you were married to him fourteen years," Neddie said.

"I know, but it feels like it happened in another life, or to somebody else, you know?" Pat said.

"Pat, that's how my whole life feels," Harmony said. "All of it feels like it happened to someone else."

"I don't like this talk," Eddie said. "It makes me want to be abducted."

"I know just how you feel, Eddie," Neddie said.

"We need music—turn on the music," Eddie said. "See if you can find Iggy Pop for me, Mom."

"Iggy Pop . . . is that a potty joke, or what?" Pat asked.

"I doubt we could find a radio station way out here that would be playing Iggy Pop," Harmony said. "We're just about to go into Arizona."

"Arizona might have Iggy Pop, too," Eddie said. "It's still in America."

"Who is this Iggy Pop?" Neddie asked. "I can't believe the things this kid has heard of."

"You must be an alien, Aunt Neddie," Eddie said. "Everybody knows who Iggy Pop is. He's on MTV every day."

Neddie kept driving.

"Mom, there's an alien driving Gary's car," Eddie said. "It has to be an alien disguised as my Aunt Neddie, because everyone on Earth knows who Iggy Pop is."

"My kids probably like him too," Neddie said, intimidated by Eddie's confident tone.

"Iggy Pop is just a rock star," Harmony said.

"You watch too much TV, it's your mother's fault," Pat said, to Eddie. "You ought to be outside, getting into mischief, like other little boys. When we get to Oklahoma your Grandpa will take you fishing. Then you'll be a lot happier."

"I'd be a lot happier if I could hear some Iggy Pop right now," Eddie said.

"If I don't get to hear Iggy I'll never be happy again," he added.

Harmony sighed, and turned on the radio. Then, to her surprise and everyone else's, she began to scream. She had not expected to scream, but then she had not expected to beat her sister Pat with the couch pillow the night before, either. Normally Harmony could track herself as she swayed out of one mood and into another, but in the part of her life that she was living at the moment, the tracking ability had deserted her. She had ceased to be able to antici- pate, even by a second or two, which way a mood might break. One moment she was packing, the next moment she was beating Pat with the pillow. One moment she was turning off the radio,

116

like a normal mom whose son had just rejected a particular song or singer, the next moment she was screaming at the top of her lungs.

"Oops, she's lost it, she's blowing wild," Pat said. "You better slow down, Neddie. She might try to jump out of the car."

"Mom, I was just teasing," Eddie said, assuming that his Mom was screaming because he had threatened to allow himself to be abducted.

To his surprise, his mother kept on screaming. She began to beat her fists against the car seat, too.

"We just passed into Arizona," Neddie said, speaking loudly so as to be heard over Harmony's screams.

"I wonder where the nuthouse is in this state," Pat yelled. "Harmony might need to go to the quiet room for a while."

"No!" Eddie said, with emphasis. "My Mom said we could go to the Grand Canyon and buy souvenirs."

"Yeah, but your Mom's gone bananas," Pat pointed out. "Shut up, Harmony. None of us can hear ourselves think with you screaming like that."

"I don't care if you think!" Harmony yelled. "I don't care if you jump out of the car! I don't care if we all fall into the Grand Canyon! I don't even care if Eddie gets abducted!"

"Mom, I won't," Eddie assured her, patting his mother's knee. "I was just teasing. I don't want to get abducted. I want to stay with you and my aunts."

To Eddie's relief, his mother began to calm down a little. She was still making a good bit of noise, but it was more like crying than screaming. He decided the threat to let himself be abducted had been going a little too far.

"My mistake, I'm sorry," he said, giving his Mom a hug.

No one said a word, for a mile or two, as Harmony gradually grew more calm. She herself wasn't sure she was really growing more calm. She wasn't screaming outside anymore, but she was still screaming inside—any second she might flip and start yelling at the top of her lungs again, even if Eddie *had* apologized for threatening to let himself be abducted.

"It's a long-looking old road, this road going into Arizona," Neddie said.

"I hope the cowboys are a little livelier than that dud I tried to pick up in Nevada," Pat said.

117

"Can we still go to the Grand Canyon and get the souvenirs?" Eddie asked. "I'm thinking of breaking my hunger strike and eating some Oreos if we're still going to get the souvenirs."

"Eddie, that's emotional blackmail," Pat pointed out.

"Pat, he has the right, I'm his mother," Harmony said, opening the package of cookies with relief.

3.

Harmony had always wanted to see the Grand Canyon, but when they got to it, a little late in the day, she didn't get out of the car. She caught glimpses of the canyon from several observation points—obviously it was a very large canyon. She couldn't see all the way to the bottom from any of the observation points, but she could see far enough down to know she wanted to stay in the car.

"Why, Mom? It's very safe, there's a wall," Eddie told her, when they were parked at the observation point that had the souvenir shop.

"You won't fall, Mom," he added. "I'll hold your hand."

"Leave her alone, Eddie—she's tuckered out from grief," Pat said. "Let's you and me go look through one of the telescopes."

"We can't," Eddie said. "Japanese people are looking through the telescopes—*all* the telescopes."

Harmony looked out the window and saw that Eddie was right. There were a dozen or so telescopes spaced around the rim of the observation deck; behind each of them was a line of Japanese people.

"It's okay," Eddie said, quickly. "I'd rather buy souvenirs, anyway."

"That's not a good attitude," Pat said. "The Grand Canyon is one of the seven wonders of the world. I've waited all my life to see it, myself. How come you'd rather buy tacky souvenirs in a stupid gift shop than look through a telescope at one of the seven wonders of the world?"

"I just would," Eddie said. "If I could go to the moon it might be different. If I could go to the moon I wouldn't care if I didn't buy *any* souvenirs.

"By the time I grow up maybe there'll be space buses to the moon," Eddie added. "I hope so. I want to meet some moon people."

"Correct me if I'm wrong, but isn't the moon uninhabited?" his Aunt Neddie asked. "I don't think the astronauts met any moon men when they went to the moon."

"No, moon people are invisible," Eddie said. "Stand me on the car and I'll look into the Grand Canyon for a minute, before we buy any souvenirs."

"That's gracious of you," Pat said.

"If I wasn't so tired I'd scream some more," Harmony said. "It felt good to scream like that."

"But it's very impolite, Mom," Eddie pointed out. "It's even impolite to raise your voice."

"What if I can't help it, Eddie?" Harmony asked. "What if a scream just comes out?"

"Well, the Japanese people might think it's Godzilla," Eddie warned her. He crawled out a window and managed to hoist himself onto the top of the car, from which he had a nice view of many Japanese people looking through telescopes at the Grand Canyon.

Far away, Eddie could see a great space, bluish in color.

"He's even heard of Godzilla," Neddie said. "What if Eddie's a genius?"

"No, he just watches *Mystery Science Theater*," Harmony said. "They show a lot of Godzilla movies."

"I wonder if they have Evel Knievel souvenirs?" Eddie said, from his post on top of the car. "He jumped the Grand Canyon on his motorcycle."

"Nope, that was the Snake River Canyon he tried to jump," Aunt Pat said. "He didn't make it, either. He opened his parachute too soon."

120

Eddie lay down on the car and edged his head out far enough that he could peek down and look his aunt in the eye.

"Don't say those words to me," he said, but he said it mildly. "I was talking about the Evel Knievel in my dream. He jumped over the Grand Canyon and landed on the moon, and the moon people gave him popcorn."

"Oh, Eddie, that was me," Harmony said. "I gave Evel Knievel popcorn in the casino one night. He used to want to have a date with me."

"No, he lives on the moon," Eddie assured her. "I guess you flew to the moon and gave him popcorn. Did it have butter on it?"

"A lot of butter," Harmony assured him.

Neddie grew tired of the silly conversation, got out, lifted Eddie off the roof of Gary's car, and proceeded with him to the gift shop. Eddie pretended he was a small Japanese prince. He bowed to several Japanese tourists, who, in turn, bowed politely to him.

"I love that kid," Pat said. "There's just something happy-making about Eddie. Just looking at him lifts my spirits."

Usually, Harmony could have said the same, and would have said the same; but at the moment her spirit was so weary that even the sight of Eddie being a Japanese prince couldn't raise it much.

"What was that about Evel Knievel?" Pat asked. She had a keen interest in the lives of celebrities—particularly their sex lives.

"He saw my show seven times," Harmony said. "Of course, he didn't have to pay. The casinos just let him in."

"Did he have the hots for you, or was he after someone else?" Pat asked.

"Pat, I don't have sex addiction," Harmony told her. "He was after me, but I never went out with him. I just bought him popcorn one day at the Trop."

"Who said anything about sex addiction?" Pat asked.

"He wanted to take me for a ride on his motorcycle, but I was scared," Harmony admitted.

"Of the motorcycle, or of getting involved with Evel?" Pat asked.

"Pat, I can't remember," Harmony said. "He had pins in his limbs from all his accidents. He walked kind of stiff, but he was real polite."

"I would hope so," Pat said. "How many celebrities have you actually slept with, Harmony?"

121

Harmony pretended that she didn't hear the question. She thought it was a rude question, particularly so under the circumstances, which were that they were at the Grand Canyon, it was hot, she was tired, and Pepper was dead. How could it possibly matter how many celebrities she had slept with?

"Pat, mind your own business," Harmony said.

"I'm just curious—when you stop being curious it's taps time," Pat said. "Taps is that song Montgomery Clift played when Frank Sinatra died, in *From Here to Eternity*."

"Dan Duryea," Harmony said quietly.

"Who?" Pat asked.

"Dan Duryea," Harmony repeated.

"Dan Duryea what?" Pat asked.

"I slept with him," Harmony said. "He was the only celebrity I ever slept with. I nearly slept with Rory Calhoun, but I didn't."

Pat blinked a couple of times, at that piece of information.

"Wait a minute, maybe I need to clean out my ears," Pat said. "Didn't you know Elvis and Frank Sinatra and Liberace and Wayne Newton—and Barry Manilow?" Pat asked.

"Yes, I knew them—at least I met them," Harmony said.

"Did you go out with any of them?"

"Sometimes they would ask me to eat, after their act," Harmony said.

"But you never slept with any of them?"

"No," Harmony said. "They were very busy. The shows took a lot out of them."

"A lot, but not *that* much," Pat said. "How could you go out with Elvis and Frank Sinatra and Barry Manilow and only sleep with Dan Duryea? It doesn't add up."

"It doesn't have to add up, Pat," Harmony said. "Add up to what?"

"Well, after all, opportunity knocked," Pat said. "Sounds to me like you would have wanted to answer the door."

Harmony put her chin on the open windowsill.

"I didn't, though," she said. Dusk was falling. The sky to the northwest was like a blue wall, over the far reaches of the Grand Canyon.

Then she saw Neddie and Eddie, walking back toward the car. As they were crossing the observation deck one of the telescopes suddenly became free. All the Japanese who had been looking through the telescopes were busy putting new rolls of film in their cameras. Neddie popped in some quarters, grabbed Eddie, and lifted him up so he could see through the telescope. Eddie looked for several minutes. Then Eddie and Neddie came walking slowly to the car. Eddie had an Evel Knievel souvenir and a small bag of popcorn.

"Here's your friend, Mom, now you can feed him some more popcorn," Eddie said. "It isn't very buttery, though. I hope Evel Knievel doesn't mind. I *asked* for extra butter, but the machine ran out."

"He won't mind, Eddie," Harmony said. "Thanks for being so thoughtful.

"I saw you looking through the telescope," she added. "What did the Grand Canyon look like?"

"Like a very huge blue hole," Eddie said. "I was hoping it would be yellow, because yellow is my favorite color. But it isn't yellow. It's blue."

"Ever heard of Dan Duryea, Neddie?" Pat asked, as they were driving away.

"Why?" Neddie asked—she was wishing Harmony could find a way, somehow or other, to cheer up.

"Pat, would you just let it drop?" Harmony said.

4.

The only motel in Tuba City that still had a vacancy when they pulled in was called the Heart of America Motel. There was an American flag, in neon, outside it, but lights for several of the stars had flickered out.

"That sign's a crock of shit," Pat said. "Why would Tuba City, Arizona, be the heart of America? Tulsa's the heart of America."

"Pat, don't make a scene about it, Eddie's tired," Harmony said.

"Tired? He's out cold," Neddie said. "He's been dead to the world for nearly a hundred miles."

It developed that the Heart of America Motel had only one vacancy.

"Our honeymoon suite," the manager said. "It's real spacious. It'll hold you all."

"The honeymoon suite?" Pat said. "This is beginning to feel like a bad joke."

"What's bad about it?" Neddie inquired, as she carried the sleeping Eddie into the honeymoon suite. "Just call up your fiancé, and see if he's still interested."

"At least it's got a king-sized bed, in case you got married to a king," Harmony said. Though no one approved, she had been

124

drinking for the last two hundred miles. She thought she might have an easier time making it through the night if she drank a few swallows of bourbon—somehow, between the Grand Canyon and Tuba City, she drank half a bottle.

"It's okay, Eddie's asleep," she told her sisters. "I promise to be sober by the time he wakes up."

Fortunately Eddie had abandoned his hunger strike, in favor of a Big Mac and fries, at the Grand Canyon McDonald's.

"French fries are rich in carbohydrates," he informed his aunts, just before falling asleep.

"What if I do call my fiancé and he *is* still interested?" Pat asked. She had decided she rather liked the honeymoon suite at the Heart of America Motel. It had its own Jacuzzi, for one thing.

"That would be a start, I guess," Neddie said.

"A start of what?" Pat asked. "He's in Tulsa and I'm in Tuba City. Rog has got a big dick but it ain't that long."

"Pat, please don't talk about sex, I'm in mourning," Harmony said. "Besides that, Eddie might wake up and hear you. He might get confused and think size is everything."

"Oh, blow it out your ear, Harmony," Pat said. "Eddie's five. He wouldn't know what I was talking about if he did hear me."

"I still don't want to take the chance," Harmony said.

Later, they all three got in the Jacuzzi. Pat went in naked but Harmony and Neddie kept their underwear on, much to Pat's amusement.

"You two look ridiculous in your undies," she said. "How come Harmony is the only one in the family with tits?"

"Ask the Lord, he made us all," Neddie said. "He just done a better job on Harmony than he done on us—don't ask me why."

Pat had always openly envied Harmony her figure. Of course, a lot of women envied Harmony her figure. Harmony had once been quite proud of it—after all, it had been her fortune for more than twenty years. But it had stopped feeling like a figure to her— it was just a body that had put on weight. It hadn't brought her happiness, or even very much love. It hadn't kept her daughter alive. It wouldn't be the factor that would allow her to raise her son well, if she managed to raise him well. Men still liked her body because she had wide hips and big breasts—she was comfortable to lie on, evidently. But for Pat to be envious just because Pat herself had small, droopy breasts seemed pretty silly. After all, Pat had all the boyfriends, despite her small, droopy breasts.

Harmony arranged a nice bed for Eddie, on a wide couch. She managed to get him undressed and into his pajamas without waking him. He did open his eyes once and say, "Teresa," but then he discovered that he had Teresa, his stuffed cow, right in his arms, after which he immediately went back to sleep.

After the Jacuzzi all three sisters lay on the king-sized bed and watched Larry King interview Richard Gere. Richard Gere talked a lot about the Dalai Lama and a little bit about Cindy Crawford, whom he had married.

"Do you think Cindy Crawford's sincere?" Neddie asked.

"I don't know, but I think the Dalai Lama is sweet," Harmony said. "Eddie thinks so too."

"Don't tell me—he saw him on the Discovery Channel," Pat said.

"No, I saw him in Caesar's, years ago," Harmony said. "I was playing keno and saw him walk by."

"The Dalai Lama was in Caesar's?" Pat asked. "Why would he come to Caesar's? He's a living god."

"I don't know—a lot of people come to Caesar's," Harmony said. "Eddie saw him on PBS and thought he was very holy."

"They never put people I'd be interested in on talk shows," Pat said.

"Who is somebody you'd be interested in?" Neddie inquired.

"Oh, Johnny Wadd or Marilyn Chambers or somebody lively," Pat said. "I think Johnny Wadd deserves to be on television at least as much as Richard Gere. Richard Gere needs to stay home and be good to Cindy Crawford."

At that point Eddie popped off the couch, wide awake. He crawled up on the king-sized bed and sat by his mother.

"What place is this, precisely?" Eddie asked.

"Precisely? Why do you need to be so precise at this hour?" Neddie asked.

Eddie shrugged, and smiled his most winning smile.

"Because I'm small," he said. "Small people need to be precise."

"Good point," Pat said. "Some large people could do with a little more precision, for that matter. Namely my boyfriends."

"Pat, don't talk about that please," Harmony reminded her. "I told you Eddie might wake up."

"Nobody answered me," Eddie pointed out. "What is this place that we're in and where is my stuffed coatimundi?"

"This is a motel in Tuba City, Arizona," Harmony told him. "Your stuffed coatimundi is still in the trailer."

"Coatimundis don't do well at high altitudes," Eddie reminded her. "Is this a high altitude?"

"No, but that's Richard Gere on TV—remember the Dalai Lama?" Harmony asked.

"Yes, are there any more Oreos?" Eddie said.

"If you ask me you eat way too many cookies," Pat said, after Eddie had hastily crammed four Oreos into his mouth.

"Maybe we ought to call Billy," Harmony said. "Maybe I ought to call Mom and Dad. Do you think they're asleep?"

"No, they stay up late—wouldn't miss Letterman," Neddie said.

Harmony remembered that it had been nearly twelve years since she had seen her brother, and almost that long since she had seen her father and mother. In a few days they would all be meeting. The thought made her stomach fluttery.

"Sure, call them," Neddie said. "Call Billy first. People in jail appreciate calls. You never can tell about the old folks. Momma might hang up on you if you interrupted some show she wanted to watch."

"Oh, I forgot Billy was in jail," Harmony said.

"Uncle Billy?" Eddie asked.

"That's right," Pat said. "Uncle Billy's been a bad boy, and he's in the pokey."

"He's not a boy," Eddie reminded her. "*I'm* a boy. Uncle Billy's much older than me. I've seen his pictures, and not only is he older than me, he's fat."

"Well, overweight would be a kinder way of putting it," Pat said. "Your uncle is a trifle overweight."

Harmony picked up the phone and started to dial, but then she lost her nerve and put the receiver down.

"You didn't dial, Mom," Eddie pointed out.

"I know I didn't, Eddie," Harmony said. "I lost my nerve. I'm afraid if I get him I'll say the wrong thing."

Neddie picked up the receiver and dialed.

"Peewee, is Billy awake?" she asked, when Peewee Mott, the night jailer in Tarwater, answered the phone.

"Too awake," Peewee said. "We're playing Scrabble and he's winning. Do you think pud is a word?"

"No," Neddie said. "It ain't a word. Give me Billy. While he's talking to Harmony maybe you can think up a word that actually is a word."

"Oh, Billy's besting Peewee at Scrabble," Pat said. "If he's winning he'll be in a good mood—you know how Billy hates to lose."

" 'Lo," Billy said, in a cautious voice.

Neddie handed the receiver to Harmony.

"Billy, it's your sister," Harmony said. "Your sister Harmony. Are you all right?"

"Right now I am, I'm thirty points ahead," Billy told her. "But it ain't a sure thing yet. Sometimes Peewee's dangerous when he's behind."

"Billy, I'm coming home—Eddie's with me," Harmony said.

There was a silence on the line.

"Billy, did we get disconnected . . . hello?" Harmony said.

"No, we ain't disconnected," Billy said. "This is big news, honey. I've got to sit here and digest it for a minute."

Then Peewee grabbed the extension.

"How about lud, is that a word?" he asked.

"That's my sister Harmony you're talking to," Billy said. "What do you think she is, a dictionary?"

"Hi, Harmony, sorry to interrupt but I'm desperate," Peewee said. "Billy's whipping me good but if I just had a three-letter word ending in d with a u before it I'd be on my way to a comeback."

"Neddie, is lud a word? Peewee's desperate," Harmony said.

"Lud ain't but cud is," Neddie said.

"Forget lud, but you could try cud, Peewee," Harmony said.

Eddie was adept at talking on the phone and became restive if conversations went on too long without him being allowed to make a comment or two.

"May I talk to Uncle Billy now?" he asked.

"Eddie, it's not a good time," Harmony said. "Uncle Billy needs to concentrate. He's playing Scrabble with Peewee."

128

"Who's Peewee?" Eddie asked. "We have a Peewee in my class but it's not his real name."

While Harmony's mind was drifting a little, Eddie grabbed the phone.

"Hi, Uncle Billy," he said. "Are you still fat?"

"Hi, Eddie, I'm still fat," Billy said. "I hear you're coming to see me."

"Yes, my Momma moved us," Eddie said. "Are there still dinosaurs there?"

"No dinosaurs, but lots of squirrels and other varmints," Billy said.

"Did you murder Batman—is that why you're in jail?" Eddie asked.

Pat giggled and even Neddie smiled. Harmony was glad Eddie had grabbed the phone. Billy's voice sounded sad, even though he was winning at Scrabble. It was obvious that Billy was making an effort to be cheerful; Billy reminded her of her friend Jessie, who also often made an effort to be cheerful when she was sad. But, despite the pretense, everyone who knew Jessie knew she would never *really* be cheerful—not unless her luck changed dramatically at some point in her life.

Harmony knew the same was probably true of her brother. He would never *really* be cheerful, no matter how happy-go-lucky he tried to seem. People who were sad but pretended to be cheerful out of consideration for their friends were heartbreaking, Harmony thought. She herself had been genuinely cheerful for most of her adult life—she rarely had to fake it. She knew it must be painful for people such as Jessie and Billy, who had to fake it day after day and year after year, in order to spare friends or family members the embarrassment of having to deal with a sad friend or family member. It made her heart go out to them, that they would try so hard and be so considerate.

"Eddie, I think Uncle Billy wants to get back to his game with Peewee," Harmony said, afraid that Billy would be put off by Eddie's efforts to find out why he was in jail.

"Hey, it's all right, Eddie," Billy said. "I didn't murder Batman. Hurry on over here to Oklahoma—I can't wait to meet you, and neither can Peewee."

"Okay, Uncle Billy," Eddie said. "Watch out for the Joker—he's very sly."

Eddie handed the phone back to Harmony.

"I think he ought to lose weight," Eddie whispered to his mother. "He sounds too fat to me."

"Well, I guess I'll let you go, Billy," Harmony said. "I just wanted to let you know I'm coming."

"Can't wait to see you, Sis," Billy said. "You can visit me in the jailhouse here, pretty much anytime in the day or night."

"I will if you're still in, Billy," Harmony promised. "But maybe they'll let you out before I get there."

There was silence on the line.

"No, yud ain't a word," she heard Billy say. "You need to give up, little buddy.

"Thanks for calling, Sis," Billy said. "That boy of yours sounds like a character."

"He is, he's the light of my life," Harmony said. "Did you hear about Pepper?"

"I did—that's real tragic, honey," Billy said. "I bet she was a fine girl."

"She was beautiful, Billy, bye," Harmony said. She felt overcome, hung up, and buried her face in the bedcovers.

5.

"I guess you care more for your brother than you do for your old mother," Ethel, Harmony's mother, said the next morning, when Harmony finally worked up to calling.

"Mom, it's not a contest, is it?" Harmony asked. "It was too late to call you when we got in."

"Not too late to call the jailbird, though," Ethel said. "My feelings are hurt so bad I spilled coffee twice and got egg on my new sweater."

"I'm sorry," Harmony said. "Neddie just thought we ought to check on Billy." Eddie was watching *Sesame Street*, Pat was putting on her makeup, and Neddie was having one last soak in the Jacuzzi.

"Maybe you shouldn't take Billy quite so much bacon for breakfast, Mom," Harmony said—she was already a little bit at a loss for conversation.

"Why not, what's wrong with bacon?" Ethel asked. "I hope you ain't raising your son on tofu and junk like that. He'll never amount to much unless he gets his protein while he's young."

"But Mom, Billy's not really young, and he's overweight," Harmony said.

"Stout, he's a good stout boy," Ethel said. "Billy's stout."

"She won't admit that Bill is fat," Sty, Harmony's father, said. Evidently he had been listening on the extension; hearing his voice made tears come to her eyes—he had a gentle voice; she had always loved her father most.

"How are you, Daddy?" she asked.

"Decrepit," Sty said.

Sty was short for Stuyvesant; no one knew why his mother had given him such a name.

"He is not, he's healthy as a horse," Ethel said. "If he had half as many ailments as I have there'd be no putting up with him."

"You don't put up with me anyway," Sty said. "You stay as far away from me as you can get, night and day."

"That's because you're cranky and you snore like a bunch of Messerschmitts taking off from an airport."

"Messerschmitts don't take off from any airport you've ever been in," Sty informed her.

"How would you know?—I was a plane spotter in World War Two and plenty of Messerschmitts were buzzing around here," Ethel said.

"She's cracked," Sty said. "There was never a Messerschmitt anywhere near Tulsa."

Neddie came in from the Jacuzzi, dripping on the carpet. She was wrapped in a bath towel.

"If that's Mom, be careful what you say," Neddie said.

"Who's in that room with you, Harmony?" her mother asked. "I just heard a man's voice."

"No, that was Neddie," Harmony told her. "You might have heard Eddie's voice, though—he's up."

"You never married that boy's father, did you?" Ethel said. "Now he'll be illegitimate all his life. How could you put that terrible stigma on an innocent child?"

"Mom, can we talk about it when I get there?" Harmony said. "We have to hit the road or we'll never get out of Arizona."

"She won't admit that Bill's fat," her father said. "Everybody can see it but her."

"I really don't think that much bacon is a good idea," Harmony said.

"Who asked you?" Ethel said. "Billy's just comfortably stout. He ain't anorexic, like Neddie."

"She thinks you're anorexic," Harmony whispered, to Neddie.

"What canyon will we see today?" Eddie asked. "Will there be a yellow canyon?"

"She's got that little boy in Arizona," Ethel said. "Ain't Arizona where they have the real bad AIDS?"

"That's Africa," Sty said. "She's so cracked she can't keep the continents separate from the states."

"Why would you bring your little boy to Arizona if there's all that AIDS out there?" Ethel asked.

"Mom, I'm going now—bye, Daddy," Harmony said. "Pat's loading the car. We'll see you in a few days if we don't decide to visit New York first."

"New York, they'll stab you in the subways if you go there," her mother said.

"Harmony, hang up, before you get us in worse trouble than we're in now," Pat said. "I need to call my fiancé anyway."

"Do you want to say hi to Grandma and Grandpa, Eddie?" Harmony asked. "You're going to meet them in a few days."

"I'll just say hi to them when I meet them," Eddie said. "Right now I'm watching *Sesame Street*." He didn't take his eyes off the television.

"He says he's looking forward to meeting you," Harmony said. "Bye, now."

"How'd you hear about the bacon?" Ethel asked. "I'd like to know who's been tattling."

"It just came up in conversation—we're all worried about Billy's health," Harmony said.

"Forget his health and worry about his soul," Ethel said. "He ain't been inside a church house in twenty-two years—he gave me that figure himself."

"Bye, honey, see you when you get home," Sty said. "We'll be looking for you."

"*I'll* be looking for them, you may be in jail too, by then," Ethel said.

"Momma, why would anybody put Daddy in jail?" Harmony asked.

"Because he steals my social security checks out of the mailbox and spends them on his girlfriend," Ethel said. "I've had enough of it."

"Don't believe her," Sty said.

"She better believe me, I'm her mother," Ethel said, just before Harmony hung up.

6.

As soon as Harmony put down the phone Pat grabbed it and called her fiancé on his car phone. When he picked up, a horrible roaring sound filled the motel room.

"Rog, it's me, Pat!" Pat yelled, over the roaring sound. "What is it, honey? Is it an earthquake or a tornado? Are you in a safe place?"

"Gas well!" Rog shouted. "Nothing to worry about. Just a little blowout."

Then there was a spewing sound so loud and terrible that Eddie stopped watching *Sesame Street* and squirmed under the bed.

"I think it's the end of the world, Mom!" Eddie said. "I think it's the Apocalypse. It's coming out of the telephone."

"Where does a five-year-old get a word like Apocalypse?" Neddie wondered. "I'm nearly fifty and I couldn't spell Apocalypse if my life depended on it."

"Rog! Rog! Are you safe?" Pat yelled into the phone.

The phone emitted horrible static for a few minutes and went dead.

"Is it the ending of the world yet, Mom?" Eddie asked, from under the bed.

"I don't think it's the ending of the world, but it might be the ending of Rog," Pat said. The minute she hung up she seemed to lose all interest in her fiancé's fate.

"Oh well," she remarked.

"Oh well what?" Harmony said. "If he was my fiancé and he was being blown up I'd say more than 'Oh well.'"

"Pat ain't the sentimental type, unless the gentleman's brand-new," Neddie observed. "The new wore off of Rog a good long while ago."

"Listen, people get blown up in the oil business every day," Pat said. "It's just an occupational hazard. Rog is a little too cocky anyway—if he gets his eyebrows singed off it might take him down a peg."

Eddie crawled out from under the bed and went to peek out the window.

"Did the world live?" he asked. "Are we going to see the yellow canyon?"

"If we can find one," Harmony said. Pat's casual attitude toward her boyfriend's fate annoyed her, mainly because she was feeling like the chances of her ever having another boyfriend of her own were remote. It might be that her sex life was over, in which case she didn't want to hear too much about Pat's, or anyone's.

"I'm not on a hunger strike today," Eddie informed them. "But I may be on one tomorrow if I don't get to see a yellow canyon. I think it would be a good idea to have pancakes, just in case."

"That sounds like blackmail again," Neddie said. "On the other hand a few pancakes wouldn't hurt."

In the coffee shop a little Indian girl with coal-black braids began to smile at Eddie, who promptly smiled back.

"I think she wants to be my friend," Eddie said. "I better go offer her my juice."

He offered his orange juice to the little girl with coal-black braids, who took it and drank every drop, while her mother and father, both large, looked on shyly.

"I guess I'll just have to order some more orange juice for myself," Eddie said, coming back to the table with his empty glass.

"That little girl was really thirsty," he added. "I asked her where the yellow canyon was, but she didn't speak to me."

"I think she's shy, Eddie," Harmony said.

7.

At the filling station down a few blocks from the Heart of America Motel Neddie asked a young attendant with long black hair where the road went that they could see stretching away to the east.

"It goes to Hopi," the young man said.

"Oh, is that a tribe?" Neddie asked.

"It is a people," the young man said. His hair was as black as the hair of the little Indian girl in the coffee shop.

"I like this place," Eddie said. "These people are good-looking. If we're not going to live in Las Vegas could we live in Tuba City sometime? I want to be friends with that little girl."

"I don't know, Eddie—it's pretty windy here," Harmony said. "Look how the dust swirls in the road. I think we'd get a lot of sand in our hair if we lived here."

"I like the way the sand swirls in the road, Mom," Eddie said. "It reminds me of snakes. We could brush our teeth and shampoo our hair *every* day to get the sand out, if we lived here. Is that a good solution?"

"I think it's a great solution, Eddie," Pat said. "I think you and your Mom could be very happy, in Tuba City."

"Shut up, Pat," Harmony said. "Eddie's just having a fantasy."

"I'm always having fantasies," Eddie said, as they wound their way up the plateau and drove across the great, empty plain toward Third Mesa.

"From a car, this country looks a lot like the Oklahoma panhandle," Pat observed. "A lot of country and not a whole lot of else."

"I think I see a cloud lying on the road," Eddie said. He was in the front seat, on his mother's lap, observing the scenery with interest.

"What about my coatimundi?" he asked. "If we're so high clouds are on the road my coatimundi might get altitude sickness."

"That ain't a cloud, Eddie, that's a herd of sheep," Neddie said. "I think I see the sheepherder and his dogs, too."

They slowed down and eased through the cloud of sheep. When they were almost through them they saw that the sheepherder was an old woman, wrapped in many shawls. She trudged quietly along the wide shoulder of the road, taking no notice of the car. As they passed she turned to see that all her sheep were across the road.

"Mom, she's very wrinkly," Eddie said. "I think she spent too much time in the sun."

"I think she's probably spent her whole life in the sun," Pat said. There was a quaver in her voice. She turned around to look at the old Hopi woman.

"What's the matter, Pat?" Harmony asked. "Are you worried that Rog might have got blown up in the blowout?"

"I'm looking at that old woman," Pat said. "What if I end up like her?"

Neddie, too, had been somewhat affected by the sight of the old sheepherding woman.

"I bet she's eighty if she's a year," Neddie said. "Poor old soul."

"Why do you think she's poor when she has so many sheep?" Eddie asked. "She owns hundreds of sheep."

"I doubt it, Eddie," Pat said. "She may not own those sheep. She may be working for three dollars a day, for all we know."

"I lived in the Oklahoma panhandle for a while," Neddie said. "I sure hope I ain't out on the baldies with a bunch of smelly ewes when I'm her age."

Harmony felt a little of what her sisters felt. She had often

138

wondered what there could be that she could earn a living doing when she reached an advanced age like sixty-five or seventy. She could imagine slipping so far that she would have to clerk at a Circle K. If she was lucky she could at least work the day shift, which was less likely to tempt armed robbers than the night shift. But there was always the chance that she wouldn't be lucky.

Twice more before they reached the first villages of Third Mesa, they saw women herding sheep. One of the women seemed to be about their age. She wore a sleeveless down vest, although it was summer. She only had about thirty sheep.

"Why did we pick this road?" Pat asked. "I don't want to see this kind of thing. It's giving me a bad feeling about the future."

They passed through the village of Hotevilla and swooped downward, near the edge of the mesa, into Oraibi. For the first time they really looked across the great space beyond the mesa—the space to the east and south. The sight startled Neddie so that she pulled off the road, stopped, looked.

"My God," she said. "Look off there."

Eddie insisted on getting out of the car at once—soon he was standing on the very edge of the mesa, a tiny boy looking out into endless space.

"There could be moons out there," Eddie said, when he came back to the car. "Moons that are lost."

"There could be," Pat admitted.

Harmony had a bad fear of heights. Low heights, such as the height of the little platform she had been lowered to the stage on, when she was a leading showgirl, didn't bother her—there were so many lights shining on her then that she didn't even feel that she was high. She was just sort of swinging in lights.

But being on Third Mesa, with the wind pushing her toward that endless space, was very different from descending on a platform toward her familiar stage. Even though her five-year-old son had walked fearlessly over to the edge of the mesa and was standing there, a dot against the deep heavens, looking for lost moons, Harmony became so frightened, when she got out, that she didn't want to let go of the car door. Finally she did let go of the door but, after two steps, she lost confidence and grabbed the radio antenna, which bent but didn't break. She felt that she didn't dare turn loose of the antenna—she might be sucked away. She even felt afraid to open her mouth—the space might pour into her and blow her up until she was a balloon, floating far above the earth.

She clung to the antenna so tightly that her knuckles were white. It embarrassed her, that she was so scared when no one else was. Eddie and her sisters were walking along the edge of the mesa, pointing out sights to one another, not at all afraid. Behind her, near one of the little adobe houses, two young Hopi women were hanging out a wash, managing the wind expertly, so that the wet sheets and shirts didn't flap across their faces. They chattered happily as they dug the wet clothes out of a brown laundry basket.

Soon Eddie and Pat and Neddie were nearly a hundred yards away. The old village, Oraibi, was very small, just a few old houses, some of them stone. Eddie seemed to be taking his aunts on a long tour. Now and then Harmony saw them stop and stare off into the mesa. Sometimes they simply stood for many minutes, looking.

Harmony felt guilty, clinging to the antenna. She felt she should be with her son, sharing the experience with him. She was missing whatever he had to say, though perhaps he would say it again to her later. But she was too scared to take even a single step toward the mesa. Instead, she crept back into the car. She didn't look out the window again; she looked at the floorboard, which had the crumpled wrapper of a Butterfinger on it.

Eddie had eaten the Butterfinger the day before, just before he fell asleep on the drive to Tuba City. He was usually careful about litter, often lecturing his mother about putting things in the wastebasket or the dirty-clothes hamper or the dishwasher or her closet or the towel shelf in the bathroom, or somewhere. But this time he had faded very quickly and let the Butterfinger wrapper slip.

When Harmony looked out again, she saw Eddie and Pat and Neddie coming around the far side of the village. They were taking their time. A small dog was with them, walking beside Eddie.

Finally Harmony looked once more into the void that had frightened her so, when she got out of the car. She could not remember a fright so deep. She wondered if Pepper knew of her fear. Eddie thought there might be lost moons, out beyond the edge of the mesa. Harmony wondered if there weren't lost spirits, too. She wondered if her daughter's spirit could be drifting somewhere in that space.

"Mom, why didn't you come with us?" Eddie asked, when he and his aunts got back to the car.

"We saw a ground squirrel and this little dog followed us," Eddie said. "He licked my face."

"Well, that's because he's friendly," Harmony said.

Neddie and Pat took one look at Harmony and decided to let her be. But she was Eddie's mother, and he was not in the habit of letting her be.

"Mom, why didn't you come?" he asked. "I think we can see to the end of the world."

"I was afraid I'd fall, Eddie," Harmony said. It was a lie, though. She hadn't really been afraid she'd fall. She had clung to the radio antenna because she was afraid she'd jump.

The small brown dog stuck as close to Eddie as he could get. He looked up at Eddie often, and if Eddie moved he moved.

Eddie squatted down for a minute, to pet him.

"I don't think this dog even has a home, Mom," Eddie said. "Maybe we should take it with us."

"Oh, Eddie, I'm sure it has a home," Harmony said. "It probably belongs to one of the families here."

"But what if it doesn't?" Eddie asked. "It could be an orphan."

"Well, it could be, but it probably has a home and a family that loves it," Harmony said.

"I'll just go ask those women," Eddie said, meaning the women who were hanging out the wash. They had almost finished. Eddie raced up the short slope to their house, the brown dog right at his heels.

"There's a little boy who wants a puppy," Neddie said.

"I favor small puppies over large puppies," Pat said. "Eddie might be right. That little dog might be an orphan. It was sitting there looking hungry, when we came up."

"Pat, don't get his hopes up," Harmony said. "It probably belongs to some little Indian family."

But in a second Eddie came racing back, his face alight.

"It's an orphan, Mom," he said. "Those women have never seen it before. They think somebody put it out on the road."

"Eddie, are you telling me the truth?" Harmony asked.

Eddie's face immediately fell.

"You don't want me to have it, do you?" he said. "You think I made up a story."

"No, I don't, Eddie," Harmony said, quickly. She felt ashamed of herself. "It just seems odd it was here in the village if it doesn't belong to somebody."

"A bad person put it out on the road," Eddie said. "It's an orphan dog. Why can't we take it, Mom? It isn't very big."

Harmony looked at the two Hopi girls. They had finished hanging up their wash and were watching Eddie and the little dog.

"Go ask them, Neddie," Harmony said.

"Why can't *you* go ask them, Mom?" Eddie asked. "It would be my dog and your dog if you let me keep it."

"I would go ask them, Eddie, but I'm afraid to get out of the car," Harmony said.

"Why, Mom?" Eddie asked, surprised. "It's perfectly safe here. It's just a little bit windy."

Harmony didn't say anything. She knew her fear was foolish; it embarrassed her that she had it. But she did have it.

"I'm sorry, honey," Harmony said. "I know I shouldn't be scared, but I'm still scared."

The two young Hopi women came walking in their direction, carrying their empty laundry basket.

"Hi," Eddie said, as they were passing the car.

The Hopi women gave him the hint of a smile, but they kept walking.

"Mom, ask them . . . *Please* ask them," Eddie said. "The puppy *might* be an orphan and he might die if we leave him."

Harmony knew she had to do something—her son was almost in tears. She managed to open the door and get out, for a moment —she held on to the door.

"Excuse me," she said, to the young Hopi women. "My son really likes this dog. Can you tell me if it belongs to someone here?"

The young women stopped. They looked very shy, now that they had been addressed by an adult. They didn't seem to want to raise their eyes, but finally the older girl looked up at Harmony.

"That dog just showed up today," she said. "He don't belong to nobody here."

Eddie's face lit up again. "See, Mom—it's just what I told you!" he said.

"Your little boy can have him, if he wants him," the girl said. "Somebody put him out on the road."

"Thank you," Harmony said, getting back in the car.

The young women gave Eddie another shy smile.

"I'll take *very* good care of him," Eddie told them. He picked the little dog up in his arms and let him lick his face.

"What do you think, Neddie?" Harmony asked.

"I think Eddie's got a puppy," Neddie said.

8.

No sooner had the car started than the little brown dog put his head on Eddie's lap and went to sleep. Eddie carefully stroked his head.

"I think he's tired from being an orphan," Eddie said.

"What will you name him, Eddie?" Pat asked.

"I don't know," Eddie said. "What do you think, Aunt Neddie?"

"I'd name him Buster," Neddie said. "He looks like a Buster to me."

"What do you think, Mom?" Eddie said. "What should his name be?"

"I'm just glad he came to live with us, Eddie," Harmony said. "Maybe you can think of a name while he's asleep."

Seeing the look of happiness on Eddie's face as he stroked the little dog made her want to cry. She had intended for months to take Eddie to the pound and get him a puppy, but she had let Jimmy Bangor talk her out of it. Jimmy's concern had been the wall-to-wall. Now Jimmy was gone and the wall-to-wall was bloodied to an extent he wouldn't have been able to live with anyway. Harmony felt guilty for having let a not-so-good boyfriend persuade her to deny her son a puppy for six months.

144

"Should his name be Jacques?" Eddie asked.

"No, it's an American dog," Pat said. "Why should it have to carry around a stupid French name?"

"Why do you think Jacques is a stupid name?" Eddie asked, regarding his aunt sternly. "Haven't you heard of Jacques Cousteau?"

"Sure, I've heard of him, but that's no reason to name a dog after him," Pat said.

"You can name him Jacques if you want to, Eddie," Harmony said. "He's your dog."

"No, he's his own dog," Eddie said. "He's just my companion."

They dipped and rose, dipped and rose, as the road wound to Second Mesa and then First Mesa. Eddie pulled the little dog into his lap and soon went to sleep himself. Harmony made herself look straight ahead, at the road. She didn't want to look south, into the great space that flowed on and on. The little Hopi villages they passed through looked very poor, except for the schools, which all looked new and well equipped.

"Why do people live here?" Pat asked. "This is a whole lot bleaker than the Oklahoma panhandle."

They passed many Hopi, men and women, little girls, high school boys, walking along the rocky shoulders of the road.

"They must not make enough cars, in Arizona," Pat said.

"I feel better, now that Eddie has a dog," Neddie said. "You need to get a grip on yourself, Harmony. Eddie was upset that you didn't get out of the car and look at the scenery. He was afraid you were having a breakdown."

"He was right," Harmony said. "When do you think we'll get to Oklahoma?"

"Honey, we've barely started," Neddie said. "It'll be a couple more days before we hit Tarwater."

"Are there any nice men at home?" Harmony asked. "Maybe it's a mistake for me to move there."

"It's a little late for that kind of thinking," Pat said. "All your earthly possessions are in the trailer."

"Maybe we should just turn around and go back to Las Vegas," Harmony said. She felt her spirits sinking to such a low point that it was beginning to be hard to breathe. It seemed insane that she was in a car, going up and down a narrow, dippy road through an

Indian reservation, with an emptiness to the south so vast that it looked as if it could swallow the world. She was driving away from the only town she had ever felt at home in, to go to a place she hadn't lived since she was sixteen. It was all because Pepper was gone. She had lost her mind when she heard the news and now was floating off in a direction that was likely to be the wrong direction. Why hadn't she just stayed where she was? Her sisters suddenly seemed like aliens to her, women from another world, who knew nothing of the casinos and the shows that had kept life interesting for her, for so many years.

"You never have to be lonely, if you have the casinos," she said. "There are always people in the casinos."

"I'm loneliest when I wake up," Pat said. "I doubt it would be any different if I slept in a casino. I'd still wake up lonely."

"Does it happen if you're with guys?" Harmony asked, remembering all the men she had awakened with, in her lifetime with men. Many times she would wake up hopeful, only to have the man she was with wake up surly and spoil her hopefulness, sometimes for the whole day.

Denny, the criminal, had been particularly bad about that. If she so much as smiled at him when he wasn't in the mood for a smile he would look as if he wanted to slug her, and, once or twice, he *had* slugged her, over nothing at all, other than a look on her face that he didn't like.

"You didn't answer my question about the guys," Harmony said.

"It depends on the guy," Pat said. "There's guys I'd just as soon not wake up in the same county with, and then there's the sweet ones you can't get enough of."

"I wonder if I would have been happier if I'd been a sheepherder," Harmony said. "I wonder if that would have been better than the casinos."

"Not for your complexion, it wouldn't have," Pat said.

Then Harmony seemed to stop thinking for a while. Her mind became as spacey as the great space beyond the mesa. They drove for two hours, Eddie and his little dog sound asleep. They went beyond the mesas of the Hopi onto a long plateau, with great white clouds the size of battleships floating above it.

"I've been in North Dakota," Pat said, apropos of nothing. "I wouldn't want to live there. Not enough to do."

146

They stopped for gasoline in a town called Chinle. Harmony got out to fill their tank and check the oil—she always used self-serve.

A cheerful Indian teenager in the office took her money and offered her a coupon in return.

"Going to the canyon?" he asked.

"Oh, the Grand Canyon—no, we've already been," Harmony said.

The boy was nice-looking; his black hair was neatly combed.

"No, our canyon," he said. "The Canyon de Chelly.

"It is not as big as the Grand Canyon," he said.

"Well, I guess since we've seen the biggest we might as well keep rolling," Harmony said.

The Indian boy smiled. "You should see our canyon," he said. "It's the place where the world began. It's only three miles from here.

"Our canyon is the most beautiful canyon in the world," the boy added.

"Okay, maybe we'll go," Harmony said. She didn't want to be impolite to such a nice young man. She didn't really want to see any more canyons, though—she was afraid she might get the feeling she had had on Third Mesa.

The nice young Indian boy came out to clean their windshield, a task Harmony had neglected. Eddie and his dog were awake. When the boy saw that Eddie's dog didn't have a leash, and couldn't be let out to go to the bathroom without the risk of being run over, he quickly produced a piece of twine and made the little dog a temporary leash.

"I hope you go see the canyon," he said, as he was finishing the windshield.

"Don't tell me we've gone in a circle and come back to the Grand Canyon," Pat said. "If we have I'll shoot myself."

"It isn't the Grand Canyon, Pat, it's a canyon where the world began," Harmony said.

Eddie and his dog had just scrambled back in the car.

"I want to go there at once, Mom," Eddie said.

"Oh, Eddie, why?" Harmony said. "We already saw the Grand Canyon and it's bigger."

"Well, I didn't like the Grand Canyon because it wasn't yellow,"

Eddie said. "And it wasn't the place where the world began, anyway."

"Neither is this one," Neddie said. "God made the world in six days and rested on the seventh."

"Eddie doesn't believe in the Bible, Neddie," Harmony said, annoyed that the conversation had veered around to religion.

"But I like Bible stories, sometimes," Eddie said. "It's okay that they didn't know whales only eat plankton."

"Neddie don't even believe that stuff about the six days, herself," Pat said. "If God did make the world in only six days, then no wonder it's so fucked up."

"Pat, please watch your language," Harmony said. "Eddie doesn't need to be hearing the *f* word every minute."

"Then I hope he wears earplugs when your boyfriends are around," Pat said. "Most of the ones I've met ain't interested in anything except the *f* word and the *f* thing."

Harmony knew there was some justice in the remark.

"I want to see the canyon anyway," Eddie insisted. "It *might* be where the world began."

"Okay, we'll just run over and take a peek," Neddie said.

On the narrow road south, to the first look-over into the Canyon de Chelly, Eddie suddenly brightened.

"I know what I'll name my dog," he said. "I'll name him Iggy, after Iggy Pop."

"Eddie, that's a perfect name," Harmony said.

"I guess so, if you happen to be one of the lucky millions who know who Iggy Pop is," Neddie said. "I ain't among the elect."

"No, and you won't be going to heaven, either," Pat said. "No woman who lusts after her own brother-in-law has a chance of getting in heaven."

"Shut up," Neddie said. "That's enough about that subject."

"Got your goat, didn't I?" Pat said.

"Pat, she has to drive," Harmony said. "She doesn't know the road, either."

"What's that got to do with heaven?" Pat asked.

"You won't be going there either—I wouldn't bring it up, if I was you," Neddie said.

"I may not go to heaven but at least I can say I wasn't frustrated while I was alive," Pat said.

148

The sun was shining brightly and the wind had died. Harmony decided she owed it to Eddie to at least take a peek into the canyon where the world began. They stopped at the first overlook and walked a short distance, over some rocks, to look into the canyon.

The moment she looked into the depths of the canyon Harmony felt her heart growing still. They went from look-over to look-over and at each one she felt the stillness growing in her. The pain was still there, but it wasn't swirling. The pain was cold inside her, like a crystal, but at least it wasn't swirling.

"Wow, Mom, I like this canyon," Eddie said.

Iggy liked it too. He raced around, chasing small ground squirrels, barking loudly.

"He's going to be sad, if he doesn't catch one soon," Eddie said. "I wish one would let him catch it. I don't think he would bite it very hard."

Pat and Neddie were silenced by the majesty of the Canyon de Chelly. They had forgotten their quarrel. They held on to one another whenever they approached the edge of the canyon.

"Look, there's people down in it," Pat said. "I see a corn patch, and some sheep."

"I'm glad the world began here," Eddie said, as they stood at the last look-over, gazing down at Spider Rock.

"Why are you glad?" Pat asked.

Eddie gave the question a moment's thought.

"Because it's good that the world began in a place where there's lots of ground squirrels," he said.

Harmony didn't want to leave the Canyon de Chelly. She felt it was so beautiful and so powerful that it might be able to turn things inside her and sort of line her up with life again. It was as if her spirit had lost its accustomed or assigned parking place; her spirit really wanted to be parked somewhere, and was looking for a place, but there were no places for a soul so dented and damaged. She just had to drift around and around the same old blocks, growing always more tired.

But the beautiful canyon, with the sun shining into its depths, made her feel rested. It was a place where she could park her spirit and let it rest.

"I wonder why they think the world began here," Neddie wondered.

"Maybe because *they* began here," Harmony said. "I guess if something has always been a part of your life and your people's lives you might think it was the place where the world began."

"Can we go see those ruins?" Eddie asked, pointing down toward the White House ruins. "There might be treasure in them."

"There might be a rattlesnake in them too," Neddie said.

"Rattlesnakes are really shy," Eddie mentioned. "They don't bite you unless you step on them."

"I'd just as soon not chance it," Neddie said. "This looks like snaky country, to me."

"What if God is a rattlesnake?" Eddie asked. "Did you ever consider that?"

"Where do you get questions like that, Eddie?" Pat asked. "Why would God be a rattlesnake?"

Eddie stared solemnly at his aunt.

"Why wouldn't God be a rattlesnake?" he asked.

"Don't provoke me, buster," Pat said. "I asked you first."

"I asked you second," Eddie said.

"Pat, can't you drop it?" Harmony said. "Eddie can have his own opinions about God, if he wants to."

"He doesn't have his own opinions, though," Pat said. "He has the Discovery Channel's opinions, and who knows what kind of atheists run the Discovery Channel."

"Maybe Harmony's right," Neddie said. "Maybe she and Eddie should just go back to Las Vegas. They may not fit in too well in Tarwater."

"I want to come back here sometime," Harmony said. "I think I'd feel better if I could come here and just look for a day or two."

"I want to put my stuffed animals in the trunk of the car," Eddie said. "I don't want them in the trailer—the altitude might make them sick."

"Eddie, the trunk of the car's the same altitude as the trailer," Neddie pointed out.

"It would be cozier, though, in the trunk of the car," Eddie said.

"That's too much trouble, get in," Pat said.

Instead of getting in, Eddie and Iggy ran off, back down the trail toward the look-over for Spider Rock. Both ran as fast as they could. Iggy ran slightly faster and tried to jump on Eddie, causing

150

Eddie to trip. Eddie fell and Iggy jumped on top of him. Then Eddie got up and resumed his run down the hill, Iggy behind him.

"Well, there goes Eddie and Iggy," Neddie said. "It might have been easier to transfer the animals."

"That kid's too brash," Pat said. "I don't know how much longer I can put up with such a brash kid."

"Pat, he's just honest," Harmony said. "I hope he doesn't run down to a cliff and fall off."

"Relax, he's over there making snowballs," Neddie said.

In the pine forests near the look-over for Spider Rock there were a few patches of snow, under the trees, in the shade. Eddie and Iggy were frolicking in one little patch of snow. Eddie threw a snowball and Iggy chased it down. When he tried to bring it back it dissolved in his mouth, which startled Iggy and made Eddie laugh.

"I wish I was as carefree as that kid and that puppy," Pat said.

Harmony opened the trailer and got Eddie's box of stuffed animals out. The box itself wouldn't fit in the trunk of Gary's car, but the stuffed animals fit. While she was fitting them in Eddie and Iggy walked up. Eddie's cheeks were red from the cold.

"Mom, my hands are cold," he said. "Thanks for moving my stuffed animals."

Harmony picked Eddie up in her arms. Iggy jumped around her legs.

"You're a permissive parent, Harmony," Pat said, with an edge in her voice, as they were driving back down the road to Chinle. It was on the tip of Harmony's tongue to ask her sisters if they would just let her out and go on to Oklahoma without her. She felt that if she could just sit and look at the Canyon de Chelly for a few days, her spirit might recover. All her life, despite what bad things might have happened, she had started her days with an optimistic feeling. Even if a boyfriend left, it would usually only take a few days for her to recover her optimistic feeling. After all, there might be a better boyfriend out there somewhere.

Pepper's death was different, though. It was final. There wasn't going to be a better daughter out there for her, ever. There wasn't going to be any daughter. Somehow life had carried her on, past the time of her daughter—a terrible fact, but a fact. She had always been the person who cheered other people up. She had even been able to cheer her own sisters up, when something bad happened in their lives. She had always been the optimistic one.

Now, it seemed to her, her sisters were growing impatient with her. They knew she had had a tragedy, but they were getting impatient anyway. They wanted her to be the cheerer-upper—neither Pat nor Neddie was cut out for that role. They probably knew they were expecting too much of her, that their need was unfair. Her sisters were realistic women; they knew they couldn't expect her to get over Pepper's death and resume her old role in only three days—yet that was what they *did* expect. They expected her to start being her old, optimistic self. That was why she felt like asking them if they could just leave her at the Canyon de Chelly for a few days. She could always take a bus to Oklahoma, once she felt a little better. That way she wouldn't have the strain of feeling that people were expecting things of her that she couldn't possibly deliver.

Harmony was trying to think of how to phrase her request—how to put it in a way that wouldn't upset Eddie, or either of her sisters—when an unexpected thing happened. She happened to look out the window, as they were going around a curve—she was hoping for a last glimpse of the Canyon de Chelly—and happened to see a U-Haul trailer going by. The trailer was passing them on the right, between them and the canyon. Neddie was driving. Pat was smoking and filing her nails. Neither of them saw the trailer going by. Harmony closed her eyes and opened them quickly, to assure herself that she was awake and that a U-Haul trailer was indeed passing them. She *was* awake, but the trailer wasn't exactly passing them, anymore. It was bouncing off at an angle, toward the beautiful canyon. It was going at a rapid rate, too.

At first Harmony wasn't totally sure that it was *their* U-Haul that had passed them. She knew that U-Haul trailers were normally attached to cars, unless they came unattached. They didn't have motors. They couldn't drive themselves. So the trailer bouncing off toward the canyon had to have come loose from *some* car. It could well be the trailer that had all her earthly possessions in it. She suspected that it *was* their trailer, but she was reluctant to look back and confirm her suspicions. If it was their trailer it might be better just to pretend she hadn't noticed its journey toward the

152

canyon. After all, it might be a serious crime to allow a U-Haul trailer to bounce into the Canyon de Chelly. The canyon was a national park—Harmony knew that much. She didn't know what the legal penalties might be for allowing a U-Haul to bounce into a national park. Also, there was the question of what the U-Haul people would think about it.

"Mom, are you sad?" Eddie asked, patting her on the leg.

"Why do you ask, Eddie?" Harmony said.

"Because you don't look right," Eddie said. "Are you getting sick to your stomach?"

"Eddie, I'm just happy we moved your stuffed animals—that's the thing I'm happiest about, right now," Harmony said. Out of the corner of her eye she saw the U-Haul cross a stretch of bare rock and disappear into the Canyon de Chelly.

"I hope it didn't hit any of the sheep," she said, trying not to allow herself to think about the other things the trailer might hit —the people who were herding the sheep, for example.

"Hit what sheep?" Neddie asked.

"The sheep at the bottom of the canyon, Neddie," Harmony said. She looked out the rear window of the car and confirmed her worst suspicion. Their trailer was gone. All she could see, out the back window, was the clear blue sky of Arizona.

"What are you and Eddie cooking up now?" Neddie asked, assuming that some kind of game was being played.

"Oh," Harmony said. Then she remembered her resolve, which was to pretend that she didn't know the U-Haul had just bounced into the Canyon de Chelly, a famous national park. She didn't say another word.

"What? I can't hear you," Neddie said.

"This is a ridiculous trip," Pat said. "I don't know why either of us thought it would be a good idea to uproot Harmony and Eddie. As soon as we get home Harmony will steal my fiancé—I feel it in my bones."

"Pat, shut up, the trailer's gone!" Harmony said, forgetting her resolve in her irritation with her sister, who seemed to have the notion that she was a sex addict too, when in fact it had been years and years since she had had a lover exciting enough that she would even have had a chance to develop sex addiction.

"What trailer?" Pat asked.

Then, at the same moment, she and Neddie got the message. Pat looked around and Neddie looked around and saw no trailer behind them.

"Oh my God, it's gone," Neddie said. "Where did it go?"

"It went into the canyon," Harmony said. "I just hope it didn't hit anything at the bottom."

Eddie stood up in the back seat and saw that the trailer wasn't there anymore.

"It went," he said. "I'm glad I got my animals out."

"Oh shit—excuse me, Eddie!" Neddie said. "You mean it went into the canyon?"

"Yep," Harmony said. "All my worldly possessions are gone forever."

"But not my stuffed animals—they're safe in the trunk," Eddie reminded them all.

9.

Neddie backed up to where Harmony thought the car was when the trailer went over the edge into the canyon. But Harmony, because she could only bear to watch out of the corner of her eye, underestimated the distance they had gone since losing the trailer. When they got out and cautiously peeked over the edge into the canyon, they saw nothing except the rocky canyon walls. Across the way, a great sheer wall of rock swooped upward, above the White House ruin.

"I guess it fell off the cliff a little farther back," Harmony said. "I was trying not to look when I saw it was going over."

"That was dumb," Pat said, with the edge still in her voice. "I guess you think all we have to do is look for the trailer with all your stuff in it."

"It wasn't dumb, it was cowardly," Harmony said. "I didn't want to watch."

"The least you could have done was mark the spot," Pat said. She sounded annoyed.

"Stop picking on Harmony—she's hurt," Neddie said. "*I'll* pick on her, if somebody needs to pick on her."

Pat suddenly burst into tears.

"Nobody likes me," she said. "Nobody ever has liked me. I wish I'd gone on and married Rog. At least I'd get laid no less than twice a week."

"Pat, it may not be too late, if he survived the gas explosion," Harmony said. The thought that her tragedy had lured Pat away from a man who had probably incinerated himself in a gas explosion made her feel bad. She had no intention of stealing any of Pat's fiancés, but she had no way of replacing one, either.

"I'm sorry if I hurt your feelings," she said.

"I'm sorry too, and Iggy's *very* sorry," Eddie said.

"I don't know what you think Iggy's got to be sorry about," Pat said. "He's a dog. He didn't hurt my feelings."

"Well, he peed on your book, though," Eddie said.

Pat had been whiling away the time between scenic stops by reading a Harlequin romance—she was never without six or seven Harlequins.

"He isn't trained good yet," Eddie said, ruefully. "He's been an orphan too long."

"You mean the little mutt peed on my Harlequin?" Pat asked. "That's the story of my whole life. I can't even read a stupid romance book without a dog peeing on it."

She picked up the paperback and threw it out the window.

"Pat, don't litter, this is a national park," Harmony said, before Eddie had a chance to make the same criticism.

"Well, then it'll make a nice present for some park ranger, provided he don't mind a little puppy piss," Pat said. "Maybe in this cool air it will dry out and be as good as new."

"Let's concentrate on one thing at a time," Neddie advised.

"I *was* concentrating on one thing at a time," Pat said. "I was concentrating on a sexual fantasy and that Harlequin was my guidebook."

"We need to find that trailer," Neddie said.

"Why?" Pat asked. "It's gone. If it's gone, it's gone."

"But all my bras are in it," Harmony said. "I can't ride all the way to Oklahoma with just one bra."

"No, but there are stores between here and Oklahoma where you can buy more bras," Pat said.

156

"None of my possessions were very good possessions," Harmony said. "Maybe it's just as well that they're gone."

"Well, my bed was a good possession," Eddie reminded her. "It was a *very* good possession. And my blankets and my pillow were very good possessions, too. I'm going to need my red pillow to sleep on when we get to Oklahoma. I don't like to sleep on pillows that aren't red."

They had to follow the canyon edge for what seemed like a long distance before they spotted the trailer. It was on some rocks, thirty or forty feet down, and it was broken wide open. Harmony's possessions were scattered everywhere. To her embarrassment she could even see some of her bras. The suitcase she had them in had burst open. Now her underwear was littering a beautiful national park.

"Oh well, cheer up, honey," Pat said. "Win a few, lose a few."

At that point Iggy began barking wildly. Harmony looked around and saw Eddie, sliding on his bottom down a steep trail toward the trailer. Below the little ledge where the trailer rested, the canyon walls fell away for hundreds of feet.

Harmony was too scared even to speak. She was about to lose her other child. It would be a miracle if Eddie could keep himself from going over the edge. Iggy was wildly upset, but Eddie was as nonchalant as if he were going down a slide at the playground.

"Oh my God!" Pat said, when she noticed Eddie.

"Keep quiet," Neddie said. "Stay calm. Eddie knows what he's doing."

"His dog doesn't think so," Pat said.

"He knows what he's doing," Neddie repeated, and she was right. Eddie stopped sliding right where most of the possessions from the trailer were scattered. He peeked into the trailer, spotted his red pillow, crawled in and took it, and started back up the canyon wall, clutching the pillow.

"I told you he knew what he was doing," Neddie said.

"Yeah, but if he had missed he'd be gone now," Harmony said.

Even so, it was on the tip of her tongue to yell down to Eddie and ask him to bring her a couple of bras. Since he didn't seem to be in any danger, he might as well be useful.

Eddie soon found that it was harder to go up a canyon wall than down a canyon wall, particularly while clutching a red pillow. Fortunately there were little bushes that he could grab, but every time he grabbed one, his pillow slipped loose and slid back down amid the debris. After he lost his pillow for the third time, he became visibly annoyed. Disgusted, he turned his small face up to them.

"Mom, I can't climb up!" he yelled. "Come and get me."

Harmony looked down into the great space that opened below the trailer.

"I can't, Eddie," she said. "I can't climb. Just rest a minute and come on up. You don't have to hurry."

"No, I'm too small, I can't," Eddie said.

"Do we have a rope?" Pat asked.

"No, why would we?" Neddie said. "We ain't ropers."

"If you'd let me seduce that old cowboy back in Nevada he might have come with us and then we'd have a rope," Pat remarked. "Then we wouldn't be in this pickle."

"No, if he'd had to put up with you for two or three days I expect he'd have hung you with that rope and we wouldn't be no better off than we are now."

"Eddie, climb on up, we need to leave," Harmony said.

"No, I'm too small," Eddie yelled.

"Just leave your pillow, honey," Pat said. "We can get you another pillow."

"No, it might not be red," Eddie yelled. He bit the pillow with his teeth and climbed a few feet, the pillow dangling from his mouth. But he was still a long way from the top.

Just then they heard a car coming along the road by the canyon. It was a pickup with a saddled horse in it.

"It's a cowboy, he'll have a rope, run stop him, Pat!" Neddie yelled.

Pat ran to the road and waved until the pickup stopped.

"She's hoping it's a guy who might be interested," Neddie said. "Look at her. This high altitude's got her worked up."

Harmony couldn't tell that her sister Pat was particularly worked up.

"I think she just wants to save Eddie," Harmony said.

158

"You don't know her like I do," Neddie said. "She's mad because we didn't take the time to let her screw that old cowboy. This one will be lucky to escape, I don't care how old he is or what he looks like."

The driver proved to be a young Navaho cowboy of somber mien. He was wearing a blue down vest and a very large hat with silver on the band. He came walking along with Pat, a lariat in one hand. It was so chilly that Harmony could see his horse's breath condensing as it waited in the pickup.

The young cowboy nodded at Harmony and Neddie, but didn't speak. He looked over the edge and spotted Eddie, who had his pillow gripped in his teeth. He was trying to climb, but the pillow was a severe encumbrance.

"Thank you for helping us," Harmony said. "I don't know what we would have done if you hadn't come along."

If the young Navaho had an opinion about what they would have done, he didn't voice it. Eddie looked up, saw him, and stopped climbing. The cowboy dangled the rope in his direction. The rope wasn't quite long enough, but it was close. Eddie only had to climb another yard to reach it. He managed to inch his way just high enough that he could grasp the rope.

Harmony had supposed that Eddie would loop the rope around his shoulders, so the Navaho cowboy could pull him to safety—in helicopter rescues on TV the rescued person always had a safety belt of some kind looped around them.

But that wasn't the way it was happening in this rescue. Eddie gripped the rope in his two little hands, while holding the red pillow in his teeth. The Navaho cowboy was as methodical as he was silent. He was careful not to bump Eddie against rocks, or pull him through the stiff little bushes that grew on the side of the canyon.

Still, all Harmony could think of was, What if he falls? He wouldn't be sliding on his bottom, this time; he might land on the ledge or he might not.

"Pat, what if he falls?" Harmony said—she was unable to keep her fear inside her any longer.

Just before Eddie got to the top he almost did fall. His pillow slipped from between his teeth and he took one hand off the rope in order to catch it. He was only two feet from the top when this occurred, and the reason it occurred was that he looked up at his mother and smiled. When he smiled the pillow slipped loose, but he quickly caught it with his free hand. Eddie seemed to be enjoying being pulled up a canyon wall by a Navaho with silver in his hatband.

"He doesn't see it from the point of view of a mom," Harmony said. Nobody was paying her any attention—her sisters didn't see it from the point of view of a mom, either, although they were moms. Now that Eddie wasn't dead they just wanted to get headed back to Oklahoma.

When Eddie was finally safe on level ground, the first thing he did was hand the red pillow to Harmony. He was pretty dusty, from being pulled up the canyon wall, but he looked perfectly content. He didn't bother to dust himself off.

"Thank you *very* much," he said, to the Navaho cowboy. "If you hadn't got me up I might have lost my red pillow."

"No trouble," the cowboy said. He seemed to find it reasonable that Eddie would risk his life sliding down into the Canyon de Chelly after a pillow.

Harmony felt a little shy. It was clear that the Navaho cowboy didn't particularly enjoy conversation. She wanted him to know how grateful she would always be that he had come along when he did and helped Eddie back to safety.

"Thank you very much, sir," Harmony said shyly. "I'm his mother. If you hadn't helped get him up safely this all could have ended differently."

The Navaho cowboy was coiling his rope. He looked up, briefly, and nodded at Harmony. Then, rope in hand, he went back to his pickup, with nothing more said.

"Do you think he was a chief?" Eddie asked, when the Navaho man was out of hearing. "He wasn't very talky. I wanted to ask him about mountain lions but I didn't because he wasn't talky."

"That's cowboys for you," Pat said. "Cowboys are all business. Very few of them are talky and very few of them know the first thing about sex, either."

"I must be losing it," she added. "That's two cowboys in two days who haven't paid the slightest attention to me."

"Stop feeling sorry for yourself," Neddie said.

"Why should I?" Pat asked.

"What is wrong with my aunts?" Eddie asked. "They're always quarreling."

"See, you two should try to be a little more pleasant," Harmony said, as they walked along the road, back toward their car.

10.

While they were having burritos at a small taco stand in Gallup, Pat's addiction began to act up.

"I wonder if there's anybody in this town I could run off with," she said, while munching a cheese-and-bean burrito.

"Pat, we're just going to ignore you when you say things like that," Harmony said. "Can't you try to be a good influence on Eddie? He's your nephew."

Pat ignored *her*. "Let's see if we could get a car phone," she said.

"She wants a car phone so she can have phone sex with Rog, if he survived," Neddie said.

"Pat, you can't, Eddie's just five," Harmony said.

"I just said I wanted a car phone," Pat said. "I didn't say a word about phone sex."

Neddie drove straight out of Gallup, without giving Pat a chance to search the Gallup yellow pages for a place that might sell car phones.

Harmony found that the loss of all her worldly possessions didn't bother her as much as she had supposed it would. In fact, when she looked out the back window of the car and saw no trailer, she felt a kind of relief. All her possessions were in a canyon in Arizona

—it was like a statement from God or something. If she had been meant to continue life with all those possessions, surely the trailer wouldn't have chosen an inaccessible spot in a famous national park to come loose and go off the road. It occurred to her that eagles and hawks might make good use of some of her stuff—her bras might make bird nests for little birds.

Now, when she looked out the back window, she was likely to see Iggy, who liked to have Eddie lift him into the little space above the back seat. There Iggy could stretch out in the sun and take naps. Sometimes he made little belching sounds, when he was napping.

"What do those sounds mean?" Eddie wondered.

"He's dreaming," Pat said.

"What would a dog's dreams be, Mom?" Eddie asked.

"Well, he might dream that he was rescued from an evil witch in Hopi land by a nice little boy named Eddie who's going to take him to live in a Christian community in Oklahoma," Neddie said.

"Slow down, Neddie," Pat said. "New Mexico is a pretty state. Why should we have to watch it hurtling by at such a high speed?"

"We could go to New York," Harmony said, somewhat to her own surprise. "We could all meet Laurie.

"We don't have the trailer," she added. "We wouldn't have to worry about having to park it in a tight space."

"I want to see the Statue of Liberty, Mom, and so does Iggy," Eddie said. "Maybe that's what he's dreaming about, when he makes those sounds."

"Why would a dog dream about the Statue of Liberty?" Neddie asked. "He's never heard of the Statue of Liberty."

"I dream about things I've never heard of," Eddie said. "Why couldn't Iggy?"

Neddie was passing eight trucks at once. Pat seemed lost in thought. Eddie listened to his dog make dreaming sounds. To the north there were some reddish bluffs. Harmony looked back, over Iggy, out the back window. A trucker, not far off their bumper, gave her a big smile and a wave. He had evidently taken a liking to her from looking at the back of her head.

"Don't encourage him, Harmony," Neddie said. "If you give him much encouragement he'll follow us all the way to Tucumcari."

163

Eddie stood up in the seat, turned around, and looked back at the trucker.

"I don't think you should smile at him, Mom," Eddie said. "He looks too much like Jimmy."

Harmony *had* smiled at the trucker, a little. She couldn't help it. During her years as a showgirl it had been her job to smile a lot. Naturally she smiled while she was on stage but she also did a good bit of smiling when she wasn't on stage. It relaxed her to sort of wander through the casinos, smiling at people—guys, mainly, but not always guys. It certainly didn't hurt business in the casinos to have a friendly showgirl passing through.

It wasn't a professional smile, though—not really. It was just the way she felt. She smiled a lot. It hadn't been a provocative smile she gave the trucker, either—it was just a normal smile, one human being indicating that she had at least a little goodwill for another human being.

"Go away, farter!" Eddie said, to the trucker—of course the trucker couldn't hear him and had no idea that Eddie had made such a horrible remark.

Harmony herself was shocked—Eddie had never taken such a negative attitude toward anyone before—or, if he had, he hadn't expressed it to her.

"Eddie, why'd you say that?" she asked.

"Well, he looks like Jimmy, he might fart too much if he was in our home," Eddie said, more mildly. "I don't think you should let him be your boyfriend."

"How could he be my boyfriend, he's in a truck?" Harmony asked, nervous. She was getting the feeling that Eddie might have been suppressing low opinions of several of her boyfriends.

"Eddie's right, casual smiles when you're not even thinking about sex is how things get started," Pat said.

"Speak for yourself," Neddie said.

"If that truck gets any closer he'll squash Iggy," Eddie said. "I don't think he has consideration for dogs. Since we have Iggy now, that's important, Mom."

Harmony didn't look around again. The trucker even tooted his horn gently, once, hoping for some response, but he didn't get one. When he finally gave up he passed them easily, though Neddie was holding steady at eighty-five.

"I doubt Gary realized what a good automobile he was giving us," Neddie said. "This car just kinda floats on down the road."

The words were scarcely out of her mouth before the car ceased to float. There was a horrible sound from inside the hood—it sounded as if a dishwasher had just blown apart, breaking all the dishes and itself besides. The car lost speed rapidly.

"Uh-oh," Neddie said.

As the car slowed, it began to buck and lurch; Neddie floorboarded it, but to little avail. The car lurched like a sick animal of some kind. Neddie had been in the passing lane when disaster struck, but she managed to wrestle it across to the right shoulder, slipping right between two speeding trucks.

"It ain't good for cars to be driven eighty-five and up," Pat said. "What do you think happened?"

"I don't think what happened was good," Neddie said. "That's as far as I'll go."

"Are we going to have to live here, Mom?" Eddie asked. They were on the outskirts of Grants, New Mexico. A few tumbleweeds were blowing across the road; they hung in the barbed wire surrounding the little shacks on the edge of town.

"No, we won't have to, Eddie," Harmony said. "But maybe we'll have to get a motel room until the car gets fixed."

"We won't be getting the car fixed," Neddie said. "This car is shot."

"Who shot it, Aunt Neddie?" Eddie asked. "I didn't hear any shots." He quickly pulled the sleeping Iggy off his warm but exposed spot above the back seat.

"I mean shot in the sense of being too damaged to repair," Neddie said.

Near the road, two teenagers were pitching a basketball at a hoop that had no net. Two skinny goats were watching them play. Every time a truck whizzed by, the car rocked for a moment from the force of the truck's passing. Harmony remembered her urge just to take Gary's car and run away from her life, as far as she could get. Probably Grants, New Mexico, was as far as she would have got, had she followed that impulse: she would have had to begin whatever life was left to her in some place pretty much like Grants, New Mexico, a place where the goats were skinny and the basketball hoops without nets.

The thought didn't really depress her. It would have been pretty much what she deserved. Only here she was, with Grants to deal with, and her sisters and her son and Gary's ruined car as well.

"Do you think God tests us, to see how much shit we can survive?" Neddie asked, smoking.

"I think God has better things to do than to heap shit on little puny human beings just to see how fast they can shovel it," Pat said.

"My teacher doesn't believe in an anthropomorphic God," Eddie said. Iggy was licking his face.

"Eddie, if you say one more big word I don't know the meaning of and don't even want to know the meaning of I'm gonna scream and run berserk through the bushes," Pat said.

"Pat, he was just contributing to the conversation," Harmony said. She felt very nervous when the conversation veered around to religion. Sooner or later it was going to come out that Eddie had never been inside a church in his life.

"But there's no bushes around here, Aunt Pat," Eddie pointed out.

"There's enough for me to run berserk through," Pat said. "This is a crazy trip. It's not doing any of us any good."

"It is too," Eddie said. "It's doing Iggy good because he's not an orphan anymore. He has a family now."

"That can be a blessing or it can be a curse," Pat said. "Right this minute it feels like a curse. Here we are broken down in some godforsaken part of the world and I don't even know whether my fiancé is dead or alive."

"If he survived, maybe this will teach you to appreciate him," Neddie said.

"I have a good idea," Harmony said. "I've been thinking about it ever since the car blew up. Why don't we just leave the car and take an airplane to New York?"

"No, what about my stuffed animals?" Eddie said. "What about Iggy?"

"They let dogs on airplanes, Iggy can come," Harmony assured him.

"Mom, I have many stuffed animals, they depend on me," Eddie said. "We'll have to take them all on the airplane—every one."

166

"It seemed like a good idea when I had it," Harmony said.

"Look around you," Pat said. "Does this look like an airport?"

"I think Harmony just wants to meet Laurie," Neddie said, in a kindly tone. "She wants to find out about Pepper. That's a natural thing."

"I don't want to leave a *single* stuffed animal," Eddie said, in a very firm voice.

"You should have let me smile at that trucker," Harmony pointed out. "If you'd just let me smile at him he might have given us a ride to the airport."

"She's got a point," Neddie allowed. "We've got a ruint car here —a friendly trucker might come in handy."

"Truckers aren't a scarce breed," Pat reminded them. "This is good old I-40 we're stranded on. A truck goes by every two or three seconds. Harmony can just get out and stand on the shoulder and smile her famous smile. In ten minutes you'll have trucks lined up all the way back to L.A., wanting to help her get her hubcaps off."

Even as she said it six or seven eighteen-wheelers swooshed by, rocking Gary's car six or seven times.

"Maybe the car isn't as ruined as you think it is, Neddie," Pat said. "Maybe it's just a minor problem with the fan belt. Maybe some genius mechanic could have us back on the road in thirty minutes."

"Maybe, but don't bet your virtue on it," Neddie said, dryly.

"Why not?—I've bet it on longer shots than that," Pat said.

11.

"I think Gary will understand," Harmony said. "Even when Gary gets mad at me he always forgives me, later in the day."

"Just tell him we ran into a deer or a cow or a buffalo or something and totaled his car," Pat said. "After all, we are out here in the country where the buffalo roam."

Harmony was feeling a little guilty for having given Gary's car away in exchange for a ride to the Albuquerque airport. A nice Navaho man had stopped to help them. About that time Harmony had begun to feel desperate. She didn't feel stable enough to continue driving around America in Gary's car, with Eddie and Iggy and her sisters and Eddie's stuffed animals. She felt she might crack up at any moment. She might jump out at a stoplight and run away. She was very conscious of her responsibility to Eddie, but even her sense of responsibility might not be as strong as the cracking-up feeling.

When the nice Navaho man offered to take the ruined car off their hands and give them a ride to the airport to boot, Harmony said yes at once, even though the man's Toyota pickup only had one seat in it, meaning that most of them had to ride in the back of the pickup all the way to Albuquerque.

Eddie spent most of the ride obsessively counting his stuffed animals, to make sure none of them had been left in a crevice in Gary's car.

"I have thirty-two stuffed animals," Eddie said. "And I have Iggy, who's not stuffed."

Fortunately he was able to charm a woman at the airline out of a box big enough to hold all thirty-two stuffed animals. The woman's name was Rosie. Eddie immediately and articulately convinced Rosie of the necessity of having a secure container for his animals. When his Aunt Pat suggested they just send the animals straight to Oklahoma Eddie chilled her out with one look.

"No way," he informed her. "The hundred-year flood might come and wash them all away."

"It's pretty dry in Tarwater," Neddie said. "I doubt the hundred-year flood will happen in the next few days."

"I'm sorry, I can't take the risk," Eddie said.

"Harmony, can't you reason with your son?" Pat asked. "What are we going to do with thirty-two stuffed animals in New York City?"

"Having his animals with him gives Eddie a sense of security," Harmony replied.

Actually, being in the pleasant Albuquerque airport gave *her* a sense of security. The terminal was airy and bright and there were nice designs on the tile floor. Harmony particularly liked the airiness. With a little space around her she didn't have to deal with the constant sense that everyone around her was just waiting for her to crack up. They could spread themselves out, in a way that had not been possible in the car. Eddie sat by himself, having a conversation with a stuffed porcupine. It was not uncommon for him to hold long conversations with his stuffed animals. Harmony wondered if that was a sign of anything bad—that Eddie didn't like being an only child, maybe, or that he resented her boyfriends because they left hairs in the bathtub or had problems controlling their wind.

In only twenty minutes it would be time to get on an airplane and fly to New York, a place Harmony had never been. The best reason Harmony could think of for going there was that there had to be something you did next. You couldn't just stop in an airport and sit there forever. You couldn't drive a car forever, or do any one single thing forever. Already her sister Pat had made the "Life must go on" statement to her several times. Harmony didn't feel that the statement was strictly true. Eddie's life would probably be a lot better if her own went on for a while, but life didn't *have* to do anything. It could go on for eighty-three years, as it had with Myrtle, or it could stop a lot sooner, as it had with Didier one morning, and with Pepper, and with Wendell's son, and many others. Jackie Bonventre's had stopped one morning while he was putting a bag of laundry in his car; Mel's had stopped in a hospital, after months of suffering that even the best drugs couldn't really dull.

Harmony supposed hers probably *would* go on: she just had no idea how the details would resolve themselves. Would she ever have a job again, or a boyfriend? If she did have a new boyfriend someday, would he have a violent side, or just be careless about hairs in the bathtub? Would Laurie be glad to see them, when they got to New York? Would her mother disown her because Eddie had never been inside a church?

"I wish I knew a little more about the details," Harmony said— meaning the details of the rest of her life. For no reason it popped into her mind that her brother was in jail.

"Why does Billy have to make phone calls?" she asked. "He's nice. Why can't he just find a girlfriend?"

Neither of her sisters had an answer.

"I guess some people would just rather get on the phone," Pat remarked.

"Billy don't think he deserves a girlfriend," Neddie said. "He's got low self-esteem."

"So do I," Harmony said. "But I still feel like I deserve a boy-friend once in a while."

"You just don't think you deserve a very good one," Eddie said, hopping on his mother's knee.

"Eddie, I just don't realize they aren't very good until it's too late," Harmony told him; she was feeling worse and worse about her record with boyfriends.

"That's still better than Billy's situation," Pat said.

"I don't feel like I deserve much better than Dick, myself," Neddie said.

"Shit, what's wrong with all of you?" Pat said. "I feel like I

170

deserve Warren Beatty. I just don't happen to know where he lives."

"You're too old for Warren Beatty," Neddie said, in an unsympathetic tone. "You'll be lucky if you've still got Rog. He's more your speed."

"Rog don't have a speed—neutral ain't a speed," Pat said.

"When we get to New York what will we do first?" Eddie asked.

Harmony looked at Neddie, who looked at Pat. None of them had an answer.

"Eddie, can't we just play it by ear?" Harmony asked. "Maybe we'll call Laurie first. Laurie was a good friend of your sister's."

"If she's not home I think we should go to the Statue of Liberty first," Eddie said. "I need to get postcards and the Statue of Liberty would be the perfect place to get postcards."

"I wouldn't have no more idea how to get to the Statue of Liberty than I would of how to get to China," Neddie said.

When they called the flight, Harmony started to cry. Her son and her two sisters ignored her. She felt sad that she was leaving the West. It had always been her home. When the plane took off she looked out the window at the beautiful sunny sky. For most of the flight Eddie kept his finger poked into Iggy's little cage, so Iggy would feel reassured. When they served the meal Eddie gave Iggy his potato.

"Will you stop crying about Pepper next year, Mom?" Eddie asked.

"I hope I can, by next year, Eddie," Harmony said. "I know it's no fun when I cry."

"It's no fun, but I have Iggy to distract me," Eddie said. "The best part of this trip so far is Iggy."

As they were coming into New York the pilot announced that the passengers on the right side of the plane would have a good view of the World Trade Center and the Statue of Liberty. Fortunately Eddie and Harmony were on the right side of the plane. It was almost sunset. Eddie held Iggy up so Iggy too could see the Statue of Liberty. Iggy didn't get the point—he yipped so much Eddie had to put him back under the seat.

"It doesn't look big from up here," Eddie said, studying the Statue of Liberty. "From up here it looks a little bit green.

"I'm still excited, though," Eddie said. "It really is the *real* Statue of Liberty. And I can even see ships down there—big ships."

Harmony looked down briefly but the plane tipped just as she did, and her stomach acted as if it was going to come up in her mouth.

"I want to go, Mom! " Eddie said. "I *love* the Statue of Liberty. When can we go?"

"I guess whenever you want to—tomorrow, even," Harmony said.

"There's sea gulls too—I can see them flying," Eddie said, as the plane sank lower and lower over the suburbs of the great city of New York.

12.

"I thought New York was in America," Neddie said, as they struggled through the corridors of La Guardia Airport, trying to find their way to the baggage claim.

"Mom, I can walk, I'm five and a half, put me down," Eddie said. He was the only one of the group who was enjoying the experience of La Guardia Airport—he had been enjoying it more before his mother snatched him up and began carrying him.

"I'm afraid to put you down," Harmony said. It was true. The airport was thick with people who looked as if they could be accomplished snatchers of little boys.

"Yeah, and if they don't snatch him, they'll snatch you," Pat said. "This is Lech City, I can sense that already."

"I don't care about that, I just wonder where America went," Neddie said. "I saw a bunch of people with turbans. I thought people with turbans lived over the sea, someplace."

"They could be visitors," Harmony told her. "We have people with turbans in the casinos, lots of times."

Neddie began to smoke too much. She seemed to be developing an obsession about America. When they finally got to the baggage claim Neddie went around looking at all the signs over the baggage

173

carousels, to be sure they had the names of American cities on them.

"I can't help it, this just don't seem like America to me," Neddie said. "A lot of these people are jabbering in languages that ain't American. I get confused real quick when I don't hear American spoken."

Eddie squirmed so that Harmony had to put him down. She had misgivings, though, and tried to keep no more than one step from him as he marched around amid the hundreds of people waiting for baggage. Eddie proceeded with complete aplomb—he loved the hustle and bustle of La Guardia Airport.

"I'm looking for my stuffed animals and when they come I'm going to look for someone to take us to the Statue of Liberty," he said.

"Eddie, I'm sure the Statue of Liberty is closed for the night," Harmony said. "We can go tomorrow. Let's don't wander off too far from Aunt Neddie and Aunt Pat. They might get lost."

"Well," Eddie said, continuing to wander. Often he said the word "Well" as if it constituted a full justification for whatever he wanted to do. In this case he seemed to be satisfied with it as a reply. Fortunately just as he spoke a red light came on and one of the carousels began to move. The very first piece of luggage that appeared was the box containing thirty-one stuffed animals—the coatimundi was in Harmony's purse.

"Aunt Neddie and Aunt Pat smoke too much," Eddie said, once Harmony had wrestled the box off the carousel. "They might give my stuffed animals lung cancer and they might even give *me* lung cancer."

While he was speaking a very small man with a wispy mustache, a turban, and no front teeth arrived with a dolly and popped Eddie's box on it, without being asked.

"I am Omar," he said. "I will help you to your car—modest fee."

Harmony decided on the spot that Omar could be trusted—he seemed sweet, and the fact that he had a wispy mustache and no front teeth was an endearing trait. She managed to locate her sisters and pointed them out to Omar.

"We don't have a car but we do have luggage, Omar," she said.

Omar winked at Eddie, who winked back.

"We're going to the Statue of Liberty sometime—but not to-night, though," Eddie informed Omar.

"My friend Salah will take you," Omar said. "All your problems sol-ved. Salah has two cars, one is no-smoking car."

"Who's this A-rab, get him out of here," Pat said brusquely, when Omar wheeled his dolly over to where she and Neddie waited.

"Pat, don't be prejudiced, this is Omar," Harmony said. "He has a friend who can take us to the Statue of Liberty."

"How about a hotel—only make sure it's in America," Neddie said.

"Not worry, all will be hunky-dory," Omar said, winking at Pat, who was just reaching for one of her bags. Omar reached more quickly, and popped the bag onto his dolly beside the box of stuffed animals.

"I can lift my own suitcase, thanks," Pat said, but Omar was undeterred.

The fact that her sisters didn't appear to like Omar made Harmony feel a little gloomy, inasmuch as it was a repeat of the story of her life. Her sisters had never liked the men she liked. They had different standards, or something. The fact that Omar wore a turban—it wasn't exactly a spotlessly clean turban, either —and had no front teeth and walked in tennis shoes so old that the little strings were beginning to show through the fabric didn't mean he wasn't a perfectly nice man. After all, she wasn't get-ting married to Omar, she was just letting him help with their bags.

"Have you ever seen an auk?" Eddie asked, walking up to Omar. "They're supposed to be extinct but I thought there might be a few left in your country."

"What *is* your country, buddy?" asked Neddie, in a tone that was fairly friendly.

"I am from Benares, City of Light," Omar said. "Omar is not my real name. At home I am called Kushwat."

"If you're Kushwat at home why are you Omar here?" Pat asked.

"Americans don't like people from India," Omar said. "They like people from Lebanon better, so I am Omar here."

Just then another man in a turban wandered up to them. He wore a bright blue shirt, dirty white trousers, and wading boots.

"Go away, I am waiting on these ladies," Omar said, before the other man even spoke. "They wish to go to the Statue of Liberty soon."

"Statue of Liberty is fifty-dollar ride," the new arrival informed them.

"He is parked illegal," Omar said. "Maybe we can hurry."

"You didn't answer my question about the auk," Eddie reminded Omar.

"The flesh of the bustard is oily," the new arrival said.

"I'm getting less and less of a feeling that we're in America," Neddie said.

"Did you eat an auk?" Eddie asked the man. "If you ate the last one that's why they are extinct."

"Salah, go away please, guard your vehicle," Omar said. "We come very soon."

"You *better* come very soon or I will be in jail with big fines looming," Salah said, with a touch of gloom.

"He is pessimist," Omar said cheerfully, watching his friend depart. "I am optimist."

"I wonder if there's anybody at all from northern Oklahoma here?" Pat asked. "I get homesick real quick when I don't have no one from northern Oklahoma to talk to. I don't know what it is about northern Oklahoma but I just love it."

"It's just a special place," Neddie said. "Lord, I miss the breeze up there on the plains."

"I don't think your friend should have eaten the last auk," Eddie said. He was carrying Iggy in his cage and Iggy was yipping indignantly. He wanted to get out and experience New York for himself.

Harmony was beginning to find the bustle of La Guardia a little exciting. At least there were a lot of people around, talking and insulting one another. La Guardia Airport was really like a big, dirty casino. There were no slot machines, but there were plenty of the kinds of people who would be feeding money into the slot machines if they were in Las Vegas. It was heartening to see the

176

activity and be part of the energy—that was what she had always liked about casinos.

"I like it here, Mom," Eddie said. "It's a little like the Circus-Circus."

"My life's ambition wasn't to be in no place where everybody wears turbans," Neddie said.

When all the baggage finally came Omar rolled it outside, where the lights of two police cars were flashing. Salah and a dark-skinned teenager with big sad eyes were surrounded by police.

"Here we are, what is commotion? VIP guests arrive!" Omar yelled. He had a surprisingly deep voice.

"What VIPs?" one cop said. "These don't look like VIPs, they don't give you no right to park in the red zone."

"Sally Jessy Raphael, she is in disguise," Omar said, pointing to Harmony. The information gave the policemen pause. They immediately began to act as if Harmony *was* a celebrity. They cast their eyes downward and kept them there.

"Seen any auks?" Eddie asked one of the cops. "There might be a few that aren't extinct."

"What's he talking about?" one cop asked.

"It's a character in a TV show," an older cop said. "You know, like them teenage turtles."

The older cop ruffled Eddie's hair, attention Eddie didn't particularly welcome.

"An auk is a bird—it isn't a teenage mutant turtle," Eddie informed him coolly. "Don't say words that are stupid to me. I want to know about auks. I hate teenage mutant ninja turtles."

"Make him be polite, Harmony," Pat said. "I was in jail once in Meridian, Mississippi, but I have a feeling being in jail here would be worse."

"Which is the no-smoking car?" Eddie asked, looking at Omar.

"No-smoking car is temporarily broken down, please get in quick," Omar said.

"Where do you think you're taking us, buddy?" Neddie asked.

"Taking you away from cops, then we can decide on destination," Omar said.

At this point Salah began to raise objections.

"This is my car, not his," he informed them. "Omar is merely

177

baggage handler. Abdul and I are car drivers. We will take you to Bayonne—you can spend comfortable night in swank motel."

"What part of the world is Bayonne in?" Pat asked.

"New Jersey part of the world," the dark-skinned teenager said. "My home is nearby—next block."

"I don't think my stuffed animals will fit in this car," Eddie said.

"They might but if they do our suitcases won't," Pat said, only to be proven wrong within a matter of minutes. Omar, Salah, and Abdul quickly squeezed all their baggage into the trunk of the car, including the box of stuffed animals. There was even room for Omar's luggage dolly, although Salah was irritated that Omar wanted to desert his post so early.

"What about night flight from L.A., many tips?" he said.

"I have heartburn," Omar replied. "I want to go home."

Soon they were all in the car. Eddie sat on Harmony's lap, and Iggy sat on Eddie's lap.

"It'll sure be nice to see Oklahoma again," Neddie said, as they pulled away from the airport.

"If we ever do," Pat said.

"Pat, shut up, my daughter died," Harmony said. Her sister's absurd worry that they would never see Oklahoma again was beginning to get on her nerves.

"What's the name of this swank motel you're taking us to?" Neddie asked Salah.

"Is called No-tel Motel," Salah said. "Is owned by my cousins."

"Mom and Dad would have a turnover in their graves if they knew we were racing around New York with a bunch of Arab terrorists," Neddie said.

"Neddie, they aren't in their graves, they're down in Oklahoma watching Letterman," Harmony pointed out.

"Lights of Manhattan, take good look," Abdul said, pointing out the window. Sure enough, there across the way were the lights of New York City. Great towers, speckled with lights, rose into the dark sky.

"I like it, Mom," Eddie said. "I like it a lot, and Iggy likes it too."

"It does look like a real town," Pat said. "There must be a guy who can step lively, over there somewhere, if I can just find him."

"Yeah, but where would you plant tomatoes, if you was in a planting mood?" Neddie asked.

178

Harmony just looked at the lights and the tall buildings. She felt as she had when she took the bus into Reno, to go back to Ross, not long after Pepper became a star at the Stardust—only the lights of Manhattan were a hundred times more startling than the lights of Reno, which, after all, was just a town with a desert all around.

13.

"Longest suspension bridge in the world, Verrazano Narrows," Abdul announced, as they were crossing a very long bridge. There had been confusion on the roads. One minute the towers of Manhattan were on their right, the next minute they were on their left. Omar had immediately passed out and, without his counsel, Salah had made a bad choice of exits. Neddie was snoring. Then, several bad choices later, no one was awake but Harmony, Eddie, Iggy, Salah, and Abdul.

Eddie was the most bright-eyed of the lot.

"I love this place, Mom," he said. "It's all bridges and skyscrapers."

"I'm glad you like it, honey," Harmony said. "I think I may like it too."

She was a little nervous, though. Just before Omar fell asleep he leaned over the seat and whispered that he was in love with her. Also, Abdul had turned the rearview mirror so he could watch her in it, considerably handicapping Salah in his efforts to get them safely to Bayonne. Salah, for his part, twisted around whenever possible in order to be able to stare at Harmony, which may have had something to do with the confusion about exits—that and the fact, revealed by Abdul, that Salah had only arrived in America two days before.

"He is new driver, always getting lost," Abdul said.

Harmony was glad that the strain of having to be somewhere other than northern Oklahoma had finally worn her sisters out. Pat was slumped against one door, Neddie against the other. Eddie looked as if he planned to stay awake forever, though.

"I don't want to miss a minute, Mom," he said. "Maybe I'll go to sleep tomorrow, after we see the Statue of Liberty." A minute later he yawned and fell fast asleep, his arm around Iggy.

"Very cute little boy, would you like to marry me?" Salah asked.

"Excuse me?" Harmony said, hoping she hadn't heard what she thought she had heard.

"We could live with my family until we get started," Salah said. "They have nice place in Queens."

"She is not wanting to get in bed with you, I can tell," Abdul said.

"You are idiot boy, don't understand women," Salah replied. "She is wanting to get in bed with me promptly when we get to motel.

"We will make beautiful children," he added.

"None of this will ever be happening," Abdul said. "You are terrible driver, we will be at the bottom of the sea pretty soon.

"No beds at the bottom of the sea," he added.

"I will learn all these roads tomorrow," Salah assured him. "I only arrived two days ago—takes a little time to learn these roads, but takes no time to go to bed with beautiful woman."

Perhaps sensing that his rivals were gaining ground, Omar woke up. When he looked out the window he saw that they were still on the Verrazano Narrows Bridge.

"Why are we on this bridge?" he asked, sleepily. Then he turned to look at Harmony.

"On bridge because no place to turn," Salah said, sulkily. "Very few places to turn in New York City."

"Millions of places to turn," Abdul informed him.

Omar turned and looked at Harmony.

"If you will marry me we will make beautiful children," Omar said, echoing Salah's sentiments of a few minutes earlier.

"He is an old man, don't listen to him," Abdul said. "He is an old man, he has no teeth. His organ is short. I am young man, good-sized organ." He smiled at her sleepily when he said it, as if he wouldn't mind having a little nap.

Harmony decided to ignore all marriage proposals, expressions of lust, and the like and just concentrate on serious matters, such as the taxi meter, which was clicking continually. Now they seemed to be heading out to sea.

"He is a boy, he doesn't know arts of pleasure," Omar said. "He is like rabbit, jerk, jerk, too quick."

Abdul merely continued to stare at her with big sleepy eyes.

"Don't look at my fiancée!" Salah said loudly. "Is forbidden by the Koran!"

"Salah, I'm not your fiancée," Harmony said, just as the taxi scraped the side of the Verrazano Narrows Bridge, waking everybody.

"Good Lord, this pond we're going over here is bigger than Lake Texhoma," Neddie said. "Why are we crossing all this water?"

At that point Omar, Salah, and Abdul began to yell at one another, while, from time to time, the taxi continued to scrape the side of the bridge.

"We will never be at motel, this man is going wrong direction, we will be in the Bronx, crack places," Omar said. "Salah is not licensed cabdriver, he is gypsy cabdriver."

"I thought he was from Lebanon or somewhere," Pat said.

"He is my uncle," Abdul said.

Harmony drowsed off for a while—it seemed to her, as she drifted into her doze, that she heard Abdul, Salah, and Omar proposing to Pat. She had a great wish to be out of the taxi and into a large soft bed, with no one in it but herself and Eddie or, at most, Eddie and Iggy.

When she came out of her little doze she smelled something sweet in her face. To her shock it turned out to be Omar's breath. He was trying to help her out of the cab, in the process stealing a kiss or two. Iggy was yipping at him loudly.

"Omar, what were you eating?" Harmony asked. His breath was unusually sweet.

"Is betel nut," Omar said, fluttering his breath in her face again.

182

"Big joke on Salah. He was looking for No-Tel Motel in Bayonne but all the time motel was in Jersey City."

Harmony could see big flares, flaring into the sky, not far away. On the ground, closer to hand, she saw several young black women with very short skirts on. The skirts were so short she could see their underpants below their skirts; the underpants were Day-Glo colors, pink and orange and aquamarine. Eddie was still sleeping like an angel, unaware that they were now at their destination, the No-Tel Motel in Jersey City. Two or three of the young black women seemed to be yelling at Abdul, who cowered behind Salah. There was no sign of Neddie or Pat.

"Omar, what happened to my sisters?" Harmony asked.

"Don't worry, they are not marrying Salah," Omar said. "They are looking over No-Tel Motel—has cable and other excellent facilities."

"What are those flares—are they oil refineries?" she asked. There had been oil refineries around Tulsa, in her youth.

"Refineries of oil, yes," Omar said. "That is why No-Tel Motel is economical facility. If refineries blow up, very big boom. Then there will be no business at Newark Airport."

One of the black girls in the very short skirts wandered over and peeked into the taxi—she looked very young and had legs like toothpicks. When she saw Eddie and Iggy she gave a big, lipsticky smile.

"I was just lookin' to see if there was any guys in this cab," the girl said.

"No, but did you see my sisters?" Harmony asked. "I was asleep and they disappeared."

"They're inside, fighting off the pimps," the girl said. "They didn't look like they live anywhere around here."

"Nope, Oklahoma," Harmony said. "Would you hold my little boy for a second, miss?"

When the girl picked him up Eddie came wide awake.

"Hello, my name is Eddie," he said. "Are you going to the Statue of Liberty with us?"

"Wouldn't mind a little trip to the Statue of Liberty with you, blue eyes," the girl said.

"What's your name?" Eddie asked.

"Oh, well, I got about thirty or forty names," the girl replied. "Some days I use one, some days I use another."

"What if you have so many names people forget who you really are?" Eddie asked, smiling angelically.

"Good question, blue eyes," the girl said. "But maybe it's good to have people forget who you really are."

"No!" Eddie said. "It's *not* good. I don't want people to forget who I really am. I want them to remember that I'm Eddie every minute of their lives."

"Ma'am, you got a live one here," the girl said, when Harmony finally managed to drag Eddie's box of stuffed animals out of the back of the cab.

"Just tell me your *best* name," Eddie said, looking at the girl.

"Sheba," the girl said. "That's my best name. But, like I say, I got a few others."

"Are those girls your sisters?" Eddie asked, looking at the other women lined up by the curb.

"Yeah, baby, my sisters," Sheba said.

"I wish I had as many sisters as you do," Eddie said. "I only had one sister and she died."

"Honey, we mustn't bother Sheba with our problems," Harmony said. Iggy had somehow entangled himself in his leash and was squirming around in her arms, yipping.

"It's okay, let him be friendly," Sheba told her. "We don't get live ones like him over here in Jersey City every day."

"I would like to meet some of your sisters—I don't know anyone in New York except you," Eddie said.

"Baby, you still don't know anyone in New York, because this ain't New York, this is New Jersey."

They were standing under a streetlight; Harmony could see that Sheba was young, eighteen maybe, or less. She was about the age Pepper had been when Pepper left for New York. Harmony felt a sadness, that the girl would have to be hooking, so young. It was not a question of blame; she was a woman herself, and knew that it was a world in which women had to get a living as best they could. Still, it saddened her that this nice, friendly girl had to offer herself to men who drove up in cars. At the curbside, not half a block away, several of the women she had called her sisters were negotiating with men who had just driven up in cars.

184

"Where do you live?" Eddie asked. "I'd like to come to your home. Is it too far for Iggy to walk?

"Iggy's my dog," he added.

"Honey, it ain't that it's too far for Iggy to walk," Sheba said. "It's just that it ain't anywhere. I one of those girls who just live where I am."

"But this is a parking lot," Eddie pointed out. "People don't live in parking lots. Cars live in parking lots."

"He's always been this way," Harmony said. She knew that Sheba meant she was homeless. Eddie figured it out almost at the same moment.

"Mom, she's homeless," he said, putting two and two together in ways that no one expected him to. "I want her to stay with us and I want it because I like her."

"Honey, Sheba might not want to stay with us," Harmony said —but it seemed that when she said it a light went out in Sheba's eyes.

"Nice try, Bright," Sheba said to Eddie. "I'm calling you Bright because of those eyes. Your Momma don't want no trash like me staying with a cutie like you."

"Sheba, I didn't mean it that way," Harmony said. "You can stay with us as long as you want to."

Nothing troubled her as much as taking away hope from people who didn't have much to spare. She had no reason in the world to let a young black hooker from Jersey City stay with her and her son—but her son wanted it, and so did the girl named Sheba.

"Can she stay with us, Mom? She doesn't have a place," Eddie said.

"Sure, honey," Harmony said, remembering some of her own hard times in Las Vegas, in the year after she tried and failed again with Ross. She was in her forties by then; she couldn't get a job in any show, and even the junkets didn't want her as a hostess. There had been a month or two when she was only one step short of having to hook herself, or else sleep in the bus station. Fortunately Gary and Jessie and Myrtle had all been true friends. They had all let Harmony stay in their places, when she was at a low ebb; then, finally, she got a job in the recycling plant.

She knew quite well, though, that she could have been standing where Sheba stood, only at a later age, when it would have been a big adjustment to have to stand at a curb all made up and hope some guy with a hard-on would like her looks well enough to give her a little money for a minute or two of sex.

Looking past Sheba, Harmony could see where the minutes of sex were taking place for Sheba and her sisters: in the parking lot of a big, all-night grocery store across the street. When one of the girls would get in a car, the driver would just do a quick U-turn and whirl into the parking lot and park over by a bank of pay phones, where the lot wasn't too brightly lit.

Harmony looked at Sheba and saw something in the girl's eyes that reminded her of Pepper; of times when Pepper had been acting as if she expected something good to happen when really she wasn't expecting anything good to happen, or anything at all to happen, for that matter. It was the look of a little girl trying to be brave; Harmony couldn't bear it.

"I mean it, honey," she said to Sheba. "You come in with me and Eddie. We'll all get a room and stay together tonight."

"Thanks, Mom, I like Sheba," Eddie said. "She's my first friend in the New York area."

The light came back into Sheba's eyes as quickly as it had gone. Eddie held up Iggy for her inspection.

"Okay, Bright, now let's have a look at this Iggy person," she said.

"I'm glad you think he's a person," Eddie said. "My aunts just think he's a dog."

Eddie and Iggy and Sheba started walking toward the office of the motel, chatting happily.

Watching them, Harmony felt too shaken to take a step. Eddie and Sheba were young; but she herself had become old. Even if she wasn't particularly old if you just counted by years, the fact was years were no way to count. Happenings were the way to count, the big happening that separated her from youth or even middle age was the death of her daughter, Pepper. That death made her realize that life, once you got around to producing children, was no longer about being pretty or having boyfriends or making money—it was about protecting the children; getting them raised to the point where they could try life as adults. It didn't have to be just the children that had come out of your body, either. It could be anyone young who needed something you had to give.

186

Some grown men were children; some grown women, too. Harmony knew that she had spent a good part of her life taking care of just such men. But now that she felt old she didn't think she wanted to spend much more of her energy protecting men who had had a good chance to grow up, but had blown it. If she never had another boyfriend—something she had been worrying about, on the plane—it might be a little dull in some areas, like sexual areas, but it wouldn't be the end of the world.

What *would* be the end of the world would be to let some little girl like Sheba get in the car with a bad man who would make a U-turn across the street and kill her right there in front of the pay phones, where pimps and crack dealers were making their calls.

With that thought in mind, she started into the No-Tel Motel. Just as the three of them were approaching the office, Neddie came out, followed by Omar and Abdul. Then Pat came out, followed by Salah. They all looked a little startled to see Eddie holding Sheba's hand while Sheba led Iggy on his leash.

"Hi, this is Sheba, does our room have a king-size?" Harmony asked. "Sheba is Eddie's first New York friend and she's spending the night with us."

Omar and Abdul took this in stride, but Salah looked horrified.

"But, is unclean woman!" he protested.

"Mind your own business, raghead," Sheba said. "I'm as clean as you."

If either Neddie or Pat was surprised to see Eddie walk up with a young black whore they hid it well.

"Hi, Sheba, he makes friends real quick, don't he?" Pat said.

"Bright, he's the quickest," Sheba said.

"I hope you've been watching the Discovery Channel for most of your life, otherwise it's hard to hold a conversation with him," Neddie said.

"Where'd you get all these ragheads, honey?" Sheba asked Eddie.

"They came at the airport," Eddie said. "Would you like me to introduce you?"

Sheba giggled appealingly, like a little girl.

"You don't need to be bothering, I know them pretty good myself," she said. "Omar, he's tricky."

187

"This is a funny motel, they rent them rooms by the hour," Neddie said. "We took twenty-four hours, I hope that's enough."

"That's plenty, I think we should just go to bed," Harmony said.

"Good idea, I will be security man," Omar, Abdul, and Salah said, in a breath.

"What is this, the Muslim Tabernacle Choir?" Pat said. "None of us are marrying any of you so why don't you just shove off?"

"Very important to have security man at the No-Tel Motel," Salah said. "Otherwise everything vanish, never see again."

"Many bad people, thugs and lawyers come here," Omar said. "Should be called Take Your Chances Motel."

"Listen, they don't need no raghead security men, they under my protection tonight," Sheba said. "Why don't you ragheads go wash your turbans?"

Eddie thought Sheba's remark was hilarious. He laughed so hard that Iggy began to yip and jump around. Iggy had taken a dislike to Salah; he snarled every time Salah came near him.

"My Mom is really sleepy, she's sort of wobbling," Eddie said, when he got through laughing at Sheba's wit.

He was right. Harmony suddenly felt so sleepy she couldn't think, talk, or even listen. It was as if her eyelids were shades that someone very strong was trying to lower. She knew she was in a strange place and that it behooved her to be especially watchful of Eddie, but Sheba was still holding Eddie's hand. He seemed okay.

"This is her key, honey," Pat said, handing a room key to Sheba. "I don't know if the bed is king-sized, though."

"I don't care about king-sized, I'm just looking for *inside*," Sheba said. "Come on, Bright."

The room didn't have a king-size, but it had two doubles, a fact Harmony didn't discover until she woke up, several hours later, to go to the bathroom. Eddie, Iggy, and Sheba were on the other bed. Sheba had taken the trouble to put Eddie's pajamas on, but had fallen asleep before she got around to turning the TV off—a Bob Newhart rerun was on, casting a blue glow into the dark room. Harmony watched it a minute, and went back to sleep.

14.

Harmony had never liked waking up to no sun. In Las Vegas it was almost never a problem; once in a while there would be clouds, but the clouds over Nevada were usually moving along, toward somewhere else; they seldom obstructed the sunlight for a whole day.

When she got up to go to the bathroom for a second time and peeked out to see what a day might look like in New Jersey, what she saw was so horrible that for a moment or two she had a lot of trouble locating her optimism. Even in the worst of times she had usually been able to wake up with the feeling that it might turn out to be a good day. Looking out the window and seeing lots of sunshine definitely helped. She liked to see the sun shining on houses across the street, on little kids riding their bikes, on the men washing down the driveways of filling stations—there would be little rainbows in the spray made by their hoses. A little sunlight sort of jump-started the day—if she happened to be headachy, or hung over, or not getting along too well with her boyfriend of the moment, at least there would be the sunlight and the bright sky.

New Jersey in the morning was a shock. Not only was there no sunlight, there wasn't really even any sky. Where the sky usually was, there was only a kind of gray murk, with, here and there, a ring of brightness from the oil flares over the refineries.

Her window happened to look out at the parking lot of the all-night grocery store across the street. A skinny black teenager was lining up the grocery carts that had been left in the parking lot the night before. He was an expert at his job, too. He had about seventy-five carts shoved together and was weaving them across the parking lot in a kind of conga line. A boom box on top of the carts provided the music. Other than that, the only activity in the parking lot was the bank of pay phones, every one of which was in use, most of them by skinny young black men not much older than the boy pushing the grocery carts.

When she came out of the bathroom Eddie was sitting up, holding Iggy. He had the remote in his hand and was working his way through many cable channels. Sheba was curled up in a ball, sound asleep.

"Mom, she wears a wig," Eddie informed her.

He was right about the wig. Sheba was thin—too thin, Harmony thought—a very skinny black girl with her hair cut very short. It wasn't cut just any old way, though—it was cut nicely. When Harmony bent to get a closer look Eddie shooed her away, even frowning a little. He was determined that Sheba get her sleep out.

Somewhere in her purse Harmony had Laurie's number. The piece of paper the number was on was a little crumpled, but Harmony smoothed it out and put it right on her bedside table, near the phone. She would have no trouble reading the number when she finally felt the moment was right to give Laurie a call and let her know that they were in New Jersey.

But the moment didn't come immediately. The number stayed right by the phone, visible and accessible, but Harmony didn't call it. Now and again she looked at it, thinking it might be a good idea to memorize it, in case the little piece of paper got lost; but she didn't memorize it. She just left it there, by her phone.

In the course of switching channels with the remote, Eddie came upon a veterinary show. It seemed to be a twenty-four-hour cable channel devoted entirely to veterinary concerns. At the moment, a young vet was explaining what to do if your dog didn't want to put all four of its paws on the ground at the same time.

190

The vet was explaining that this behavior didn't necessarily mean the dog had a broken leg. There were various other occurrences that might cause a dog to walk on only three legs from time to time—sprains and stickers and bites of various kinds.

Eddie, a dog owner, was fascinated.

"Mom, this is important," he said, crawling over into her bed. "It could help us know what to do for Iggy if he got sick. It's a good thing we didn't have Iggy when we lived in Las Vegas."

"Why?" Harmony asked.

"Because we didn't have this channel in Las Vegas," Eddie said. "I thought they had all the channels in the whole world, but they didn't. New York has a lot more channels."

"Eddie, would you do me a big favor?" Harmony asked.

Eddie wrinkled his nose. He liked having his mother ask him favors.

"How big?" he asked.

"Big, big," Harmony said.

"Just big big?" Eddie said. "That's not very big."

"What would be very big?" Harmony asked.

"Fourteen bigs—that's as high as I can count," Eddie said.

"Oh, Eddie, you can count higher than fourteen, you just don't like to," Harmony said.

"No, because I get dizzy in my brain if I count higher than fourteen," Eddie informed her.

"Anyway, it's a big favor," Harmony said. "I want you to dial a phone number for me and say hello if someone answers."

"That's not even big big," Eddie said. "Show me the number."

When Harmony showed Eddie the number he immediately dialed it, but since he hadn't dialed 9 first, he only got the hotel operator.

"Can I help you?" the operator asked.

"You can help my Mom," Eddie said, handing the phone to his mother.

Harmony apologized to the operator, who sounded weary and told her how to dial New York.

"If you want to send your little boy down to the office I'll give him a doughnut," the operator offered. "He sounds like a cute little thing."

Eddie reached for the phone. "Is it a glazed doughnut or chocolate?" Eddie asked. Just hearing him ask brought back a little of Harmony's optimism.

"Well, we got glazed and we got chocolate and we got some with goo in the middle," the operator said. "We have a variety to choose from."

"The problem is I would like to bring Iggy but he isn't awake," Eddie said. "Could you save me one glazed?"

"Is Iggy your little brother?" the operator inquired.

"No, he's my dog, he was on the Hopi reservation being an orphan and I found him," Eddie said. He went on to tell the operator a number of things about Iggy, so many that by the time he hung up Harmony had forgotten her original plan, which was to have Eddie call Laurie.

"That was a nice conversation but you didn't do me the big favor yet," Harmony said. "I still need for you to dial the number and say hello."

"Sorry," Eddie said. Harmony gave him the sequence and he immediately dialed the number.

Before he could ask for instructions, Laurie answered the phone.

"Hello?" she said.

"Hello, who am I speaking to, please?" Eddie asked.

"Hi, Eddie, you're speaking to Laurie," Laurie said. "What a pleasant surprise. I know it's got to be you because I spoke to you a few times when your Mom called your sister."

"I don't remember but it's me all right," Eddie said. "Iggy's still asleep and so is Sheba."

"Iggy and Sheba—could they be parrots?" Laurie asked. "I remember you and your Mom had a parrot once."

"We did, but he pooped too much and we gave him to the zoo," Eddie said. "Iggy's a dog and Sheba's a person like me and my Mom, only she's black."

Laurie laughed. Harmony had her ear close to the phone—she heard the laugh. Laurie had a low voice and a pleasant laugh.

"This is the nicest thing that's happened to me in a week," Laurie said. "To tell the truth I'd been hoping you'd call someday, Eddie. I've been wanting to talk to somebody in your sister's family."

"Were you my sister's friend?" Eddie asked.

There was a silence, and then a kind of gulp from Laurie. She was trying to control herself.

"Yes, I was, Eddie," she said. "I was her friend."

"What is your name?" he asked.

"Laurie," Laurie said.

"Would you like to be my friend?" Eddie asked. "I only have Sheba for a friend here and she's asleep. Last night everyone was tired and three men with turbans brought us to the motel."

"Is it a nice motel?" Laurie inquired.

"Well, there's supposed to be doughnuts in the office but I haven't been there yet," Eddie said.

"The cable has a lot of channels," he added. "There's a vet who tells you what to do if your dog only wants to walk on three legs."

"I love that channel," Laurie said. "Only I think they could use a nicer vet. The one they're using now is a little stiff."

"Would you like to speak to my Mom?" Eddie asked.

"Eddie, I'd *really* like to speak to your Mom," Laurie said.

"After you speak to her would you like to go to the Statue of Liberty with us?" Eddie asked. "We're going today. Sheba's going too."

"You are the nicest boy," Laurie said. "I think I better speak to your mother before I decide but if it's all right with her I would like to go to the Statue of Liberty with you."

"Okay, here's my Mom," Eddie said.

Harmony felt a little shaky, taking the phone. She liked listening to Eddie talk to Laurie—actually she liked listening to Eddie talk to anybody. Eddie had even had interesting conversations with Jimmy Bangor, something Harmony had never really managed, herself.

Having to talk to Laurie herself was different. Harmony wanted to, but she wasn't sure her voice would work correctly. After all, Laurie was with Pepper when she died. It might become such a sad conversation that her voice would stop working or something.

"Hi," she said—though it was only one syllable, her voice quavered.

"I know how you feel," Laurie said. "I'm glad you're here. Where are you?"

"I think it's in New Jersey," Harmony said. "It's called the No-Tel Motel."

"The No-Tel Motel?" Laurie said. "Are you sure that's safe?"

"I'm not sure of anything," Harmony said. "Can we meet you? That's why we came."

"I need to meet you so badly. . . . I guess I was afraid you wouldn't want to," Laurie said. Then she did the little gulping sound again.

"Honey, why?" Harmony said. "Why would you be afraid?"

"Because I'm gay," Laurie said. "I was afraid you might think I had something to do with Pepper getting AIDS."

"Laurie, I know you loved her—my best friend is gay," Harmony said. She remembered Gary, running across the street and almost getting hit by the taxicab, as they were leaving Las Vegas.

"People have attitudes—I couldn't be sure," Laurie said. "Should I call you Harmony or should I call you Mom?" Laurie asked.

Harmony choked up. It had never occurred to her that anyone besides Eddie would ever call her Mom again. Even Pepper, when she was alive, had only once or twice called her Mom.

"What's Laurie saying?" Eddie asked. He hated to be left out of phone conversations, or any conversations, for that matter.

"I'll talk now, give me the phone," he said, when Harmony didn't immediately respond.

"Laurie, call me whatever feels best—I think Eddie wants to talk to you again," Harmony said. She shoved the phone at Eddie and buried her face in the pillow. Just then there was a knock at the door. Harmony ignored it. Eddie pointed at the door and Sheba, yawning, got up to answer it. When she did Neddie and Pat walked in, both in their bathrobes.

"What happened to your hair, child?" Neddie asked—without the hair and the lipstick Sheba did indeed look like a child.

"It's on the floor, over there," Eddie said, pointing at Sheba's wig.

"Eddie wanted it, so I gave it to him," Sheba said, with a sleepy grin.

"I was showing my aunt where Sheba's wig went," Eddie said, to Laurie. "I didn't mean not to talk to you."

"Relax, Eddie," Laurie said. "I don't have a job right now, so we can talk at our own pace."

194

"That's good because if you had a job you couldn't go with us to see the Statue of Liberty," Eddie said.

"Well, it's good from every point of view except the point of view of not starving to death," Laurie said.

"Oh, are you from Somalia?" Eddie asked. He had paid close and concerned attention to the famine in Somalia, a problem no one else in Las Vegas wanted to think about.

"No, I'm from California," Laurie said. "I just meant that if I don't get a new job pretty soon, I'm going to run out of money, and when I run out of money it's going to be hard to buy food."

"Well," Eddie said—it was his drawn-out, philosophical "well" —"I think you should come over here right now and we'll go to the office together and have chocolate doughnuts. They also have glazed doughnuts, the kind with goo in them."

"Sounds like a winner to me," Laurie said. "Did your mother go back to sleep?"

"She's just crying . . . it's because my sister deaded," Eddie said. "It makes her sad."

"It makes me sad too . . ." Laurie said, making the gulping sound again.

Eddie took the phone away from his ear and looked at his aunts.

"Everybody's sad today," he said. "We all need doughnuts and then we need to find the turban men and go to the Statue of Liberty *soon*."

"It's a good thing we got Bright," Sheba said, looking at Eddie and Harmony. Everybody could hear Laurie's sobbing, through the phone.

"Who were you talking to, Eddie?" Pat asked.

"Laurie," Eddie said. "She's not from Somalia but she might starve if she doesn't get a new job."

"Tell her to get her butt over here and we'll see that she don't starve," Pat said.

Eddie covered the receiver. "I won't say 'butt,'" he said. "It's where farts come from. Anyway, I already invited her and she's going to come when she stops being sad."

"Bright, do you think I could take a shower?" Sheba asked. "Would anybody mind? I ain't had a good long shower in a week."

"Honey, go take one," Harmony said, rousing herself briefly.

"If this room is like our room you'll have to dry off on the washrag," Neddie said. "They ain't lavish with towels up here in New Jersey."

"Wait!" Eddie commanded, as Sheba was drifting off toward the bathroom. "What is your doughnut preference?"

"Glazed, see if you can snatch about three," Sheba said.

Eddie picked up the phone and spoke to Laurie. "You should come very quickly, so we can go get the doughnuts," he said.

"I would come immediately if I knew where to come," Laurie said.

Pat managed to find the address on a piece of stationery in a drawer. She took the phone and read the address to Laurie.

"Wow," Laurie said. "You really are in Jersey City. I'm having a hard time imagining how that could have happened."

"Honey, it will be crystal-clear once you meet the family," Pat said. "Not a single one of us has ever done anything right."

Eddie looked shocked, to hear his aunt make such a remark.

"Well, my Mom did something right, she had *me!*" he pointed out.

Both Pat and Laurie laughed.

"You got me there, cutie," Pat said.

15.

When Sheba emerged from her long shower she looked even younger. She put on Harmony's bathrobe and went with Eddie to the office to get doughnuts.

"How old do you think that child really is?" Neddie asked.

Harmony was thinking about the men in cars and the sex that happened across the street, in the parking lot in front of the pay phones. It seemed hard to believe that the girl walking down the hall with her five-year-old son had been getting in cars with those men for who knew how long.

"Was she doing what I think she was doing, when we drove up?" Pat asked.

"Pat, she's homeless," Harmony said. She knew it wasn't exactly an answer to the question.

"If kids that age are whoring, then New Jersey's even raunchier than Oklahoma," Neddie said.

"Laurie will be here soon," Harmony said. "I just want her to get here."

"I bet Eddie's breaking some ice down in the office," Pat said. "That kid's got panache."

"I'm getting kind of lonesome for the farm," Neddie said. "I wonder if we can meet Laurie, see the Statue of Liberty, and get headed home tonight?"

"No, we can't, I ain't even set foot on the Great White Way," Pat said. "I want to shop at Macy's too, while I'm here."

"I can only take so much city," Neddie said. "I get lonesome for the plains. You can live on the Great White Way. I'm heading home to Tulsa pretty soon. I'd rather even be in the Tulsa airport than be in a motel in New Jersey that don't even have no towels."

Just as she said it there was a knock on the door. Harmony immediately felt the shaky feeling she had felt earlier.

"Don't be nervous, I'm sure Laurie's nice," Pat said.

"Mom, we have doughnuts, and we also have a surprise," Eddie said, through the door.

Harmony opened the door and saw that the surprise was Laurie, a tall girl with short brown hair and big sad eyes.

"Laurie came and paid for the doughnuts," Eddie said.

Sheba came in with a paper plate heaped with doughnuts, but Harmony just stood and looked at Laurie, who was wearing black jeans and a black blouse.

"Hi," Laurie said. Then she and Harmony hugged.

"I can't believe you're in this motel," Laurie said. She still had her arms around Harmony, who had the wish that life could just stop right there, while she was hugging the young woman who had been her daughter's friend. But of course life couldn't stop right there, she finally had to stop hugging Laurie and step back.

"Don't ask us how we ended up in this motel," Pat said. "We just did."

Harmony noticed Sheba looking sad. Maybe she thought that because a white girl had arrived she would be thrown out or something, though no one had said a word to make her feel that way. Nonetheless, the girl's face was sad. Probably she thought that being with Eddie and his family was a brief, nice dream that was about to end.

"Eddie, could you serve the doughnuts?" Harmony asked. "Give Sheba one first—she looks real hungry."

"Ain't so much hungry as scared," Sheba said. "Otis gonna be coming around looking for me pretty soon." Then, to everyone's dismay, she began to cry. She stuck her head under the covers and cried.

198

"I wonder who this Otis is," Pat said. "Maybe we should have hired the turban man as security after all."

"I think Sheba may have low blood sugar," Eddie said. "I should have fed her a doughnut sooner."

"No, I think Sheba's just sad," Neddie said. "I wake up feeling that way half the time myself. Them moods hit me and I just feel, What's the point? Why feed the chickens? Why slop the hogs? Why take the dog to the vet? Why milk the cow? Why rake up the cowshit down in the lots? Why put gas in the pickup when there's no place I want to go? Why go to the feed store when I hate every animal on the place? Why talk to Dick when I ain't had a word to say to him in twenty years? Why talk to my kids?—they don't listen anyway. Why go to church?—the preacher's a lech. Why keep paying insurance on a house I don't want?"

She stopped and looked around. Everyone had fallen silent.

"Why even live?" she concluded.

There was a silence.

"I think Aunt Neddie's got low blood sugar too," Eddie said, handing her a doughnut. "Be careful, this one's got goo in it."

"Those doughnuts look pretty stale," Laurie said. "I think they may be yesterday's doughnuts. Why don't we all go into Manhattan and have a nice breakfast at my place?—Sheba too."

"But what about the Statue of Liberty?" Eddie asked. "The turban men are coming to take us soon."

Just then there was a knock at the door.

Sheba flung the covers back and darted into the bathroom.

Laurie opened the door and there stood Omar, Abdul, and Salah, all of them considerably cleaner than they had been the night before. Their turbans were spotless.

"Taxi and bodyguards for trip to Statue of Liberty," Omar announced.

"My God, they're back," Pat said.

"Our swains," Neddie said, dryly.

Harmony was kind of glad to see the three men. They didn't seem like such bad guys, to her. Omar had sweet breath, although he didn't have teeth.

"Talk about a melting pot, get all of us in here and we'll have one," Pat said.

"You want pot, we can find, small fee," Abdul said.

Meanwhile Laurie was whispering in Eddie's ear. Eddie looked annoyed.

"Do you have a boat?" he asked Omar. "Laurie says you have to have a boat to get to the Statue of Liberty."

"No boat immediately at hand," Omar admitted.

"You don't have a boat, so you can't take us to the Statue of Liberty," Eddie said. "Besides, you scared Sheba and now she's hiding."

At that moment, Sheba came out of hiding. She looked a little less frightened.

"Omar, you seen Otis?" she asked.

"Otis is asleep in Dumpster," Omar said.

"Yeah, he always asleep in Dumpster," Sheba said. "That's why I ain't got no roof over my head. Did he say anything?"

"His heart is broken into a thousand bits," Salah said.

"Million bits," he added, after some thought.

"Yeah, but did he *say* anything?" Sheba asked.

"You his woman, he loves you, he is very broke, please loan fifty dollars," Abdul said.

"Not till he gets out of my Dumpster," Sheba said. "I ain't sharing no Dumpster with that man till he do a lot of apologizing."

"Sheba, do you work for this Otis or what?" Harmony asked.

"Work for him—I'm *married* to him!" Sheba said. "Only he stole all my stuff and sold it and now he wants me to come back to the Dumpster and live with him."

"Otis sounds like a typical male," Pat said.

"I feel like I took the subway and got off at the Comedy Channel," Laurie said.

At the mention of the Comedy Channel Eddie brightened.

"Do you like the Kids in the Hall?" he asked.

"I like them very much and besides that one of them's my cousin," Laurie said. "Your sister and I were even in a skit once— we sat at a table and smoked. I happened to be visiting my cousin and they put us in."

"If I'd known my sister was in it I would have watched harder," Eddie said, at which point Laurie's face fell and she looked very sad.

"You mean Pepper was on TV?" Harmony asked.

"We were just extras," Laurie said. "Just in one scene. We vis-

200

ited the set, and we were dressed sort of funky and the director just decided to stick us in. I have a tape of the skit. I could give it to you."

"I'd like to watch it, I think," Neddie said.

"Want to go to Laurie's and watch it, Mom?" Eddie asked.

Harmony didn't answer, for a bit.

"Eddie, I think we better just go to the Statue of Liberty," Harmony said.

16.

"Is this Otis a big bruiser?" Neddie asked Sheba, a little apprehensively. They had decided to go as a group and confront Otis, in the Dumpster behind the Shop and Sack, where he was staying. For Pat, Neddie, and Harmony, it was their first walk on the streets of New Jersey. Eddie walked between Laurie and Sheba, holding hands with each of them.

"No, he ain't big, he just has fits," Sheba said. "If he can find some glue to sniff he's apt to have a fit anytime. People need to stop throwing away glue. It gets in Dumpsters and Otis finds it and pretty soon he's having a fit. I get scared he'll bite me with them bat teeth of his."

"Oh," Neddie said. She and Pat were both walking carefully, cheerfully, taking tiny, cautious steps. Both of them seemed to feel that the streets of New Jersey might swallow them up, if they didn't exercise caution. Eddie kept looking back at his aunts, puzzled by their inhibited way of walking.

"Maybe they think this is an Indiana Jones movie," he suggested. "Maybe they think a trapdoor is going to open and let them fall into a pit of boiling oil."

202

"It could happen, Eddie," Pat said. "Trapdoors can be any-where."

"If the streets of Las Vegas were this dirty no one would ever come there and the casinos would all close," Harmony said. She was rather enjoying the walk—she liked seeing her little boy walk along with Laurie and Sheba; she liked it that Eddie was so wel-coming—it was a good trait for a little boy to have, Harmony thought.

It had to be admitted, though, that the streets of New Jersey were filthy streets, at least in the part of town where the No-Tel Motel was. Most of the garbage cans had been knocked over and their contents raked onto the sidewalks or into the streets. A small gray Yugo with its doors open and its windshields smashed out, its hood up, and three of its four tires missing, was parked right on the sidewalk. The fourth tire was flat. Around it on the sidewalk were empty wine bottles, empty whiskey bottles, syringes, cotton swabs, condoms, pools of vomit, and several squashed tomatoes. The sky was the same color as the Yugo, gray. It was the opposite of all Harmony had been used to; in Las Vegas they made a point of keeping the streets real clean—they didn't want some tourist or junketeer to step out of the casino and be revolted by condoms or squashed tomatoes or little torn-up cars.

Still, Harmony didn't feel too bad. Having Laurie and Sheba and Omar and Abdul and Salah sort of made things less lonely.

"Yuk, you can get AIDS just from walking down this sidewalk," Pat said.

"You cannot, it's just a few syringes, just watch where you step," Harmony said.

"Otis ain't been himself lately—he might have another woman," Sheba said. "It wouldn't surprise me."

"What does it mean that he has bat teeth?" Eddie asked. "Does he suck people's blood like a vampire?"

"You'll see when you see him, Bright," Sheba said. "I'm glad there's a bunch of us coming. I ain't up to having Otis throw no fits this morning."

"Mom, we have to remember to recycle glue," Eddie said. "It will help Sheba if we do."

"Help Otis too," Sheba said. "He's the one sniffing up his brain. Otis got a good brain when it ain't filled up with them glue fumes."

"Would be more pleasant to be going to Statue of Liberty," Omar reminded them. "Is not pleasant to see brokenhearted man."

"Too much weeping," Abdul said.

"I am homesick, I don't like New Jersey," Salah said.

"What about us?" Pat said. "You think we don't miss Oklahoma?"

"There's my Dumpster," Sheba said. "That's Otis's motor scooter. I guess the man at home."

A small yellow motor scooter was chained by the Dumpster. The Dumpster itself was green.

"He might have his new woman in there, if he's got one," Sheba said.

"What kind of woman would want to live in a Dumpster?" Pat asked without thinking.

"The kind that ain't got nowhere else to live, like me," Sheba said.

Sheba stopped, suddenly. They were in the parking lot of the Shop and Sack, only about twenty yards from the Dumpster Sheba claimed as her own.

"He's doin' it!" Sheba said. "I can tell."

"Doing what?" Neddie asked.

"Doin' *it!*" Sheba said.

"I think she means making love," Eddie said, in his clear, cheerful voice.

"Oh, Eddie, you're just five, you don't know what making love means," Harmony said, hoping she was right. She was embarrassed by the turn the conversation had taken.

"Isn't it when the daddy puts his penis in the momma's vagina?" Eddie asked.

"Well, that's close," Pat said.

"At Eli's house they call it sexual intercourse but at Maggie's house they just call it 'it,' " Eddie said.

"He's a bright little boy, active soon," Omar said.

"Don't rush him," Laurie said.

"Yeah, who asked you?" Neddie asked.

204

"Omar only talks about sex—he is too old to perform," Salah volunteered.

"Can we go to the Statue of Liberty now?" Harmony asked. "Sheba can visit Otis when we get back."

"No, I ain't going till I see my man," Sheba said.

"Then go see him," Laurie said. "The Dumpster's right there."

"I see the Dumpster, it's what's going on in the Dumpster that's got me worried," Sheba said.

"Maybe he's just taking a nap," Laurie said. "I have a friend who naps in Dumpsters. It's not that unusual."

"Go look, Harmony," Pat said. "If the man's busy we can come back some other time."

"Why me? I don't even know Otis," Harmony said.

"Yeah, but you live in Las Vegas," Pat said, as if that were reason enough as to why Harmony should be the one to find out if Sheba's husband was committing adultery in a Dumpster behind the Shop and Sack.

"Pat, I don't live anywhere," Harmony reminded her.

"That's okay, Mom, I'll go see if he's doing sexual intercourse," Eddie said. Before anyone could stop him he raced toward the Dumpster. The minute he got there he climbed up on the motor scooter in order to be able to peek in.

"Oh no," Harmony said. "Why is this happening?"

"Well, when he gets to the farm he's apt to see the bull doing it with the cow, anyway," Neddie said. "Or the boar doing it with the sow. Or the rooster doing it with the hen."

"Neddie, shut up," Harmony said.

"Yeah, we're not talking about Noah's ark here," Pat said.

"Hey, look at that," Sheba said. "Look at him climb. If they're doin' it, Bright's seeing it."

Eddie stood on tiptoe on the motor scooter and peeked into the Dumpster.

"Oh my God," Harmony said. "I just hope nobody's completely naked."

"They could cover up with sacks, if they're naked," Laurie said. "Usually there's lots of sacks in a Dumpster that size."

Eddie, unconcerned, seemed to be holding a pleasant conversation with the people in the Dumpster.

"That kid will talk to anybody," Neddie observed. "I've never seen it fail."

"No, but male organ can fail," Salah said, looking at Omar.

"Shut up about the male organ, it's all you talk about, Salah," Pat said.

After a moment more on the motor scooter, Eddie jumped down and came racing back across the parking lot. Several black men standing around the pay phones looked at him with amazement, and then amusement—a small white boy with golden curls racing across their parking lot was a sight that seemed to amuse them. There was a flash of white teeth.

"Eddie takes the world with him, doesn't he?" Laurie said. "He just sort of makes things his own."

"He's just a little boy," Harmony said. "He shouldn't have to worry about things that older people worry about." The thought of Eddie having to concern himself with the uncertainties and turmoil of the sexual life made her heart ache.

Eddie himself was untroubled by whatever he had seen. He raced up to Sheba and leapt into her arms.

"They're not doing it," he announced.

"Who *they?*" Sheba inquired.

"Rosie and Otis," Eddie said. "Rosie's just changing her clothes."

"Otis is a small," he added. "He's not very big at all, but he does have bat teeth."

"You think he's small now, wait till you see how small he is when I rip his little squirrelly head off," Sheba said.

She handed Eddie to Laurie, who gave him a kiss. Sheba started off across the parking lot. When she was nearly to the Dumpster a large black girl in a blond wig climbed out and ran off behind the Shop and Sack at the fastest clip she could manage. Sheba yelled something at her but the black girl kept running.

"I think they may have been doing it just before Eddie arrived," Pat said.

"No they *weren't doing it!*" Eddie said, with emphasis. "Rosie was just changing her clothes. Don't say stupid words to me!"

"He gets mad if people contradict him," Harmony said, to Laurie.

"I can tell he has firm opinions," Laurie said. "That's good,

206

though. People who have firm opinions don't get pushed around as much as people who don't.

"I don't have firm opinions, I'm a jellyfish," she added.

"I'm a sponge, myself," Neddie said. "Everybody I know pushes me around."

"Neddie, it's not attractive to feel sorry for yourself," Harmony told her sister. "It makes people feel guilty."

"People *are* guilty, Harmony," Neddie said. "Looks like you'd have figured that out by this point in life."

"If people aren't guilty, who is?" Pat asked.

"Mom, I don't want Sheba to tear Otis's head off," Eddie said. "She shouldn't tear his head off just because he has bat teeth. He could go to the dentist and get his bat teeth fixed."

"I think there were other problems, Eddie," Harmony said.

Just as Sheba reached the Dumpster Otis started to crawl out. When he saw how close Sheba was he decided he had no chance for a getaway and dropped back into the Dumpster, out of sight.

"It's true he's not very big," Harmony said. "I hope she doesn't hurt him."

"Why are you always on the man's side?" Neddie asked. "He was doing it in a Dumpster with a fat girl in a blond wig—why wouldn't she rip his head off?"

"You are wrong!" Eddie said, indignantly. "You are saying stupid words! I don't want to hear those words! Otis is nice."

"The war of the sexes," Laurie said, smiling. "I guess it starts at birth."

"Otis is my new friend," Eddie said. "I now have Laurie and Sheba and Otis, and Rosie and Omar and Salah and Abdul. That's almost as many friends as I had in Las Vegas. Now I won't be lonely."

Everyone was silenced by this passionate outburst, except Sheba, who was screaming into the Dumpster. When she got through screaming she went to the back of the Dumpster and managed to push the heavy lid closed. It closed with a loud clang. Several of the black men at the pay phones jumped when the lid clanged.

"It's a good thing Otis didn't have his head sticking over the edge when that lid dropped," Pat said. "Sheba wouldn't have had to rip it off. She could have Dumpstered it off."

"Why doesn't anybody like Otis?" Eddie asked. "You haven't even met him. It's prejudiced to not like people you don't even know."

"Well, he's certainly got a point there," Laurie said.

"It's pretty suspicious that Rosie got in the Dumpster to change clothes," Pat remarked.

"She's homeless," Eddie said. "She could have changed clothes in our hotel room, but she didn't know us then. There's nothing wrong with changing clothes in a Dumpster if you're homeless."

"Well, he's made another point," Laurie said. "Maybe we better go over and help mediate this quarrel."

"I'm old enough to know better than to stick my hand in a dogfight," Neddie said.

"They're not fighting now anyway," Pat said. "Sheba just locked him in a Dumpster."

Sheba then took a sizable padlock out of her purse and padlocked the Dumpster.

"Why did she do that?" Eddie asked. "Now Otis can't get out. I asked him to go see the Statue of Liberty with us. I don't want to go without him—it might make him sad."

"That's a nice thought, Eddie," Harmony said.

"I always have nice thoughts," Eddie said. "The only times I don't is when Eli steals my lunch."

"It's going to be a pretty crowded cab ride, over to the ferry," Laurie said.

"No cab, we talked to cousin who owns school bus," Omar said. "He can take us all, very modest fee."

"I better go talk to Sheba," Eddie said. "She'll listen to me. I have to explain to her that she has to let Otis out so he can go to the Statue of Liberty with us."

"I would say you're just the man for the job, Eddie," Laurie said.

Harmony saw that Laurie was sad—it showed in her eyes. She had a big mouth and a nice smile but above the smile were two sad brown eyes.

Eddie ran across the parking lot again, traveling at his usual fleet pace.

"I never met anyone quite like Eddie," Laurie said. "What did you do before you had him?"

"I can't remember very well," Harmony said. "It seems like I've always had Eddie."

"You're not supposed to give kids too much responsibility too young," Neddie said. "It messes them up."

"Yeah, they might not get to enjoy their childhood to the full," Pat said.

"They don't think I'm a good mother," Harmony explained. "They think I give Eddie too much responsibility."

"I don't think it's a question of *giving* Eddie responsibility," Laurie said. "He just seems to take it and run with it. Not many kids that age would realize that it hurts people to be left out."

She said it with a sad note in her voice. Harmony could imagine that being gay might have caused Laurie to be left out, particularly if she had discovered that she was gay in high school, when almost any behavior that was a little unusual could cause a person to be left out.

"Eddie's like the man of the house, and he's only five," Pat said. "Somehow that don't seem right."

"Pat, it *isn't* right—why do you have to pick on me in front of Laurie?" Harmony said. "If I could find some grown man to be head of our house don't you think I'd let him? I just don't happen to have a boyfriend right now. That's the only reason it seems like Eddie's the head of the house. But there isn't a house, and there wouldn't be anything to put in it if there was one."

"All her stuff fell into a canyon and we left it," Neddie explained.

"It fell into the Canyon de Chelly," Harmony said. "That's in Arizona."

"I know, I've been there," Laurie said. "My uncle's a park ranger. He worked there for a while."

Down by the Dumpster Eddie could be seen remonstrating with Sheba. Once in a while Eddie put his ear to the Dumpster, indicating that Otis was being allowed to participate in the conversation too—at least with Eddie.

Then Sheba unlocked the padlock and attempted to raise the lid of the Dumpster; she had been strong enough to push it over from the rear, but she wasn't strong enough to raise it. Several times she gave it a push and it went up a little way, before clanging back down.

"Hope Otis don't stick his head up," Laurie said. "He'd be Dumpstered for sure."

There was no sign of Otis, however.

"I think we better go help now," Laurie said. "I don't know how good Eddie is at taking orders. He might try to climb in, and get Dumpstered himself."

She started across the parking lot, slowly.

"I like her but she sure is sad," Neddie said.

"Well, she lost the same person I lost," Harmony said.

"Very beautiful girl, Abdul should marry her," Salah said. "Girl with gentle manner—make a good wife for Abdul."

"I don't want to marry—I want to go to Atlantic City, get rich," Abdul said.

"She's not interested in men, Salah," Pat pointed out.

Harmony started walking too. She didn't feel like listening to her sisters explain to Omar and Salah that Laurie was gay. Since leaving Las Vegas she had felt a growing need to stay close to everybody: to her sisters, to Eddie, to old friends and new friends. Of course, it was no longer possible to stay close in the physical sense to Gary and Jessie and Myrtle. But she could stay close to her sisters and to Eddie, and now there was also Laurie, not to mention Omar and Salah and Abdul—Sheba and maybe even Otis. The thing that was happening that might become a little bit of a problem was that she only seemed to feel like adding people; she didn't want to subtract anyone in her immediate circle, not just at that time. The reason that could be a problem was that there were only so many people who could be fitted into a taxi or a motel room. Very likely there were only so many people who could be fitted into a life, too. For most of her years in Las Vegas she had depended on only a few people, not counting other show-girls, who sort of had a tendency to come and go, particularly after the casino scene improved in Reno and Tahoe.

Now, though, she had the feeling that she didn't want to let a single person go. She wanted to keep adding, for a while. Maybe Omar's cousin with the school bus would rent it to her for a small fee, while she added people to her life. None of the people, nor all of them together, could be expected to fill the gap left by Pepper; but having a lot of them, surrounding her life with their lives, made her feel a little safer—if nothing else she could distract her-

210

self with their problems, their foibles, their little sorrows and little dramas. It was better than just thinking always of what had been lost, or of what might have been.

"Don't you think there is a limit?" she asked Laurie, when she caught up with her.

"A limit to what?" Laurie asked, turning.

"A limit to how many people I can collect so I won't be without company?" Harmony said. "We only got here last night and I already have five or six new people that I know."

Laurie stopped and looked at her.

"I guess you can collect as many as you can find," she said. "The main problem with sort of letting it grow is transportation. Maybe the guy who is supposed to bring the bus is our solution for the moment. If he actually shows up to take us to the ferry, then I guess a busload is probably your limit."

Harmony walked on and Laurie linked her arm in hers.

"Do you mind?" she asked.

"No, Laurie," Harmony said. "I don't mind."

"I guess I have the opposite way of dealing with it," Laurie said. "I've been mostly alone since Pepper died. I find even talking to people very wearying. Some friend will come by and I'll think I'm glad to see her at first and then within a few minutes I'm so tired I can hardly talk. It just wears me out to be with even my best friends now."

"Laurie, you really don't have to go to the Statue of Liberty," Harmony said. "Not if it's that bad." There was a weariness in Laurie's face that made her feel that she should make helpful suggestions, if she could.

"Oh, no, I don't mean you guys," Laurie said. "I love being with you guys. It's like the young give me energy or something. I mean, just being around Eddie for a few minutes charges me up. Sometimes I volunteer at a day care and it works the same way. When I'm with the kids I'm hardly depressed at all. Energy just sort of flows off them, or something.

"I don't know why I'm telling *you* that, though," Laurie added. "You live with Eddie."

"He's up on the motor scooter and he doesn't want to get off," Harmony said. "Sheba had to grab him. He must have really liked Otis."

Indeed, Eddie and Sheba were faced off in the parking lot, and the lid of the Dumpster was still closed. Harmony and Laurie strolled over. Eddie did not appear to be angry, but he did appear to be sad. The look he wore was the look he only got when his sensibilities had been bruised.

"Bright, don't you cry on me," Sheba said. "I didn't mean to hurt your feelings."

"But you did—you made me sad," Eddie said. "I want Otis to be my friend."

"I didn't say he can't be your friend," Sheba said, squatting down so as to bring her face closer to Eddie's. "I just said I ain't ready to let him out of the Dumpster yet."

"You called him a creep and you said he had bat teeth," Eddie said. "Those words aren't very nice. If he's my friend you shouldn't say such words about him."

Sheba looked at Harmony.

Eddie's lip trembled. His eyes had tears in them.

"What do you do with him when he gets like this?" Sheba asked.

"She's my Mom, she doesn't make me sad," Eddie said. "Only other people make me sad."

Harmony picked up her son. "Eddie, I do too make you sad, sometimes," she said. "Remember when I made you leave Las Vegas without saying goodbye to your friends?"

Eddie didn't speak; his lip still trembled and his eyes were filled with tears.

"That made you sad," Harmony said, again.

"It still makes me sad," Eddie admitted. "It made me sad because it was rude."

"He's right," Harmony said. "It *was* rude. We should have waited till morning to leave. I guess I was just too upset to wait."

"I miss Eli very much," Eddie said. "I really miss Eli."

"Aw," Laurie said.

"I miss Otis, too," Eddie said, tears on his cheeks. "I wish you'd let him out of the Dumpster now."

Sheba was so horrified by Eddie's tears that she looked as if she might cry herself.

"You got it, Bright, he's coming out," Sheba said. "Somebody want to help me get the lid up?"

"Sure, I'll help you," Laurie said.

Neddie and Pat helped too, and soon the lid was up. Eddie wiped his wet cheeks with the back of his hand and a smile immediately came back to his face.

"That's nice," he said. "I'll just dry my tears and we'll go help Otis out."

"He don't need no help," Sheba said. "He's in and out of that Dumpster all day and all night."

"But you made him a prisoner, he might be scared," Eddie said. He climbed back up on the yellow motor scooter and peered into the Dumpster.

"Hi," he said, to Otis. "Do you want to come out and meet my mother?"

A very small black man, with a soft face, hair that was combed straight up, and a wispy Fu Manchu mustache, peeked cautiously over the edge of the Dumpster.

"Hi, white folks," he said.

17.

"Ain't you gonna say hi to *me?*" Sheba asked immediately. "I'm here, but I ain't white folks."

"No, because you call me too many names," Otis said. "I ain't as bad as you say I am."

"You worse," Sheba said.

But she walked over to the Dumpster and helped her husband out.

"Baby, I didn't mean to make you so mad," Otis said, looking at Sheba anxiously. His front teeth *were* rather pointed. Harmony decided it was probably that his family couldn't afford an orthodontist.

"I always making her mad," he said to the group, with a little smile. "Don't know how it happens."

"It happens because you don't never think of nobody but yourself, you little jerk," Sheba said.

"Jerk isn't a very nice word to call Otis," Eddie said. "I want everybody to say nice words, just for one day."

"That's a good idea, Ed," Otis said. "Sheba always be saying these ugly things to me. It kinda gets me down, you know."

She turned her back and walked off, into the center of the

214

parking lot. The boy whose job it was to gather up the grocery carts was just coming through the lot with an even longer conga line of carts. He was pushing hard, and the carts were undulating like a long shiny snake. On impulse, as the carts were passing, Sheba jumped on top of them.

The boy pushing the carts was not pleased.

"Get off, girl," he said. "You making me wobble."

The parking lot was slanted slightly. When Sheba jumped on the carts, the whole long line of grocery carts began to veer downhill, toward an exit onto a busy street.

"Uh-oh, Sheba's gone wild again, she's headed right for the exit," Otis said.

He began to race across the parking lot, angling so he would be able to intersect the line of carts before they shot into the street. Just then the line of carts broke in two. The boy pushing the carts was left with about twenty, and Sheba sailed along on the rest. She managed to get to her feet, and did a little dance as she sped past the pay phones. The pimps at the bank of phones looked around in amazement.

"She's like Lillian Gish on the ice floe," Laurie said.

Then she started running herself, to help Otis. The two of them fell in beside the carts and began to slow them down. They turned them just enough to make them miss the exit to the street, and coasted them to a halt behind the Dumpster.

"That's fun," Eddie said. "I wish Sheba had taken me with her."

"Yeah, and if she had, and if those carts had gone into the street, you'd have been squashed like a bug," Pat said.

"No, I would not have been squashed like a bug," Eddie said. "I would have been squashed like a boy."

Sheba and Otis were holding hands, by the Dumpster. Laurie came walking back. One of the pimps by the pay phones whistled at her, but she ignored him.

Harmony thought Laurie looked lonely—a nice tall girl, but sad.

"Harmony, we can't be adopting everybody," Neddie said, as if reading Harmony's thoughts.

"Think what Mom would say if we brought this whole gang home," Pat said. "It'd almost be worth doing, just to hear her."

Just then a grimy white school bus came veering into the parking lot, honking loudly.

"Good, here is G.," Omar said. "Now plenty of room for everybody. We can go to Statue of Liberty boat."

"That's a good-looking bus driver," Pat said, when the man, who had a handsome black beard, parked his bus and stepped out. "What did you say his name is?"

"His name is G.," Omar said. "He is Sikh man from Delhi."

"Uh-oh, just my luck," Pat said. "What's he sick with?"

"No sick, Sikh!" Omar said. "He is my cousin."

"He could be your cousin and still be sick," Pat said.

G. got back in the bus and began to honk. He was listening to a Walkman.

"G. is listening to Pink Floyd," Abdul said. "He is always listening to Pink Floyd."

"It's weird that his name is G.," Pat said. "Is it G-e-e- or what?"

"No, is spelled G.," Omar said.

When G. got back on the school bus he closed the doors behind him. Omar, Salah, and Abdul began to bang on the doors but G. sat behind the wheel listening to Pink Floyd. He paid no attention.

"I don't want to get on his bus anyway, till I find out what he's sick with," Pat said.

"I think Omar just meant he's a Sikh—it's a sect," Laurie said. "He's a Sikh like you're a Baptist—if you're a Baptist."

Eddie was walking around in circles, holding a new red dog leash Laurie had bought him at the Shop and Sack. Iggy had chewed the old leash in two. Eddie sometimes walked around in circles when he was in a happy mood.

Harmony was glad her son was in a happy mood. She herself was beginning to feel a sinking of spirits. For a few minutes she had enjoyed having so many people around—despite the squalor of the streets it had been kind of fun to walk around New Jersey, with her sisters and Laurie, and Sheba and the turban men. But somehow the fun had begun to have little cracks in it, little cracks through which she couldn't help seeing the real facts of her life: Pepper was dead, she and Eddie had left Las Vegas, she really didn't know where she might have to live or how she would make a living for herself and her son. Having all the people there, even Eddie, made it impossible to do what she really wanted to do, which was be alone and cry.

"Mom, don't look that way," Eddie said, noticing that his

216

mother's face had a sad look on it. "We're going to get Iggy and we're going to the Statue of Liberty *right now*."

"Okay, honey," Harmony said. Sometimes the easiest thing was just to obey Eddie, if she could. She knew it wasn't fair to make a five-year-old be the boss—but there were times when it was the best she could do.

"Hard to get to the Statue of Liberty if G. won't open the bus," Sheba said.

"Eddie can fix that," Laurie said. She picked Eddie up, took him around to the driver's side of the bus, and lifted him high, so his face would be at the level of the bus driver's. Eddie rapped politely on the window of the bus, near the driver's head. G., still listening to Pink Floyd, gave no sign of noticing.

"Wave your arms, Eddie," Laurie said. "Maybe he'll see you."

"But they're just little short arms," Eddie said. "I'm very small, really."

But he waved his arms anyway and G., the bus driver who liked Pink Floyd, suddenly noticed that a child with curly hair was waving at him.

Very methodically, G. turned off his Walkman and opened the window.

"Hi," Eddie said.

"You the spokesman, Bright," Sheba said. "Do some of your good talking."

"Hello," Eddie said, to G. "Could you open the door so we can all get in and go get my dog, Iggy, and then go straight to the Statue of Liberty?"

G. looked down at Eddie, and smiled. His teeth were very white, against his black beard.

"I am waiting for Omar," he said, in a very deep voice.

"There's Omar," Eddie said. "He's beating on your door *right now*."

G. looked, and saw the angry faces of Omar, Abdul, and Salah, all pressed against the glass of his door.

"They are looking angry, always looking angry," G. said. "I am happy man, no fuss."

"So do you know where the Statue of Liberty boat is?" Eddie asked. "We've come from Las Vegas, Nevada, and we need to go now."

G. opened the door of the bus and Omar, Abdul, and Salah all spilled in, all talking at once.

When Laurie set Eddie down he immediately began to herd everyone onto the bus.

"Come on, we need to go now, right *now!*" he said. "It's time to see the Statue of Liberty."

He grabbed Harmony's finger and began tugging her toward the steps of the bus.

"Come on, Mom, hurry," he said. "The Statue of Liberty might close, if we don't hurry."

"Eddie, it won't close," Harmony said.

I wish I could be anywhere on earth but where I am, she thought. I wish it could be another day. I wish I could be in a faraway place where I don't know anybody. I wish nobody at all was with me. I wish I could just be in bed alone, with my head under the covers.

But she wasn't in a faraway place, of course, she was just in the parking lot of a Shop and Sack in Jersey City. She wasn't alone, either. She was with a lot of people, some of them people she had just met. There was no chance at all that she was going to get to be alone.

"Come on, Mom, we need to go *now*," Eddie repeated.

Omar was still yelling at his cousin G. when Harmony allowed her son to lead her onto the bus.

18.

On the ride to the Statue of Liberty boat, Harmony sat alone. Even Eddie abandoned her.

"She's too sad about my sister," Eddie said. "Let's just let her ride in the back seat until she feels better."

He himself spent the trip happily chatting with Laurie and Sheba, and admiring Iggy's new red leash and black collar.

"Laurie bought them just for Iggy," he said.

Pat sat on the front seat and flirted, as best she could, with G. but G. kept turning around and flashing his beautiful white teeth at Neddie. It made Neddie uncomfortable and Pat mad.

"That man's mixed up, I don't care what his religion is," Pat said. "I'm the one flirting with him, not you."

"Don't blame me," Neddie said. "I'm ignoring him for dear life."

Despite little irritations, on the order of G. flirting with the wrong woman, the group was mostly a happy group. They were all so cheerful that Harmony wished her part of the bus would just drop off—just detach itself, like a railroad car that had come unhooked, and coast to a stop somewhere with her in it. She didn't have the spirit to be part of a happy group; she felt she had more in common with winos and derelicts and aging people of every sort, quite a few of whom were visible on the streets of New Jersey.

Even on the boat to the Statue of Liberty she found a place on the rail by herself, near the stern. Cold spray from the harbor hit her face and mingled with the tears she cried from time to time. Eddie, proud of Iggy and his new leash, walked all around the boat, letting all the tourists see what a nice dog he had.

None of them knew at the time that Iggy was about to become the most famous dog in America, if not the world, the only dog in history to fall from the top of the Statue of Liberty and live.

"He did not *fall*, he *jumped*," Eddie was later to insist: he insisted it, with mounting indignation, on *Larry King Live*, on the *Today* show, on *Good Morning, America*, and, finally, on Letterman, on all of which he and Iggy appeared in the space of two whirlwind days. During most of those days Harmony holed up in Laurie Chalk's bedroom on East Ninth Street, looking at pictures of Pepper in Laurie's scrapbook.

Looking through the scrapbook was actually good—it was a little cheering in some way. In many of the pictures Pepper looked happy; the pictures helped convince Harmony that Pepper had mostly had a happy, not an unhappy, life. In many of the pictures Pepper was with dancers or other show people; she was invariably the most beautiful girl in the picture, too. In most of the pictures, Pepper was smiling. She was a beautiful girl with her brights on. Harmony wished she had worked up the nerve to override Pepper's prickliness and come east and see her; she would have liked to meet some of the people in the pictures—Pepper's friends.

Meanwhile, while Harmony sipped tea and spent time with her regrets, Eddie and Iggy were on all the talk shows. They were even on the cover of *People* magazine. Laurie and Sheba, who sort of started new careers as Eddie and Iggy's business managers, were even getting calls from manufacturers who wanted to make Eddie and Iggy dolls. All this was because Iggy hated sea gulls and had tried to bite one that happened to be flapping off the topmost parapet of the Statue of Liberty. When they got off the boat Iggy had tried to run off and bite a couple of sea gulls but Eddie hung on to the new red leash and wouldn't let him. Iggy bided his time until they were on the very top of the statue, looking across New York Harbor to the great towers of Manhattan, before he went

220

after another sea gull, in this case the one that happened to be flapping off the parapet.

Eddie was looking away at that moment, at the Hudson and America beyond it, when Iggy suddenly jerked the leash out of his hand and made a leap at the gull, after which he disappeared, plummeting straight down toward what should have been his death.

"Oh no, he can't fly, Mom, he's not a bird!" Eddie said. "Will he be deaded forever when he hits?"

Nobody answered the question, because they all certainly expected Iggy to be deaded forever. It was a long drop from the top of the Statue of Liberty. The only optimist in the crowd was Eddie, and Eddie was only half convinced.

"But somebody could catch him, he's a very small dog," Eddie said, to reassure himself, as they were hurrying down. The only person who wasn't crying was G., the driver, who had only known Iggy for an hour. Everyone else was trying to think of what they might do to console Eddie, who, though he had tears on his cheeks, was still trying to think of optimistic outcomes.

"A tourist could catch him," he said, in the elevator. "A professional football player might be standing there—Iggy is shaped like a football. I'm sure a professional football player could catch Iggy if he was standing in the right spot."

It seemed a forlorn hope, to everyone else in the crowd.

"That would be a long shot, Bright," Sheba said. "It ain't even football season."

"Don't say sad words to me," Eddie said. "I don't want to hear sad words right now."

But there was not much energy in his complaint; the force of his optimism was waning.

"We bit off more than we can chew, coming up here to New York," Neddie said. "We should have gone straight to Oklahoma, where we belong."

"What do you want us to do, turn back the clock?" Pat asked. She was annoyed with Neddie anyway, because of G., who was still peering at Neddie with big soulful eyes.

Harmony was thinking that she was cursed. Probably she should never have attempted motherhood. Her son had had to wait many months to get a puppy, because of Jimmy Bangor's conservative views on the upkeep of wall-to-wall carpet, and then the little puppy Eddie finally got had to fall off the Statue of Liberty. What could be more like a curse?

Then the miracle that soon captured the hearts of America: Iggy was alive. Before they even got out of the Statue of Liberty they heard Iggy barking, just outside.

"Iggy!" Eddie said, wiggling out of Sheba's arms. "See! I told you someone could catch him."

Iggy was outside, yipping at some tourists. An old man with freckles on his bald head was attempting to feed him a cookie.

"No thank you, he's not allowed sweets," Eddie said, politely grabbing Iggy's leash. "Besides, he just fell off the Statue of Liberty and his stomach might be upset."

Iggy was a little muddy, but otherwise seemed to be entirely unharmed. He had fallen into some mud at a construction site behind the statue. Several tourists, who had seen a small dog plummeting downward, were muttering and shaking their heads.

"It's a miracle, God done it, that puppy ain't got a scratch on him," an old lady from somewhere said. "Where's the TV cameras when you need them?"

"I've heard that more than three hundred people have fallen out of airplanes and lived," the old man with the cookie said. "I guess there's no reason it couldn't happen to a pup."

"He was an orphan, I found him in Arizona," Eddie said, happily holding Iggy in his arms.

Pat burst into tears. "It's just relief," she said. "I couldn't have stood another tragedy right now."

Soon little disposable cameras began to flash their flashes. In no time more than a hundred tourists were trying to take pictures of Eddie and his dog. Eddie giggled and smiled, as he explained that for some reason Iggy had a strong dislike of sea gulls.

"He was after one when he jumped off," he said. "It's very lucky that he isn't deaded."

"Is that kid happy, or what?" Laurie said. She came close to Harmony and put her arm around her. Harmony leaned close to Laurie. She didn't want to reveal her shameful secret, which was that she had felt only a kind of distant flicker of sadness when it seemed certain that her son's puppy had been killed. The sadness had flickered, but it had only been like a quick flare of lightning

222

on the far horizon. If Iggy really had been dead, she wouldn't have known how to comfort Eddie. Sheba or Laurie or her sisters would have had to do it.

"We were very lucky, weren't we?" Laurie said. "Most of all Iggy."

Harmony didn't answer. Something in her felt stilled, so stilled that she knew she had to leave her son to the care of others, for a bit. Fortunately, others were there: Laurie and Sheba. Otis was helpful too. Soon nearly a thousand tourists had heard of the miraculous event. Otis persuaded the officials that they had a major media event on their hands: a small American dog had fallen off the Statue of Liberty and lived; besides that, the dog belonged to a cute, curly-haired five-year-old from Las Vegas.

Before they even left the Statue of Liberty the Mayor called— he had heard a news flash on the radio and wanted to meet Eddie and Iggy himself, ASAP.

"Yep, ASAP, the boss man said," Otis informed them.

"ASAP, is that a medal or a drug?" Neddie asked.

"It just means as soon as possible," Laurie said. "Everybody in New York always wants everything ASAP."

"Oh, like Pat wants sex," Neddie said. "ASAP."

"Shut up, Neddie, you don't have to kick me when I'm down," Pat said.

Harmony too was bothered that Neddie wouldn't let up about Pat's sex addiction.

"Neddie, none of us are perfect," she said.

"I know, but it's a matter of degree," Neddie said. She didn't seem inclined to yield much ground.

Harmony found herself wishing Gary had come with them. Nobody would have enjoyed Eddie's new celebrity as much as Gary. Two TV crews had already arrived, by helicopter, and were filming Eddie and Iggy—maybe Gary would get to see them on national TV.

The thing that surprised Harmony a little was how thrilled all the tourists were that Iggy had fallen off the statue and lived. Particularly the older tourists were thrilled. Some of them who had been at the top with their group, just before Iggy fell off, had been pretty apathetic. Some had even been quarrelsome; being at the top of the Statue of Liberty didn't thrill them as much as they

223

hoped it would. It wasn't that different from just being alive, or being in the marriages they were in, or whatever. They had come to the Statue of Liberty because they thought it was their duty as Americans, or their duty as tourists, or something. But they had been vaguely disappointed, and Gary would have been the perfect person to sympathize with them, because Gary was always getting his hopes up about little trips to places he hadn't been; then he would take the little trips and come back vaguely disappointed; either a boyfriend had been uncooperative or the place he had taken the little trip to hadn't been as beautiful as it looked in the travel brochures. It hadn't made life different enough, and the same seemed to apply to the tourists who trudged into the Statue of Liberty. They weren't fired up about it, as Eddie had been— and Eddie hadn't been a bit disappointed, either. He *loved* the Statue of Liberty, right up until the moment when his dog had fallen off it.

The tourists, particularly the older ones, didn't love it that much, but they did love the fact that Iggy had fallen off it and lived. Their faces were all lit up, and they were chattering with one another, excited by the fact that the little boy and his dog had not been separated by a tragic happening. Seeing Eddie and Iggy miraculously reunited didn't just make their day; it made their whole trip. Perhaps it even lifted up a whole part of their lives.

Harmony wanted to be lifted up by it too, but the lifting feeling —usually a common feeling with her—just wouldn't come.

More and more helicopters came though, bearing more and more camera crews. The pressures of celebrity proved too much for Iggy. Despite all the lights and flashing flashbulbs, Iggy went to sleep in Eddie's lap. Eddie himself was holding up fine—he seemed to be fully in command of the situation, as he usually was of most situations.

Laurie and Sheba had both become protective of Eddie—they watched the newsmen and the tourists like hawks, to see that no one got too pushy, or asked questions that were inappropriate. Otis drifted over to where Harmony stood.

"Ed got Broadway written all over him," he said. "Plus he got two tough women looking after him. Anybody try to do anything bad to Ed, Sheba rip his head off."

"I'm glad you came, Otis," Harmony said—it was all she could

224

think of to say. Otis seemed sweet, if a little frail. Harmony wondered if he had sniffed a little too much glue.

Of course the newspeople wanted to get the mom of the little boy whose dog had fallen off the Statue of Liberty into their stories, but Harmony just shook her head, she wasn't in any mood to be making comments on TV. The turban men, including G., who looked very formidable with his full black beard, stood in front of Harmony and hid her from the cameras. The turban men definitely enjoyed being on camera themselves, though. They all brought out their best smiles. One roly-poly assistant on one of the camera crews grew a little annoyed by the fact that the turban men kept popping up every time his camera swung Harmony's way.

"Come on, ragheads, move it," he said. "This isn't a story about Islamic fanaticism, it's a story about a boy and his dog."

"Boy and his dog over that way," Omar said, unimpressed. "Point camera that way if you want to show boy and his dog."

Then a giant black helicopter, bigger than all the little TV helicopters put together, came whirling across from Manhattan. The big black helicopter had CITY OF NEW YORK written on the side.

"My God," Laurie said. "I think it's Mayor Dinkins himself."

"Boss Dinkins, that's who it is," Otis said. "Sheba gonna flip out. She thinks Boss Dinkins is one cute dude."

In a moment a dapper-looking black man, surrounded by aides with walkie-talkies, stepped out of the helicopter and headed for the cluster of tourists and news crews surrounding Eddie and Iggy. Harmony knew she ought to be excited; after all, the Mayor of New York had come in a helicopter to see her son. It was undoubtedly an honor, but it still didn't produce the lifting feeling inside that would have made it possible for her to be thrilled by it, or something.

She drifted away and sat down on the steps near the Statue of Liberty. Neddie wandered over. Then Pat came; all three sisters sat on the steps, watching the sea gulls wheel and cry above the crowd of reporters and the Mayor's aides.

"I thought that stocky fellow over there in the cowboy hat was Randall Yard, but he ain't," Pat said. "He could win a Randall Yard look-alike contest any day, though."

"Why would there be a Randall Yard look-alike contest?" Neddie asked. "Randall Yard ain't famous and he ain't good-looking, either."

"That's a matter of opinion," Pat said. "He was good-looking enough to me that I broke up his marriage. I don't usually break up a marriage if the guy's ugly."

"You don't seem like yourself today, honey," Neddie said, to Harmony.

"That's an understatement," Pat said. "Harmony's sad as shit."

"Oh, I know that," Neddie said. "That's not what I meant. I'm sad most of the time, but I'm still *myself*, sad or not. Harmony just seems like she's draining away. She's not gonna have no self at all unless she can get a grip."

"I don't know how," Harmony said. "I would get a grip if I knew how."

They sat for a while, just looking across the harbor, watching the big boats cut through the water. Across the way they saw the great skyscrapers.

"What if Iggy has internal injuries?" Pat asked. "What if he just keels over, after a while?"

"You ought to be in therapy, Pat," Neddie said. "If you was a healthy woman you wouldn't have such thoughts. That little dog is fine."

Actually, Harmony had been having the same foreboding as Pat. What if, just as Iggy got to be a national hero, he fell over dead? She looked up, at the top of the statue. It was so high it made her dizzy, just to look up. Harmony tried to imagine what Iggy felt as he plummeted downward—it occurred to her that maybe he didn't feel anything, maybe he just thought it was a dream he was having. Perhaps it just felt like floating, to Iggy.

Harmony shut her eyes—a few tears squeezed out. She tried to imagine what it would be like not to have any ties, not even a tie to gravity. If she could manage to avoid gravity she would never have to hit ground anywhere, she could just float on toward the heavens.

"Harmony's having suicidal fantasies again, I can feel her having them," Neddie said.

"Neddie, I was just hoping Iggy didn't have internal injuries," Harmony said, dishonestly. She knew her fantasy of floating was mostly a fantasy of giving up.

They sat for a while; Eddie was still in the thick of the camera crews.

"Don't either of you talk to me about it, anymore," Harmony said. "You're making it like a pressure, and I don't want any more pressures, right now."

"Okay," both sisters said.

The last thing Harmony remembered about their visit to the Statue of Liberty was Laurie and Sheba coming over, herding Eddie and Iggy between them. Iggy was awake again, he was straining at his leash; Eddie wasn't taking a chance on any more accidents happening.

"Mom, I'm going to be on TV, is it okay?" Eddie asked.

"Sure, honey—go be on TV," Harmony said.

"Oh boy, is this a circus," Laurie said. "What if Sheba and I and Otis go with Eddie, to look after him? You girls look tired. Why don't we have Omar and his friends take you to my apartment. You can rest."

"We'll take care of Bright," Sheba assured her. "Rate things going right now, Bright might be a millionaire before the day is over."

"What if these turbanheads can't find your apartment?" Pat asked.

"Don't worry, I told G. where I live, and gave him the key," Laurie said. "Sikhs are pretty reliable. He'll take you there."

"Mom, are you sadded again?" Eddie asked, looking at her. "If I give you a thousand hugs, will you not be sadded?"

"Even one hug might do it," Harmony said.

Eddie gave her the hug. A man in a suit came while he was giving it.

"Hi, could you hurry it, please?" he said. "The Mayor's on a tight schedule."

"Mom, we're going to be in a big black helicopter," Eddie said. "I'll hold Iggy *very* tightly, so he won't see a sea gull and jump out."

Eddie blew her five or six kisses, for good measure; soon he was whirling high, in the black helicopter with CITY OF NEW YORK written on it. Just for a moment, as the helicopter took off, Harmony saw his tiny face in the window, and Iggy's even tinier face beside it.

As Harmony sat on the steps, watching the big helicopter whirl her son away, an elderly woman who had spilled powder on the front of her blue suit came walking up.

"That's a cute boy you got," the old lady said. "Bright too. You got a lot to be proud of, having a boy that bright. Our boy had that dyslexia but they never figured it out until he was in the service."

An old man in a suit the same color as his wife's came up beside her.

"Yes, that's the truth," he said. "Our boy never learned to read until he was nearly twenty-five years old."

The old couple walked on into the Statue of Liberty.

"Why do people tell me things like that?" Harmony asked. "Even at the recycling plant they told me things like that. They even tell me about their sex lives. Why would I want to know about their sex lives?"

"You ought to listen, you might learn something," Pat said. "It's never too late to learn a new trick or two."

"Pat, just because I don't have a boyfriend right now doesn't mean I don't know about sex," Harmony said.

"Use it or lose it, that's what they say," Pat said.

"You'll be the last to lose it, then," Neddie said.

"I hope I am," Pat said.

19.

"I'd feel better if I had a shotgun," Pat said, looking out the window of Laurie's apartment on East Ninth Street, just off Second Avenue.

"Pat, the door has double dead bolts," Harmony reminded her. They were watching Bob Newhart reruns, waiting for Eddie to come home from his TV appearances. They had watched a couple of his TV appearances themselves, but then the mere sight of Eddie made Harmony miss him so much that they switched to cable. Neddie had fallen asleep in a chair, but Pat was looking down at the street, watching the action on Second Avenue.

"You're no judge of what's safe and what isn't," Pat said. "Anyway, you're so sad you wouldn't care if you got murdered."

Bob Newhart reminded Harmony of Ross, Pepper's father; the memory made her feel guilty, because she had not yet made an effort to find Ross and tell him the tragic news.

"The problem I have with this show is that I can't believe a woman as attractive as Suzanne Pleshette would marry a drip like Bob Newhart," Pat said.

"Pat, he's sweet," Harmony said. She had a sense of déjà vu—sometime, long ago, she had had the same argument about Bob

Newhart and Suzanne Pleshette. The argument had taken place on one of her sisters' visits to Las Vegas. While she and Pat argued Neddie had made Pepper corn bread, which she loved.

"You didn't answer my question about Ross," she said.

"No, even Bob Newhart is a whole lot cuter than Ross," Pat said. "Ross is one of those guys who wouldn't know how to get laid if he was in a whorehouse."

"Pat, he was Pepper's father," Harmony reminded her. "He did know how to get laid."

Just then the double dead bolts began to click and Laurie and Sheba and Otis returned with Eddie, who was sound asleep. Harmony took him in her arms and smelled him, and was reassured that he smelled like her own little boy, her Eddie. He didn't smell like a celebrity, or anything. Sheba carried Iggy, who was also asleep. They had to step over Omar, Abdul, and Salah, all of whom were asleep on the floor, wrapped up in rugs.

"Did Eddie have supper?" Harmony asked. "It's very important that he get his meals regularly."

Actually, she felt guilty for sort of having dropped her maternal responsibilities for a while. The guilt hit her the moment she saw Eddie's little face in the Mayor's helicopter. Her son's dog had fallen off the Statue of Liberty, but she herself had been almost no help. It was as if the accident had occurred at a moment when her maternal emotions were unavailable. For all of her five and a half years with Eddie she had been pretty much always on call; the emotions required to handle this problem or that had been right there where they needed to be, in her heart.

But then the news came of Pepper's death, and the bombs of grief began exploding. The part of her heart where the maternal emotions stayed sort of got smacked by one of the bombs. The emotions were still there, somewhere, but they were buried beneath the rubble and dust, like the homes of people in Sarajevo. Every now and then, while Eddie was rolling the cable channels with the remote, he would release the button at CNN, and there would be shots from Yugoslavia or Israel or somewhere, showing people whose homes had just been bombed or otherwise destroyed. The people who had lived in the homes, if they survived, would just be wandering around looking blank, as if they could no longer quite get a grip on what life meant, or think of what they were supposed to do next. Some dug in the rubble with spades, hoping to unearth a possession or two, but most just wandered around looking blank.

Harmony sympathized; she thought she knew a little of what they felt—or maybe, how they didn't feel. Mainly, that was how it was with her, a sense of not feeling. She had had it that afternoon at the Statue of Liberty, but it wore off while they were in G.'s dirty white bus, stuck in the Holland Tunnel. Harmony hadn't realized they were in a tunnel, at first. She was sitting in the back of the school bus, and hadn't really been paying much attention to the road. The bus had been stopped about five minutes, inching into the Holland Tunnel, before Harmony came out of her numbed state sufficiently to realize that something unusual was happening. She realized it when she saw Pat trying to rip the blue seat cushions off a row of seats in G.'s bus. All the turban men except G. himself were looking at her sternly, and trying to get her to stop ripping the cushions off the seats.

G., though, with only about a sixteenth of an inch separating his bus from a shiny white stretch limo, had to concentrate on his driving and couldn't take part in the defense of his seats.

"Do not rip up seat!" Salah said, frowning.

"Little children need to sit on these seats, very important," Omar said. "Many little children need to sit on the seat, every day."

"This cushion might save my life if this tunnel cracks open and the ocean comes pouring in," Pat said. "I got a right to use any flotation device I can find, and this is the only one I can find."

"Neddie, what's she doing?" Harmony asked. "Where are we? Why would Pat need a flotation device?"

"Because we're under the ocean, or whatever this body of water is that's on top of the tunnel," Neddie said.

"We're under the *ocean?*" Harmony said, suddenly remembering that she was still a mom; she also suddenly remembered that she was very claustrophobic.

"Why do we have to be in a tunnel—couldn't we find a bridge?" she asked. The walls of the tunnel were only a few inches from the sides of the school bus; she was beginning to feel *very* claustrophobic.

"If you two believed in predestination—it's Baptist doctrine—

then you wouldn't be having fits," Neddie said. "If we're meant to die in a tunnel under the ocean then we will, but if we ain't meant to die in a tunnel under the ocean then there's nothing to worry about and Pat don't need to be tearing up G.'s seats."

"I thought there were bridges, where's Brooklyn?" Harmony asked.

G. succeeded in edging just in front of the stretch limousine, but the bus was still pointing down, deeper into the tunnel. Harmony was beginning to remember that her claustrophobia wasn't just a minor thing, it was a major thing—it was just that in a desert city like Las Vegas there were no tunnels to activate it. About the worst Las Vegas had to offer was the parking garage at Caesar's, which had real low ceilings.

"G. is accomplished driver, he knows best routes," Abdul said, shocked that a bunch of infidel women would think to question G.'s decision to use the Holland Tunnel.

"Bridges under construction," Omar said, just as they approached a flashing orange sign blocking the right lane of the tunnel. The sign said: TUNNEL UNDER CONSTRUCTION: EXPECT MAJOR DELAYS.

Harmony had been told by someone, probably Gary, that the best cure for claustrophobia was to chew gum vigorously. She began to rummage in her purse, hoping to find some gum that she could chew vigorously, but she couldn't find any.

Neither Pat nor Neddie had gum. Pat was annoyed that Harmony would even bother her with such a request, when she needed to devote all her strength to ripping the cushion off her seat.

"It pisses me off that the last person I made love to was Rog," she said. "If I'd known something like this was going to happen I'd have tried to find someone a little more studly."

"You're heartless, Pat," Neddie said. "For all you know, that poor man was blown to smithereens in a gas explosion."

Harmony suddenly recovered her maternal feelings; she had a great longing to see Eddie.

Salah began to stare at Pat intently. Her dissatisfaction with what she assumed would be her final love act aroused his sympathy —and his sympathy was not the only thing it aroused.

232

"Organ available for love act," he announced. "Plenty bus seats available for pleasing actions."

"Why are these Arabs always talking about their dicks?" Pat asked.

"Because they're guys," Harmony said. "I hope Laurie and Sheba remember that Eddie doesn't like cauliflower. If they try to serve him cauliflower he might go on a hunger strike."

She was beginning to shake a little.

"Harmony, it's just a tunnel," Neddie said. "Everything will be fine. At least it will be if we don't have to watch Pat get seduced by Salah."

"No way, I'm holding out for someone American-made," Pat said.

"Pleasant coition on bus seats," Salah said, though his hopes were fading. "Much joy comes from good-sized organ."

"Salah is braggart," Abdul said. "Organ is nothing special."

"Besides that, he needs a shave," Pat said.

Harmony's claustrophobia was getting worse. The fact that nobody had any chewing gum made her feel a little desperate, so desperate that when Omar finally understood her problem and offered her some betel nut she immediately accepted it, much to her sisters' dismay.

"Harmony, you don't have to take some weird drug just because we're in a tunnel," Pat said.

"This seat must have been glued on with Super Glue," she added, sinking down on the seat she had hoped to use as a flotation device.

"That's a foreign drug, Harmony," Neddie said.

"You got no room to talk, you're addicted to all kinds of prescriptions," Pat told her.

"Mostly just codeine cough syrup," Neddie said. "It's not as bad as taking some Arab drug that you never heard of."

"We may be in this tunnel all night," Harmony said. "I feel like getting out and taking my chances on foot."

G. turned and looked stern.

"Do not leave bus," he said. "Take more betel nut."

Harmony took G.'s advice. At least it gave her jaws something to do, other than just being clenched from the tension of her claustrophobia.

"We was in that tunnel forty-seven minutes," Neddie said, when they finally emerged and were in New York City. Another of Neddie's odd habits was her habit of timing events, or even things that didn't feel very much like events.

"I guess if I was getting strangled you'd time it," Pat said.

"I don't see what harm it does to time things," Neddie said, a little offended that her sisters thought there was something weird about her timing their passage through the Holland Tunnel.

Now they were all safe in Laurie's apartment, though, and Eddie was back from six TV appearances. Iggy had been sleeping in Otis's coat pocket: Otis wore an old green parka with capacious pockets. Once Iggy was awake, though, he began to scamper about as if he had lived in Laurie's apartment all his life.

"There's plenty of room here for you guys," Laurie said, to Sheba and Otis. "Just grab a blanket and roll yourselves up somewhere." Otis accepted a blanket, but Sheba just took off her wig and curled up on the end of the couch.

"Keeping up with Ed wore everybody out," Otis said, covering Sheba with his blanket. He lay down on the floor and pulled the hood of his parka over his head.

"Sure nice not to be in no Dumpster," he said. "Too many old soggy tomatoes gets thrown in that Dumpster."

"Harmony, you have a famous child—would you like some tea?" Laurie asked.

"Isn't there a better neighborhood than this, in New York City?" Pat asked.

"Plenty of better neighborhoods, I just can't afford them," Laurie said. "I didn't make much money even when I had a job, and now I don't have a job. I'll probably have to sink even lower than this, if I want to stay in New York."

Harmony was hoping everybody would go to sleep—maybe when they did Laurie would talk about Pepper. She had already looked through Laurie's scrapbooks two or three times. As she watched Laurie move about the apartment, serving tea or putting blankets over people, she tried to imagine how it must have been with just Laurie and Pepper living there together. She tried to see a kind of movie in her mind, of Laurie and Pepper in their days of happiness. She wanted to know where Pepper sat, and whether she had been helpful in the kitchen—of course Pepper had been brought up to be helpful in the kitchen, but she had been a teen-ager when she left for New York, she might have forgotten those habits. Also, Harmony wanted to know if Laurie and Pepper held hands and were friendly and sweet when they were alone together, or if they bickered like women sometimes did, or what.

"I can't even glance around this place without having some memory of her," Laurie said later, when everyone but herself and Harmony had nodded off. "Come on into the bedroom and let me show you some of her clothes. Pepper had good taste right to the end. She would have spent every cent we have on clothes if I'd let her."

"She always had better taste than I did," Harmony admitted, as they were looking at Pepper's clothes. "She always thought I dressed a little tacky.

"Did you two disagree a lot?" she asked Laurie.

"Well, she bossed me," Laurie said. "I hate quarreling, so I didn't get my way very often."

Harmony took Pepper's outfits out, one by one, and looked at them. They all looked very Pepper-like—outfits you had to be as beautiful as Pepper to make work. As she handled the clothes, her mood started yo-yoing: one second she wished that she had never left Las Vegas, that she had just let Pepper's life in New York be a mystery, and her death a mystery; but the next second it was all she could do to keep from clinging to Laurie, and finally she did cling to Laurie, standing at the foot of the bed, Pepper's outfits strewn on the bedcovers. Harmony began to tremble so badly that she felt she might have fallen if Laurie hadn't been hugging her.

"It might just be claustrophobia from the tunnel," she said.

"I don't think it has anything to do with the tunnel, Harmony," Laurie said. "I think it has to do with your loss."

Then Laurie began to shake too.

"If only it had never happened," Laurie said. "I'm going to put Pepper's clothes back in the closet—she hated having them strewn all around."

Crying, she hung Pepper's clothes back up, as quickly as she could.

"I even keep them in the order she hung them in, do you think that's sick?" Laurie asked.

Harmony felt too weary to deal with the issue, or any issue. As soon as Pepper's clothes were hung up, she lay down on Laurie's bed. About the time she closed her eyes she felt Laurie sink down on the bed beside her.

"Laurie, is your mother alive?" she asked.

"My mother is dead," Laurie said. "She was killed on the Santa Ana Freeway about a year ago. A truck flipped over and landed right on her and her little Honda."

"Maybe you ought to pretend to be my daughter, just for a while," Harmony said. She didn't really know why she said it, she just felt like saying it.

"Yeah, you know, why not?" Laurie said. "I don't miss my Mom near as much as I miss Pepper, though."

"Maybe it would help us both," Harmony said.

"Yeah, maybe it would," Laurie said, before they both let it all go, and went to sleep.

20.

Eddie and Iggy came into Laurie's room, very early. For a moment Eddie pretended that he was going to be very quiet, and not wake his Mom.

"Be *very* quiet," he told Iggy loudly.

But Iggy didn't know how to be very quiet. Eddie had on his sneakers, and Iggy began to tug at the shoelaces. While he tugged he growled. He growled more and more loudly and then he began to yip, as he had yipped at the astonished tourist just after he fell off the Statue of Liberty.

Harmony saw it was no use; she opened her eyes—anyway she wanted to see Eddie, and there he was, smiling like an angel.

"I *told* him not to yip, Mom, but he yipped anyway," Eddie said. "He doesn't know how to behave. He's just a puppy—he isn't educated yet."

"I think Iggy's a candidate for obedience training," Laurie said, in a very sleepy voice.

"Are there going to be pancakes?" Eddie asked.

"Not unless we go out and get some pancake mix—I guess the mice ate all I had," Laurie said.

"I don't see any mice," Eddie commented.

"Well, mice are sly, they had to be," Laurie said.

"How many mice have you counted?" Eddie asked, patting Laurie on the shoulder.

"Eddie, can't I just sleep a *few* more minutes?" Laurie asked. "I haven't counted the mice lately, but I think there's about forty running around here."

"Iggy hasn't seen any mice either," Eddie said.

Neither Harmony nor Laurie responded.

"Mom, I have to be on many television shows today," Eddie said. "If I don't get some pancakes pretty soon, I'll be starved and won't be able to tell them about Iggy falling all the way off the Statue of Liberty."

"Why can't Iggy tell them about it himself?" Laurie asked. "He can sort of yip it out."

"No, he's just a dog, he isn't supposed to talk," Eddie said.

"I'm a human, I'm not supposed to make pancakes at this hour, either," Laurie said.

"Mom, why don't you say something?" Eddie asked. "You look like you're deaded."

"Honey, I'm just tired," Harmony said. "So is Laurie. Go see if Sheba's awake—maybe she and Otis can take you for pancakes."

"Omar's snoring," Eddie said. "That's why I woke up. When he snores it's like an animal's about to eat you."

"Maybe he has a nasal obstruction," Harmony said.

"Maybe he has a monster that lives in his head," Eddie said. "When Omar goes to sleep the monster roars and it comes out his mouth like a snore."

"I like that theory," Laurie said.

"The monster is the color of puke . . . *green* puke," Eddie said. Then he giggled.

Iggy was still tugging at Eddie's shoelaces.

"He likes my shoelaces," Eddie said. "Maybe he thinks they're pasta."

Laurie opened her eyes and sat up.

"This kid's not going to give up," she said.

Harmony agreed. Sleep never seemed more delicious than at some moment when Eddie insisted she wake up and feed him pancakes.

"Sheba doesn't have her wig on," Eddie said. "I don't think she would take me for pancakes unless she puts on her wig, because she doesn't want to be seen on the street without it, because her hair is too short."

"In her view," Laurie said. "Personally I think she looks better without the wig."

"Mom, they sprayed my hair when I was on television," Eddie said.

Laurie put her hand over Eddie's mouth, like a gag, and he giggled into the gag. Harmony opened her eyes and saw that Eddie's eyes were full of mischief.

"Eddie, go and see if anyone's awake in the other room," she said. "Maybe someone else wants pancakes too."

"Aunt Neddie's the only one awake—she's smoking," Eddie said. "It's bad. It means her lungs will turn black."

"Go make Iggy bark at them and wake them up," Laurie said. "We have to take a team approach if we're going to get through the day."

"He won't bark at them because he's *very* polite," Eddie said.

"Well, you're not especially polite, go pull their hair or something and get them up," Laurie said.

Immediately it was apparent that Laurie had made an ill-considered remark. The giggly look left Eddie's face, to be replaced by a solemn look. In a moment his eyes got wide and filled with tears.

"Hey, don't look that way, it was just a joke," Laurie said, horrified.

"She didn't mean it, honey, it was a joke," Harmony said.

"But she *said* it," Eddie said. "She said I wasn't very polite."

Tears slid down his cheeks.

"Eddie, don't cry, I was kidding—sometimes people kid," Laurie said, looking at Harmony, to see if she could offer more help.

Harmony was willing to help, but once Eddie got his feelings hurt, making them unhurt was no simple matter.

"I didn't want to hear those words," he said.

Then he slipped off the bed and started disconsolately out of the room.

Laurie jumped off the bed and swooped him up in her arms.

Eddie began to kick and struggle, but Laurie carried him back to the bed and hung on until he got tired of kicking and struggling.

"He doesn't hold grudges," Harmony said. "He gets over things."

She said it because Laurie looked as if she might cry herself.

"Yes I do hold grudges," Eddie said. "I hold them forever and forever and forever until it's the end of the world."

"You mean from now till the end of the world you're going to hate me just because I made a stupid joke?" Laurie asked. "You're going to hate me for one little stupid comment forever and forever?"

"Yes," Eddie said. Then he looked at Laurie's face and changed his mind.

"Well, I won't *hate* you," he said. "You made me sad because of those words, though."

"If you hated me I couldn't bear it, Eddie," Laurie said.

"Well," Eddie said again. It was his philosophical "well."

"I apologize, how's that?" Laurie said. "How about if we just move on to pancakes?"

"Yes, let's move on to pancakes," Eddie said. "We'll take Otis and Sheba because my Mom looks too sleepy to go down to the street."

"What if I tie your shoelaces?" Laurie said.

While Laurie was tying the sneakers Iggy began to try to bite the strings even though Laurie's fingers were in the way.

"He thinks he owns my shoelaces," Eddie said.

"He thinks he owns *you!*" Laurie corrected.

"He doesn't own me and I don't own him," Eddie said. "We're friends. He's a dog and I'm a person."

"I don't think Iggy realizes he's a dog, though," Laurie said. "I think he thinks he's a person too.

"I *know* he thinks he's a person," she said, picking Iggy up. "He's looking at me right now the way a person would look if another person were holding him up."

"I like to hold him up because he's small," Eddie said. "Anyway, he's not a person, he's a dog."

He looked at Iggy and reflected on the business of who was a person and who wasn't.

"He might think he's a person now because he lives with me and my Mom," Eddie said. "Before that he was an orphan and some-

240

body put him out on the road in Arizona, where the Hopi people live."

"Okay, those sneakers are tied and even a dog who thinks shoelaces are pasta can't get them untied," Laurie said. "Now can we go see about those pancakes?"

A minute or two later Harmony looked out the window and saw Laurie and Eddie walking down the littered street. Laurie was holding Eddie's hand. Neddie wandered in and looked down at them too.

"She's sweet, ain't she?" Neddie said.

"She's sweet," Harmony said.

21.

While waiting for Eddie and Laurie to get back from having pancakes, Harmony decided she couldn't wait any longer to check in with Gary—it was the longest she had been out of touch with him in almost thirty years. In the back of her mind was the hope that maybe Gary would have had some contact with Ross, who still didn't know that his daughter was dead.

Of course it would have to be chance contact, because Gary didn't like Ross and Ross didn't like Gary; still, Las Vegas was a pretty small world, they might just sit down by one another at Burger King or something. Sometimes she would just be having a burger or maybe a taco and some showgirl she hadn't seen in years would wander in and sit by her; or maybe it would be a stagehand or a light man or even an old boyfriend who had sort of passed beyond the hots and still had a little tender feeling for her. She herself had tender feelings for quite a number of guys who had been in her life for a while and then passed on. After all, why hold grudges? Life or maybe just love or certainly the hots had that temporary aspect to it—somebody was around, making lots of waves and occupying a lot of space, and then, one day, they weren't around, or maybe they were still around but occupying less space and less space until they just gradually stopped occupying any space.

Harmony didn't really expect to get Gary on the first try, usually it took seven or eight calls, and messages would have to be left with people who might run into him, but this time she was lucky and got Gary on the first try.

"Harmony?" he said, when he answered. His voice didn't sound quite right, it had a different tone.

"So did you see Eddie on TV? He's a big celebrity because his dog fell off the Statue of Liberty and lived," Harmony said at once.

"Really?" Gary said—his voice still didn't sound quite right.

"Gosh, if I had a TV I'd turn it on," Gary added. "Has he been on Letterman yet?"

"That's today," Harmony said. "Why don't you have a TV? I gave you my old one, remember?"

"Of course I remember, I'm not a mental defective," Gary said —Harmony was shocked that he would be so bitchy right off, when they hadn't talked to one another for quite a few days.

"Gary, do you have a hangover?" she asked.

"It's not a hangover, it's a broken neck," Gary said. "All I have left of that TV you gave me is the remote. I'm clicking it right now but nothing's coming on because Derek stole the TV set."

"Gary, who's Derek? I never heard of him, why do you have a broken neck?" Harmony asked.

No wonder he doesn't sound right, she thought—if he had a broken neck his vocal cords might have been affected.

"I have a broken neck because Derek knocked me off a wall I was sitting on," Gary said. "It was about a ten-foot drop and the worst part of it is that I landed on a grill where some people were barbecuing, so I got a bad burn and now it's infected.

"I knew something like this would happen if you went away and left me," he said, in a sort of accusing voice.

"Gary, you could have come, you were already in the car, it's not my fault you jumped out," Harmony said, annoyed that he was trying to make it sound like it was her fault because his boyfriend pushed him off a wall.

"Okay, forget it, when are you coming back?" Gary asked. "I have to have an operation in six weeks, I was really hoping you could be here."

"Oh my God, why do you need an operation, is it for your burn?" Harmony asked.

"No, Harmony, it's for my broken neck," Gary said. "They have to take a piece of bone out of my hip and graft it into the place that got broken in my neck."

"Gary, that sounds horrible," she said. Thinking about Gary with part of his hip somehow stuck onto his neck made her want to cry. It was as if there was no direction she could turn her mind's eye to that didn't present a horrible sight, unless she turned her mind's eye toward Eddie, who was never a horrible sight. Probably even now he was getting happily sticky from eating pancakes.

"It is horrible, I imagine I'll lose my job, too," Gary said, morosely.

"I don't know Derek but if I see him I'm going to rip his head off," Harmony said. The thought that someone would cause Gary such a terrible injury made her feel like slapping whoever did it.

"He's just a little faggot, he had no idea they were barbecuing that chicken on the balcony below," Gary said.

"Yeah, but it wasn't just the burn—he broke your neck," Harmony reminded him. "Can't you make yourself love someone nice for a change, Gary?"

"You're no one to talk," Gary said. "How long has it been since *you* loved someone nice?"

"Never mind, I'm sorry I ever brought it up," Harmony said. She knew she was no one to talk, although it had been a while since a boyfriend had done anything as bad as what Derek had done to Gary. She had never had anyone break her neck, although a boyfriend named Randy had slugged her so hard she couldn't do aerobics for six months, she had dizzy spells whenever she bent over.

"Harmony, please just say you'll come for the operation and all will be forgiven," Gary said—he sounded like he needed to know that he still had his best friend. It occurred to her that he had forgotten that she had left Las Vegas forever—that had been her feeling anyway, when they loaded Eddie's bunk bed and all his stuffed animals and took off.

"Gary, of course I'll come for the operation," Harmony said. "I don't live anywhere now, so I don't know where I'll be coming from, but I'll come. Have you seen Ross?"

244

"No, why would I see that ugly son of a bitch?" Gary asked. He had always taken the attitude that Harmony had degraded herself by sleeping with Ross and getting pregnant by him—probably it was because Ross only had a seventh-grade education. Ross was from Kentucky and in Kentucky it was not uncommon for kids to drop out of school about the time of the seventh grade—Harmony had only been through the tenth grade herself and didn't see that it was such a big deal, but Gary felt differently.

"You have natural smarts," he told her one time, when the subject came up. "Ross on the other hand has natural dumbs.

"He's ugly besides," Gary had added, unnecessarily in Harmony's view. That was even before Ross had gone bald, too.

"Eddie didn't have a dog when you left Las Vegas," Gary said. He had figured out that he needed to change the subject.

"No, we picked him up on the Hopi reservation," Harmony said. "He was an orphan and now he's a national hero."

"It sounds gimmicky to me," Gary said. "How could a dog fall all the way off the Statue of Liberty and live?"

"Gary, are you in a bad mood because your burn's infected, or are you just mad at me for leaving?" Harmony asked. It was trying her patience a little, that Gary was being so negative.

"What kind of mood would you be in if your best friend left town and you had no TV and your burn was infected and all you had to look forward to was having part of your hipbone transplanted to your neck?" Gary asked. "Plus, probably losing your job. What kind of mood would all that put *you* in?"

"I wish you hadn't been gay, so we could have got married," Harmony said, unexpectedly.

There was silence on the other end—Gary hadn't expected such a comment, probably.

"Harmony, did I hear you correctly?" Gary asked, in a subdued, almost shocked tone.

"Gary, I can't help it," Harmony said. "You're the only man I trust."

"Well, I was bi at one point, but I didn't know you then," Gary said. "It's kind of a pity."

"Yeah," Harmony said, but she didn't want to emphasize how big a pity she thought it was, it would only make Gary feel guilty. She felt she must have gone a little crazy, as a result of her grief.

She had been around Gary for years and had even slept in the same bed with him without ever really feeling the urge to have sex with him, but now that she was two thousand miles away in Laurie Chalk's apartment in New York, she was wondering if maybe it would have been fun to have sex with Gary.

"You never acted like you were attracted to me," Gary said.

"Gary, it's just that I don't trust anybody else," Harmony said. "It seems like it would be better if there could be some trust and some sex with the same guy."

"I see your point, you sure couldn't trust any of the guys you sleep with, at least not the ones I've known.

"I haven't felt too sexy since Derek pushed me off the wall," Gary said. "My burn is pretty bad, I imagine that's the reason."

Then there was a long silence. Harmony felt a little embarrassed by what she had said. Ever since she had been afraid to get out of the car on the Hopi mesa, for fear of being sucked away, she had sort of had the feeling that she wanted to be married again, to someone who would want to always be with her. Gary was just the sort of person who came to mind, if the trusting and the always being there were part of the qualifications.

"I never should have said it—now I've upset you," she said. "I didn't plan to say it, Gary. It just popped out."

"Harmony, I'm not upset," Gary said. "No guy is going to be upset by the thought that you might want to sleep with him. Even if I'm gay I'm still a guy, and it's flattering. After all, you were the most beautiful woman Las Vegas has ever seen."

"Gary, was I?" she asked.

"Absolutely—Mr. Sinatra even said that to me once," Gary said.

"But now it's past," Harmony said. "I'm in a different time of life. I'm older and I don't know what to do next, other than raise Eddie."

"Harmony, can we put the part about getting married on hold, until you come out for my operation?" Gary asked.

"On hold—how do you mean?" she asked.

"I mean just sort of not rule it out a hundred percent," Gary said. "It's a pretty flattering thought. It's even taken my mind off my burn for a few minutes, and it's pretty hard to get my mind off my burn these days."

246

"Okay," Harmony said. "Okay. If it will help with your burn that's fine. Let's just put it on hold."

"I wish I had a TV, that's all," Gary said. "It's pretty boring not to have a TV when you're burned. Sometimes I click my remote and try to imagine the shows that would be there, if I had a TV."

"I should have left you my new one," Harmony said. "Now it's gone forever."

"What?" Gary said. "You mean some jerk stole your new TV?"

"No, it went over into a canyon, all my possessions did," Harmony said. "The trailer came unhitched and all was lost except Eddie's stuffed animals. Those were in the trunk of your car."

"Speaking of my car, how is it doing in New York?" Gary asked.

"It isn't in New York—it had a bad explosion in New Mexico," Harmony said. "We had to fly to New York."

"Hey, easy come, easy go," Gary said.

Then there was another silence—a longer silence.

"So, okay, the marriage stuff is on hold. I don't want to think about it too much or I'll get nervous," Gary said. "I'm supposed to try and keep the stress levels down between now and the time of my operation."

"Fine, it's on hold, don't give it another thought," Harmony said.

Rather than take the chance of any more silences developing, they hung up.

"What was that all about?" Neddie asked. She had been eavesdropping on the last part of the conversation.

"Oh, nothing. Gary and I were thinking about getting married but he has to have surgery first," Harmony said.

Pat wandered in just as she said it.

"You and Gary? That's the dumbest thing I ever heard," Pat said. "Correct me if I'm wrong, but isn't Gary gay?"

"Shut up, Pat," Harmony said.

22.

"My opinion is, we ought to be thinking about how to get back to Tarwater, the quickest way," Neddie said, when everybody was awake and they were trying to decide what to do with themselves.

"Can't leave before Eddie do Letterman," Sheba said. "Those Letterman people be mad as hops if we do that."

"Well, but when's that?" Neddie asked. "We've already seen the Statue of Liberty—I'd like to get started home sometime today.

"Anything could be happening, back in Tarwater," she added.

"But, Neddie, you're *here*, in the greatest city in the world," Laurie pointed out. She and Eddie had just returned. Eddie was feeding Iggy a piece of pancake he had brought home in a napkin.

"Don't mean much to Neddie," Pat said. "She'd rather get back to Tarwater and listen to the wind blow."

"Ed got to take advantage of all these opportunities while he's hot," Otis said. "Nobody stay hot but two or three days, not in New York. By tomorrow people be starting to forget about the dog that fell off the Statue of Liberty."

"You should at least go out and walk the streets a little," Laurie said. "It's a great place to people-watch."

248

"Yeah, but too many of the people watch back," Pat said. "Like muggers and rapists and winos and the homeless."

"You should be kind to the homeless," Eddie said, a little sternly. "Sheba was homeless till she met us, and Otis lived in the Dumpster."

"Yeah, and I be homeless again when you go, Bright," Sheba said. "Who knows if Otis even let me in the Dumpster."

"This place a lot nicer than the Dumpster," Otis said, looking around Laurie's cheerful apartment. The floor was bare and there was not a lot of furniture, but the apartment had high windows and the sun had just come out and was shining through them brightly.

"Wait a minute," Eddie said, to Sheba. "What did you say?"

"What *did* I say?" Sheba asked, a little startled by Eddie's statement.

"You said you'd be homeless again, once Ed leave," Otis said.

"Yeah, that's right, I was just speaking the facts, Bright," Sheba said.

"No way," Eddie said. "I'm not going to Oklahoma unless Sheba and Otis come with me, and Iggy's not going either, and that's final. I *don't* want to leave my new friends.

"Then there's Omar and Abdul and Salah and G.," he added. "I don't want to leave anybody out. It might make them sad."

"It might make them sadder to live in Tarwater," Pat said.

"Oh, shut up, Pat," Harmony said. "Eddie's not pessimistic, like you are."

"Harmony, that's twice you've told me to shut up in twenty minutes," Pat said.

Laurie had brought pastries from a local bakery. She put big white plates on her table and divided the pastries between the plates.

"These are knishes," she said.

"I don't think I want to eat something if its name starts with *k*," Neddie said, looking at the knishes suspiciously.

"Boy, are you weird, Neddie," Pat said. "It's a dish. What difference does it make what letter of the alphabet its name starts with?"

"They're very good knishes," Laurie said.

"Every time you say the name of them I get the shivers," Neddie said, and she gave a little shudder, to prove her point.

"You eat kraut, don't you?" Pat said. "Kraut starts with a *k*."

"Not the kraut I eat," Neddie said. "I only eat sauerkraut, which starts with an *s*."

"Oklahoma must be one funny place," Otis said, not unkindly.

"It is, Otis—it's a great, friendly place," Neddie said, responding to the kindness.

"To tell you the truth, Otis, it's only friendly if you're white and have lived there all your life, and it ain't *that* friendly even if you *are* white and *have* lived there all your life," Pat said.

Just then the phone rang. Laurie smiled at Harmony before she picked it up. Harmony thought Laurie probably grinned to reassure her that she wasn't disturbed by Neddie's refusal to eat the knishes. After all, everybody's relatives were a little bit out of the ordinary—Jimmy Bangor had had a sister who was quite out of the ordinary: she weighed four hundred and sixty pounds and wore see-through nighties.

"Hello," Laurie said, picking up the phone.

"Oh my gosh, is this a joke?" she said, looking nervous all of a sudden.

"Oh my gosh, I guess it isn't, Mr. President," she said. "He's right here."

Then she offered the phone to Eddie.

"It's the President," she said. "He wants to talk to you and Iggy."

"Oh," Eddie said. "I guess he heard about Iggy on TV."

"The real President?" Pat asked.

"It's the real President," Laurie said.

"Hello, thank you for calling," Eddie said, in the new, brisk voice he used now that he was an experienced talk show celebrity.

"Iggy's fine," he said, listening a moment. "He's right here but I don't know if he can talk because he's a dog and he might not feel like yipping."

The President spoke again and Eddie listened.

"Well, I could *come* to see you because we have a school bus," Eddie said. "But I don't know where you live. I'm with my Mom and my aunts and some friends, and I have to be on TV today. So I *could* come later, if I knew where you live."

Everyone was gathered around the phone, listening to Eddie

talk to the President, who was puzzled by the reference to G. He asked for clarification.

"G. is his name!" Eddie insisted. "He's a turban man and he has a beard and it's black.

"Well, where is she?" he asked, after another pause. "I don't know if Iggy will yip at her, either—he's not very yippy today, although he usually yips when he's on TV.

"Mrs. President wants to talk to me," he informed the eager crowd, after the President had signed off.

"She's not Mrs. President, she's the First Lady," Otis said, quickly assuming the role of chief of protocol.

"I call her Mrs. President," Eddie informed him, firmly. "Because he's Mr. President and she's Mrs. President."

"Okay, Ed," Otis said.

"Hi," Eddie said, when the First Lady got on the line. "Thank you for calling."

Then he listened a moment.

"Well, he's an orphan," he said. "Somebody put him out on the road and I found him when we were up high on the mesa."

Harmony thought how strange life was. Her son, who was only five, had just talked to the President and now was talking to the First Lady. Her sister Neddie had just refused to eat any food whose name started with a *k*. She herself had just told her oldest friend, who was gay, that she wished he wasn't, so they could marry. Four men with turbans were there, and two black teenagers who lived in a Dumpster in New Jersey. She herself had no job and no prospects and her brother was in jail in Tarwater for making obscene phone calls. Pepper, her daughter, was dead of AIDS.

It was a lot to adjust to, if adjust was the right word. Harmony had the fear that maybe she wasn't capable of adjusting to so much. Even at that moment she wasn't really taking part in any of it. She had just sort of faded into the background and let people who were more connected with life figure out what her son should do. She had always been an active mom, too, but now she was just sitting in an apartment in New York, not even that eager to know what the First Lady was saying to her son. She could tell that Otis and Sheba and Laurie and even Neddie and Pat were really excited that Eddie was talking to the White House. Eddie was just being friendly and informative, he might have been talking to Gary or his friend Eli or just someone he met in a store about Iggy's amazing fall.

"Okay, I'll ask my Mom, and I'll ask G., because he's the man who drives the bus," Eddie said. "Maybe we could come and see you and Iggy could run across the lawn. There wasn't much grass for him to run on in Arizona—there were cactus and he had to watch out for prickles."

Then he listened a little more.

"Somebody has to write down the number so we can go visit Mr. and Mrs. President," he said. "Laurie, could you please do it?"

Laurie took the phone and wrote down the First Family's phone number.

"Wow," she said, when she hung up. "I never thought I'd be chatting it up with Hillary. I sure have led a more interesting life since you came into it, Eddie."

"Wait till they hear about this in Tarwater," Neddie said. "When Mom and Dad find out Eddie talked to the President it'll get him off the hook for not believing the whale ate Jonah."

"Why don't you believe the whale ate Jonah, Bright?" Sheba asked.

"Whales don't eat people, they eat plankton," Eddie said, matter-of-factly.

"Well, but maybe this was an old-timey whale that didn't know about plankton or whatever it is," Sheba said. "Maybe it ate Jonah before it knew it wasn't supposed to."

"No, it *didn't eat Jonah!*" Eddie said, with great emphasis. "Mrs. President says they have a very big house and it has a fence and if we come see them Iggy can play on the lawn. Don't you think he'd like that, Mom?"

"I'm sure he'd like that," Harmony said.

Already she was nervous about not having anything to wear. She didn't own any clothes except the clothes she had on and two pairs of slacks, two bras, and two blouses that she had bought at a Kmart in Albuquerque. They weren't clothes she could show up at the White House wearing, although she knew the Clintons were from Arkansas and weren't that different from people who lived in Tulsa or any other place in that part of the country; but they

252

weren't living in Arkansas anymore, they were living in the White House—just from watching them on TV now and then, she could tell that they dressed nicely and probably didn't buy their clothes from Kmart anymore.

"So can we go, Mom?" Eddie asked. "Mrs. President wanted me to decide if we were coming. The reason we have to decide is because Mr. and Mrs. President are going on a trip to China.

"They want to fit us into their schedule, if they can," he added, coming over and taking a knish, which he ate with a good appetite.

Harmony didn't answer. She felt totally incapable of making a decision about whether they should see the President and the First Lady. In the normal part of her life she would have thought it an exciting possibility—in her younger days she had always loved to meet celebrities. Not all of them were nice but still they were celebrities; it was interesting just to see what kind of clothes they wore, or if they used cologne or aftershave if they were guys, or how they did their hair if they were women. After meeting a celebrity she would sort of have the feeling that she had added something interesting to her life; at least she would have an anecdote or two to tell the other showgirls—about whether the guys behaved like gentlemen or whether they dressed tacky and hadn't bothered to shine their shoes, things like that. It did seem to be true that a great many celebrities didn't bother to shine their shoes.

But that had been in another time—for herself she couldn't work up any interest in meeting the President or the First Lady, or visiting the White House; but she was a mother still, and it would certainly be a fine opportunity for Eddie. She knew she had to try and think of it that way. Her son shouldn't have to miss exceptional opportunities just because his mother had stopped being interested in anything.

Once Eddie got on a subject, he liked to stay on it until he got it resolved.

"We have to decide soon, Mom," he said, after finishing his knish. "Mr. and Mrs. President are going to China very soon, and they were just hoping to meet Iggy before they go.

"Mrs. President said it wasn't a very far drive to where they live," he went on. "She said we could make it in one day if we had a good school bus."

Then Eddie got an impish look in his eye.

"Uh-oh, I don't like that look," Sheba said. "That's a bad look. What you thinking about now, Bright?"

"The Washington Monument," Eddie said. "I've seen it on TV a million times. What if we went up it and a sea gull flew by and Iggy jumped off the Washington Monument and he fell all the way down and landed in some very soft grass and he still wasn't deaded. Then we'd have to go on *one million* TV shows."

"Eddie, that's a horrible thought," Laurie said. "You don't want Iggy to be taking that kind of chance. You want him to be safe from now on."

"Well, but if he fell into some very very soft grass he would be safe," Eddie insisted. "He wouldn't be hurt at all."

"Let's not push our luck, Eddie," Pat said.

"You should just think about him being safe, Eddie," Laurie said. But she didn't say it in the same voice. There was a catch in her voice, this time, and before anybody could say anything else she began to cry. At first it was silent crying, just a few tears running down her cheeks.

Eddie was appalled that something he had said made Laurie cry. He went right over and began to pat her on the knee.

"I was just joking, I'm very sorry," he said.

"Oh, Eddie," Laurie said. "The creatures we love don't live forever, honey. We should always just think of what could make them safe."

"Well, I will try to make Iggy be safe," Eddie said. "I won't let him go up on anything high where there could be *any* sea gulls. I promise, I promise, I promise."

Despite Eddie's promise, and his pats, Laurie lost control of her sorrow and began to sob so hard that she had to run out of the room. She went into her bedroom and closed her door.

"Poor thing, she's been shouldering a big load of grief," Neddie said.

"I guess she really loved that Pepper," Sheba said, quietly.

"Mom, I *really* didn't mean to make Laurie sad," Eddie said.

"I know, honey," Harmony said. "Laurie knows you really don't want Iggy to fall off the Washington Monument."

Still, they could all hear Laurie sobbing, through the thin door of her bedroom.

"Mom, can't you go make her better?" Eddie asked. "I feel very bad now about what I said."

"You could go give it a try, Sis," Neddie said. "It's you and her who have had the worst loss."

"Mom, go on," Eddie insisted. "I don't want to hear that bad crying."

"Sometimes people just need to cry, Eddie," Pat said.

"No they don't, they *never* need to cry! Don't say those words to me!" Eddie said, crying himself.

"I'll go," Harmony said. She got up and knocked gently on Laurie's door.

"Laurie, can I come in? Eddie's very sorry," Harmony asked.

There was no answer from Laurie. Harmony looked around, at Eddie and Neddie and Pat and Sheba and the turban men, all of whom expected her to make Laurie feel better, even though Pepper was dead and Laurie couldn't really feel better. Harmony knew she couldn't, it was impossible; but her son expected her to try, so, after a moment, she opened the door and went in anyway.

Book
Three

1.

"She slept with some dirty little boy," Laurie said, once she had cried herself out. "All she had to do was step outdoors and she'd be infested with them. If she walked to rehearsal she'd pick up three or four, and she wouldn't stop sleeping with them. If a guy looked at Pepper and got a hard-on she felt she owed him sex.

"I gave up arguing with her about it—I just gave up," Laurie said.

Harmony felt a throb of guilt, remembering how many times she'd ended up in the sack, with a guy she'd just met on top of her, for no better reason than that the guy had managed to make her feel responsible for the fact that he had a hard-on.

"I mean, we had a sex life and it was plenty okay with me," Laurie said. "I wasn't cut out to be celibate, any more than anybody else. I wanted so badly to be enough for Pepper—I can't tell you how much I wanted that. But I never was enough."

"Laurie, it wasn't your fault," Harmony said, disturbed by the hopeless look on Laurie's face.

"It wasn't my fault but it was my life," Laurie said. "We were together three years and she was my life the whole time. I don't know how many times I came home and found Pepper fucking some boy. She wasn't careful, either. For Pepper safe sex was sex you might as well not be having."

Then she bent over, pressing her hands against her head as if she were about to break into sobs again—but she didn't. She just rocked back and forth on her knees for a minute, taking deep breaths.

"But my God, you *raised* her," Laurie went on. "I just can't imagine how it would be to have Pepper for a daughter and then lose her."

"I wish it was just something I had to try to imagine," Harmony said. Though Laurie had cried a long time, and was very sad, Harmony was still glad to be alone with her finally, and glad to be having a talk about Pepper, even though what was being said was not happy stuff. It couldn't be happy stuff, and yet talking to Laurie about it—even though Laurie was desperate—seemed more right than trying to talk to her sisters about it, or even Gary, usually a good person to talk to about any problem.

The difference was that Laurie had loved Pepper enough to put up with the fact that she slept with guys; fine people like Laurie gave up on perfection without giving up on hope, or the possibility of good times and things that were worth sharing. It didn't always have to be sex that was worth sharing.

The fact was, Laurie was the person who had been closest to Pepper, not only in her last years but in *all* her years—in her whole life. Mel, her husband, hadn't been that close to her; Harmony didn't even feel that *she* had the right to claim that she had been that close. Mainly, Pepper didn't want people close, though there had been exceptions. When Pepper was about nine or ten Myrtle had been an exception.

Mainly, though, Pepper just hadn't been the kind of child it was possible to be very close to. She kept her thoughts for herself, and her feelings for herself, too.

"You know what I'd like?" Laurie said. "I'd like for all the people in the other room to just go away for about eight hours, so you and I could be together. We don't have to talk, if we don't want to. There may not be that much to talk about. I'd just like them all to go away so we can have a day of privacy. Maybe later you'd feel like taking a walk around New York.

"It's not a bad place to be if you're grief-stricken," she added. "If

260

you want to talk to people about your grief, they'll talk, but if you don't want to talk, they'll definitely respect that and leave you alone."

Harmony didn't answer. For the moment she was as afraid of New York as she had been of the great Hopi mesa. She had the feeling that she might get sucked into the crowd, or maybe the subway or something, and just vanish. She knew it was a silly feeling—it had been silly on the mesa too. But it was still how she felt, silly or not.

"I haven't eaten in a long time," she said. "Maybe when they all leave to take Eddie to his TV shows, I'll feel like having a sandwich.

"But what about the President and the First Lady?" she asked. "They invited us. What do we do about them?"

"You don't have to mother the President and the First Lady," Laurie said. "They can take care of themselves. If it works out that we can visit them, we will. But you don't have to decide the fate of the world right now, Harmony. Just let it go for a day. Stay with me.

"I need you," she added. "I need you just to be with me. Okay?"

While the others were getting ready to leave, Harmony lay on Laurie's bed. At the bedside was a picture of Pepper in her dancing leotard, just standing on a stage somewhere, smiling. Harmony put a pillow under her head and stared at the picture for a long time. Looking at the picture was a way of looking back through time, to the years when Pepper had been a dancer in New York. Only, once she began to look back through time it was like she was on a fast rewind or something, she went far back in her memory, rewinding through Pepper's life, to her childhood—to the years, just three years, when Pepper had been a very little girl and they had lived with Ross, in a little apartment just off the Strip, a few blocks from the Stardust. Pepper was just a sweet, normal little girl then. It was long before the stage of keeping her feelings to herself. Then she was always hugging her Mom and her Dad, whispering secrets in their ears, eating cereal, watching cartoons, and doing all the other things normal little girls did.

For three years Ross tried to be a normal father to Pepper, too. On Saturday mornings, even if he'd worked the late show at the Trop, he would make an effort to wake up early, so he could watch cartoons with his little daughter. Often he would fall back to sleep, while the cartoons were running, but at least he was there on the couch, so Pepper could sort of crawl around on him and color in her coloring books while she watched cartoons. One of the reasons Harmony had always felt sympathetic to Ross, even to the point of sleeping with him again after quite a few years of separation, was that he had at least made the effort to be a good father. The effort fizzled—in the end adult responsibilities that went beyond the level of maybe reading a story now and then or maybe watching the cartoons on Saturday morning left Ross exhausted. He simply wasn't up to continuous parenting, or continuous husbanding either—not for long. One day he got up from the breakfast table, where he had been quietly eating a bowl of Frosted Flakes, and walked up the street to the Sandy Scenes Apartments, where he got his own place.

When Harmony asked him why—was it something she did, or something she didn't do?—Ross very sweetly took all the blame. He explained that it was probably genetic. In his family, situations that required continuing along, day after day in a responsible pattern, just didn't survive. In his family, work came first, as Ross put it. He couldn't afford to get so tired from watching cartoons with Pepper that he couldn't get the spots on the right performer at the right time. Mr. Sinatra or Elvis or Liberace needed to know that whoever was working the spots was reliable—Harmony was a performer herself, she understood the requirements for being a light man for the big floor shows at the casinos. As a top showgirl for many years the spots had often been on her. So when Ross went up the street to the Sandy Scenes, Harmony tried to be understanding. Mainly she got sad about it on Saturday mornings, when there was no Daddy there to watch cartoons with Pepper or help her color in her coloring books.

Still, Ross didn't completely desert Pepper—once he sent her a stuffed bunny, and another time, a leather giraffe. Even though he had stopped being there on Saturday mornings, at least he was a better father than Webb, who wasn't there on *any* mornings to watch cartoons with Eddie, or do anything else for Eddie, either. Ross was an occasional father, but Webb was a could-have-cared-less father, which was why Harmony was less sympathetic when Webb showed up with problems. Webb had even made overtures, if he happened to run into Harmony in the casino or somewhere; they were just automatic overtures, Webb didn't know what else to do if he encountered a woman he had slept with in a casino.

Eddie wasn't like Pepper, though. Eddie didn't keep his feelings to himself; he told anybody he happened to meet what his feelings were. He told Sheba, he told the President, he told the cops at La Guardia Airport. Having no father to speak of hadn't kept him from being a little boy it was easy to get along with. Eddie went on TV, and had conversations with the First Lady; Pepper picked up boys and slept with them but kept her feelings to herself.

Harmony knew she could look down the tunnel of time forever and not figure out why her children were so different. Looking at the lovely picture of Pepper at Laurie's bedside wasn't a wrong thing to do, though. The picture showed how graceful Pepper had been, how she sort of ducked her chin when she faced into the camera. She had had grace and beauty—not everyone could say that, Pat for example. Pat was dumpy and accident-prone. Neddie was bony and weird; the business about no foods that began with *k* was way out in left field. She herself had never been graceful, in the way that Pepper was.

Harmony had the thought, looking at Pepper's picture, that maybe grace of body such as Pepper had was as good as love. Maybe to have it even for a few years was as good as living a long time. When she looked at the picture, looked and looked at it, her feelings began to grow still. For most of the trip east they hadn't been still at all. They heaved and shook and dripped, like clothes in a washing machine. She couldn't turn off the washing machine, either; she *was* the washing machine. At times on the trip she thought the heaving would go on until she became too exhausted to function; she had been afraid they would have to put her in a hospital somewhere, and leave her.

It was such a relief just to feel a little calm again, calm enough that she could maybe do little tasks for her son—choose his clothes, or make him a waffle—that she didn't want to do anything that might put the calming at risk. What helped was the sense she had that she could put herself in Laurie's hands, for a time. She was really too weak to do anything *but* put herself in Laurie's hands.

Just before Eddie left to do the TV shows, Laurie had brought him into the bedroom for a minute. He was dressed in jeans, with a little red snap-on bow tie at his collar.

"Eddie, I never saw that bow tie before," Harmony said, surprised at how spiffy he looked.

"No, you haven't, because Sheba bought it for me yesterday, from a person on the street," Eddie said. "The person had bow ties *and* watches but Sheba didn't buy me a watch."

"Maybe I'll buy you the watch," Laurie said. "Can you tell time?"

"I can tell time and I can count to fourteen," Eddie assured her. "We're going to the TV places now, Mom. Sheba gave Iggy a bath and now he's clean."

"I'll watch you on TV," Harmony assured him. "Mind Sheba and Otis and mind your aunts, while you're gone."

Eddie considered that order.

"Well, I'll mind Sheba and Otis and I'll mind Omar but I won't mind my aunts and I won't mind Abdul or Salah."

"Uh-oh," Laurie said. "Why won't you mind your aunts?"

"Because they don't believe that whales eat plankton," Eddie said. "They think the whale ate Jonah, and the whale did *not* eat Jonah, so if they believe something stupid like that then I don't have to mind them."

"Okay then, why won't you mind Abdul and Salah?" Laurie asked.

"Because they're silly, that's why," Eddie said. "I might mind G., but G. does not speak."

"That's true, G.'s the strong silent type," Laurie said.

"Please don't forget to call Mrs. President, Mom," Eddie said. "She has to plan her trip to China and she has to plan it soon."

"Eddie, I'm just so tired," Harmony said. "Will you be very disappointed if we don't go see the President and the First Lady?"

Eddie pursed his lips and got a faraway look in his eye. It was a look he often got when he was not especially pleased with the direction events were taking.

"Well, I won't be very disappointed, but the President and Mrs. President will be sad," Eddie said. "They wanted to see me and they wanted to meet Iggy."

"Eddie, you can't please everyone," Laurie said.

"Well," Eddie said. "Why can't you please everyone?"

"Because it's too tiring," Laurie said—she was not sure it was exactly an answer Eddie would accept.

"But you could nap on the bus," Eddie pointed out. "You could *nap* all the way to the White House. And there's a big lawn and Iggy could run around on it and enjoy the grass.

"That wouldn't be very tiring," he added.

"Well, but there's your aunts, and all the rest of us to deal with," Laurie said.

"It will make them sad," Eddie insisted. "I *know* it will make them very sad."

"Too bad, they'll get over it," Laurie said.

"I don't like your words today," Eddie said, but he said it mildly, as if he was not disposed to fight with Laurie, just then.

"Well, I don't want to go see the President just now, so there," Laurie said.

" 'So there' is not a very nice word," Eddie commented. "See you in the funny papers."

"Eddie, who told you that?" Harmony asked. "I haven't heard that in years."

"Aunt Neddie," Eddie said, just before Laurie carried him out the door.

2.

In the afternoon Laurie went down to a little deli a half block away and brought Harmony some wonderful vegetable soup. She also brought some cheese, and some very thin salami that was better than any salami Harmony had ever had. Laurie also got some fresh rolls from the bakery next to the deli; she and Harmony sat at the plain wooden table in Laurie's kitchen, looking down on East Ninth Street, while they ate.

Harmony didn't think she would be able to eat—since the moment she read Laurie's letter she had had no appetite; eating was something she was out of practice at. It was almost as if food belonged to a different period of her life; as if eating with pleasure was something you surrendered for good, once you had lost a child.

But the first spoonful of the vegetable soup was so delicious that Harmony ended up eating most of the soup, three rolls, many slices of the thinly sliced salami, and some very good cheddar cheese.

While she was eating, Laurie made her tea, and put a lot of honey in it.

"I believe in honey," Laurie said. "Sometimes I just eat it by the spoonful. If I buy local honey—it has really good antibodies in it."

Harmony had never been too clear about antibodies—she knew good ones were supposed to be in mother's milk and that was one reason it was good to breast-feed, if you could. She had no problem breast-feeding Pepper but had had to stop fairly soon with Eddie due to the medications she had to take because of the complications. Harmony liked the honey, even if she didn't know what antibodies were.

Thanks to the tea, and the soup, and the salami, she began to feel better. She liked looking out of Laurie's window and seeing the New Yorkers walking along East Ninth Street. She liked the way the tea smelled—smelling it was almost as good as sipping it. She liked Laurie's kitchen: there were still pictures of Pepper stuck everywhere, on the refrigerator door and the doors of Laurie's cabinets. A nice one of Pepper on a boat, in white jeans and a blue sweater, stood on the windowsill. Harmony thought it was brave of Laurie, to keep pictures of Pepper all around the kitchen and in the bedroom.

"People don't leave your life until you stop thinking about them," Laurie said, noticing that Harmony kept looking at the pictures. "I'll never stop thinking of Pepper and remembering the things we did. I know that time will sort of change it and there'll be gaps when I'm not thinking about her every five minutes, like I do now. But Pepper and I had too much—she'll never be out of my life entirely."

There was a trembling in Laurie's voice when she said Pepper would never be out of her life—a trembling and a defiance, too. Laurie was so bound up with what she felt for Pepper that she was defying life to do anything to change the feeling. It made Harmony a little sad. It was brave of Laurie, to pit herself against life like that, but it was also foolish. Life always won those contests—at least it always had when Harmony had pitted herself against it by trying to hold on to some feeling for someone who was gone. The big example was Didier, her first love and her best love, the man who made her appreciate herself for the first time. She had wanted to go on loving Didier forever, but Didier had died when she was only eighteen, and forever had gone on too long. She still loved his memory, though, despite many intervening guys. None of the intervening guys were Didier's equal—they didn't even come close —but the years did pass; the deep feeling she had had for Didier was no protection from the years. Probably there had just been too many years.

Harmony couldn't tell that to Laurie, though—couldn't try to warn her that there would be too many years for Laurie too. It made her feel guilty, that she could offer no comfort to Laurie—it was just that what she knew about such things wasn't comforting.

"I know you think that's too foolish, that I'll forget her and get somebody else," Laurie said. "I guess it's in the cards that I will get someone else, but it won't happen for a long time and whoever it is won't replace Pepper."

"Laurie, could we take a walk?" Harmony asked.

"Sure, but let me ask you, are you scared of what you might say if we talk about Pepper?" Laurie asked. "Don't be scared. If there's something you want to ask, just ask."

"Did she know the person who gave her AIDS?" Harmony asked.

"Most likely it was a guy named Terry, he's dead now too," Laurie said. "But that's just a guess."

"I don't really have many questions," Harmony said. "She was a lucky girl, in some ways."

"Why do you say that?" Laurie asked, looking at Harmony in some surprise.

"Because she had you, and you were devoted to her," Harmony said. "Wild as she was, she was lucky to have someone nice devoted to her."

"I have to admit I'm curious about Mel," Laurie said. "Was Pepper actually married to him?"

"Yes, he was very nice to her—he died," Harmony said.

"It's hard for me to imagine Pepper married," Laurie said. "I'm the married type, but Pepper wasn't."

"Mel was devoted to her," Harmony said. She was not really anxious to talk about Mel. For one thing, Laurie might be jealous —but that wasn't the main reason she didn't want to talk about Mel. The main reason was that she thought Pepper had treated him disgracefully. It had taken Mel a year and a half to die and Pepper had never come to see him once. Mel could say all he wanted to about loving people for their flaws, it still didn't seem right. Mel had given her his kindness; he had even given her his name. A visit as he died would have meant a lot to him, Harmony

268

knew. She didn't want to mention it to Laurie, if she didn't have to.

"Are you sure you want to walk?" Laurie asked.

In truth Harmony didn't want to, much. But she had become a little afraid of talking to Laurie. There was too much pain floating around just beneath the surface—too much for both of them. It kept seeping through the cracks, into their conversation—Harmony grew fearful that it would do more than seep, which is why she agreed to the walk.

It was raining a little. Harmony borrowed an old poncho from Laurie, and they set out. Pretty soon the walk surprised her, in the way that the lunch had—the walk proved a lot more enjoyable than she had expected it to be. They drifted down Lower Broadway and cut across into some little side streets, just walking in the drizzle, now and then stopping to look in a shop window. Laurie had an interest in antiques. Harmony liked them too, but she had no money to buy them with and no home to put them in; she couldn't let herself get too involved with possessions, much less with costly antiques; she had to be careful with her money. After all, Eddie would be needing new school clothes, pretty soon.

"Let's ride the subway uptown and back downtown," Laurie suggested. Harmony was a little fearful; her impression was that the subways were dangerous—but Laurie marched her right down the steps and through a turnstile and into a subway car. Soon they were rattling along, under New York City. Harmony had no idea where she was going; she was just grateful that no one on a particular subway car looked like a murderer or anything.

They got off near a great museum, with hundreds of people on its long steps.

"That's the Metropolitan—are you much of a museumgoer?" Laurie asked.

"No, but Eddie's been to museums," Harmony said. "He went on a school trip already." She was glad Laurie didn't suggest going into the big museum. The steps looked like a long climb, but the main reason Harmony was glad Laurie didn't suggest it was because she was afraid she would reveal her total ignorance about art. From the age of sixteen until she was too old to be a showgirl she had mostly been working two shows a day at one of the casinos. She didn't take trips, really, unless it was just a drive to the lake with some guy. None of the guys she had gone to the lake with had exactly been museumgoing types.

"Let's just walk across the park and see a little of the West Side," Laurie suggested. As they walked Harmony began to relax a little about New York City. It was plain that most of the guys they met weren't rapists or murderers. In Central Park there were lots of old ladies and an equal number of little old men. There were lots of mothers with children, some fathers with children, and a fair number of children who were just goofing off in the park, on their own. There were some very well dressed people who gave off an aura of wanting to be alone; obviously they were thinking over some problem, or maybe just brooding about life in general. There were quite a few policemen on horses. Across the park, on both sides, were huge, towering buildings that looked mysterious to Harmony. She couldn't imagine living in huge towers in New York. The towers were nice to look at, though. While looking at some of the great towers on the West Side Harmony was nearly hit by a speeding bicyclist she had stepped in front of. There were plenty of joggers in the park, men and women, but the joggers didn't present any problem because they weren't nearly as speedy as the people on bicycles.

The bicyclist who nearly hit Harmony yelled the word "Cunt!" as he swerved to miss her.

"Ring your bell, asshole!" Laurie yelled after him.

It was a nice park, but after her near miss, anxiety about being hit by a bicycle kept Harmony from enjoying it to the full. Laurie, though, didn't seem to give the cyclists a thought.

"Do you have a man in your life, Harmony?" Laurie asked, as they were waiting at West Seventy-fifth Street for the light to change.

"No," Harmony said. "My boyfriend left ten minutes after he heard that Pepper was dead."

"I've never had any restraint," Laurie said. "I just come right out and ask people the facts about their lives."

Harmony was about to say that she didn't mind, Laurie was welcome to ask her anything she wanted to ask, when she looked across Seventy-fifth Street and saw that the man on the opposite curb, the man that would be coming right toward them as soon as the light changed and the taxicabs stopped swishing by, was one

270

of the very people her instincts had always told her to give a pretty wide berth to.

"Oh my God, that's Sonny Le Song," Harmony said.

"Oh my God, he'll recognize me for sure."

"Who?" Laurie asked. She looked across the street and saw a short man in cowboy boots and old jeans and a trench coat, waiting for the light. He was looking down, watching the shallow stream of brown water swish along below the curb.

"That's a man I know," Harmony said. "Turn around quick, before he sees us."

Laurie obeyed without question. They whipped around and started back down the sidewalk, walking at a much faster pace than they had been walking previously.

"I can't believe it," Harmony whispered to Laurie, as they hurried along. "All these millions of people, and my first walk in New York and I have to run right into Sonny Le Song."

"You have to be joking about that name, Harmony," Laurie said. "Nobody could be named Sonny Le Song."

Harmony was afraid to argue, for fear that Sonny would somehow catch the sound of her voice, even over the traffic, even if she whispered. Sonny had always claimed he would follow her forever —he was that in love—and now it looked as if he *had* followed her forever.

Harmony was wondering what the chances would be of ducking into an apartment building. Maybe they could pretend to be in the wrong apartment building just long enough for Sonny to pass. All the apartments had doormen standing in front of them, and the doormen looked pretty formidable—still, anything was preferable to Sonny catching up with them.

"Do you hate him?" Laurie asked.

"Is he still behind us?" Harmony asked. She was having an unkind fantasy, which was that the water swishing along the curbs was not a shallow little runoff but a deep pool that Sonny would step into and drown. It wasn't that she hated him so much, either, it was just that she hoped to avoid him for the rest of her life.

"Let's just edge over to the right," Laurie whispered. "If we turn real quick he might see you, but if we give it another block or two and then turn, maybe we can get over to Columbus Avenue and hit the subway."

"He might recognize me from my walk," Harmony pointed out.

They gave it one more block, edging west as they walked. When they came to Seventy-third Street they just slid around the corner. After they had walked half a block, toward Columbus Avenue, Harmony couldn't stand the suspense, she had to know if Sonny was still behind them.

She turned her head and there he was, not a yard behind her, looking at her out of the same big dumb brown eyes he had always had.

"I guess you thought I wouldn't recognize you by your walk," Sonny said. "Always playing hard to get."

"Sonny, my daughter died, just let me alone, please," Harmony said. "I have to take the subway."

"I heard about Pepper, I was at a club in the Poconos—this guy she danced with told me about it," Sonny said, holding his ground. "It's tragic, kiddo."

"Bye, Sonny, I have to take the subway," Harmony said.

"All the more reason why you need the Cowboy," Sonny informed her. "Muggers will be on you in the subway like ticks on a coon."

"She doesn't want to talk to you, buddy," Laurie said. "She just said so in plain English. Will you excuse us now?"

Sonny's big brown eyes didn't change expression. He held out a hand.

"Sonny Le Song, ma'am," he said. "I have no intention of intruding on a mother's grief."

"But you *are* intruding on it," Laurie pointed out, not unkindly. She had been prepared to be abrasive, in the manner of the New York streets, but something about the small man's look stopped her. He just looked dumb and scared.

"I've been in love with Harmony since the day we met," Sonny said.

"Oh, Sonny," Harmony said. He was just one of those men who were easily hurt—even now, on West Seventy-third Street, he looked as if he might cry, just from the fact that she hadn't been exactly welcoming.

"Do you want him to come home with us, Harmony?" Laurie asked. Then she walked away several steps. She had been ready to slam the guy on the sidewalk, but now she felt uncertain. She felt

272

strange. Just when she was able to get Harmony to come to life a little—to eat, to take a walk—they start across Seventy-fifth Street and run into a little yokel who happened to be an old beau of Harmony's—or at least an old would-be beau. Harmony had freaked at the sight of him, but now she seemed to be a little ambivalent.

"Sonny, could you just give me a day or two?" Harmony asked. "This is my first day to be with Laurie—I wasn't planning on male company right now."

"I knew you were in town, babe," Sonny said, more or less sidestepping Harmony's request. "I saw your little boy on TV—talk about star quality. I wouldn't be surprised if Caesar's signed him up—maybe the pup could do a diving act or something."

Harmony wished he would just stop looking at her with those eyes. Sonny couldn't stand rejection—it was the only reason she had ever slept with him. He got so upset if he was rejected that it was easier just to sleep with him; it took less time. She knew that Laurie probably wouldn't think that was very good grounds for a relationship; probably it wasn't, but it was what had kept Sonny Le Song in her life for the better part of a year. Basically she did it with him as a means of avoiding listening to him cry. Sonny explained that he couldn't help it, his feelings lay close to the surface; he didn't feel he should be blamed for bursting into tears because of his close-to-the-surface feelings. Harmony had been hopeful for a while that there might be a part of Sonny that *wasn't* so close to the surface; after all, she developed a few tender feelings for the guy; even if she was just sleeping with him because she didn't want to hurt his feelings, still, she *was* sleeping with him.

But if there was a part of Sonny Le Song that didn't lie close to the surface, Harmony never located it. All he liked to do was sing and screw, and he wasn't exactly casino class in either department. So far as Harmony could remember, he never got higher in Las Vegas than a lounge act at the Best Western, and, in the romance department, Harmony got the sense that Sonny never got higher than her. But those were just reflections; they didn't help her know what she was going to do with the guy now that she had had the misfortune to bump into him on her first and only walk in New York.

273

There he stood, with his "I'm gonna cry if you send me away" look on his face.

"How old are you now, Sonny?" Harmony asked. She was really just stalling, hoping he could be distracted into a normal conversation. Maybe they could walk along together to the nearest subway, after which maybe Sonny would just go one way and she and Laurie would go another.

"Not too old to cut the mustard, babe," Sonny said. He had a short upper lip—probably it was one reason he never got higher than a lounge act at the Best Western. When he smiled there was something a little chipmunky about Sonny—people just didn't go to shows in Las Vegas to be sung to by a man who reminded them of a chipmunk.

Later, she knew, Sonny had sunk considerably lower than the lounge at the Best Western; he had even been forced to try country-and-western for a while. Once, when she had borrowed Gary's car and stopped to fill it up at a brand-new Chevron station on the Strip, there was Sonny, dressed in rhinestones, with a little mike and an audience of four or five old couples who had pulled in to fill up their RVs, singing "Behind Closed Doors." It turned out that the Chevron station was even more brand-new than she had thought; it had only been open about two hours—Sonny had been hired to entertain at the opening. There was a little sandwich board propped over by the airhose that said:

SONNY LE SONG
STAR OF STAGE AND SCREEN
(appearing exclusively for Chevron)

For a second or two Harmony thought that maybe she could just gas up and head on down the Strip, but while she was gassing up, Sonny spotted her. There was no way she could leave without hurting his feelings, so she sat on the fender of the car and listened to a few songs. Being polite didn't work out too well, either. Quite a few people turned out to be more interested in getting her autograph than in listening to Sonny sing—he had never had perfect pitch, exactly. Of course it was the middle of the day and it was pretty hot over by the airhose—that might have thrown Sonny's pitch a little further off than usual.

Finally he finished his set and came over to say hi. Several old couples who had seen Harmony on stage wanted to snap her picture. Harmony didn't care, it was part of her job to welcome vacationers to Las Vegas. Sonny promptly squeezed himself into the pictures. One or two of the old couples weren't too happy with that development, and neither was she, to be truthful. What if one of the old couples sent her a copy of the photograph and Jay, her boyfriend, who was definitely the jealous type, happened to open the mail that day and saw Sonny Le Song practically sitting in her lap? On the whole, she was glad when Sonny's break ended.

Little did she know that trouble was coming with Jay anyway, and it didn't involve Sonny or the photographs the old people took at the opening of the Chevron station. Jay had accidentally happened to walk through the casino one day and noticed Harmony chatting with Hank, the captain of the cleaning crew. Hank was sitting on the seat of a big, silent vacuum cleaner that he swished around on, sucking crumbs and other trash off the floor. Harmony had known Hank for years, since long before he became head of the cleaning crew at the Stardust. They were just chums —they had never even gone on a date, none of which mattered to Jay, of course. Jay didn't accept the chums part, he took the position that there was more going on; or, if there wasn't more going on already, there would be more going on sooner or later; in his view men and women could never be chums. He came over and got huffy with Hank, who just turned on the big vacuum cleaner and swished away. Harmony felt a little hurt that Hank hadn't stayed around to explain, but of course he had his position to think of, he had an important job; people liked the casinos to be clean. Hank couldn't afford to be in a controversy on the casino floor— he just smiled, and left her to her fate.

Later, at home, Harmony tried over and over again to explain to Jay that she wasn't romantically interested in Hank; she had just stopped to chat—after all, she and Hank had worked at the same casinos several times. But all her talk fell on deaf ears—Jay didn't even listen. He yelled at her, and called her a slut in front of Pepper—after which he slapped her hard enough that she fell over the back of a couch. Then he stalked out the door and Harmony never saw him again.

It was during that time that Harmony gave up and slept with

Sonny Le Song. His real name was Butch Gussow, but of course you couldn't go on stage in Las Vegas with a name like Butch Gussow. Sonny's gig at the Chevron station was for three days—she would drive by and see him, with his white suit on and the mike in his hand, singing some country-and-western song to three or four old couples—well, somehow it touched her.

In a town where Elvis and Mr. Sinatra sang to millions, over the years, the thought that Sonny wanted to be a singer so badly that he would keep trying, even though it was just to old couples at a Chevron station—couples who were just taking a little break from driving around America in their declining years—well, you had to admire persistence, at least she did.

When it turned out that Jay had no interest in making up—he was soon sleeping with a checker at the Big Bear supermarket—Harmony opened the door a crack to Sonny. She knew it was a mistake, he wasn't her kind of guy, but then her kind of guy wasn't working out too well—it wasn't helpful to Pepper to hear her mother called a slut, not to mention having to watch her get knocked over a couch. She decided that maybe someone with a milder approach would be better, and Sonny seemed mild. She just hadn't reckoned with his problem with rejection, really it was a major problem. Once they finally did become lovers Sonny's problem with rejection took some pretty extreme forms—for example, he expected her to hold his dick all night, if she even took her hand off it long enough to scratch her nose or turn out the bedside light Sonny would begin to feel rejected. At first it was a little endearing, that he wanted her to stay so close, but later it definitely presented some difficulties. He didn't even like Harmony to go to the potty by herself—if she went in her own bathroom and started to close the door he got a desperate look on his face.

"Sonny, I'm just going to the bathroom," she would say, hoping he would see that it was no big deal.

"Do you have to close the door?" Sonny asked.

"Well, it's more private if I close the door," she said. "I don't follow you when you go to the bathroom, do I?"

"No, but I wish you would," Sonny said.

"Sonny, I don't want to watch you use the potty," Harmony said. "I think you should have a little privacy."

"Why, if I don't want it?" he asked.

276

Some of their conversations made Harmony feel a little crazy; they made her realize she should have given Sonny a pass and stuck with her kind of guy. At least none of them got a desperate look in his eye if she needed to use the potty. They hadn't insisted that she hold them by the dick all night, either.

Now Harmony could tell just from a brief moment of eye contact that Sonny Le Song was still a man whose emotions lay close to the surface. Why did I have to meet him? she kept asking herself, or asking God or fate or whatever power had caused Sonny to show up on West Seventy-fifth Street at that particular time. It was probably the one moment in her whole life when she would be on the opposite street corner. But nothing gave back any answer, not Sonny, not the heavens, not anything. The fact was, she met him, in his cowboy boots and his old mashed hat, on a rainy day in New York.

The question that had to be answered was what to do next. Laurie was being very patient, but Harmony could tell that she thought it was a little odd that she would give him so much attention. "Hi, how are you, hope I can see you again when I have more time," would have been Laurie's approach.

"Sonny, could you just give me your phone number?" Harmony asked. "Laurie and I have to get home—but if you'll give me a phone number I'll call you in the morning."

"Babe, if you only knew how I missed you," Sonny said, but at that point Laurie Chalk whipped back into her aggressive New York mode and cut him off.

"Buddy, she said she'd take your number, which I think is certainly generous under the circumstances," Laurie said. "If I were you I'd just give her the number so we can go. She's had a tragedy, you know. She needs to get some rest."

Sonny just ignored Laurie, as if she didn't enter into the matter at all.

"Let's go, Harmony," Laurie said, grabbing her arm. "We asked this man politely to let us be. I don't know what his problem is, but it's his problem, not ours."

"I don't have a phone number," Sonny admitted. "Sometimes if I have a gig they let me sleep under the tables. But I think I'll be getting a situation in the Poconos in about a week. I think things will be looking up."

"You mean you're homeless?" Laurie asked.

"Well, until the situation in the Poconos comes through," Sonny said. "I have a gig tonight though. I expect I'll have a place to sleep tonight."

"Where's the gig?" Laurie asked.

"Way uptown," Sonny said. "It's an old folks' home—a lot of old Jewish grandmothers. They won't turn a nice boy like me out on the streets."

"Well, nice to meet you," Laurie said. "I hope it works out in the Poconos."

Harmony had no idea what the Poconos were—the name just rang no bells. She felt a little torn, though—she *had* offered to call. Maybe knowing Sonny wouldn't be so bad if she could just know him over the telephone. It was pointless, though; he was homeless and had no phone.

"Is it the old folks' home on a Hundred and Tenth Street, south side?" Laurie asked.

"That's it—if you want to come to the show I'm sure I can get you on the list," Sonny said.

Evidently he considered them dumb enough to believe there would be a waiting list for his concert at the Jewish old folks' home. Even Laurie, who lived in New York City and considered herself unshockable, was a little shocked by the novelty of that idea.

"Oh, Mr. Le Song, it's too bad," she said. "We have to get home. Eddie's going to be on the Letterman show tonight, and we promised we'd watch."

A second later she wished she hadn't said it. How was the little dope going to feel? Harmony's five-year-old was going to be on the most popular talk show in America, and Sonny Le Song was singing—*if* he was singing, even that small claim could be a lie—at an old folks' home on 110th Street. Why in God's name did we have to meet him? she asked herself—but, like Harmony, she got no answer.

"I know that old folks' home," Laurie said. "If they let you spend the night they'll let you stay for breakfast. That's when Harmony will call."

Sonny Le Song didn't answer. He just stood on the sidewalk, mute, looking at Harmony with the same needy brown eyes that

278

he had trained on her years ago, when he wanted her to hold his dick in her hand for a few hours.

"Bye, Sonny," Harmony said, as she allowed herself to be led away. After a while she looked back and saw that Sonny was standing right where he had been when they left.

Laurie looked back and saw the same sight.

"We can bring him home if you really want to," she offered.

"I don't really want to," Harmony said.

"Do you still have a soft spot for the guy, or what?" Laurie asked.

Harmony shook her head. It wasn't really a soft spot. Mainly it was just the memory of him singing at the Chevron station that touched her.

"Maybe it was the rhinestones," she said, thinking out loud.

"What rhinestones?" Laurie asked.

"He used to wear rhinestones when he sang country-western," Harmony said.

3.

"**W**ere you in love with that guy?" Laurie asked, once they rounded the corner onto Columbus Avenue. Sonny Le Song still stood right where they left him.

"If there was ever to be a movie of your life Joe Pesci could play him," she added.

"I was never in love with Sonny Le Song," Harmony said. She had been inclined to let the question slide by, but that didn't seem fair; after all, it was an easy question to answer. Of course, Sonny didn't know she had never been in love with him, he was so naive that he assumed women only slept with men they were in love with. He didn't consider sympathy or the hots or any of the various other reasons why a woman might find herself in bed with a guy she wasn't in love with.

"I bet he was in love with you, though—not that that's *your* problem," Laurie said.

"It wouldn't have been my problem if I had walked down another street and never met him," Harmony said.

"It still isn't your problem," Laurie said. "He's a grown man. His clothes were clean. It's not like he's been sleeping under bridges or something. He may have a girlfriend here, for all you know."

"He was always neat," Harmony remembered. As to the question of girlfriends, who could say? Even when Sonny was so in love with her that he hated to leave her side long enough to allow her to answer calls of nature, he still found time to keep in touch with all three of his ex-wives, all of whom lived in Las Vegas. Now and then he would show up in the evenings and she would catch a whiff of a perfume that was not her perfume, but Sonny always maintained that it was fans who had just been particularly enthusiastic about hugging him after his set at the Chevron station or wherever he was performing at the time. Sonny wasn't much of a singer; it was hard to imagine fans being *that* enthusiastic. Now and then she had the suspicion that there might be girlfriends but she didn't really have time to press any investigations.

That was about the time when she was beginning to see Ronnie, who did a lariat act at some of the smaller casinos during the afternoon lull. In fact, she began to have regular dates with Ronnie —he had a blue pickup with a campershell where he kept his ropes, and he was very proud of the fact that he had been able to squeeze a waterbed into his pickup. The waterbed even had a wave mechanism. Harmony wasn't too fond of the wave mechanism; in her experience sex on waterbeds was tricky enough even without the wave mechanism. Particularly it was tricky if you had a guy who had gymnastic expectations of the sex act, as Ronnie did. Still, she and Ronnie had regular dates for a while; crawling into the campershell with Ronnie was pretty exciting—exciting enough at least that the question of whether Sonny had a girlfriend was not uppermost in her mind. She had always been of the live-and-let-live persuasion, herself; one of her problems was that she had never run into a man who was of the same persuasion. Ronnie certainly didn't have a live-and-let-live attitude—he just couldn't take Sonny seriously as a rival, Sonny was too chipmunky. Anyway, Ronnie was totally vain about himself as a lover, so vain that it never dawned on him that a woman who could sleep with him on his waterbed with the wave mechanism would have the slightest interest in sleeping with anyone else at any time for any reason.

"Are you real upset about leaving Sonny on the street?" Laurie asked.

"No," Harmony said. She had begun to feel very tired, though —what she really wanted was to sit down. She felt sort of saggy.

"How far is the subway?" she asked, so tired that she felt like she might be stumbling in a few more steps.

Laurie stopped her for a moment, and felt her forehead.

"I think you're feverish," she said. She immediately waved for a taxi. Before the taxi even started moving again, Harmony closed her eyes.

"I wish we hadn't met Sonny," she said, as they were walking up Laurie's stairs. "I know I'm going to think about him now."

When they got to Laurie's apartment nobody was there. While Laurie was making tea Harmony took off her clothes and wrapped up in an old bathrobe Laurie loaned her. She lay down for a minute, to wait for the tea, and when she opened her eyes again Eddie was sleeping in the bed with her—he had his pajamas on, too. She awoke to a New York morning, and the smell of tea. Laurie had put a big cup of tea on the bedside table. Eddie was still asleep, and so was Sheba. Laurie sat in a rocking chair by the bed. She had just washed her short brown hair and was rubbing it with a towel.

When Harmony was a little more awake she noticed that there were tears on Laurie's cheeks.

"What's the matter, honey?" she asked.

"Just the same thing," Laurie said. "Just the same thing that's always going to be the matter."

She rubbed her wet hair again, and then put her face in the towel for a moment.

"Don't mind me, drink your tea," she said. "Everyone said Eddie was terrific on Letterman."

Harmony felt surprisingly rested. She felt like it might be a day when she could get Eddie dressed, and make him a waffle, if Laurie had a waffle iron. She also felt it was time to have a few goals. One goal—the main goal, at the moment—would be to go home.

"Laurie, could we go to Oklahoma today?" she asked, whispering so as not to wake up Eddie and Sheba.

Laurie looked a little startled by the question.

"Have I upset you?" she asked. "I was really hoping we could have more time. We haven't got to talk about Pepper very much."

"Laurie, I didn't mean go without you," Harmony said. "I want you to come too."

Then she remembered Sonny Le Song.

282

"Laurie, can I get the number of that old folks' home?" Harmony asked. "I think I better call Sonny. If I don't I'll feel guilty all day."

"You don't have to feel guilty, and you don't need the number," Laurie said. "Look out the window.

"I'll go with you to Oklahoma," she said. Then she put her face in the towel again.

Harmony got out of bed and hugged her. Laurie made room for Harmony in the rocking chair—fortunately it was a large rocking chair. Harmony hugged Laurie real close, while Laurie sobbed. Laurie was too thin—probably she hadn't been eating correctly since Pepper's death.

While she was rocking Laurie, Eddie opened his eyes and took in the scene. Harmony put her finger to her lips, to let Eddie know that she and Laurie were sharing a private moment. She hoped that Eddie would be patient and not pop up and start making breakfast demands until Laurie had had an opportunity to pour out a little more of her sorrow. After all, that was why they had come to New York and accidentally made it possible for Iggy to fall off the Statue of Liberty: so she and Laurie could grieve together about the girl they had both lost.

Eddie seemed to understand perfectly—he lay very still, with a solemn look on his face. Iggy was sleeping at his feet, which was a good thing. With Eddie and Iggy both awake there was going to be some noise: they were little boys, after all.

Finally Laurie calmed, and just in time too, because Eddie reached the end of being able to be still. He began to tickle Sheba on the neck, pretending that his fingers were a spider. Sheba twitched and kept on sleeping but Harmony knew it wouldn't last long; pretty soon Sheba would have to accept the fact that Eddie wanted her to wake up.

"Did you see them?" Laurie asked, when she wiped away her tears with the wet towel that smelled of shampoo. Laurie even managed a smile at Eddie.

"See who?" Harmony asked. Then she remembered that she had forgotten to look out the window.

"Don't ask me how he found us, but he found us," Laurie said.

Harmony looked down: Sonny Le Song was sitting on the steps of a building across the street. Her sister Pat sat on one side of him, and her sister Neddie sat on the other. All three were smoking, and all three had Styrofoam coffee cups in their hands.

About that time Eddie popped out of bed and looked out the window too.

"Who's that person, he looks like a chipmunk, Mom?" Eddie asked.

"His name is Sonny," Harmony said. "I used to know him before you were born."

"Oh, then it was a real long time ago," Eddie said. Then he wandered back to the bed and did some more spider fingers on Sheba's neck. After he had done the spider fingers for a while, Sheba began to twitch. Finally she rolled on her back.

"Who doing spider fingers on me?" she asked, without opening her eyes.

Harmony stood at the window, looking down at Neddie, Pat, and Sonny Le Song.

"I guess your Aunt Pat has started smoking again," she said.

4.

When Neddie and Pat brought Sonny up to Laurie's apartment Harmony got a little irate for a minute; if there was one thing she wasn't going to tolerate it was the idea that some little jerk of a lounge singer, who could only get gigs by singing at old folks' homes or for the openings of gas stations, was following her around.

"Sonny, I never thought you'd turn into a stalker, if you are one I never want to see you again!" Harmony informed him, to the astonishment of everyone, even G., who was so impressed by the anger in Harmony's voice that his black beard began to twitch. Otis had been dozing behind a chair; he didn't really wake up but he did pull the hood of his parka over his head.

"No, no, no," Sonny said, in response to the stalking charge.

He said no several more times before he could get Harmony calm enough so he could explain how he happened to be sitting across the street from Laurie's place, with Neddie and Pat. His explanation was that when he found out Pepper was in town he waited outside one of her rehearsals and introduced himself and walked her home.

"Then how come she didn't mention it to me?" Laurie asked, skeptically.

"If she walked home with a friend of her mother's I think she would have mentioned it," Laurie said.

"Not if it was me," Sonny said. "I'm the kind of guy who seldom gets mentioned."

Before anyone could stop him, Sonny Le Song sank into despair, mainly at the thought of his own lack of mentionability.

"I haven't been mentioned in years," he said, his face growing longer and longer. Even with his face at its longest he still looked a lot like a chipmunk.

"Mom, you made him sad," Eddie said. "Say something so he won't be sad."

But it was too late.

"I haven't been mentioned since my mother's funeral," Sonny said. "Even then the minister got me mixed up with my half brother."

"Well, you poor soul," Neddie said. "That's awful."

"I do have nine half brothers," Sonny said. "I know it's a lot to remember."

To everyone's horror, he began to cry. Soon tears were dripping off his chin, onto the lapel of his trench coat.

"Oh, Sonny, I didn't mean it, I know you're not a stalker," Harmony said. She went over and hugged him—what else could she do? Even while she was hugging him she felt a little annoyed, though—not so much at Sonny as at life. Why, with all her troubles, and no certainties in sight anywhere except Eddie, did she have to be the one to make it up to Sonny Le Song because he wasn't mentionable? The truth was, he seemed even less mentionable than he had been when he was working in Las Vegas. What was she supposed to do about it?

"Not only that, I lost my clippings," Sonny said. "Now I don't even have my clippings. At least when I had my clippings I had something to show to groups that might need an entertainer."

"I see what you mean—just showing them yourself probably wouldn't convince them," Pat said. Harmony suspected that she was in one of her surly moods.

"Pat, why do you have to kick him while he's down?" Harmony asked.

286

"Where did you lose your clippings?" Eddie asked. "Maybe we can just all go and find them. It can be like an Easter egg hunt."

"Hey, he's like his mother—tries to be helpful," Sonny said.

"So how did you lose them, Sonny?" Harmony asked. She herself had drifted off from her own clippings several years earlier. For a while they had been in the bottom drawer of her chest of drawers, which she usually kept in the bedroom. But her bedrooms kept shrinking once she wasn't working steady; it became harder and harder to fit a large chest of drawers into her apartments. Finally, at a time when she was approaching the eight-dollar level in her bank account—that was the time when Eddie had a bad infection; doctor bills were mounting up—she agreed to let Myrtle put the chest of drawers in her permanent floating garage sale, just to see if anybody wanted it. To everyone's surprise an old man heading home from Wisconsin stopped by the garage sale and bought the chest of drawers. He just put it in the back of his pickup and headed on to Wisconsin.

After that, two or three weeks passed before it dawned on Harmony that she had forgotten to remove her clippings from the chest of drawers. For about an hour it was a terrible shock—after all, those clippings were a record of her whole life in Las Vegas. They were the sort of thing Eddie might have wanted to look at someday, when he was in the mood to know what his mother had been like when she was younger.

But then a few days passed and instead of feeling sad about the loss of her clippings, she began to get a little perspective; in a way it was a relief not to have the clippings anymore, she would be less likely to be reminded of what a comparatively glamorous life she had led before she got too old to be a showgirl and had to go to work at the recycling plant. After all, she still had quite a few scrapbooks that she kept on a shelf in her closet—she could always look at the scrapbooks if she wanted to remember what she had looked like in the years of her youth and beauty. Eddie could look at them too, and in fact did, from time to time, if he happened to be using the bar in her closet as a jungle gym or something.

Then a miracle happened: The old man got home to Wisconsin and started to put his socks or his underwear or something into the bottom drawer of the nice chest of drawers he had bought at a garage sale in Las Vegas. There were Harmony's clippings. The

287

old man wrapped the clippings in brown paper and tied them neatly with a string and sent them to the Stardust casino—by a miracle Jackie Bonventre's daughter, Josie, was working in the mailroom the day the package came in—Josie was kind enough to bring it to her.

The clippings were doomed, though; during their short stay in Wisconsin Harmony had stopped caring whether she had them or not. By chance she had a very jealous boyfriend at the time, named Monty; it was hard to describe Monty other than to say that his nose had been broken four times and he was very jealous. He hated the fact that Harmony had had a time of youth and beauty and had spent some of it with other men; thanks to his feeling that all her years of youth and beauty and sex—particularly sex—should have been his, Monty developed a resentful attitude toward her clippings and one day while she was at the recycling plant the whole package of clippings got mixed up with a couple of months' accumulation of racing forms, all of which he threw out. Harmony didn't exactly hold it against Monty; it was only thanks to a miracle that the clippings had made it back from Wisconsin anyway.

It was plain from the look on Sonny's face that he had not yet acquired a good perspective on his own lost clippings, though.

"It's hopeless," he said. "I lost them over a year ago—left them on a bus in Utica. I was up there entertaining at a bowling tournament."

Harmony had a brief vision of Sonny trying to sing his little off-key ballads over the sound of crashing bowling pins. It would be even worse than customers at the Chevron station slamming down hoods or revving up their motors to see if their radiators were sturdy enough to make the trip across the desert.

"I went home with this girl I met," Sonny said. Harmony was hoping he wouldn't launch into graphic descriptions of his love life, not with Eddie standing there, five years old and all ears.

"We were taking the bus, she didn't have no car, she wasn't really a girl, she was a little bit older," Sonny went on, recalling the tragic scene of the bus ride in Utica, and the girl, and his clippings. But the memory became too difficult; he began to gulp and his eyes watered again.

"I guess I left them on the bus, it's what I get for chasing skirts," he said, and then he sort of collapsed in Harmony's arms and sobbed and sobbed.

"Saddest man I've met in a *while*," Otis said.

Omar seemed to agree. "Saddest mans in town," he remarked.

Eddie was walking around in circles, wearing the goofy look he often wore when he walked around in circles. Iggy, thinking something must be up, was walking around in circles, too, right at Eddie's heels.

"Mom, I know what might cheer him up," Eddie remarked. "We could take him to Washington with us and maybe he could sing for the President and Mrs. President."

"I don't think so, Eddie," Laurie said, horrified at the prospect of Sonny Le Song arriving unannounced at the White House, expecting to sing.

"You have to have a very special invitation before you can sing at the White House," she added.

"Honey, couldn't we go in the bedroom?" Sonny asked, lifting his face to Harmony. "I hate to cry my eyes out in front of all these people—some of them don't even know me."

Harmony had a different interpretation of why Sonny suddenly wanted to go in the bedroom, and it wasn't because he wanted to hide his tears. After she had been hugging him for a few minutes she felt something male bumping against her lower thigh. The little jerk was actually taking advantage of her sympathy hug to the extent of getting a hard-on, never mind that her son and most of her family were three feet away. Of course he still had his trench coat on, nobody was going to notice that Sonny was bumping himself against her leg.

What she could do about that was end the hug, which she did. If Sonny had recovered enough to be thinking about going to bed with her, then it was time all of them forgot his lost clippings and went on with their day. After all, there were some big decisions to be made—for example, who was going to Oklahoma and when and how.

"Sonny, just have some tea," she said. From the look on his face she could tell that he was a good deal more upset by her refusal to go into the bedroom with him than by the knowledge that he had left his clippings on a bus in Utica.

"I don't know about the rest of you, but I need to get started

289

home on the plains today," Neddie said. "I may have to hitchhike but I'm heading that way. I'm getting the urge to smell the prairie breeze."

"We already said we were going, you don't have to clobber us with sentimental speeches," Pat said.

"Can I come?" Sonny asked—Harmony knew he was just thinking of bedrooms he might get her in down the road.

Harmony did a quick head count, arriving at the figure of twelve.

"There's twelve of us, if we all go," she said.

"The whole population of Tarwater is just two hundred and thirty-five," Neddie said. "They'll have to do a new census, once we get there."

"This is absurd," Laurie said. "What are all of us going to do in Tarwater?"

"Some of the titty bars in Tulsa don't have much in the way of singers," Pat observed. "Maybe Sonny could support us by singing in titty bars."

"Pat, he lost his clippings, he might not be able to get a job," Harmony said. The thought of Sonny tagging along made her nervous. Her sisters didn't know him like she did; if she even relaxed for a moment and put her arm around him he'd be bumping his hard-on against some part of her.

"First of all, we should ask G.," Laurie said. "It's his bus. What if he doesn't want to take us to Oklahoma—then what do we do?"

G. failed to respond. He was looking out the window, and wore an inscrutable expression.

"G. is not going, due to worries about leaving family," Omar said. "G. has one dozen children."

"By how many wives—is he one of them bigamists?" Pat asked. "Just from looking at him . . ."

"G. has only one wife," Omar said. "He is not going to Oklahoma."

"He is going to Oklahoma," Salah said. "He is confiding in me a desire to see America. Will accept small fee."

Omar was annoyed because Salah had contradicted him.

"Give me back my taxicab," he said.

"Taxicab is in Bayonne," Salah reminded him.

290

"Give me back the key," Omar said. "Go be shoeshine boy. Abdul will drive the cab now."

"Abdul is passionate boy, only wanting women," Salah said.

Abdul, the passionate boy, had developed a terrible crush on Laurie Chalk.

"I am going to die when Laurie dies," he said, to everyone's surprise.

"Abdul, you don't have to," Laurie assured him.

Just at that moment Sheba danced out of the bedroom. She had already done her makeup, and looked snappy.

"Good morning," Eddie said—he liked Sheba.

"Good morning, Bright," Sheba said. "Man, I like this sleeping in beds."

"I think we have to settle the question of whether G. wants to take us anywhere," Laurie said. "We need to sit down and discuss this sanely."

"Discuss what?" Neddie asked.

"Well, our next move, or the rest of our lives," Laurie said. "There's twelve of us and we all just met. We're from different places and we don't know one another very well. It's worked fine so far, but what if it stops working when we're in the middle of Tennessee?"

Eddie had been walking around in circles, but he stopped and got the tough look in his eye that he sometimes got when he didn't like the direction a conversation was going.

"I mean, what if we all start hating one another's guts, in a day or two?" Laurie asked.

Harmony saw her point. Unusual circumstances had brought them together. It was true that lots of things fizzled and went bad; that would describe every romance she had ever had. It was nice to think they could all just get on a bus and set off for Oklahoma and be friends forever, but what if it didn't work out that way?

"She don't want us to go," Otis observed, mildly.

"That isn't it, Otis," Laurie said. "It's not about not wanting any one of us to go. I don't know that I want to go myself, but, by the same token, I don't know that I *don't* want to go. We're all from different places—I'm just worried."

"She's right, I might be missing Jersey City pretty soon," Sheba said. "I ain't never lived noplace but Jersey City—Oklahoma don't mean shit to me."

"I mean, we don't all *have* to go," Laurie said. "It's like an option we should all consider for a few minutes."

"Those words are *wrong*, we do all have to go!" Eddie said. It was startling how emphatic he could be when he put his mind to it.

"We *do* all have to go and we have to go *today*!" Eddie added.

"Well, but why, Eddie?" Laurie asked. "Why do we all have to go?"

"Because that's what families do," Eddie said. "They go on trips together, with their dogs."

"Bright's got an answer for everything," Sheba said, smiling at Laurie.

"If we go off down to Oklahoma, time we get back somebody else have the Dumpster," Otis said, looking at Sheba.

"Let 'em have it, who wants to live in an old rotten-egg Dumpster anyway," Sheba said.

All of a sudden G. delivered himself of a long statement in his native tongue. Because of his deep voice, everyone listened. The only person who wasn't listening was Sonny, who was offering Harmony little smiles, obviously hoping she would soften up, take him into the bedroom, and do something about his hard-on.

"What is he saying?" Laurie asked.

"G. is saying he needs to change the oil in school bus," Omar informed her. "Then he is saying he wants to see America, Washington Monument and giant redwoods. He is requesting that we leave in one hour's time."

"I'm for that," Neddie said.

"Hey, I know how to change the oil in a school bus," Pat said, fluffing her hair. "I drove a school bus for years. Maybe I'll go with G."

Laurie got up, looking upset, and went into her bedroom. Harmony decided she ought to see what was wrong. When she got in the bedroom Laurie was staring at herself in the mirror.

"Laurie, are you upset that we're all going?" Harmony asked.

"No, it's Abdul—do you ever wish you could make yourself less attractive?" Laurie asked.

"Laurie, it's just a crush," Harmony told her.

"I wish I could be completely plain," Laurie said. "I'd like to pass unnoticed through life from now on."

Harmony was a little shocked by what Laurie said, and by the way Laurie was looking in the mirror. Lots of times she had looked in her own mirror and hadn't exactly seen herself looking her best. There had been mornings when she was hung over; she wasn't a big drinker but now and then she forgot to stop drinking and went on until she was really drunk. There had been mornings when guys had punched her, or mornings when she had cried for an hour or two for no reason—probably she cried just because life was the way it was. There had been mornings since Eddie arrived when the complications in the way of female problems meant that her color wasn't too good. But at least her hope had always been to be attractive, if not immediately, then later in the day. She had every intention of doing her best to look attractive—maybe it was just her showgirl training.

But Laurie obviously meant what she said; she wished to make herself less attractive.

"Is it because you don't want to be hit on by guys?" Harmony asked.

"*Or* girls," Laurie said. "I don't want to be hit on by anyone. When someone acts like they think I'm attractive I get real disturbed. I was happy about being a girl while Pepper was alive, but now I'm not."

"People will always be able to tell that you're nice, Laurie," Harmony said.

"I try to be, but I don't think I am, really," Laurie said.

"Well, we're not angels," Harmony said. "Gary says that. In fact he says it about forty times a day."

"Who's Gary?" Laurie asked.

"He's my best friend—he's a costume manager," Harmony said. "Didn't Pepper tell you about him?"

"Nope—she didn't like to talk about Las Vegas," Laurie said. "Pepper wasn't a big talker. Dancing was her way of talking."

Even so, Harmony felt sad. She couldn't help drooping a little. If Pepper didn't like to talk about Las Vegas it was probably because she hadn't really liked the part of her life that she lived at home. Harmony felt some of her old guilts rising—why *should* Pepper have liked it particularly? They moved too much, they never had a car, guys came and went—it probably hadn't been that enjoyable a home environment, and whose fault was that?

"Don't look so gloomy, we have to decide about Oklahoma," Laurie said. "You were a good mom, and I'm a nice person. I don't want us to get the mopes, not right now."

"Okay," Harmony said—nonetheless, her spirits weren't as high as they had been when she got up. It only took a chance remark to remind her of all her mistakes, and Laurie had made the chance remark. Harmony couldn't help thinking how hurt Gary would be if he knew Pepper hadn't even mentioned him to the woman she lived with. Gary adored Pepper, he would go into a major decline if he knew Pepper had just sort of forgotten him once she moved away.

"This trip seems like madness," Laurie said. "What are any of us going to do in Oklahoma?"

"Meet my family," Harmony said. "I think you might like Billy, he has a good sense of humor."

"Who's Billy?" Laurie asked. She picked up a brush and began to brush her hair.

"My brother—he's in jail for making obscene phone calls," Harmony said.

Laurie shook her head, but at least she smiled.

"I thought you were trying to sell me on this trip," she said.

"I am, but Billy being in jail just happened to be the first detail that popped into my mind," Harmony said.

"If that's the first detail, maybe you better not hit me with any more," Laurie said. "One or two more details like that and I might decide to do something sensible, such as stay here and get a job."

"Laurie, you have to come," Harmony said. "Eddie would be heartbroken if you don't."

"Or else he'd be mad as hell," Laurie said, smiling. "Would you come with me to the record store before we leave? I want to pick out some tapes."

5.

Harmony decided she was not inviting Sonny Le Song to go to Oklahoma with them no matter what—she had only included him in the count of twelve because he happened to be standing there. The fact that he had already had the nerve to make a sexual overture was highly annoying.

Then it turned out that Pat and Neddie had invited him earlier that morning, while they were all having coffee. That was pretty annoying too—what business did her sisters think they had inviting her old boyfriends to go places?

"If we take him with us I'll have to introduce him to Mom and Dad," Harmony pointed out, while they were examining their clothes to see if they had any clean enough to get across America in.

"So what? We'll have to introduce this whole zoo to Mom and Dad anyway," Pat said. "They're gonna think a lunatic asylum showed up on the porch."

"They're gonna be right, too," Neddie said. "I don't care, though. I just want to get home and smell the breeze."

"If it's blowing in the wrong direction all you'll smell is the fertilizer plant," Pat said.

"Pat, you don't know Sonny," Harmony said. "He doesn't have a cent and the only jobs he can get is to sing in old folks' homes."

"Good, he can sing to Mom and Dad then," Pat said. "Don't gripe at me. All I did was be friendly to your old sweetheart."

"Are you sure it was just friendly?" Harmony asked.

Pat stopped raking through the pile of wrinkled clothes in her suitcase and looked annoyed.

"Harmony, he's not my type," she said.

"That's odd," Neddie said.

"Why is it odd—don't I have a right to a type?" Pat asked.

"Sure, but out of a hundred guys you can usually find ninety-nine that are your type," Neddie said.

While they were packing, Eddie and Iggy ran up and down Ninth Street with two little Chinese girls they met in front of a bakery. Everyone on the street recognized Eddie and Iggy from their TV appearances—several people stopped to wish them well. Pat and Neddie chatted with some ladies outside a beauty shop. Meanwhile, G. insisted that all baggage be strapped to the top of the bus, although it was a big school bus and there was lots of room inside. None of them had much luggage. Sonny Le Song didn't even have a clean shirt. He just had a toothbrush and a razor.

"Omar, why do the suitcases have to go on top?" Harmony asked. "All Eddie's stuffed animals are in that big suitcase. If they blow away he's going to be really upset."

"G. is from Bangladesh, suitcases must go on top of bus," Omar assured her. "G. is saving room, there may be more peoples coming."

"Forget that," Laurie said. "We've got quite enough peoples here right now and half of us aren't too sure about this trip, anyway."

"Yeah, me," Sheba said. "Don't they have cows in Oklahoma?"

"Any kind you want," Neddie said.

"I don't want *no* kind," Sheba said. "I don't want no cowboys, either."

Harmony thought Sheba and Otis looked the most scared. The turban men seemed happy to throw in their lot with Pat and Neddie and herself, but Sheba and Otis looked like frightened chil-

296

dren. For a moment Harmony thought they shouldn't even go, but then she remembered what they had been doing when she met them. Sheba was a parking lot whore and Otis had been sniffing glue in a Dumpster. Going to Oklahoma might give them a little different perspective.

Just as she was worrying that maybe it was wrong to take Sheba and Otis out of their lives, even though they didn't have great lives, Eddie came dashing up at top speed and jumped up into Sheba's arms. As soon as Sheba had a good grip on him he leaned back and gave Otis a high five. Otis smiled and they did a little high-five game that Otis had taught Eddie. The little Chinese girls, their black hair neatly combed, stood on the sidewalk watching.

"Aren't those little Chinese girls cute?" Neddie asked. "There's Asian people in Tulsa—they're real good at science."

Pat came walking up with Sonny Le Song. They had gone to a T-shirt stand two blocks up and bought Sonny some T-shirts, so at least he could make a clean appearance on the trip.

"Pat's a sucker, I bet she shelled out the money for those T-shirts," Neddie said, observing her sister. "There's nothing she'd rather do than steal one of your boyfriends, either."

"He's not my boyfriend, Neddie," Harmony said. "Every man I bump into on the street is not my boyfriend."

"That's not how Mom will look at it," Neddie said. "How she'll look at it is how you brought home this deadbeat who doesn't have a dime and you'll expect her to feed him."

"I don't expect her to feed him," Harmony said. "I don't even expect her to feed me."

"If you think Mom was tight when we were growing up, you ought to see her now," Neddie said.

"Neddie, don't talk to me about it, I don't want to be discouraged before I even start," Harmony said. Then she stepped on the school bus and almost immediately had to break up a fistfight between Omar, Salah, and Sonny Le Song, all of whom assumed that they would get to sit by her during the trip. Omar started to sit by her and Sonny practically knocked him over in his effort to get there first.

"That's my seat," he said. But he didn't quite dare sit down, because Harmony was glaring at him.

297

"I was sitting here—lady is teaching me English lessons," Salah said.

"Give me key to taxicab," Omar thundered. Evidently he was still mad about the insult.

"I want to sit by Laurie, if you gentlemen don't mind," Harmony said, to all three men. "You need to be a little better mannered. We have a long trip ahead."

Sonny Le Song got a puzzled look on his face; probably he had figured out that Laurie was gay. Feeling as he did about his own dick, it was no doubt a big shock that a woman he was interested in would rather sit by someone who was gay than sit by him.

Laurie was the last one on the bus; she looked a little wistful at the thought that she was leaving the streets of New York. Harmony could understand that; people got dependent on their routines. Time after time she had stayed with some guy mainly because he had managed to become a habit. Obviously Sonny Le Song was hoping to become a habit again—little did he know he had no chance.

"Mom, I'm going to sit with Sheba, she's never been on a trip before and she's scared," Eddie said. "Iggy and I are going to stay with her all the way to Oklahoma so she won't be scared."

"He has the sweetest impulses," Laurie said, looking at Eddie fondly. She managed to ruffle his curls, as he was passing down the aisle toward Sheba and Otis.

"I wish he got to see his father more," Harmony said. It was one of the sorrows of her life that Eddie, who deserved excellent fathering if any little boy ever did, had had no father to speak of. She tried never to mention his father to him—if she did he got a hopeful look in his eyes; she couldn't bear to see the hopeful look in Eddie's eyes because it meant that he was only going to be disappointed.

Harmony had been dreading the tunnel so much that G. agreed to leave Manhattan Island by way of the George Washington Bridge. Laurie worked it out with him. G. was respectful of Laurie and always did what she asked.

Harmony was glad they were going over a bridge rather than through a tunnel. It also meant that she got to have a peaceful look at New York City, as the bus made its way from downtown to uptown. As she looked out and saw all the people on the streets,

298

old and young, fat and thin, blond and dark, rich and poor, she had the sense that she was leaving New York before she had even arrived. It wasn't that New York hadn't been there, with all its noise and beauty, its buildings and taxicabs, it was that *she* hadn't been there. She had only brushed by the city; she hadn't been able to be there because events had removed her from herself—she had been a little like a ghost during her hours in New York. She thought that maybe someday, when Eddie was grown and she didn't have responsibilities, she could come back to New York and mingle with the people, as she had mingled with people in the casinos all her life. Just mingle, walk, have a cup of coffee here and a bagel there, chat a little, hear about people's problems, maybe mention a few of her own if she happened to sit by someone who had a friendly ear; it could be an old lady in a coffee shop, it could be a guy waiting for a bus—it could be anyone. She had the fantasy, as the bus was going up Sixth Avenue, that maybe she and Laurie Chalk would stay friends for the rest of their lives, so that someday she could come back; then the two of them could walk around New York together. Maybe on that visit she could connect with all the things she hadn't been able to connect with this time, because of her ghostly state.

"I'm getting a little excited," Laurie said, with a smile. "Despite myself, I am. It's going to be an adventure, isn't it?"

"I hope it's a good adventure," Harmony said. "I hope we don't go off in a canyon or something, like my trailer did."

"I haven't heard about many canyons between here and Oklahoma," Laurie said. "I wonder if we could stop and buy a map, at some point. I'm not sure G. understands where Oklahoma is."

"Neddie will tell him, she's a homebody," Harmony commented. "She's not going to go past it or anything."

When Laurie smiled she was very appealing. It was easy for Harmony to see why Pepper had fallen in love; what wasn't so easy to see was why Pepper hadn't let the boys go and just had a life with Laurie. She knew, though, that Pepper's problems with boys weren't anything she should dwell on. They were about to go onto the George Washington Bridge—she wanted to take a last look at New York. When she was sixteen she had fully intended to go to New York to seek her fortune; it was just an accident that she chose Las Vegas instead. The accident had occurred because Con-

299

tinental Trailways was giving a special discount on tickets to Las Vegas—undoubtedly the casinos had made some sort of deal with them, to encourage people to head that way. It had worked for Harmony, she didn't really have enough money for a ticket all the way to New York. Her plan had been to stop and work for a few months in some city like Chattanooga or Baltimore; in a few months she should be able to save enough to get a bus ticket on to New York. But the special rate at Trailways made it so much easier to get to Las Vegas that she got on that bus instead of the bus going east.

Now she was on a bus going west again, out of the city she had missed because Continental Trailways had offered special prices, all those years ago, before she even had a real boyfriend. Of course she had done well in Las Vegas; well professionally at least. She had no skills to speak of; she could type a little but she couldn't do shorthand; she had not been particularly employable, except as a showgirl. Fortunately being a showgirl didn't require any skill except good looks.

"We're crossing the Hudson," Laurie said.

The George Washington Bridge was so large that you couldn't just look down off it, as you could most bridges. Harmony had to look far away to see water. Then they got off the bridge and sort of swung around into some other state; Harmony wasn't quite sure which state it might be, but she did look out the window at the great buildings of Manhattan one more time. For a moment she felt a keen regret—she felt she might have made a wrong choice, all those years ago; maybe if she had not been tempted by the cheap ticket and had come to New York she would have had a better life—it wasn't just herself she was thinking of, either; it was her children. New Yorkers all seemed so ambitious, maybe she could have developed ambitions too, if she had come there as a young woman. She might have managed to go to college, at least she could have taken Spanish classes or something—she had always meant to learn Spanish but she never had; once she had done a show in Acapulco for two weeks, but still she had felt handicapped by not being able to talk to the Mexican people.

Mainly what Harmony felt, as she looked across the Hudson at the great city she had missed, was that if she hadn't missed it she

300

might have done better by her children: Eddie might have a father who cared about him, and Pepper might not be dead. Gary was right when he said that most of the guys in Las Vegas were jerk-offs. It was a pessimistic view for sure, but there was a lot of truth in it. Harmony had always tried to be a nice woman, and yet she had never really even been able to find a man who cared enough about her to help her raise her children. Gary was the man who had helped her the most—by far the most, in fact—and Gary was gay. Probably the person who had meant the most to Pepper, her daughter, was the girl sitting beside her, Laurie, who was also gay; what that said to Harmony was that the fact that you slept with a member of the opposite sex didn't make you a helpful person necessarily.

Then Eddie came up the aisle of the bus and crawled up in her lap. He had a solemn look on his face.

"Sheba's sad, Mom," he said. "She doesn't want to leave her friends. What are we going to do?"

"Well, you didn't want to leave your friends, either," Harmony reminded him. "You were very sad about it, but you got over it in a few days."

Eddie looked at her with his most solemn look, and shook his head.

"No, I *didn't* get over it," he said. "I'm still sad. I wish I could be on the bus with Eli, going to my school."

"I guess I was just hoping you were over it so I wouldn't have to feel guilty."

"Well," Eddie said, brightening a little, "you won't have to feel guilty if you'll let me see the President and Mrs. President."

"That solves *your* problem, but what about Sheba's?" Laurie asked. "She doesn't really want to go to Oklahoma, does she?"

"No, she wants to get off the bus," Eddie said. "Otis does too. They're afraid somebody will get their Dumpster if they leave."

Harmony got up and went to the back of the bus, leaving Eddie with Laurie Chalk. Sheba was crying and Otis looked bleak. Harmony was remembering that Gary had almost been hit by a taxicab when he jumped out of the car. They were on a pretty big freeway —for sure she didn't want to take any chances of Sheba and Otis getting hit by cars.

"Honey, you don't have to go to Oklahoma," Harmony said. "You don't have to go anywhere, if you don't want to. Eddie's going to miss you, but he'll get over it."

"No, I won't," Eddie said—he had followed her to the rear of the bus. "I'll never get over it, but I don't want Sheba to be sad. And I don't want Otis to lose the Dumpster."

"Probably already gone," Otis said. "Ten people probably living in it now."

"Yeah, all of them your girlfriends—dumb sluts," Sheba said. Even so she was holding Otis's hand.

"I don't want to leave Bright and I don't want to leave you, because you kind," Sheba said, looking at Harmony sadly. "Nobody's been kind to me like you have, letting me stay in your room right off the bat. But me and Otis be like fish out of water, down in Oklahoma. They ain't gonna like two New Jersey niggers coming in on them. How we going to make a living down there?"

Eddie crawled up in Sheba's lap, and clung to her, sobbing.

"I hate to lose my friends," he said. "I hate to lose Sheba, most of all."

"Oh, Bright," Sheba said, hugging him.

"We might not be able to find no Dumpster, in Oklahoma," Otis said—obviously leaving the Dumpster had been a big step, for him.

Harmony felt overwhelmed. She gave up, and went back to sit with Laurie. Eddie's big thing was keeping people together, yet it was the one thing his own mother had never been able to manage. Despite her best intentions, she had never been able to keep even three people together for very long, much less a busload.

"I don't know what to do," she said, to Laurie.

"Eddie got attached, and so did Sheba and Otis," Laurie said. "Maybe I can talk them into going at least as far as Washington—we could send them back on a bus."

She went back to chat with Sheba and Otis, and when she did Sonny Le Song immediately sat down in her seat beside Harmony.

"That's Laurie's seat," Harmony informed him immediately. Omar glared at him and Salah stood up and shook his fist.

"Oh, sit down, Salah," Harmony said. "I'll make him move when Laurie comes back."

302

Sonny Le Song got the look on his face that he always got when his feelings were close to the surface, but Harmony didn't care. She wasn't about to let him sit in Laurie's seat.

"I don't want to sit by you and I didn't invite you to Oklahoma, either," she said. "And I don't care how close to the surface your feelings are."

"Your sisters invited me," Sonny said. "They took pity on me because I'm down on my luck. You used to take pity but I guess you ain't got a soft spot for old Sonny, anymore."

Harmony didn't say anything—she knew him well enough to know that talk would only make him worse.

"Is it because I made a pass?" he asked. "I know it was bad timing, but I miss you so much I couldn't help it."

Harmony kept silent—New York City was receding in the distance. She still felt her regret when she saw the tall buildings growing dim behind them.

"Remember when you used to come to the Chevron to hear me sing?" Sonny asked. "The guys at the gas station thought I was lucky, to have the prettiest showgirl in Las Vegas check out my gig."

Why is this man talking to me, what does he think it will change? Harmony thought. She kept a close watch on his hands, while she maintained her silence.

"Harmony, I was missing you *that way*," Sonny said. "That's what caused the bad timing."

"Sonny, it wasn't the pass, it's that I have absolutely no interest in having you in my life right now," Harmony said. She knew it would sound like total rejection, but she didn't care. He shouldn't have been so quick to take Laurie's seat. Besides that, he had shown up outside Laurie's apartment—in her book it was stalking; she had had other old boyfriends stalk her on occasion and it was not something she could feel tolerant about in her present state.

Sonny looked at her as if he was about to cry, but this time she knew he wasn't about to cry; mainly what she saw in his look was belligerence; he didn't like it that she said what she said about not wanting him to be in her life anymore. The bottom line, in her view, was that Sonny Le Song was a jerk-off from Cleveland or Wyoming or somewhere and he wanted to be the one to decide whether he got to be in her life or not. How dare he poke his dick at her leg when her sisters and her son were both in the room, it would have been rude enough if nobody had been in the room.

"You never used to be so hard-hearted when you were younger," Sonny commented—definitely she heard some belligerence in his voice. Probably Sonny was smart enough to realize that bursting into tears wasn't going to work, not with Harmony, not at the present moment, so he switched to the macho mode instead.

Harmony didn't respond to the hard-hearted comment—why should she? Saying goodbye to Sheba and Otis was going to be sad; she had no space in her to worry about whether Sonny Le Song thought she was hard-hearted. She knew he was just trying to make her feel guilty enough to sleep with him at some point; the first time they were alone or even if they weren't alone he would be shoving it against her leg again, or against whatever part of her he could reach.

Laurie came walking back up the aisle. When she saw Sonny in her seat she got an annoyed look on her face. She came on along the aisle and tapped Sonny on the shoulder.

"Can I help you?" he said, looking up at Laurie as if he had never seen her before.

"Yes, you can help me, you can give me back my seat please," Laurie said.

Sonny stood up and peered at the seat as if he were looking for something, but he didn't move into the aisle so Laurie could sit down.

"I don't see no name on this seat," he said, in a tone that was neither friendly nor polite. "It don't say reserved for dykes or nothing. Maybe you better sit somewhere else, honey."

Laurie flushed with embarrassment, she didn't know how to react but Harmony reacted: she stood up and punched Sonny in the mouth as hard as she could, which was hard enough to split his lower lip open—it might have split his upper lip too if there had been any upper lip to split. It was a solid enough punch that it knocked him across the aisle into the seats on the other side of the bus.

"You ditsy cunt, you busted my lip!" Sonny said. He put his hand to his mouth and looked at the blood on his fingers.

"Watch your language, buddy, there's a child on this bus!" Laurie said. Sonny tried to slap her, but he was off balance and Laurie was on guard—the slap didn't come anywhere close. Then Sheba came dashing up the aisle; evidently Sheba *really* disliked Sonny: she waded right in and punched him in the eye.

"You black whore!" he said, but before he could say more Omar and Salah pounced on him, and Otis rushed up to help Sheba; it was such a melee that all Harmony could see of Sonny was the blood on his shirt, from the lip she had split with her first punch.

The bus was kind of rocking from the struggle; Harmony could tell G. was not pleased, but he kept his eye on the road and slowly eased the bus off on the right shoulder and brought it to a stop. Harmony was grateful to him; it was reassuring to have a driver who kept his presence of mind even when a fight was going on in his school bus. Harmony glanced around to see what her sisters were making of it—after all, they were the ones who had invited Sonny to come along on the trip. Both of them were watching with surprised looks on their faces; probably they had been dozing or something and had no idea why Harmony had suddenly punched him. She was grateful to G. for stopping the bus, and to Sheba and Omar and Salah for coming to her defense; but, still, it was her fight. He was *her* old boyfriend; she was the one who should have to reap the consequences of having made such a dreadful mistake as to sleep with him in the first place.

"Let him go, Salah," she said, stepping into the aisle. Salah was the one who was mostly holding Sonny; Salah was bigger and had an arm across Sonny's throat—unfortunately blood from the split lip was getting on Salah's nice clean white smock, probably it wasn't a smock but Harmony didn't know what else to call it.

"But he is a crazed man," Omar protested.

"No, he's not crazy, he's just selfish," Harmony said.

With some reluctance, Salah released Sonny. Sheba and Sonny were glaring at one another; Sheba had a look in her eye that was a little scary. Obviously, given the chance, she was going to go for Sonny again.

"I want you all to go to the back of the bus, please," Harmony said. "Sonny's getting off. I just want to say a few words to him."

"Why's he getting off, what's happened?" Pat asked.

"Pat, he's getting off, mind your own business," Harmony said; she was not in the mood to have to explain things to her sisters.

"I just asked," Pat said. "I nap for five seconds and the next thing I know, you're throwing the man off the bus. Can't I even be curious?"

Neddie took her arm.

"Let's go back where we can smoke in peace, Pat," she said. "If Harmony's got something to settle with the man, let her settle it."

There was some huffing and puffing on Salah's part, and on Sheba's, but finally everybody moved away. Sonny stood there feeling his lip, which had nearly stopped bleeding. Pat handed him a Kleenex, before she moved back up the aisle.

"Why were you waiting around my daughter's rehearsals?" Harmony asked—she was feeling some very ugly feelings toward Sonny Le Song right at that moment. The fact that he knew exactly where her daughter had lived was a disturbing fact, in her book.

For a moment Sonny looked as if he might spit it out, he still had a belligerent look in his eye, but then he lost it, he shifted, he let the macho go. Probably he picked up something in Harmony's attitude, the something being that she was going to kill him if he made a wrong move, or said a wrong word. He shrugged, stopped huffing, made himself look smaller.

"I seen her picture in the paper, that's all," he said. "I thought, What's Harmony's little girl doing up here all by herself? I thought maybe I could be helpful, that's all. I only seen her like a maximum three times."

Harmony was having the impulse to grab Sonny by the throat and squeeze until his guts popped out; never in her life had she had such a terrible impulse to rip into a man's body with her bare hands. For all she knew, she was looking at the man who had given her daughter the disease that killed her—among Sonny's many bad habits was a tendency to use the needle when he could afford it. Obviously there were only two reasons why Sonny would go to the trouble to find Pepper at a rehearsal. One was to mooch, to see if she could help find him a booking agent, or introduce him to a producer, or help him get gigs. The other reason was to fuck

306

her: that was the one that was making Harmony want to rip a hole in his throat and pull his entrails out through the hole.

Harmony had a notion from the scared look in Sonny's eyes that she knew which one it had been—not that it couldn't have been both.

"Hey, forget it, I don't want to interfere with your trip, I'll just get out and hitch," Sonny said; he even forgot his new T-shirts in his hurry to get off the school bus. G. opened the door and Sonny popped out so quickly that some of the oncoming traffic on the expressway honked at him—maybe they thought they had a suicide on their hands, though Sonny's main thought was probably just to get out of the bus before Harmony strangled him. He was right about that one, too—if he hadn't fled and she had actually got her hands on Sonny Le Song he might have been dead before anyone could have pried her loose.

"G., could we just go?" Harmony asked.

G. immediately shut the door and eased the bus back into the traffic; the problem of where to drop Sheba and Otis was a problem they would have to cope with later. Harmony sat back down—for a while, no one came to sit with her or speak to her. Probably she had scared them all, she didn't know. The thought that Sonny Le Song might have seduced her daughter was so disturbing that if she let the thought settle in her mind, even for a second, it made her want to take the wheel of the bus herself and go back and run over Sonny—not just once but over and over again, until she had ground him into the asphalt; until there was nothing left, not even a stain. All he was was a stain anyway: a stain on her memory, a stain on her motherhood, a stain on her conscience, a stain on her life.

After the bus was moving along smoothly, Eddie came down the aisle and crawled up in Harmony's lap. He peered out the window, to see if he could see Sonny Le Song, but Sonny was somewhere back down the road, around a curve. All Eddie could see was traffic, and a last outline of the buildings of Manhattan.

"I like it that there's towers," Eddie said, as the towers became shadows against the gray sky. "Demons and monsters and warlocks could live in the towers. And men with trunks like elephants."

Harmony was still feeling like doing terrible bodily injury to

Sonny Le Song—she couldn't concentrate on her son's vision of men with trunks like elephants, in the towers of Manhattan.

"You pummeled him, Mom, didn't you?" Eddie said.

"No, but I socked him," Harmony said.

"Salah pummeled him, though," Eddie said. "I think Omar pummeled him, too, and Sheba poked him in the eye."

"Eddie, he said a very rude thing to Laurie," Harmony said. "I didn't want him to go with us to Oklahoma."

"I didn't either," Eddie said. "I think he was fart, and fart makes bad smells in the bus."

Neddie and Pat came up and sat down across the aisle. They looked puzzled and depressed.

"We're trying again," Neddie said. "Why'd Sonny jump off the bus so quick? Now we've lost the one person in this whole gang who was like a normal American."

"Neddie, he left because I was about to kill him," Harmony said.

"You were about to what?" Pat asked. She had Sonny's little sack of T-shirts in her hand.

"Kill him," Harmony repeated. "He got out just in time."

"He said a rude thing to Laurie and he was fart," Eddie informed them.

"You mean you had a fight, or what?" Neddie asked. "I don't understand. He seemed like a decent little fellow to me."

"Yeah, we were getting along with him fine," Pat said. "Now we got a bunch of ugly T-shirts that nobody at home is gonna want to wear."

"Pat, are you saying it's my fault?" Harmony asked; it was very annoying to her that her sisters were sitting there with long faces, defending Sonny Le Song just because he was male and looked like he might live in their part of the country. It was so annoying to her that she wondered why she was even going home. Obviously she and her sisters had different values: what was the point?

"If it was just a spat he could have sat in the back with us, for a while," Pat said.

"What if I threw him off because he was a child molester, would it still be my fault?" Harmony asked. Some of the anger that had made her want to pull Sonny's guts out of his body spilled into her tone when she looked at her sister Pat.

"Uh-oh, I think we better let this one lie," Neddie said. "Harmony might know something about him that we don't know."

"Neddie, I know a million things about him that you don't know!" Harmony pointed out. "Why would you think it was my fault because I threw a little jerk off the bus? Haven't you ever met a jerk you wanted to throw off a bus?"

"There's a limited number of jerks in Tarwater, that's how bleak the scene is," Pat said.

"You're my sisters, you shouldn't always think it's my fault," Harmony said—she was still upset. "Why can't I even get support from my sisters?"

Both sisters were a little taken aback by the anger in her voice.

"Wow," Pat said, a little defensively.

"Shut up these loud words!" Eddie commanded. "I want to talk to my Mom about men with elephant trunks, but I *can't* talk to my Mom when there's loud words all the time."

"So do you two think it's always the woman's fault no matter how much of a scumbag the man is?" Harmony asked.

"Pat always gives them the benefit of the doubt," Neddie said.

Harmony gave up and hugged Eddie, who was in a smiley mood and was so sweet to hold and look at that a little of her bad mood began to drain away. There was not much she could do about her sisters; mostly, they meant well. The sun came out and the white school bus went sailing along the freeway at top speed. But just as her spirits began to come back to normal another sorrow arrived; this time it was Sheba and Otis getting off the bus. Harmony looked out and saw the oil refineries she had seen from the window of the No-Tel Motel. They were back in Jersey City, not far from the Dumpster where Sheba and Otis lived.

"I'm going quick, otherwise I be crying so hard I fall right on my ugly face," Sheba said; she bent and gave Eddie a quick kiss. At first Eddie tried to keep his hands over his eyes; he refused to let his eyes see that Sheba was leaving. But then he gave up and gave her a big hug and a kiss. In only seconds Sheba and Otis were off the bus. At this departure everybody cried except G. He was impassive and kept his eyes on the road. Soon the bus was moving, sailing down the freeway again as if the two young people had not just severed themselves from the group, probably forever. Abdul cried and Salah and Laurie; Neddie and Pat looked bleak, and Harmony couldn't look out the window at all; she didn't want to see those two nice black kids standing by a freeway in New Jersey.

Eddie buried his face in Harmony's lap; he had always been supersensitive to departures and this one was particularly hard, the reason being that Eddie loved Sheba so much.

6.

"This is the Jersey Turnpike," Laurie said, after a while. Once again she took her seat beside Harmony. She reached over and smoothed Eddie's curls, but he kept his face in his mother's lap.

"I don't blame him for being upset," Laurie said. "This is all so odd. You can't blame two black kids from New Jersey for freaking out and wanting to go home."

"Laurie, I'm sorry Sonny called you a dyke," Harmony said. "It's just too bad we met him on the street."

"Forget it," Laurie said. "What I was really worried about was that you might be going to get involved with him again."

Harmony didn't answer. Probably the truth was that if Sonny had taken the trouble to be even halfway nice it could have happened, not right away, not on the bus trip, but someday. He would just have had to be patient and wait for the soft spot to grow. But it was hard to know: maybe the soft spot she had had when Sonny was singing at the Chevron station was gone anyway; maybe all she had left was the memory of a soft spot.

"I know I'm not strong, Laurie," Harmony said. "I never have been strong, where guys are concerned. I just don't know how to be. But I can be pretty strong where Eddie is concerned."

The question of Pepper and Sonny was hanging in the air. Harmony wanted to ask if Laurie had an opinion, but the question never came out; she let it be a question there would never be an answer to.

While she was letting the question die away, Eddie sat up.

"We'll see Sheba and Otis again *someday*," he said. "We can go to the Shop and Sack and find them when we come back to Jersey City, or we can ask Beth at the No-Tel Motel and we can find them and have doughnuts *and* bagels."

Neither Harmony nor Laurie could bring themselves to answer —it was a bit of self-reassurance on Eddie's part. He didn't like it that his friends Sheba and Otis were gone forever. After all, only the day before, they had been shepherding him around New York, seeing that he got good treatment on the TV shows. Now he was just a little boy on the bus with his family again, traveling along toward Oklahoma.

A little later Eddie asked Laurie if she would go to the back of the bus and read him a few stories.

"Why, I'd be glad to, Eddie," Laurie said. She gave Harmony a little kiss before she left. Neddie and Pat were both asleep. Probably the strain of not being in Oklahoma had worn them out.

After Laurie moved to the back of the bus Omar stood up and asked politely if he could sit by Harmony for a few minutes.

"I am sorry you lose daughter," Omar said, once he sat down. "I have lost three children, but I have many more—tens more.

"You have fine little son, though," he added.

"My daughter died of AIDS," Harmony said—she had an urge to pour it all out to somebody, preferably somebody she didn't know very well.

"Your daughter is at peace, no suffering," Omar said, patting Harmony's leg.

"Children have own fates," he added. "My boys all marry bad womens, French womens, have no respect. I throw them out, with their French womens."

Then Omar got up and went back to his own seat, looking very sad. He had a strange look in his eye, as if he had gone into his own space; maybe the space was memory, and maybe he was remembering his earlier life, before his children died and his sons took up with French women.

Harmony looked around. Eddie was sprawled on the back seat, his head in Laurie's lap. Laurie was reading him *Beauty and the Beast*. Eddie was listening closely. Eddie always gave stories his full attention, even if they were stories he had had read to him many times before.

She felt guilty for having made Omar feel sad. She hadn't asked him any questions, but even one question could be the wrong question if you asked it at a bad time, or if memories were there that could open beneath you like a trapdoor.

The problem was, once a tragedy had happened, or not even a tragedy, just the troubles that went with being alive, memories were always there, they could always open beneath you like a trapdoor; you could just be riding along on a bus and suddenly the trapdoor would open and plunge you downward, into the depth of your regrets. It was a fact that could make you fearful, if you let yourself think about it very much.

Harmony decided she wanted to be with Eddie and Laurie.

"The beast isn't really bad, Mom," Eddie said, once she sat down by him. "He only *looks* a little bad."

"Well, he can't help that," Laurie said. "None of us can help how we look. I think that thought every morning, when I get up and look in the mirror."

"But that's a good thought because you look nice, Laurie," Eddie said, giving her a pat.

"Not to myself," Laurie said. "I think I look really blah. Sort of like how a pancake would taste without real maple syrup."

"I'm glad the beast isn't really bad," Eddie said again. "He looks really scary but he isn't really bad."

"Well, not too many things in this world are *really* bad," Laurie commented. "Although a lot of things are a little bad."

"Yeah, shots are a little bad," Eddie said. "My school bus driver was a little bad because he yelled at Eli because Eli stood up in the seat."

"Eddie, he was just thinking of safety," Harmony said.

"Harmony, are you nervous about going home?" Laurie asked.

"But the beast's paw is hurt, you have to keep reading," Eddie said. "My Mom can listen too."

"Can't I get the answer to one question before I have to read?" Laurie asked. "After all, you were talking about Eli just a moment ago."

"I was, but now I need to know about the beast because his paw is hurt—it's a *very important* part," Eddie said.

"Laurie, it's not just about going home, I'm nervous about everything," Harmony said. "Do you ever get the feeling that you just don't know how to live? That's how I feel. I just don't know how to live."

"Yes you do know how to live, don't say silly words," Eddie protested. "How to live is you fix my breakfast and help me get ready for school, and then you go to your job at the recycling plant and when your job is over I'll come home and we'll eat macaroni and cheese and we'll watch some TV shows and if Gary comes over we'll play cards and then I'll take my bath and you can read me a story and I'll go to sleep and that's how to live."

"Wow, no wonder this young man was on TV," Laurie said, grinning. "He's only five and he actually understands how to live."

"Five and a half, my birthday is in October," Eddie said.

7.

Eddie got his way about the White House. He kept harping on the First Family's impending trip to China until Laurie finally got off the bus in Baltimore and called the White House number. She did it mainly to convince Eddie that an effort was being made to be polite to the First Family, but, to everyone's bewilderment, the call went through and a meeting was arranged.

"I guess the President isn't doing much today," Laurie said, when she got back on the bus. "Now if we can just get over to Washington and find the White House, Eddie and Iggy are in business."

"I don't have to go in, do I?" Harmony asked, horrified at the thought that she'd have to meet a dignitary looking the way she looked.

"Nobody has to go in but Eddie and Iggy," Laurie said. "A Marine will take Eddie in and a Marine will bring him back."

"Why can't my aunts go in?" Eddie asked. "They don't have much to do."

"Forget it, Eddie," Pat said. "I feel like I fell off the Statue of Liberty myself. I don't want to meet nobody, much less two people from Arkansas."

"What's wrong with Arkansas?" Neddie asked. "There's good fishing over there in Arkansas."

"I've had my share of bad experiences in Arkansas," Pat said, without elaborating.

"It ain't the state's fault that you pick assholes for boyfriends," Neddie said. "At one point me and Dick thought we might move over to Arkansas and try life over there but we never got around to it."

"I still don't see why my aunts can't come in," Eddie said. "It would be a good experience for the President and Mrs. President to meet my family."

"Well, that's one good experience they'll just have to do without —end of conversation," Pat said.

"Pat, why do you have to be so negative?" Harmony asked. "Eddie was just asking a simple question."

"He wasn't, either, he was trying to pressure me and Neddie into going into the White House with him, when all our clothes are wrinkled and we wouldn't know what to say anyway."

"Be quiet with these words, I don't want to hear any more of these words right now," Eddie said.

"Well, but we don't take orders from you, Eddie," Pat said. "We're grown-ups and there's free speech in this country. That means people get to say whatever words they want to say."

"Pat, it was just a suggestion," Harmony said.

Eddie put his fingers in his ears and went back to where Laurie sat, at the back of the bus.

"I think you hurt his feelings," Harmony said.

"I did not hurt his feelings," Pat insisted. "I love Eddie but I'm not taking any more lip from him. I'm beginning to wish I'd gone on and married Rog."

"Marry him—you don't even know if he's alive," Neddie reminded her.

Harmony enjoyed looking at Baltimore, as they passed through it; as a town, it definitely had a funky look. She was thinking that her family had a habit of simply forgetting people. Pat had forgotten Rog and she had forgotten Ross, among others.

"Neddie, have you ever forgotten anybody—I mean a person who was important to you for a while but then became forgotten?" she asked.

"Well, there's Dick, I forgot him years ago, even though I'm still married to him," Neddie said.

"That's *why* you're still married to him," Pat said. "If you remembered him for ten minutes you'd probably get divorced."

"I couldn't live up here where it's so old," Neddie said. "They don't even have yards back here in Baltimore. I didn't see none in New York either."

"I don't want to talk to you, you make rude comments," Eddie said, to Pat.

"You don't believe in free speech, that's your problem," Pat said.

Nonetheless they all got tears in their eyes when Eddie went marching across the south lawn of the White House, with Iggy on his leash. Two Marines led the way. G. had found the White House on the first try, not long after they entered Washington. The guards behind it were friendly and let them park in a little space off the street that was mostly filled with black limousines. Evidently the staff had been fully informed of their arrival; there was not the slightest problem about parking, even though two security men did come on the bus with little portable metal detectors, to sweep them all down and make sure they were not armed.

"Eddie looks so tiny, it breaks my heart," Laurie said, as they watched Eddie and Iggy being led into the White House by the two tall Marines in their blue uniforms.

Harmony was having a hard time believing in the reality of what was happening. It didn't seem possible that they could really be in Washington, D.C., parked beside the White House, so that her own son, aged five and a half, could have a few words with the President and the First Lady. Yet there they were, and her sisters and Laurie and the turban men were all watching.

As for Eddie himself, he could hardly wait to get out of the bus and go meet the First Family. He loved telling the story of Iggy's famous, foolhardy pursuit of the sea gull, and his miraculous fall from the Statue of Liberty. His only problem with the visit had involved his clip-on bow tie, which really wasn't all that easy to clip on. Eddie tried, but grew so frustrated that he was about to cry. Finally he let Laurie do it.

"Eddie, be polite," Harmony had said, giving him a kiss as he

317

got off the bus; then some television people showed up, and the Marines; she didn't get to say much more.

"Why don't we never have a camera at a time like this?" Neddie asked. "I've bought at least twenty cameras in my life, but I never have one when I need one and if I do either the flash doesn't work or I don't have no film."

"It'll be on TV, we can get it on tape," Laurie assured them.

All of a sudden everyone on the bus got hyper at the same time; it was probably the excitement of being at the White House. They all had been what Laurie would call blah on the trip from Baltimore. Harmony was wondering why they were bothering at all, it all seemed sort of pointless. Neddie was still griping because there didn't seem to be any lawns in the part of the country they were driving through.

There was a lawn at the White House, though, and the sight of Eddie and Iggy walking across it sort of made everyone feel keyed up. While they were feeling keyed up an even more exciting thing happened: the President and the First Lady and several aides suddenly appeared on the lawn with Eddie and Iggy. Although they were a good distance from the bus it was easy to see that it was the President and the First Lady.

"My God, it's them," Laurie said.

"I'm glad it's Eddie out there, and not me," Neddie said.

Then Eddie disappeared amid the aides and Marines—in a minute or two, though, he came in sight again, dashing after Iggy, who had been turned loose to scamper on the green lawn behind the White House. Eddie and Iggy scampered around for a while, watched over by the President and the First Lady.

There was a helicopter parked on the White House lawn, not far from where the group was. Eddie ran back to the President and pointed at it. Evidently the President was about to go somewhere not too formal, he just had on a windbreaker and khakis. When Eddie pointed at the helicopter the President started waving and pretty soon he and the First Lady and some of the aides and Eddie and Iggy got in the helicopter. The helicopter immediately took off.

"How do you like that, Eddie's taking a ride in Helicopter One," Laurie said.

318

"Maybe they took Eddie to Camp David—I know they go off to Camp David a lot," Pat said. "I think they eat popcorn."

Several aides and the two Marines were still standing on the White House lawn. The aides' hair was badly ruffled when the helicopter took off. They all watched it go. The Marines still seemed to be standing at attention. To her surprise, Harmony saw that the four turban men were standing at attention too, even G., who had his hand on his heart, as if he were about to recite the Pledge of Allegiance. Omar had tears in his eyes. Being that close to the White House and seeing the President touched them all. Harmony felt a little guilty. Why was it that everyone was more patriotic than she was? She felt that it was nice of the President to give her son a ride in Helicopter One but it didn't make her want to recite the Pledge of Allegiance. What she really wanted to do was get back in the bus and take a nap; not only would that be unpatriotic, it would also be being a bad mother; after all, what kind of mother would take a nap in a school bus while her son and his puppy were aloft in Helicopter One?

While they all watched, the big helicopter veered over toward the Washington Monument, circled around it for a minute, and then disappeared in the direction of the Capitol. They had passed right in front of the Capitol themselves, on the school bus.

In only five minutes the big helicopter came back. Meanwhile, Pat and Neddie had wandered off to get coffee and Laurie and Salah, Abdul, and G. had drifted around the White House fence, somewhere—they wanted a better view of how the First Family lived.

When the helicopter landed, the President didn't get off—only Eddie and Iggy and two aides got off. Then the other aides who had had their hair ruffled when the helicopter first took off got on the helicopter, which rose in the sky and whirled away.

Eddie and Iggy came hurrying back across the big green lawn, flanked by the two Marines.

"All because little dog chase sea gull," Omar said.

"What?" Harmony asked—she had been watching her son sprint across the White House lawn; after all, it might be the only time in her life she would get to witness that sight. So many sights were sort of onetime sights. Probably that was why she felt wistful so much of the time; you usually only got one look and then you never got that look again. Maybe that was why certain sights were so sweet—the sweeter the sight the more likely that it would never come again: for example, the sight of Eddie and Iggy racing across the White House lawn, quite a distance ahead of the two tall blue-uniformed Marines. Even if Eddie made it back to the White House at some later date, he wouldn't be five and a half and Iggy might not be with him.

"Lucky boy," Omar said.

"Lucky dog, too," Harmony said.

"Lots of life is lucks," Omar said. "I don't have very much lucks. If I have little dog, chase sea gull, fall off Statue of Liberty, just be dead dog, no TV, no Helicopter One. Just be dead dog, because I have no big-time lucks."

Harmony thought she knew how Omar felt, but it was not a thought to dwell on, it could only lead to self-pity, and Didier Korn himself had warned her sternly against self-pity; his argument was that no one blessed with her good looks had any business feeling sorry for themselves. Life might not be perfect, it might even be tragic, but if you had looks enough to be voted Miss Las Vegas Showgirl three years running you should not be indulging in self-pity. Didier had been a foreigner too, like Omar; he didn't have a view of life; but Harmony had never known a man she respected more. For that reason she did her best to be loyal to his memory by avoiding self-pity. She tried to bat it away every time she felt it creeping up.

"Mom, we went right over the Washington Monument," Eddie said, jumping up in her arms. "We went right over it and Iggy didn't fall out—Mrs. President was holding him."

"Oh, Eddie, that was nice of her," Harmony said. "What did she say?"

"Well, she said she wished she had curls like my curls," Eddie said. "And Mr. President said he wished they had a dog like Iggy at the White House—they only have a cat."

"Socks," Omar said.

"That's right, their cat is named Socks," Eddie said. "I didn't know if Iggy liked cats so they didn't meet."

"Eddie, you should thank the Marines, they were very nice to walk with you—it might have been scary on such a big lawn," Harmony said.

"No, it wasn't scary at *all*, it was the President's lawn!" Eddie said, with emphasis—but he marched back and thanked the two Marines anyway. Both Marines gave Eddie a salute and after it one of the Marines gave Harmony the eye; fortunately he was on duty, it was just a look or two. It made her remember Dave, a guy with a Marine background who had fed her K rations once before seducing her. She had survived plenty of not too successful seductions; the one preceded by the dinner of K rations was one never to repeat, and in fact she never had repeated it, although Dave had kept coming around for years, he had not expected the K rations to have such a turning-off effect. He himself liked them so much that he kept a pantryful, although he had not actually been a Marine for many years.

Neddie and Pat took their time getting coffee; long before they returned Harmony fell asleep on the back seat. As she was dozing off Eddie got out a tablet and began to play many games of tic-tac-toe with Abdul. Eddie won easily, too—Abdul had trouble grasping the essential principles of tic-tac-toe.

When she woke up, it was dark, she was hungry, and they were lost. Omar, Abdul, and Salah were yelling at one another, and G. was trying to keep driving while reading a map by the light of a small flashlight he held in his mouth. Laurie was trying to talk him into letting *her* read the map, but so far G. remained in firm possession of the map, the flashlight, and the wheel.

"Where are we?" Harmony asked, when she sat up.

Eddie sat beside her, quietly studying a story about an octopus.

"Some octopuses are very small, about the right size to be a pet," he informed his Mom.

"Where are we?" Harmony asked again—she was too drowsy to give much thought to letting Eddie have an octopus as a pet.

"Oh my God, we're lost in a crack neighborhood," Pat said. "I knew this would happen if we hung around up here where people don't have lawns."

Harmony looked out the window—she couldn't tell that it was a totally great neighborhood, but, after all, they were in a bus, there was no reason to panic that she could see.

"Pat, it's just a black neighborhood, calm down," Harmony said. "Did we miss the freeway or what?"

"We're looking for the airport, the last plane for Oklahoma City leaves in forty-five minutes and we don't even have tickets," Neddie said. "I was sure hoping to get home and smell the prairie breezes tonight but I don't know, it looks like another lost cause."

"But we were supposed to be *driving* to Oklahoma, what happened while I was asleep?" Harmony asked. The thought of being in Oklahoma in a few hours brought her wide awake in a hurry.

"G. says it's too far to the giant redwoods, he doesn't want to go and neither does Salah or Omar or Abdul," Eddie said. "They want to go back to New York and it makes me very sad."

"Well, Eddie, they have families, I guess they miss them," Harmony said, putting her arm around him for a minute.

"I wanted there to be a family that has us in it," he said. "I wanted it to be Sheba and Otis and the turban men but if they have to go home we'll just have to find another family that has us in it, won't we, Mom?

"I guess it was just a pretend family anyway," he added, with a sigh.

"Sometimes it's hard to tell the difference between pretend families and real families, Eddie," she said, giving him a hug. "Sometimes pretend families are even better than real families."

"Well, but it would just be nice to have it settled, wouldn't it, Mom?" Eddie said. He seemed a little bit wistful.

"Just look at the road, we're almost there," Laurie said, loudly, to G., pointing at a descending airplane. The plane seemed to be descending almost on top of the bus. But the plane didn't land on them and they got to National Airport with thirty minutes to spare. Neddie was so anxious to get home and smell the breeze off the prairie that she dashed into the airport and put all their tickets on her Visa card.

"I'll take up a collection when I get home," she said, but there was another setback. The flight to Oklahoma City was full. The best they could do was a flight to Dallas. Neddie was so anxious to get back that she booked them on the Dallas flight and didn't tell them about the little setback until they were actually in the air. They thought they were flying to Oklahoma City but they weren't. Then they had almost missed that flight too because Eddie talked

322

the airlines out of another box and very carefully and slowly packed his stuffed animals in it. He didn't like to put incompatible animals next to one another; he even had a discussion with the airline woman about whether a buffalo and a sheep could ride together on an airplane happily. Finally he decided they could and the box was sealed and they all raced for the plane. They didn't have time for very much in the way of farewells with the turban men, but the turban men were distracted anyway. A Sikh taxi driver with a beard as big and black as G.'s came rushing up while they were getting the bags off the bus. He turned out to be G.'s brother-in-law. In a way it made the parting easier—at least they were leaving Omar and Abdul and Salah and G. with a family member, it was not as bad as just racing off from them at an airport. Even so Omar and Abdul cried; they had become attached. Salah had gone inside to compare baggage-handling possibilities at National Airport with those at La Guardia—they didn't get to say goodbye to him—and G. had his brother-in-law to deal with, the brother-in-law seemed to want him to come immediately and start driving a taxicab in Washington.

Once they were in the air, trying to catch their breath—it had been a pretty sudden departure, at least Harmony thought so—Neddie revealed that they were not exactly bound for Oklahoma City, they were bound for Dallas.

"Why would this many people want to go to Oklahoma City in the middle of the night?" Pat asked, on hearing that the plane to Oklahoma City had been full.

"I guess as many people would want to go to Oklahoma as would want to go to Texas," Neddie said, in an annoyed tone.

"Chill out, I was just wondering," Pat said.

"Wait a minute," Laurie said. "You mean we're on a plane for Texas?"

"Yeah, but it's just about fifty miles back across the river to them red Oklahoma hills," Neddie said. "Dallas was as close as I could put us down."

"No quarrels!" Eddie said. "My Mom has had a very hard day and besides, quarrels disturb my coatimundi because we're in an airplane and it's *high* altitude!"

Harmony felt like putting her fingers in her ears—she almost felt like asking the stewardess for a parachute so she could jump out of the plane. Maybe she would float down on a nice little country road somewhere and a nice family would pick her up and let her live in a barn or a shed or something until she felt a little better. She had just been adjusting to the bus. She could lie on the back seat with Eddie, or sit with Laurie by a window and feel that she had found a little calm. She liked the turban men, they were all gentle men; she had confidence in G. as a driver, too. He was a patient driver who never took chances that might lead to an accident.

But now the turban men were gone, and they were squeezed into two rows of a hot airplane and Neddie and Pat were bickering, as they had bickered all their lives. Laurie looked anxious—she hadn't counted on going to Texas, and Eddie was sad from having to give up another pretend family on short notice.

It would be so nice just to float downward in a parachute, to that nice country road, in an area where nobody would be too shocked at her appearance. But of course that was just a fantasy, the stewardess wasn't going to give her a parachute and even if she would Eddie wouldn't want his Mom just jumping out of an airplane in the night; he might think it had to do with too many stuffed animals or something.

"Neddie, it's a long way up there to Tulsa, what if your Visa's maxed out and we can't rent a car when we get to Dallas?" Pat asked. "We'll just be stuck down in Texas, with all them ugly Texans."

"The Dallas Cowboys' cheerleaders ain't ugly, you have to admit that," Neddie said. She always had an answer for anything Pat said —usually it was an argumentative answer too.

"Yeah, but I doubt the Dallas Cowboys' cheerleaders will be waiting for us at the airport in the middle of the night," Pat said. "Even if they are, so what? It won't get us home."

Eddie unbuckled his seat belt, stood up in his seat, and leaned over toward his aunts, who were across the aisle.

"*Stop bickering!*" he yelled, putting so much force into the yell that his face turned beet-red and a little vein in his forehead stood out.

"It's *very* inconsiderate," he yelled, with only slightly less force.

An old man in a checked shirt, sitting on the aisle behind Neddie and Pat, looked up when Eddie yelled. The old man had bright blue eyes, a steelier blue than Eddie's, and he was reading a magazine called *Soldier of Fortune*, which had a soldier who looked a little bit like Rambo on the cover.

"Say, I know you, sonny," the old man said. "You're the little boy whose dog fell off the Statue of Liberty and lived. I saw you on the Letterman show."

"Hi," Eddie said. "Excuse me for yelling, but my aunts were bickering."

"Females, that explains it," the old man said, turning to his wife, who wore a Baltimore Orioles baseball cap. "This one here that I've been married to fifty-one years would talk back to a fireplug if a fireplug could talk."

"I guess you're a saint then," his wife said, without looking up from the romance novel she was reading.

"Nearer to being one than you are, by a damn sight," the old man said.

Then he turned back to Eddie.

"So how's that little dog?" he asked.

"Harmony, make your son sit down and tell him to mind his own business," Pat said. "I can bicker with my sister if I want to."

"Well, it's very inconsiderate," Eddie said, again.

"The Bible says respect your elders—I think a few trips to a good Sunday school wouldn't hurt you," Neddie said.

"The Bible said the whale ate Jonah and that's a lie," Eddie reminded her. "Whales only eat plankton."

"He's got a tongue on him, ain't he?" the old man said.

"It takes one to know one," his wife said, again without looking up.

"See, I told you, talk back to a fireplug," the old man said.

"This is my Mom," Eddie said, patting Harmony on the shoulder. Sweet as Eddie was, Harmony still kept having the fantasy of jumping out of the airplane. The only thing that had changed about the fantasy was that she no longer had the parachute—she just saw herself falling, free, through the darkness. The good thing about the fantasy was the darkness, not the falling. In the darkness no one would be able to see how she really felt. She could let her face show what it felt like showing, secure in the knowledge that no one, not her son, not Laurie, not her sisters, would see the sadness and be disturbed.

325

"I'm military, but even so I've been around my share of bickering women," the old man said, at which point Pat got out of her seat, stood in the aisle, and glared at him.

"I'll bicker with my sister if I want to, mister," she said. "Keep your fucking opinions to yourself."

"Oh-oh, she said the *f* word, Mom," Eddie said. "I think she's angry."

"Pat, please sit down, it's not that important, it was just a comment," Harmony said.

"See, your big mouth's got you in trouble again," the man's wife said. She looked up and smiled at Pat, from underneath her Orioles baseball cap.

"Why, I just asked about the puppy," the old man said. "It's not every day I meet somebody who's been on the Letterman show."

"It's not every day I have to sit in front of an old fart who doesn't know how to mind his own business, either," Pat said. "Maybe I wouldn't be so aggravated if I wasn't on my way to a state I hate."

Then she sat down.

"What's wrong with Texas?" the old man asked, in a quieter tone. He seemed to be addressing the question to his wife, but Pat heard it and twisted around in her seat, in order to answer.

"What's wrong with it is that it's filled with nosy old turds like you," Pat said.

"I told you your big mouth would get you in trouble," his wife said, still reading.

The old man winked at Eddie—he didn't seem very abashed.

"We're on this plane with a lot of tough women, ain't we, sonny?" he said.

Eddie ignored him and sat down.

"What about *Alligators All Around*?" he asked, turning to Laurie.

"You know *Alligators All Around* backwards and forwards," Laurie informed him. "You've known it backwards and forwards for years."

"Well, I still want you to read it to me," Eddie said. "It's just a tiny book."

While Laurie was reading to Eddie, Harmony dozed off. She had a dream in which she was giving a birthday party for Pepper, and Ross remembered to come. The odd part about the dream was

326

that Eddie and Laurie were at the birthday party too. Pepper and Eddie blew out the candles together. The dream was still flickering, like a TV that somebody had forgotten to turn off, when the plane landed in Dallas. Eddie was sound asleep, Laurie had to carry him, but he woke up while they were traveling around the big airport on a little train that was supposed to take them to the rent car place. It was late at night—the airport looked eerie because of the white lights everywhere.

"Mom, did we land on the moon?" Eddie asked, when he was awake enough to notice that they were on a train at night, in an eerie place.

"No, but it would be more fun if we were on the moon, honey," Pat said.

"At least we're only fifty miles from Oklahoma," Neddie reminded them. "The air will be smelling sweeter, pretty soon."

"I never thought I'd be in Texas," Laurie said. She was a little nervous.

"Well, I don't think we are in Texas," Eddie said. "I think we're on the moon. I hope we see some moon people pretty soon."

Iggy began to race up and down the aisles of the little train, yipping his loudest.

"He doesn't like the moon," Eddie observed. "He wants to return to earth because there is *no* dog food on the moon. Can you blame him?"

"I can blame him for making that noise, I got a hangover," Pat said. "There must have been something wrong with that vodka—I don't usually get this hung over on six or eight drinks."

Harmony felt like she had jumped out of the plane, just like in her fantasy, only instead of landing on a peaceful country road somewhere she had landed at a weird place that *was* a little like a place on another planet. The train seemed to be taking them along an endless track, under the bright white lights. The only other people who had been on the train at all were two or three Asians who gave Iggy strange looks.

"I think those Asians wanted to eat Iggy," Eddie remarked, after they got out.

"Airline food probably got to them, if they flew all the way from China," Pat said. "Even a rat terrier might look good if you'd been on a plane that long."

The train finally stopped, Neddie's Visa card was not maxed out, and soon they were all piled into a blue Cadillac—since it was a late hour Neddie decided to splurge—and racing up a freeway toward Oklahoma. Eddie, wide awake, suddenly remembered that his Aunt Pat had called Iggy a rat terrier. He demanded to know why.

"Because he's the kind of dog you keep around the house to kill rats," Pat said.

"That's not very nice," Eddie said. "Iggy doesn't kill rats."

"Just because he hasn't yet doesn't mean he wouldn't if he got the chance," Pat said.

"He wouldn't, because he would want it to be his friend," Eddie said.

"Just don't mention the Discovery Channel to me right now, Eddie," Pat said. "If you do I'm going to scream and jump out of this car."

"Discovery Channel, Discovery Channel, Discovery Channel," Eddie said, grinning.

"Oh, Eddie, why do you have to call my bluff when I'm hung over?" Pat said. "Couldn't you let your old auntie win, just once?"

"Discovery Channel, Discovery Channel," Eddie said.

8.

When Harmony opened her eyes her father was looking at her through the window of the rent car. The window was down—she could smell the prairie breeze that Neddie was so fond of. Her father was bending a little, his elbows on the door of the car. He was looking at her over the frame of his old spectacles, with his kind eyes. He had on a blue, short-sleeved work shirt; his arms were deeply freckled from the sun. When he looked at her Harmony remembered that no one's eyes were as kind as her father's.

"How are you, darling?" her father asked—behind him stood her parents' house. Part of the lawn had been mown, and part was shaggy. The freshly mown grass smelled sweet.

"Oh, Daddy, Daddy," Harmony said—a flood of tears came out. She tried to reach through the window and hug her father, he tried to reach through the window, but it didn't work, the window was too small. Finally she got out of the car and let her father squeeze her in his thin arms. He was so skinny she could feel his ribs when he squeezed.

"Dad, you're skinny, do you eat well?" Harmony asked, when she stepped back a little, to look at him. She thought she smelled a whiff of whiskey on his breath.

"You aren't drinking, are you?" she asked, before he could speak.

"I just drink when I'm mowing the lawn—boredom," her father said. "If I have to follow a dern lawn mower around and around, I'd rather be drunk when I'm doing it."

"Daddy, what if the mower cut your foot off?" Harmony asked —she was having paranoid fantasies.

"Oh well, that would be the end of me if I cut my foot off," her father said. "Ethel would just let me die. She can't remember nine-one-one anymore, you know."

"She can't?" Harmony asked.

"Nope," her father said. "We had a grease fire in the kitchen yesterday and I yelled at her to call nine-one-one. She dialed her sister in Altus and talked for twenty minutes. If the fire truck hadn't been passing by on the way back from a grass fire there wouldn't be no house for you to come back to, sweetheart."

"Oh, Aunt Etta?" Harmony asked. "What did she talk to Aunt Etta about?"

"Menopause," her father said. "Smoke pouring out the windows and she took the Portaphone and went to the bathroom and talked about menopause."

"Momma's in her eighties," Harmony said. "What's so interesting about menopause?"

"The way she sees it, she ain't never paused," her father said. "I paused, but she didn't. That's been one of her main topics of conversation for the last forty years."

"What about Aunt Etta—did she pause?" Harmony asked.

"Etta's crazy as a bedbug, always has been," her father said. "I have no idea what her feelings are on the subject of menopause."

"How about Uncle Mo?" Harmony asked—it was amazing how good the green grass smelled. Mowing part of it seemed to have released more smell into the air.

"Oh, Mo's dead—died back in 'seventy-four, I think it was. I remember the year because he died not long after Billy got arrested for the first time. I remember your mother stopped by the jail and left Billy some bacon before we drove over to Altus for Mo's funeral."

Harmony felt a twinge of guilt—Aunt Etta had made her cookies and let her stay up late, long ago in her girlhood. Now Uncle Mo, who took the screen off the bedroom window in their farmhouse so he could spit tobacco out it, had been dead for nearly twenty years and she herself had not been aware of it. She wondered what Aunt Etta would think if she sent her a sympathy card twenty years late—maybe it would be a case of "Better late than later," a saying that was a favorite of Gary's. In Gary's case it was a useful saying because he was always late. But Aunt Etta was not Gary—she might take offense that Harmony had waited twenty years to acknowledge the passing of her husband. It was one more example of Harmony not being too good at keeping up family ties.

"Sty, get in here, what are you two doing standing down there and what business does Neddie think she has renting a Cadillac?" her mother yelled, from just outside the back door of the house. Harmony waved at her mother—she seemed tinier, but she was wearing lipstick. Eddie had come outside with his grandmother. He suddenly spotted a small box turtle, making its way through the new-mown grass—he ran right over to it. Iggy ran with him and began to yip at the turtle, employing his fiercest yip.

"Mom, can I pick it up?" Eddie yelled. "I want it to be my pet—it's very small."

Before Harmony could answer, Eddie picked the turtle up and held it off the ground as high as he could, which wasn't very high. Iggy continued to yip, between jumps at the turtle.

"Mom, Iggy's jealous, what do I do?" Eddie yelled.

"Put that filthy thing down, don't you know old turtles tinkle on little boys, where was you raised, anyway?" Ethel said.

Eddie glanced at her as if she might be a troll he had happened to meet—actually, his grandmother was not much larger than a troll—and brought the turtle to his mother.

"It hasn't peed yet," he said. "Hi, Grandpa."

"Get up here, I ain't coming there," Ethel yelled. "My shoes will get wet in that wet grass and the toes will curl up."

"Ethel, the grass isn't wet," Sty informed her. "We're in a drought—that's why there was a grass fire yesterday, over at the Hilburn place."

"Oh hush, my shoes would curl up," Ethel said. "Tell Eddie to put that filthy turtle down."

331

"It is not filthy, it's my pet," Eddie yelled at his grandmother. He employed almost as much force as he had used on the airplane, when he was trying to get his aunts to stop bickering.

"Even if it was filthy we could wash it with the hose," Sty said, winking at Eddie. "I wonder why womenfolks want everything to be so clean."

"Well, I don't know why," Eddie said, pleasantly. "Maybe we should wash my turtle off with the hose anyway, Grandpa. Maybe he's a little filthy, inside his shell."

"Okay, let's do it," Sty said, with a wink at his daughter. "Then let's have a big breakfast and then let's go fishing, how's that strike you?"

"Well, it doesn't strike me but it interests me," Eddie said. "Will we scuba dive and look at the fish before we catch one, Grandpa?"

"No, we'll just drop a hook in the water and hope for the best," his grandfather said.

"Get that boy out of that wet grass, he'll have chiggers up to his neck," Ethel yelled, still standing on the back step.

"She can't get it through her head that it's a dry year," Sty said. "A chigger would starve in weather like this."

Then he looked at Eddie.

"Scuba diving wouldn't work because the water's too brown," he said. "A fish could be two inches from your nose and you wouldn't see it—water's too brown."

"Well, you can't see through brown and besides we have no scuba equipment," Eddie said. He went off with his grandfather to hose down the turtle. Iggy had worn himself out, from leaping and yipping. He tagged along behind Eddie and Sty, looking like a tired little dog.

"Now where are they going?" Ethel asked. "Neddie's about got the pancakes ready."

"Momma, they've gone to wash the turtle," Harmony said. Despite what her father said, the new-mown grass was a little wet. Probably the moisture was dew. She remembered that in her girlhood the grass had been very dewy in the mornings. She could look out her bedroom window and see the sunshine sparkling on the dew, almost every morning. On the way to the school bus she would carry her socks and shoes in her hands, until she got to the road. Even in those early years her mother had been worried that even a little bit of moisture would make shoes curl up.

"Your hair's a mess, want me to make you an appointment with Barbara?" her mother asked, just before they hugged. Harmony had to bend over to make the hug work—her mother had always been short but now she seemed even shorter. Why is it always my hair? she thought, trying to remember a homecoming that had not begun with her mother making a comment about her hair—usually a negative comment, too. Even in the days when she had had really beautiful hair it had never been beautiful enough for her mother, or, at least, it had never been done the way her mother thought it ought to be done. The first words out of her mother's mouth were always an offer to get her a quick appointment at the beauty parlor in Tarwater.

"Who's Barbara?" Harmony asked, just to have something to say.

"Well, she does me and Neddie," her mother said. "Pat's stuck-up, she goes to some fancy place in Tulsa where they charge forty-eight dollars just to ruin her looks."

"Mom, can't we eat first, we drove all the way from Dallas," Harmony said.

"Suit yourself, but Barbara's hard to get, she ain't the best hair-dresser in Tarwater for nothing," Ethel said, in an annoyed tone. She had never liked to have her suggestions disregarded.

"Where's that old fool taking that boy?" she asked, peering across the yard. Her eyes seemed a little faded; Harmony knew that she should try to remember that her mother was really old, although she was neatly dressed and clean as a pin.

"I think they just went to wash Eddie's turtle," Harmony reminded her. "After all, you were the one who said it might not be clean."

"It ain't Eddie's turtle, it's just a turtle that happened to be passing through the yard," Ethel said. "Turtles give you warts and they pee on you too. Turtles belong outside."

"Well, it *is* outside," Harmony said. "They're just washing it."

"You shouldn't be letting that little boy keep any critter he happens to pick up," her mother said, still peering with her vague old eyes around the yard.

"Mom, Eddie's not in his home right now, he needs a pet for security," Harmony said. "We'll just put it in the car or somewhere until we get a place."

The problem with that was, she already had a feeling that she didn't want to get a place, at least not a place near enough by that her mother could criticize her hairdo every time she saw her.

But, through the screen door, she could smell Neddie's pancakes, they smelled so good it made her hungry. She had to resist the impulse just to pick her mother up like a doll and carry her into the house.

"I can't see Sty at all, I must have put on the wrong specs today," her mother said. "I have to watch him though."

"Mom, why? He's perfectly safe, he just went to wash a turtle off with the hose," Harmony said.

"That's all you know—he's got a girlfriend in Bartlesville," her mother said. "If I don't keep him in sight he's off and gone."

Harmony was a little shocked; she didn't know why. With her mother being so critical it wasn't that hard to imagine that her father might want a woman who was a little less critical, at least to be his friend.

"Momma, could we just go eat?" she asked. She felt it might be best to skirt the issue of her father's other woman, if he had one—at least it would be best to skirt it until after breakfast.

"No point in telling you about it anyway, you always side with the man," her mother said, looking her over closely. Harmony knew her mother was looking her over from the hair down, finding nothing to please her along the way. For one thing, she wasn't wearing nail polish, a choice that wasn't going to sit well. Her mother was a firm believer in bright red nail polish.

"Mom, you didn't want me to be a feminist," Harmony reminded her. She had always had trouble thinking of anything to say when her mother made wild accusations. She didn't remember her childhood very well, but she did sort of remember siding with her father, most of the time. After all, he was the nicer person—why not side with him?

"He's taken up with some old hussy at the nursing home in Bartlesville," her mother said. "I have to hide the pickup keys or he'll be gone for a week at a stretch, leaving me with the chickens to feed and the pigs to slop. I'm too well mannered to be slopping pigs at my age. I think I got a right to resent that kind of stuff, but that don't make me a feminist. I don't even know what a feminist is—bra burners, I guess you mean."

Harmony looked down toward the old barn—once it had been red but now it was gray; the prairie breeze Neddie was so fond of had slowly peeled the paint off the family barn. A few cows were standing around idly, but she couldn't see any pigs. Quite a few chickens milled around in the chicken yard, which was about halfway between the house and the barn.

"Let's go in, you don't want to hear my troubles, you never have," her mother said, with a sigh. "Sty may be off to Bartlesville, I don't see him anywhere. I'll call Barbara right now and see if she can work you in at the beauty parlor."

Harmony followed her mother inside—the ceiling and one of the walls had been smoked black as tar. The smoky smell was still very strong.

"As you can see, this house nearly burned up," Pat said. "Looks like the time's finally come to hire Mom and Dad a cook."

"That time came about twenty years ago," Neddie remarked. She was sitting in a chair, smoking. She seemed more content, now that she was home where she could smell the breeze.

Seeing how black the kitchen was made Harmony wonder if her parents were really capable of looking after themselves. Her father looked perfectly spry, but the kitchen was perfectly black, too.

"I can run off any cook you two can hire," her mother said, sounding determined. "I ran off the last one and I'll run off the next one, too. Nobody's cooking for me in my house, while I still got two hands and two feet."

"How about two eyes, Momma?" Pat asked. "If you had any vision I imagine you could have seen that that frying pan was on fire. This kitchen's still so smoky it ain't fit to eat in."

"Well, I had on my wrong specs yesterday," Ethel said. "Don't you ever put on the wrong specs?"

"No," Pat remarked.

"*I* wear specs," Neddie said. "If you're so blind you can't tell your daughters apart it might be time to think about retiring from the kitchen."

"You two shut up about that grease fire," Ethel said. "I was frying Billy his bacon and just looked off for a minute. Anybody can look off for a minute, while bacon's frying."

"If you'd looked off another minute we'd be living in the yard," Sty said, coming in the back door. "I think it's time to hire a cook myself. Not only would it be safer, it might be better grub. At least it would if the new cook could cook at all."

Eddie, Iggy, and the turtle came in behind him.

"I've decided to name my turtle Eli, after my friend Eli," Eddie said. "Grandpa washed him and now he's clean."

"I don't like animals in my house, much less reptiles," Ethel said. "You need to learn to mind your grandmother. This is the first visit we've ever had and let's start it off right by leaving all the animals and reptiles outside."

Eddie regarded his grandmother silently, as if she were a different order of being, one that required prolonged and careful study.

"Animals belong *outside*, that includes dogs," Ethel continued, emphatically.

"Mom, I don't want to hug Grandma, she's being rude," Eddie said.

Both Neddie and Pat laughed loudly.

"Momma's finally met her match," Neddie said.

"I'm not sure—I think the outcome is still in doubt," Pat said. "What we have here is a battle of the Titans."

"Little boy, I'm older than you," Ethel said.

Eddie ignored her. He marched over to the table and put Eli the turtle beside his plate.

"Turtles don't eat pancakes up but Eli can watch," Eddie said.

"Sty, make him get that filthy thing off my table," Ethel said. "I won't be bossed around in my own kitchen by no five-year-old."

"I'm five and a half, Grandma," Eddie said politely.

"Let's eat, before this tasty food goes to waste," Sty said. "All my daughters are good cooks. I can't say the same for my wife, not without fibbing a little."

"Is it real maple syrup, Aunt Neddie?" Eddie asked, climbing into his chair. Iggy yipped to be lifted up, but no one lifted him up. Harmony knew her mother wouldn't put up with a dog *and* a turtle on her table, particularly since she had never before even

336

allowed an animal to come in her house. Iggy continued to yip; he was annoyed that he couldn't sit in Eddie's lap and eat pancakes.

"It's the only maple syrup we have, let's hope it's real," Neddie said.

"I *do* hope it's real," Eddie said. "I do not like syrup that isn't real maple syrup."

"That child's spoiled rotten," Ethel said. "Somebody get that filthy turtle off my tablecloth and pitch it out in the road where it belongs. Ned, you're closest."

"I'm closest but I'm letting it lie," Neddie said.

Eddie looked his grandmother over with a cool eye.

"I don't think she's a grandmother," he said. "I think she's an alien pretending to be a grandmother."

"Could be," Pat said. "She never has been quite normal.

"Just kidding," she added, after a glance at her mother.

"*I* wasn't kidding," Eddie said. "I think Grandmother is an alien and the reason I think so is because she's rude to turtles and dogs. Eli is a nice turtle and Iggy is a nice dog."

Laurie came downstairs at that point. She had washed her face and combed her short hair. She smiled at everyone, but she looked nervous. Harmony could tell she felt a little out of place; after all, it was a family gathering except for her.

"Just sit anywhere, young lady," Sty said, sitting down himself. "If you like turtles sit by Eddie."

"Well, she does like turtles because she's my friend," Eddie said. "And I love her and she's always going to be my friend."

"Yes, I am always going to be your friend," Laurie said, sitting by Eddie. "That's a really cute little turtle."

"Be careful, it'll tinkle on my tablecloth," Ethel said. She ladled up a big plate of pancakes and set them in front of Eddie, along with a butter dish filled with butter.

"If you don't like the syrup it's your problem," she said. "It's all the syrup there is."

"Well, it's your problem if you don't like Eli, Grandma," Eddie said. "He's the only turtle I've got and I just met him and he's my pet."

Then he considered his grandmother solemnly for a minute. He gave her one of the looks that made people a little nervous if they happened to notice that he was looking at them that way.

"You could be my friend, too, Grandma," Eddie said. "Because I don't have any other grandma and you could be my Grandma and my friend too. Do you want to, Grandma?"

"Yep," Ethel said. Then she gave Eddie a lipsticky kiss and, a second later, burst into tears.

"Whoa, there she blows," Sty said. "Now we're in for it."

"Momma, what's wrong?" Harmony asked. She had forgotten how horrible it was to see her mother cry.

Eddie regarded his grandmother's tear burst coolly.

"Everybody's against me, they always have been," Ethel wailed. It was a wail all her daughters had heard many times—usually when her mother figured out that she wasn't going to get her way about something.

"No, everybody *isn't* against you," Eddie insisted. "Eli isn't and Iggy isn't and I'm not. And my Mom's not and Laurie's not and my aunts are *not* against you. Maybe you just need to see a psychiatrist, Grandma?

"Mom, I think Grandma's paranoid, maybe you better call a psychiatrist," he added, turning to Harmony.

"A psychiatrist—where would your mother meet a psychiatrist, little boy?" Ethel asked.

"She meets her in her office, her name is Dr. Short," Eddie said, sampling a pancake. "Don't you have a psychiatrist you could talk to, Grandma?"

"No, and I don't want one and no one in this family needs one, either," Ethel said. "Why would anyone go listen to a woman psychiatrist anyway? What would an old woman like that know about other women?"

"Dr. Short isn't old, Mom—she's younger than me," Harmony said.

"I don't think Grandma likes psychiatrists, Mom," Eddie said. "She glares out of her eyes when she talks about them."

"My mother didn't approve of them either," Laurie said, smiling at Ethel.

"A psychiatrist is just a doctor who doctors you when your emotions hurt, Grandma," Eddie explained. "Everybody needs one sometimes."

Harmony was hoping that Eddie wouldn't mention that he had gone to the counselor a few times himself, when he was feeling

338

unhappy—maybe it was about his father never coming to see him, or maybe it was about her boyfriends, who farted too much or had other bad habits. But of course Eddie had no bias against psychiatrists and no reason to hold back, he promptly revealed to his grandparents that he had a counselor all his own.

"My shrink is named Dr. Prichard and she's pretty and she helps me when I'm hurt in my emotions," Eddie said.

"My Lord, she's ruint that little child already, Sty," Ethel said. "We can't tell a soul about this."

"We talk about what hurts my emotions," Eddie went on, blithely. "Sometimes I get a sucker when I leave, like at the bank."

"Can't tell a soul what?" Sty asked. Harmony knew he turned down his hearing aid when he was in the house; that way he didn't have to be involved in every single argument that was going on. It seemed like a sensible policy; after all, her mother never seemed to do anything but argue. At least that was all she had done since they got home.

"Why don't you like psychiatrists, Grandma?" Eddie asked, looking at her curiously, as if he had not completely abandoned the notion that she might be an alien.

"Because I don't need one and no one in this family has ever needed one or ever will," Ethel said. "You're not even six years old yet, you couldn't possibly be crazy. Why would you need to talk to some old woman?"

"Dr. Prichard isn't old, she's pretty I told you," Eddie said. "Don't you ever listen to other people's words, Grandma?"

"No, she wouldn't see any reason to listen to other people's words, son," Sty said. "She knows it all already—why listen?"

"Nobody pulled your string, I'm trying to save this whole family from disgrace," Ethel said.

"You're too late by forty years or so, if that's what you think you're doing," Pat said. "I think I'll go home and see if I got any love letters, or if anybody sent me flowers."

"I'm going home and spread a little manure, myself," Neddie said, in her matter-of-fact voice. "That always relaxes me after a long trip."

"What'd you think of New York City, girls?—you didn't say," Sty asked. "Here all of you went to New York and we ain't even had a postcard."

"They really didn't have time to see much of the city," Laurie said.

"I didn't know what to make of it, really," Neddie said.

"I could probably have made something of it if I'd got to the right dance spots," Pat said. "But of course these stick-in-the-muds wouldn't take me."

Ethel took a big sponge out of the sink and began to scrub the blackened wall beside the stove. All she accomplished was to move some of the smudge over to a part of the wall that had been cleaner. Nonetheless she kept on sponging vigorously.

"Mom, she's just making it worse," Eddie observed at once. "Make her stop before the whole wall gets smudgy.

"Maybe she has on the wrong glasses," he added generously.

"Telling Momma to stop would be like telling a fly to stop buzzing," Neddie said.

"Eddie, she's my mother, I can't make her stop," Harmony said.

"What about Billy—has everybody just forgot him?" Pat asked, looking at Harmony. She seemed a little truculent, to Harmony.

"Don't talk nasty about your brother just because he's in jail," Ethel said, instantly. "All Billy needs is a good woman. He certainly don't need them psychiatrists they keep sending him to."

"What is she talking about, money?" Sty asked. "That's all she usually talks about. Ethel likes money better than she likes anything else."

"See how far gone he is, he can't even follow a conversation," Ethel said. "Talking to him is like talking to a fence post—boring."

"I'm going to make more pancakes, if no one minds," Laurie said.

"Nobody minds, but this is not real maple syrup," Eddie said. "It's good but it's not real maple syrup.

"I think it's *cabbage* syrup," he said, giggling at his own wit. "I think it was made from big green cabbages."

"Well, Ed's about through with his vittles, I think we'll gather up the equipment and go see if we can hook a fish or two—if we can't we can just have a conversation somewhere where there ain't no females," Sty said. "I don't know about Eddie, but I'm about out of the mood for females."

"If you meet anybody while you're fishing don't let on that Eddie's seen a psychiatrist," Ethel said. "We got our good name to worry about." She was still sponging the smoky part of the wall onto the clean part.

"What's that I'm not supposed to tell 'em?" Sty inquired.

"Dad, just ignore her, she's crazy," Neddie said.

"Shut up, don't tell your father to ignore me when I'm giving instructions," Ethel said. "He better not ignore me—it's never too late for divorce."

"How many fishermen around Tarwater are going to care whether Eddie's been to a shrink or not, Momma?" Pat said. "Get real."

"I can't hear a word anybody's saying," Sty complained.

"Well, I hear their words but I don't like them," Eddie said. "They're not very nice words."

"Got any Velveeta cheese?" Sty asked, addressing the question to Ethel. "Eddie and I might fish all day. It would be nice to have some cheese and crackers to nibble on in case the crappie are biting."

"I can't believe a daughter of mine was foolish enough to take her son to a psychiatrist before he was even six years old. I'd go see my minister about this if he wasn't such a blabbermouth."

"Momma, I live in Las Vegas, people have a different attitude there," Harmony said. "I really wish we could change the subject."

"That minister's from Kansas—they're too talky up in Kansas," Ethel said. "They oughtn't to let preachers from way up in Kansas preach in Oklahoma."

Laurie was at the stove, making pancakes. She looked over her shoulder at Harmony and smiled a nice smile. It was a smile to let Harmony know that she sympathized where Ethel was concerned. Probably Laurie's mother wouldn't get off an awkward subject either, once she got on one. When the pancakes were ready Laurie gave some to Harmony, who passed them on to Neddie—she would need to eat if she was going to spread manure.

"My stomach feels funny—maybe it's just from being home," Harmony remarked.

"Maybe it's because there's an alien in the kitchen," Eddie said, with a grin. "Mom, would you watch my turtle while I go fishing? He doesn't move very fast. I think he'll be easy to watch."

He gave her a sticky kiss before going off to wash his hands.

"I'm going to get rid of that filthy turtle," Ethel said. She came

341

around the table and tried to snatch Eli, but Harmony saved him just in time.

"No, Mom—it's Eddie's pet," she said. "Didn't you hear me tell him I'd take care of it?"

"We could tell him it escaped—turtles are filthy," Ethel said. "This is my house. I've never kept a reptile in it and I don't intend to start."

Harmony felt a little emotional as she watched Eddie and her father get ready to go fishing. It was something her father had been mentioning for years. He seemed to think the prospect of fishing would bring them home.

"We'll just put the turtle in a box, so it won't hurt anything," she said, to placate her mother.

"It has a name, Eli," Eddie reminded her as he was leaving.

9.

Later in the day Harmony took a nap, on an old purple Sears and Roebuck couch, on her parents' back porch. Eli the turtle took a nap with her, in a shoebox by her side—Harmony knew her mother would throw Eli out if she could find him, so she hid him under a quilt. The quilt was the same blue Arkansas quilt that had been there in her childhood.

Iggy had gone fishing with Eddie and her father—nobody trusted Ethel in relation to Iggy, either.

Laurie, too, took a nap. She simply went outside and stretched out on the newly mown grass.

"That girl will get chiggers—they'll be up to her undies," Ethel warned. "If she don't get chiggers she'll get pneumonia—that ground's sopping wet underneath."

"Momma, you can't see underneath the ground," Harmony pointed out.

"No, she can't even see the top of the ground, much less the bottom," Pat said. "If someone offered her a million dollars to find a june bug she couldn't find one in a week, and this place is crawling with june bugs."

"Shut up and go home!" Ethel said—actually Pat and Neddie

were just waiting for Neddie's husband, Dick, to arrive. Harmony tried gamely to stay awake, so she could say hello to Dick, but she didn't make it. It felt so relaxing to lie on the old couch that despite herself, she drifted off. As she was drifting off, she heard her mother complaining to Neddie about Dick's problems with his tractors.

"He oughtn't to be driving tractors at his age, anyway," her mother said.

"Momma, he's just sixty," Neddie said. "I'd like to see someone try to stop me from driving my tractor because I'm sixty years old.

"Which I won't be yet for quite a while," she added quickly.

"Tractors flip over and when they do the driver is always killed, that's a well-known fact," Ethel said.

"Don't argue with her, she's cracked," Pat said. "I wish Dick would hurry. I'm in one of those moods where I might become a serial killer, and I might start with my mother."

Harmony remembered, as she was fading, how happy Eddie had looked when he climbed into the old blue pickup, to go fishing with his grandfather. Except for Gary, Eddie had lived all his life with women: finally, there was a man who was paying some attention to him, and not just a man off the street, either. The man was his grandfather. When Eddie shut the door of the pickup she couldn't even see the top of his head, but she could hear his voice, relaying to his grandfather some fish facts he had learned on the Discovery Channel. It was a good sound to go to sleep with; better, for sure, than her mother's complaining.

When she woke up, Eddie was standing by her, holding three small green fish on a string.

"Mom, these are perch, I caught them!" Eddie said. "I caught them on a hook and Grandpa and I are going to *clean* them. They'll be very clean and then we'll cook them in a pan and eat them."

"Perch are too bony to eat," Ethel said, popping back onto the porch. "If you eat them you'll get a bone in your throat and we'll have to run you to the emergency room and they'll take it out with tongs."

But Eddie had already run off in search of his grandfather, the three perch jiggling on the string.

"Oh, Eddie, I knew you'd be a good fisherman," Harmony said, though he probably didn't hear her—he was too excited. It was one of those moments when parenting was mixed; it was difficult. Now Eddie was happy in Oklahoma. He was going to want to stay with his grandfather for a while, and learn more about country living, whereas she herself had been thinking about calling Gary and asking him to meet her at the airport in Las Vegas. She was thinking of going right back, and it wasn't because her mother was so critical, either.

One reason she felt comfortable on the porch was that it really wasn't in her mother's house—the porch was just sort of tacked on. She had not even gone upstairs yet, to see the room that had once been hers. The stairs to the second floor were pretty narrow; she felt she might get claustrophobia if she tried to squeeze through. It wasn't just the stairs, though. The whole experience of being home was making her feel that she just wanted to go, even though she knew that to be a good parent she should get a room or something and give Eddie time to soak up some attention from his grandparents.

"Where's Laurie?" she asked—it was almost evening.

"She got up and walked off down the road without a by-your-leave," Ethel said. "You slept all day. I guess she got bored. Why'd you bring a girl like that all the way to Oklahoma?"

"Momma, she was Pepper's best friend, I wanted to spend some time with her," Harmony said. "We need to be with one another for a while."

"Why didn't her husband come?" Ethel asked. "Does he just let her run all over the country like a chicken?"

"Laurie's not married," Harmony pointed out—of course she had no intention of mentioning that Laurie was gay.

"Then what's she doing wearing a wedding band?" Ethel asked. "The first thing I notice when I meet somebody is whether she's wearing a wedding band."

Harmony remembered then that Pepper and Laurie had exchanged wedding bands, they were just cheap ones bought on a street corner, Laurie said.

"I think it was just a ring, Momma," Harmony said; she saw no reason to be more specific.

"Well, it's fishy," Ethel said. "Just because I've lived in the country all my life don't mean I can't tell when something's fishy."

Harmony got up and walked off the porch—usually that was the best way to end a conversation with her mother; sometimes it was the only way. Probably her departure for Las Vegas at sixteen had been a way of walking off from the sound of her mother's voice.

The moon was just coming up. It was a big moon, more yellow than it seemed to be in other places. Harmony's plan was to walk down the lane and find Laurie, but then she noticed Laurie over by the barrel where fish got cleaned. She was helping Eddie and Sty clean the fish, so Harmony just waved and walked on down toward the pond. She thought it might be nice to walk a little and watch the moon rise. Already she heard frogs croaking, from the pond, and heard the bullbats call, as they swooshed over her head.

The pond was right beside the road, so close that when her boyfriends brought her home from dates, in high school, they would try to flip beer bottles over the car and into the water. Usually they could get the bottles to fall into the pond. Sometimes the beer bottles didn't sink right away—sometimes they would still be floating the next day. If her father came by the next day and noticed beer bottles floating in the pond, there would usually be a scene. Her father had been strict when he was younger. He didn't want boys who threw beer bottles in the pond to be going out with his daughter.

Harmony decided to climb through the fence and watch the moon rise over the water—she was hoping there wouldn't be snakes watching the moon rise with her. Getting through the barbed-wire fence was a little difficult. She nicked her blouse a time or two, but at least the barbs didn't stick in her butt, as they had from time to time when she was a teenager.

After she made it past the fence, Harmony picked her way through the prickly grass to a stump on the dam, on the east side of the pond. Once a great sycamore tree had stood on the tank dam—Harmony could remember it a little from her early childhood. She could remember the hard little balls the tree made, which had become puffballs once they dried up. But, one day, some vagrants driving along in a car in winter saw the sycamore and stopped and cut it down for firewood. When her father came back from work in the fields that day and saw that the sycamore was gone he was so stunned he couldn't eat supper—his own mother had planted the tree almost seventy-five years earlier.

346

Ethel said it was the only night of their marriage that Sty had been unable to eat; his shock and grief over the loss of the sycamore became a family legend.

"Even seeing his own son arrested for naughty phone calls didn't affect him as much as the loss of that tree," Ethel said, many times. She always referred to Billy's calls as naughty. Even after it had happened five or six times, naughty was the strongest word she would use.

Though Harmony didn't really remember the sycamore itself very clearly, she did remember every detail of its destruction by the vagrants. Everyone in the family remembered every detail of its destruction by the vagrants, and remembered, particularly, the effect of the destruction on their father.

"He wouldn't eat no steak, he wouldn't eat no gravy, he didn't touch the peach cobbler I made him and he didn't do nothing under the quilts, neither," was how her mother described that day. "Usually on Thursday night Sty does something under the quilts, but he didn't that night, nor the next Thursday either. Who would think an old tree falling over would make that happen to a healthy man?"

"Under the quilts" was her mother's euphemism for sex.

"I've seen Sty lots of times with his behind dragging nearly down to the floor but it didn't stop him eating and it didn't stop him under the quilts, either," Ethel added. "I think he went off in his head and never came back, that's what I think."

"It was a shock to me that any people would be so ignorant as to cut down a shade tree, in this country," her father said, when he discussed the loss of the sycamore. "There wasn't no trees in this country a-tall, when my folks settled here. My mother ordered that tree and planted it with her own hands. I doubt Dad was much help to her, either. Dad worked so hard he didn't notice whether he was in the shade or in the sun. But Momma carried water from the well to water that tree—that was long before we scraped up a dam and made this pond. My mother watered it herself and it finally took root and grew. There wasn't a better shade tree in this whole county. How could people be so ignorant that they'd cut down a shade tree for firewood, on the plains?"

Usually, when he thought of the lost tree, her father would grow melancholy. He would go off alone and sit with his mule for a while. For an hour or two he would be so wrought up that he couldn't stand human company.

"I think he misses his mother," Neddie theorized. Harmony wasn't sure. In her childhood she dreaded occasions that reminded her father of the tree. It was as if the fact that the thoughtless vagrants had cut down the tree said something bad to her father—bad about human nature itself. When he dwelled on it too much he always decided that he preferred the company of mules to the company of humans, for a while.

Harmony's own memories were more wrapped up with the stump than with the tree. It was a big stump—big enough that two people could sit on it. Sometimes the same boyfriends who threw the beer bottles in the pond would work up their nerve and kiss her while sitting on the stump. Sometimes, while she was necking on the stump with some boy, the boy would try to get his hands inside her bra—that was about as far as even the boldest boyfriends ventured, in those days.

Also, many of her talks with her father had taken place on the stump. Often, at the end of the day, he would walk down to the pond and sit on the stump for a while, to smoke and fish. Sometimes Harmony would go with him. They would sit together, watching the dragonflies skim the surface of the pond, watching the bullbats circle, listening to the coyotes yip, as they often would at sundown. If her father happened to catch a fish he would usually throw it back—having a line in the water just seemed to fit with the occasion. Sometimes they would sit long enough to see the moon's reflection in the water—then her mother would begin to yell at them to come and eat dinner. Her father would wince a little, when they heard Ethel's voice.

"She reminds me of a squeaky gate," he said, more than once. "I can't figure out how I ended up married to her."

Harmony had often wondered about that herself—but then it was hard to figure out why anybody ended up married to anyone. Neddie married Dick because there wasn't much of anyone else to date when she was dating age. Pat had ended up married to various men because she slept with them a few times and got carried away. She herself had ended up married to Ross because he looked so helpless she thought he might not survive if she didn't move in and

348

take care of him. Those things happened—afterward, particularly many years afterward, it was hard to remember why.

This time, just as she was settling herself on the stump, she felt something pass between herself and the moon and looked up in time to see a great blue heron, flying away. It had been feeding in the marshy grass at the edge of the pond. For a second she was scared—the heron's wings were so long. But when she saw the heron in the sky, flapping away toward the fields, she lost her fear. After all, it was just a bird.

Harmony watched the little swallows skim the water until it was so dark she could only make out the water when a bird skimmed its surface. The water would be touched for a moment with a little fleck of moonlight.

Watching the heron fly, or the birds skim the water, reminded her of the time—most of her life, actually—when she had enjoyed just watching various aspects of life—not beautiful aspects, always, but interesting to watch. She had taken a part of her happiness just from looking at living things, whether it was Eddie or Pepper, or a little bird or a large bird, or a man sliding into bed with her, or people in the casino, or the way the other showgirls did their hair. It could be almost anything, for example a little baby just learning to stand alone that would sometimes turn loose of whatever it was holding and just stand there a few seconds, not realizing what was taking place. She had taken pleasure just in the way guys laughed, or in the way certain dealers handled their cards, or even just in the way the sun shone on sunny mornings in the desert outside Las Vegas. The external world was a neat place; she could never get enough of looking at it. Even during low periods, after a breakup with some guy, when the salt had sort of lost its savor, there were always things to watch. Once Eddie came along there was always Eddie to watch—watching him had kept her perky for five and a half years.

The nicest thing so far about coming back to Oklahoma was that Eddie liked her father so much, and her father liked him. Having a grandfather to take him fishing, and to take an interest in his point of view, would make up for having no father; at least it would make up for it a little bit.

But, apart from Eddie and Sty, her homecoming really didn't

feel as if it was going to work out. She was sitting on the old sycamore stump she had sat on in her girlhood, on a beautiful evening with a full moon rising over the plains, with birds flying around, and yet she didn't have much sense that she was even there. She couldn't get out of herself, not even under the beautiful moon. Pepper's death had taken away the external world, the very world whose beauties had sustained her for so long. The external world was still there; she could look at it; it hadn't vanished. But it might as well have vanished because she couldn't reach it anymore.

Always, before, she had found it easy to get out of herself—easier to get out than to stay in, for that matter—but now, even though the moon was full and the prairie breeze did smell good, she wasn't outdoors in her spirit. She was inside, with her grief about Pepper. All she could see was the hole in her life, where once there had been a person who would never be there again. Only the hole would be there—and in the hole was a darkness so dark that the light of the world couldn't reach it; only, now and then, there might be a flicker, like the streak the moonlight made on the water when a little bird touched the surface.

"Why are you sitting there?" Laurie asked. "Are you sad?"

She was trying to crawl through the fence and seemed to be a little snagged. She finally got through, though, and picked her way toward the pond.

"Can I sit with you, or are you too sad?" she asked, when she finally made it to the stump.

Harmony made room on the stump; of course Laurie could sit with her.

"Eddie and his grandfather really connected," Laurie said. "I thought I ought to leave them alone, so they can make up for lost time."

"I should have brought Eddie sooner," Harmony said—it was obvious that Eddie and his grandfather should have had a chance to know one another years ago.

"My grandfather was killed in World War Two," Laurie said. "He might have taken me fishing or something if I'd met him.

"My good grandfather, I mean," she added. "In my fantasies I've made him the perfect grandfather, and the fantasy will never be tested, because he's dead."

350

"What about your other grandfather?" Harmony asked. "Is he dead?"

"No, but everybody wishes he was," Laurie said. "He's never showed any interest in me, only in my brothers. He didn't particularly like my mother and I think he expected me to turn out like her. Boy, was he wrong."

"What does he do?" Harmony asked. She felt she ought to show some interest in Laurie's family, but in the state she was in—the state of not being able to get out of herself—it was hard. Laurie seemed to realize it was hard.

"He plays golf—let's talk about something else," she said.

"What about your Dad?" Harmony asked. She wasn't trying to be polite, exactly; she was trying to get out of herself, to breathe the same air other people breathed. In that air people had some curiosity about one another's families.

"Dad fell in love with a twenty-seven-year-old, and divorced Mom, and married her," Laurie said. "He plays a lot of golf too.

"I think you came here to be alone," Laurie added. "Maybe I should go back to the house."

Harmony *had* come to the pond to be alone, only the pond wasn't far enough away to provide much aloneness. Across the pond, across the lane, across the yard, she could see the lights in the windows of her parents' house. Eddie was probably there, talking a blue streak, while her father cooked the fish. Her mother didn't cook fish, and never had. When there was fish, Sty cooked it and Ethel stood in the kitchen and complained. "Fish belong in water, steak belongs on my stove," she often said.

"I want you to stay," Harmony told Laurie. She was thinking of Eddie and her father, when she said it; she didn't want to intrude on their time together. It was her problem that she could no longer breathe the air other people breathed. It was her problem that she couldn't find aloneness, even by the old pond, even in the dark. It was hard to be alone when you had memories: where could you go, other than death, to be beyond memory? All she knew was that she didn't want to go upstairs, in her parents' house—up the stairs to the bedroom she had left at sixteen. The thought of going up those narrow stairs that led to the past made her feel sick.

When she asked Laurie to stay, she took her hand.

"Of course I'll stay," Laurie said, squeezing Harmony's hand.

"I don't know what's to become of me," Harmony said. "I have to stay alive, because of Eddie, but I don't know what's to become of me. I don't have any money. I don't know if I could hold a job —not an everyday job, not right now."

"I can hold a job," Laurie said. "I'll live with you and support you."

Laurie did look confident. Undoubtedly she could hold a job. Yet she was the young one; Harmony felt she ought to be taking care of Laurie, not the other way around.

"I've had twenty-three jobs, since I left college," Laurie said. "I only got fired twice and that was because I had bosses who wanted to fuck me and I wouldn't. But mostly I didn't get fired, I just happened to get jobs with infirm businesses. Quite a few of the businesses just slowly expired."

Just then, from across the pond, they heard a thin but desperate squeaking. A frog had been a bit careless, careless enough that a water snake had caught it. Now the frog was going to be swallowed, and was squeaking out its last few frog sounds before the end.

"What's that?" Laurie asked. Harmony remembered that Laurie was a city girl. She wouldn't know how a small frog sounded as it was being swallowed by a water snake.

"That's a frog," Harmony said. "A snake's swallowing it."

"Well, we're about to swallow Eddie's fish, I guess that's nature," Laurie said.

Harmony didn't know whether she had been right to identify the sound for Laurie. Some people were delicate. Even though they knew the facts of life they might not welcome the news that a squeaky sound by a pond was the sound a frog made as it was being swallowed. Gary had once ruined a little dinner party of hers by recounting an experience he had had in Singapore—the experience of ordering a puppy in a Chinese restaurant and then eating the puppy after it had been killed and cooked. Actually it was Gary's boyfriend who ordered the puppy; Gary had once been so in love with a rich Asian kid that he followed him to Singapore. Gary claimed he had only been able to choke down a bite or two of the puppy—Gary was of the try-anything-once school—but it was definitely Gary who told the story and ruined her dinner party.

Harmony was thinking of Pepper, though. She had died of a disease that held her and slowly swallowed her, as the water snake was surely swallowing the frog. Laurie had been with her as the swallowing took place, too Now she and Laurie were hearing the sounds of the end of a life—a frog life, but still a life. It was silly to feel so disturbed just because she told Laurie about a little fact of nature of the sort that occurred all over Oklahoma many times a day. Yet she *was* disturbed: she felt as if a million eggshells might break inside her, if she misspoke.

"I was thinking of Pepper," she explained. "Anything bad, even a little frog getting eaten by a snake, makes me think of her now."

"You're right," Laurie said. "AIDS swallowed her. One day she was fine and the next day it had her by the leg. Two months later she was dead. The only difference is, Pepper didn't squeak. She just gave up.

"Pepper had no fight in her really," Laurie added, after a moment. "Even if we just happened to have a squabble, she wouldn't fight. She just gave up. I wanted her to try some experimental treatments, but she wouldn't. She preferred to give up. It only took her eight weeks to die."

Just as she said it, the frog stopped squeaking. There were crickets singing around the pond, but no sound from the frog. Somewhere in the mud at the pond's edge, the snake was slithering away, with the frog inside it.

"I wish we could stop thinking about her," Laurie said. "I think it's unhealthy, that we can't stop, but the fact is we can't. I was thinking this morning that I shouldn't have come with you."

"Why, Laurie?" Harmony said—she was shocked.

"Because if we're together how are we ever going to stop thinking about her?" Laurie asked.

"Mom, come eat the fish—I caught it," Eddie said, from somewhere near the yard. "Mom, you have to come and Laurie has to come."

"The voice of our leader," Laurie said. "We better stop moping and go eat those fish."

Somehow Harmony caught herself before the million eggshells cracked. It was close, though. One more sad tone from Laurie and they might have cracked, all million of them at once.

But Eddie's tone wasn't sad. He was proud that he had caught a fish.

"I have a question for you," Laurie said, as they were walking back up the lane. From time to time Eddie yelled a command. He was getting impatient.

Harmony was hoping the question wasn't about Pepper; she didn't feel up to any more questions about Pepper, not right then.

"How did you stand your mother?" Laurie asked. They were almost to the yard.

"I didn't, I left," Harmony reminded her.

"Do you think that's why your brother makes obscene phone calls? To get back at her?" Laurie asked.

"Laurie, it's probably because he can't find a girlfriend," Harmony said.

10.

Eddie insisted that his mother eat the first of the three perch he caught—he ate the other two. Then, as soon as supper was over, he fell asleep on the purple couch on the back porch, just as Harmony had, several hours earlier. As he slept he clutched a pocketknife that his grandfather had given him. It was a knife Sty had used for many years, and had sharpened many times—he used it to cut twine, or clean fish, or pare his toenails. The main blade of the pocketknife had worn thin, from many sharpenings. Eddie was very proud of the knife. Despite his grandmother's frequent injunctions about cutting his finger off, he kept opening and closing the knife until he went to sleep.

Iggy, exhausted from a day of following Eddie around, slept at his feet; the turtle was in his shoebox beside the couch, but on the side near the screen, where his grandmother, with her poor eyesight, would be unlikely to find it and release it.

"Don't let that child sleep on the porch," Ethel said. "The night air's bad for children—he'll wake up with pneumonia and if he don't get pneumonia a spider might bite him."

"She's cracked," Sty said. "There's no spiders on that porch."

"You don't know, you're blind as a bat," Ethel said.

"*I'm* blind as a bat?" Sty said, in surprise.

"Blind as a bat," Ethel repeated. "If there was a tarantula spider crawling right on this table I doubt you'd even see it."

"Mom, the night air's the same air that's out there in the daytime," Harmony pointed out. Neddie and Pat had gone home while she was napping—now she missed them. Even though they bickered, she had gotten so used to having them around that *not* having them around made her feel strange. Anyway, arguing with her mother was a full-time job for three people; it was a good bit more than any one person could manage.

Laurie offered to do the dishes. She started clearing the table, but she made the mistake of yawning while she was carrying a couple of plates—Ethel, bad eyesight or not, saw the yawn.

"You're sleepy, young lady, just leave them dishes, Harmony can clear the table," Ethel said. "She hasn't turned a hand in this kitchen in Lord knows how long."

"Momma, that's rude, Laurie just wanted to help," Harmony said. "It's only a few dishes."

"Well, that girl's sleepy, she might drop five or six plates," Ethel said. "I can't take the chance. Your father steals all my money, you know—he just takes my social security check right out of the mailbox and cashes it. I wouldn't be able to replace this crockery if that girl broke it."

"If I *didn't* take your social security check out of the mailbox it'd sit there and never get cashed," Sty said. "You haven't been to the mailbox in years, and when you do go you won't stick your hand in because you're afraid of black widow spiders."

"Black widow spiders make their home in mailboxes, everybody knows that," Ethel said.

Laurie quietly cleared the table; Ethel didn't notice.

"Ethel, that was excellent gravy," Laurie said, referring to the cream gravy Ethel made with every meal. "I'm a little sleepy. If no one minds I'll go to bed."

"Don't open your window no more than a crack, there might be bats flying around outside," Ethel said. "Besides that, snakes climb walls."

"Ethel, there's a screen on the window," Sty reminded her. "There's screens on all our windows. Even if Laurie opened her window all the way to the top a bat couldn't get in, much less a snake."

"You don't know everything, Sty," Ethel said. "In fact, if you even still know anything, I don't know what it is."

Laurie kissed Harmony and then went up to bed.

"Is that girl adopted?" Ethel asked, once Laurie had gone.

"No, Momma, she's not adopted," Harmony said. "Why do you ask so many rude questions?"

"What's rude about the truth?" Ethel asked. "There's something funny about that girl, I thought she might be adopted. What's she doing kissing you?—you're not her mother."

"It was just a goodnight kiss," Harmony said. Her urge to be somewhere else was getting stronger. Ever since she woke up from her nap she had been thinking how nice it would be to be in a motel room, alone, just to piddle, or watch TV. She wanted to be someplace where her mother wouldn't always be there to ask rude questions, or make rude statements, or just look at her rudely and think suspicious thoughts.

"Momma, would you mind if I went to a motel? I feel like being alone," she said.

Ethel looked shocked.

"Drive all this way after being gone for years and then not even spend the night?" her mother asked. "What kind of behavior is that?

"Which motel?" she asked, before Harmony could even reply. "Have you got some man stashed away here that we don't know about?"

"I don't have a man anywhere, Mom," Harmony said. "I've been under a lot of strain and think I'd sleep better if I could be alone."

"Go in your room and shut the door, that's alone enough," Ethel said. "Why would anybody want to be alone when they could be with their own mother? That's awful. Drive all this way to be with your mother and then go off to a motel to see some man?"

"Ethel, Harmony's grown," Sty said. "She's middle-aged, and this is a free country. If a middle-aged woman wants to be alone that's her business."

"She's my daughter, I don't care how old she is," Ethel said.

357

"I didn't want to be alone when I was middle-aged. Why should Harmony be any different from me?"

"Momma, I *am* different from you," Harmony pointed out, feeling tired. Even when she was sixteen, arguing with her mother had made her feel tired.

"It's middle-aged women who usually have some old boy stashed away," Ethel said. "Look at Pat. It's a disgrace, how she behaves. They've had to send her away to those old sex doctors I don't know how many times. I thought it was a waste of money. If that's her thing, whose business is it but hers?"

Sty looked exasperated. "That's just what I said to you about Harmony," he said. "If being alone in a motel is her thing, let her do it."

He handed her the keys to his pickup.

"There's a Best Western about six miles down the highway," he said. "They have a nice clean coffee shop. I expect it's the best Tarwater's got to offer."

Ethel picked up the sponge and began to sponge the smoky wall again.

"I doubt she knows how to drive a pickup," she said. "If she don't, too bad—my Buick is unavailable. You let the oil get dirty and now I'm afraid to drive it for fear it will burst into flames while I'm on the way to town.

"I got no friends left anyway, I don't need to go to town," she added, still sponging the wall. "What if there's a nuclear attack while she's off in the pickup—what'll we do, Sty?"

"Ethel, the cold war's over, there won't be a nuclear attack," Sty said. "Just watch CNN."

"I don't believe everything I hear on the radio," Ethel said.

"CNN ain't radio, it's TV," Sty reminded her. "I guess it don't matter, you can't see well enough to tell the difference."

"If we could get all the way to Texas we might survive," Ethel said, still working on the premise of a nuclear attack. "I don't know that that fallout would fall all the way to Texas."

"She's cracked," Sty said. "Go on, honey. Get a good night's sleep. Me and Eddie will do the milking in the morning. Once we get the chores done we might fish a little more. Sleep late if you feel the need."

"Why would she need to sleep late?" Ethel asked. "She hasn't done anything but sleep since she got here. I thought she might want to talk to me, but so far we ain't talked five minutes. I've got funny daughters, none of them care about talking to their mother."

Sty stood up and walked Harmony to the door.

"Don't stand around waiting for the last word to come out," he said. "If you do that you'll never leave. There's no such thing as a last word, with your mother. I've been waiting over fifty years for the last word, and so far I've waited in vain."

Harmony kissed her father, and made sure Eddie's blanket was tucked close around him before she let herself out the screen door.

"How do we know she's even got a driver's license?" she heard her mother say, while she was still on the step.

The seat of the pickup was just about worn through—Harmony could feel the springs, when she sat on it. The highway was visible, about two miles away. She could see the lights of big trucks purring along it. There was a glow to the south, where Tulsa was.

Harmony took it slow, going over the dirt road—she wasn't used to pickups. She knew if she had a wreck her mother would complain forever, mainly to her father, since it was her father who gave her the keys.

She had only been on the highway about two miles when she came to the Tarwater exit. The town was just a sprinkle of lights, a mile off the interstate. She had been looking forward to being in the motel alone, but she had a sudden urge to see her brother; it was odd that they had seen so little of one another, over the years, because they had always been close. When Harmony was in high school she thought Billy was the best-looking man in Oklahoma, if not the world. He quarterbacked the high school football team and took them to the state championships twice, winning both times. There was even a commemorative cannon on the court-house lawn, with the dates of the victories printed on the barrel.

In high school, Billy had all the girls in love with him. He dated the most beautiful girl in the school, Tammy Dawson; it was assumed they would marry, but to everyone's surprise Tammy married a lawyer and moved to Dallas.

It was about then that Billy began to let success slip through his fingers. He was a sophomore at the University of Tulsa, and had been on the dean's list four straight semesters, when he got arrested with some friends of his for stealing oil field equipment. Since it was a first offense, Billy didn't have to go to jail, but definitely the slipping began about that time. He came back home and tried to farm with his father, but that effort didn't last long; Sty had his own way of doing things, and that was that. Pretty soon Billy left and went to New Mexico, where he got in some trouble that everyone had always been sort of vague about. Neddie thought there might be a child born out of wedlock, out in New Mexico, but that was just her guess. Billy never said anything to anyone about a child. Then he got caught coming out of Mexico with some kind of ore in his trunk; some people thought the ore was gold and some people thought it was uranium, but in either case it was a little bit illegal. Billy had to go to jail for six months as a result. When he got out of jail he didn't do much of anything for a few years, except gamble on sports and play dominoes with the brothers who owned the Conoco station in Tarwater. Billy was the best domino player in the state; he had always been exceptional at anything he did; but it was still a limited life. Of course the very fact that Billy had even been in Mexico caused Ethel to fret for years; she had worried while he was in prison, but even that worry paled beside the worries she had about all the diseases Billy probably was infected with as a result of being south of the border.

Harmony had been south of the border quite a few times herself; she had even had a boyfriend named Enrique, from somewhere south of the border; of all her boyfriends, many of whom had been pretty hard to shake, Enrique ranked as probably the most obsessed. Specifically he had been obsessed with her clitoris, why she could never figure out. Most men, once they reached the state of being obsessed, fixed on her breasts but Enrique got obsessed with her clitoris and stayed obsessed with it until she finally managed to shake him, which was quite a few months after the obsession began. Never again had her clitoris come in for quite so much attention as it got while Enrique was obsessed with it.

Of course the fact that Enrique had been obsessed with her clitoris was way off the track from wondering what had caused success to slip away from Billy; it was just a memory that came back to her once in a while when she was low—at least with Enrique around she had always known she was wanted.

One reason she drove so slowly as she entered Tarwater was

because her mother's last-minute intuition had been right on the nose: she didn't have a driver's license. Somehow, the last time her license came up for renewal, she had never got around to sending it in. It was one of those times when her bank account had eight dollars in it, exactly the amount that it cost to renew her driver's license. She didn't think it made sense to spend her last eight dollars on a driver's license when she didn't have a car anyway.

So, as she approached the center of Tarwater, she drove especially slowly. The two policemen in Tarwater—there had always been two—didn't have that much to do. They sat in their cars and waited, most of the night, and they loved to pounce on speeders. Also, she had the feeling that her father's pickup was not too well equipped for night driving. Only one headlight seemed to be working; either that or her vision was weird.

Still, the town looked awfully peaceful, maybe because it was such a relief to get beyond the sound of her mother's voice. There was not a single car moving on the streets of Tarwater when Harmony drove up to the jail. Tarwater had no buildings more than two stories high—it was essentially a one-story town. Across the stretch of prairie to the south she could clearly see the sign for the Best Western. Just being able to see it was kind of reassuring; if the other headlight went out on the pickup she could probably just walk to the motel, it wasn't that far.

Only a single police car was parked in front of the jail when she pulled up, but there were six teenagers sitting there, on the curb. At first she thought it might be a youth gang that had been let out of jail. There were three girls and three boys. When she stepped out of the car they all said "Aunt Harmony" at once, it was a big surprise. Then it dawned on her that the youth gang was composed of her nephews and nieces—Neddie had a girl and two boys, Pat a boy and two girls.

"We knew you'd come to see Uncle Billy, we just wanted to meet you, you're the most famous person who ever lived in Tarwater," a skinny boy said. Harmony knew he was Neddie's just from his skinniness.

"Aren't you Dickie?" she asked. "And you're Don and you're Donna. And you're Dave and you're Deenie and you're Debbie."

For some reason her sisters had given all their children names that began with D. Harmony thought she had done well to get their names right. Once the introductions were over, nobody had much of an inkling of what to say next. Harmony certainly didn't, although she was touched that they had all wanted to meet her so badly that they had parked themselves on a curb in Tarwater, in the middle of the night. It certainly showed that they cared about their auntie.

Another fact that kind of soaked in was that none of her nieces and nephews were all that young; she was not seeing the little kids she remembered from Polaroids. They all seemed to fall in an age group between seventeen and maybe twenty-five. She had stayed away too long—much too long—to get to see them as kids. It seemed only a short while ago that she had been getting pictures of their earliest birthday parties, or snaps of the boys in their Little League uniforms—pictures from childhood. But already the childhood of the children in those pictures was gone; they just weren't children anymore.

"You're all grown up," she said. "Can I give you all hugs?"

Before she knew it they were all hugging her; it was as if they had been waiting for the hugs for years and years—all their lives, really. She was thinking, as she hugged them, that none of them looked too happy—not in an overall sense; not happy as Eddie was happy. They seemed older than their years, as if life in Tarwater had aged them too quickly. It was a little confusing; it was supposed to be city kids that grew up too quickly; but her nieces and nephews seemed to have grown old as they grew up. All but two already had children, and several had had more than one marriage.

"Aunt Harmony, you're still beautiful," Debbie said.

"We're sorry about Pepper," Don said. "We only got to meet her once."

"Maybe if she had lived in Tarwater she wouldn't have got AIDS," Deenie suggested; Harmony knew she was just trying to be comforting, but the way it came out wasn't comforting. The very thought of Pepper living in Tarwater was confusing. She might have already had babies and an ex-husband and have been abandoned; she might never have known Laurie or the nice bakeries of New York. If she could have lived, Pepper would have had good things ahead of her. Harmony was having a hard time imagining what good things the nice young people in the street had ahead of

362

them, other than more children, more divorces, more husbands and wives who weren't much different from the husbands and wives they had got the divorces from.

"Aunt Harmony, did we make you sad?" Deenie asked. Probably she felt Don had done the wrong thing, in mentioning Pepper.

"Honey, it's just a sadness I have," Harmony said. "You didn't cause it. Have you been in to see Uncle Billy?"

"He doesn't want to see us," Dickie said.

"He thinks we're all fuckups," Debbie said. "He told Peewee not to let us in the jail."

"We all want to meet Eddie, real bad," Donna said. "We saw him all over the place on TV."

"He's so cute," Deenie said. "We're going to go out to Grandpa's in the morning and take him to breakfast."

"Try to find a place with real maple syrup," Harmony advised. "He's kind of picky about things like that."

"I don't guess I'd know real maple syrup if I was eating it," Don said.

"Mom says he's a match for Granny," Debbie said. "I'm glad somebody's a match for her, none of us are."

"I'm a match for her," Donna said. "I'm not letting some cranky old lady push me around."

Harmony was looking at the little town, empty even of cars; not one single thing open at ten at night except the jail. The sight of it was making her want to go to the airport. She had never before had such a strong feeling of needing to go to the airport; she wanted to be someplace where at least a few things other than the jail stayed open past ten at night. It was touching that her nieces and nephews had wanted to meet her so badly that they would come to the jail in the middle of the night; it was touching, but also complicated. She had missed their lives—what could she and they do with one another now? She knew she ought to get a good night's sleep and start right in the next day meeting their children and learning their husbands' and wives' names and finding out what jobs they worked at; but the thought of doing that made her feel hopeless, it was too late. She had missed being an aunt—it wasn't her calling, as Gary would say.

"I have to go now, Auntie," Don said. "My girlfriend works at a Circle K in a bad part of Tulsa—I have to be there in twenty minutes to pick her up. If she has to stand around, guys try to pick her up."

"They don't have to try very hard, either," Donna said, with a kind of flatness in her voice that reminded Harmony of Neddie.

"Donna thinks Jeanie's a slut," Debbie said.

"She's not a slut, she just likes to be picked up on time," Don said. "It's hard for an outsider to make much headway with this family."

"Oh, bullshit," Donna said. "Anybody who's not a slut can get along fine with this family."

Something about the look on Don's face touched Harmony—it was a hopeless look. Perhaps he knew in his heart that Donna was right and that his girlfriend really was a slut. Probably she wouldn't wait two minutes at the Circle K before going off with some guy, if Don wasn't right there to meet her. The look made Harmony want to hug him, really hug him. Maybe he had just taken the only girl he could get because he was too lonely to do anything else. Harmony could see, from looking around the empty streets, that it would be easy to get lonely enough that it would keep you from being picky. She had been that lonely even in Las Vegas, and certainly there were plenty of guys to choose from in Las Vegas.

When Don left they all began to leave, too—they just kind of drifted across the street, with a wave or two—they all had cars parked on the other side of the square. Harmony waved too; she felt ambivalent about seeing them leave. When they were standing around her, close, they all looked old, but now that they were wandering across the street they all looked young again—very young, just a bunch of skinny kids who had grown up in the same family in the same small town. They all seemed too skinny, but in ways that had nothing to do with their bodies. It was their experience that was skinny: they had too much experience of a flat place and not enough experience of the big world and the interesting things it held. She wished that at some point she could have scraped up the money to fly them all to Disneyland—then they could tell all their friends that their famous aunt had flown them there. It occurred to her that maybe she could still do it, someday; it might be even better because now some of them could even take *their* kids. It would be killing two birds with one stone. Even so,

Harmony couldn't help feeling how much more advantaged Eddie was. He had been to Disneyland when he was four, and meant to go to Disney World in Florida pretty soon, too.

"I need to go there before I'm eight, at the *latest*," he said, often.

Then her nephews and nieces came convoying around the square in their cars. The only one who didn't have a car was Don, who had a motorcycle. He rode it without a helmet, too. Except for Don the boys drove large rattly cars whose mufflers weren't the best, and the girls drove small economical cars that all looked a little bent, as if they might have been involved in a few fender benders.

All the nephews and nieces waved at her before they disappeared up the road, to wherever they lived their lives. She knew Eddie would be thrilled to have breakfast with them, if they remembered—sometimes people's memories just weren't as good as their intentions.

Harmony decided to walk around the courthouse before she went in to see Billy. She was definitely the only person walking around the courthouse at that hour; it should have been a peaceful stroll, but in fact she felt a little unsettled. Being among her family, so suddenly, was sort of like arriving unexpectedly in a country she had visited once previously, long ago. She was vaguely familiar with the customs and the language, but only vaguely. Since she *had* been to the country long before, she had expected that things would soon fall into place. She would learn what to do and what not to do, what to say and what not to say. Still, she felt a little rattled: the country was more different than she had expected it to be. The fact that she had come back after a long absence gave her a power she wasn't comfortable with; mainly, it was the power to wound: to make people feel their manners were bad, just because their manners were different. She didn't want to make her nephew Don feel like he was a hick just because he couldn't tell real maple syrup from fake maple syrup, even though her five-year-old son could make that distinction from one lick of the spoon. She knew she had to be real careful not to give her nephews and nieces the impression that she thought their lives were skinny, although she did think that. Lots of young people worked with her at the recycling plant in Las Vegas, but with those young people she had a sense that just about anything could happen—they could move to New York, they could go to college; one she knew was even writing a book; another was a ranked tennis player. His rank was around seven hundred but in her book that wasn't bad, considering how many people there were who played tennis.

With her nephews and nieces, though, she *didn't* have a sense that anything could happen; mostly she had a sense that anything couldn't happen; only a few things could happen. Mostly the young people who had just driven away were going to live lives their parents had lived, only with different hairstyles, in different clothes, driving different cars. Mainly, it would be external things that would be different; the internal things probably weren't going to be different at all.

It didn't take very long to walk around the courthouse. Before Harmony could even halfway sort out her feelings she was back at the jail. At least the walk had helped to wake her up. Often in Las Vegas she would kind of get buzzy in the middle of the night, get a second wind or something—usually, when it happened there, she would just wander over to a casino. Maybe she would bump into somebody she had worked with and they would chat for a while. She could always find someone to talk to, in the casinos, even if it was three o'clock in the morning.

Things weren't that way in Tarwater; in Tarwater there was only the jail. If there had been a convenience store in sight, Harmony would have walked to it to buy some gum, she felt she would be a little less nervous if she had some gum to chew. But there was no convenience store in sight, and no one in sight, either, when she went in the jail, although, on the counter, there was a little bell you could ring. Beside the counter was a whole wall of wanted posters; she had not realized there were so many people out there who were wanted by the law, although she probably should have realized it; two or three of them had been her boyfriends. Back in her earlier days she had been reckless; she had liked to hook up with the wild guys, once in a while.

She did a quick scan of the posters to see if any of her boyfriends were still wanted; mainly the scan was a way of putting off ringing the bell. It was a little like checking into a small hotel in the middle of the night; probably the person who would have to check her in was already asleep. But, finally, she rang the bell.

366

The minute the bell jingled Peewee appeared—he got there so quick Harmony felt like he must have been standing on the other side of the door. Peewee had only been a grade behind her in school, but now he was almost bald. He had just a little bit of hair around the edges of his head.

"Harmony, my gosh, we thought you'd never come," Peewee said. "Billy's been waiting. All them nephews and nieces of yours kept coming in to use the bathroom."

Peewee smiled a little smile—it reminded her of Ross, whom she still hadn't called. The way Peewee smiled touched Harmony, though. It was a smile that told her he didn't expect much. So many men smiled that smile: maybe they had expected to be sports heroes or make a lot of money or marry a movie star; or maybe they didn't even aim that high. Maybe they just thought they could run a nice little business, or have a happy family life or something; but, then, before they knew it, a lot of life slipped by, with none of the above happening. Then it seemed they began to expect less and less, until the day came when they didn't expect anything at all—maybe they still expected to breathe, or to watch television, maybe see a ball game now and then, but that was about where such men's expectations seemed to stop.

Peewee swung open the little door and showed her into the jail proper. At that moment Harmony remembered that she wasn't wearing any makeup, although it was her first visit to her brother in years; she should have fixed herself up a little, for such an important occasion, but it was too late, she was already in the jail, and, anyway, she had driven into Tarwater without so much as a comb.

There was Billy, though, in the back room of the jail, sitting on an old couch watching TV. He was bigger than when she had seen him last—a lot bigger; obviously the bacon had had some effect, over the years. It was horrible to think of all that greasy bacon going into her brother, year after year; no wonder he looked so sad.

"Hi, Sis," Billy said. Even though he was big, he was still graceful and athletic. He got off the couch and gave her a nice hug and a kiss.

"Oh, Billy, I've missed you," she said. It was true, too—in some ways she had always missed her brother, and relied on his counsel, even if she had to get it over the telephone.

"I hope I haven't come too late at night," she added—actually she had no idea what time it had gotten to be.

"Oh, no, the later the better in this jail," Billy said. "Me and Peewee, we're the town's two night owls.

"Otherwise this whole town nods off about nine o'clock," he added.

"Once in a while the juvenile delinquents will go on a tear and make a little noise," Peewee said. "But mostly the nightlife consists of me and Billy and Dick Van Dyke."

A Dick Van Dyke rerun was on the TV at that moment; Harmony had forgotten that Mary Tyler Moore had ever looked that young.

"Billy's up later than me," Peewee said. He seemed nervous. Harmony remembered that he had had a big crush on her when they were in high school, maybe still had a little bit of the crush or something, which might explain the nervousness.

"I usually like to be asleep by three a.m.," he added. "I usually am, too, unless Bonzo acts up or something."

When Billy hugged her, Harmony noticed that his clothes smelled like they weren't being laundered too well—they smelled a little musty; she wondered if there was a way she could do his laundry for him, while she was home; it would be nice if her brother could at least have clean-smelling clothes while he was in jail.

"Who's Bonzo?" she asked—it was an odd nickname.

Billy looked at her strangely, as if she had said something unusual.

"He's your nephew," he said. "Little Davie."

"Davie—I just met him," Harmony said. "He was kind of solemn."

"He's solemn when he's sober, but that ain't when he becomes Bonzo," Peewee said. "It's when little Davie turns into Bonzo that the wilding starts. Sometimes it takes all the police in two or three counties to get him under control."

"He likes to take off all his clothes and race around naked with two or three whores in the car, honking and carrying on," Billy said. "If they can't get him off that nose candy I expect Neddie and Dick will end up losing their farm."

"You mean cocaine?" Harmony asked.

368

She could hardly believe they were talking about the same quiet boy who had just given her such a nice hug; though, of course, she knew from experience that quiet boys weren't necessarily quiet *all* the time. Maybe the whores were understandable; there had always been whores in Tulsa. But the part about Neddie and Dick losing their farm because of Davie's habit seemed hard to believe, though of course she had only met Dave for a few minutes.

"He's ruint their credit," Peewee explained.

"Yep, put it right up his nose," Billy said. "David ain't a bad kid, either—that drug's just got ahold of him."

Harmony was wondering why her sisters hadn't said a word about Davie having a drug problem—why wouldn't Neddie have at least mentioned it?

"Why wouldn't Neddie tell me?" she asked Billy.

"It's hard to come out with news like that," Billy said. "Neddie and Dick are honest people. Dick's a little dull, but then lots of people are a little dull. Neither of them deserve to have a son who would take their whole life's work and stuff it up his nose."

"What about the rest of those kids?" she asked.

"They're fuckups," Billy said. "Don's already got two out-of-wedlock children he has no way to support."

"What about the girls?" Harmony asked. "They seem like sweet girls."

"Oh, they are, far as sweet goes," Billy said.

"They sing in the choir, too," Peewee said.

"On the other hand, not a one of them's ever slept with anyone who doesn't have a criminal record," Billy said. "They just naturally gravitate to criminals. I can't trust 'em in my house because if I do they'll come by when I ain't there and steal my stuff, so they can sell it to buy dope for their creepy boyfriends."

"What little they ain't already stole," Peewee said. "It's a good thing you're still in jail, if you ask me. At least we got a couch you can stretch out on. At home you don't even have a couch."

"Or a TV to watch, if I did have a couch," Billy said. "Those kids have about picked me clean."

"Deenie's the one who worries me," Peewee said. "If she don't get the shoplifting under control they'll send her to the pen, one of these days."

"Deenie?" Harmony asked.

"Yep, she steals so she can buy dope for her boyfriends," Billy said.

Harmony felt confused. She had only been with her brother maybe five minutes and already she was learning all sorts of unhappy stuff about her sisters' children—the very ones who were eager to meet Eddie and take him to breakfast. Already she was feeling that it was sad that her nice brother had to be in jail, and that his clothes smelled musty, and that he was overweight, and that his only companion was Peewee, a man who had lost his expectations. Now it was beginning to sound as if her whole family had lost their expectations, which was not good.

"Then there's little Debbie, she's got the same problem her mother has," Billy said. "She's dick-struck—if she was selling it instead of giving it away she'd be a millionairess by now."

"What about Donna?" Harmony asked. "She seemed pretty stable—but of course I just met her for a few minutes."

"Donna's the one you don't want to cross," Billy said. "When I think how mean little Donna is I don't feel so bad about being in jail."

"Safest place in Tarwater," Peewee agreed. "So far Donna ain't attacked the jail, but I wouldn't put it past her."

"Yeah, it's pretty peaceful in here, Sis," Billy said. "I don't have to worry about getting mugged by one of my sisters' kids. About the worst it gets is when they bring Bonzo and stick him in a cell. Then we have to listen to him snore."

"I've had old worn-out tractors that don't make as much noise as Bonzo makes when he snores," Peewee said. "Most of the time we don't try to bring him in. We just mace him and leave him in his car."

"Mace Davie?" Harmony asked. She was getting the sense that her hometown was a pretty strange place. "Why would you mace him? Is he violent?"

"No, but he just sulks when they get him pulled over," Peewee said. "He won't roll down the window or cooperate at all."

"Some cop in Tulsa invented a little squirt hose they can slip through the crack of the door so they can mace Davie," Billy said. "I guess it's a pretty clever little device. They use it all over the country now, but it was invented right here in Oklahoma, for use on your own nephew."

"I think Davie should be in the *Guinness Book of World Records*, myself," Peewee said. "I mean for speeding tickets. Not too many people can rack up a hundred and eighty-six speeding tickets in one year's time."

"I don't know, they got some pretty wild drivers up in Kansas," Billy said. He got up, went to a little refrigerator toward the rear of the jail, and took out three beers, one for Peewee, one for himself, and one he offered to Harmony, who took it.

"Billy, when do they plan to let you out?" Harmony asked. "I think your clothes need to be laundered better."

Peewee chuckled. He may not have had expectations, but he did have a sweet smile.

"The whole town needs to be laundered better," he said.

"Can't the woman you've been calling just get her phone number changed?" Harmony asked.

"Well, it ain't quite that simple, Sis," Billy said. One thing he hadn't lost was the twinkle in his eye. Billy had always found life amusing, and evidently still did.

"Ain't simple at all," Peewee commented. "Billy's got connections—he can get unlisted phone numbers in less time than it takes you or me to call information."

"If I leave jail but don't leave town Jack might shoot me with his hunting rifle," Billy said. "Jack's a pretty fair shot, too. He gets a deer just about every season."

"Who's Jack?" Harmony asked.

"Mildred's husband—he owns the Exxon station," Peewee said. "He says he won't shoot Billy as long as he stays in jail, which is why Billy's still here. Watching Dick Van Dyke with me beats being shot by Jack."

"But Billy, you can't stay in jail all your life," Harmony said. "Can't you just promise Mildred and Jack not to do it anymore?"

"I could, but it would be a lie, and they know it," Billy said.

Harmony found herself wondering what her brother actually said, in his phone calls.

"If I'm out wandering the streets, once in a while I get the urge to call up Mildred and make suggestions," Billy said.

"Billy don't want to be cured," Peewee said. "That's the whole problem."

Actually, the jail seemed pretty comfortable—at least it was neat. Harmony had never been in Billy's house, but she understood from her sisters that he wasn't a neat housekeeper; Billy had always had a tendency to let the chores go. So maybe it wasn't entirely bad that he was in jail, but it wasn't entirely good, either. Billy was sweet and nice—what was he doing spending his life in a small-town jail?

Harmony suddenly had the urge to see her brother alone. Peewee was behaving, but Harmony could tell he still had some of the crush he had in high school. The fact of the crush made it hard for her to relax and enjoy her visit with her brother.

"Peewee, would it be against the law for me to take Billy for a walk?" she asked. "We haven't got to visit in a long time. Maybe we could just take a walk, or ride around a little."

Peewee and Billy exchanged looks—neither of them had been expecting the suggestion. "Well, I guess that would be all right, Harmony," Peewee said. "You got to promise not to give him no quarters, though—or let him get hold of a screwdriver. If Billy has a screwdriver he can make a pay phone work in no time."

"Do you want to go, Billy?" she asked. After all, maybe she shouldn't disturb him; maybe he would be more comfortable just staying where he was.

"Sure, let's take a cruise," Billy said, getting up. "We've about run out of beer, anyway. Maybe I can pick up a twelve-pack or two, while I'm out."

"Jack opens the Exxon at four a.m.," Peewee said. "If you ain't back by then kind of avoid the main drag, if you can. Jack gets pretty hot when he sees Billy."

"He keeps that deer rifle right by the cash register, too," Billy said. "Remember that time he shot old Pete Rutherford's tires out because the old fart tried to drive off without paying Jack for the gas?"

"Yep," Peewee said. "I doubt old man Rutherford done it on purpose, though. He was probably just addled in the head."

"I don't know, that old man is sly," Billy said. "I think he meant to sneak himself a tank of gas while Jack was in the john."

A minute later Harmony and Billy were out on the sidewalk. Billy hadn't even had to sign out. At first, Billy took a cautious approach. He looked around carefully before he stepped off the curb.

"Billy, are you afraid he might kill you, even at night?" Harmony asked.

"It could happen," Billy said. "Jack's pretty crazy about Mildred.

"Of course, so am I," he added. "Let's just slip into the pickup and move on out."

Harmony was thinking about Eddie—it would have been nice to have him along.

11.

A mile from the Best Western there was an all-night convenience store, where Billy could buy beer. He came out with two twelve-packs.

"One for now and one for later," he said.

"I wish you'd stop letting Momma stuff you with bacon," Harmony said. "That much bacon is not good for anybody."

Billy smiled, and didn't answer. Billy was driving, though it turned out that he didn't have a driver's license, either. He too had failed to renew.

"Why waste money on a driver's license when I'm mostly gonna live in the slammer anyway," Billy said.

"Could we get a room at the Best Western in case we get sleepy?" Harmony suggested. "This pickup doesn't have but one headlight. If we get stopped and neither of us has licenses I don't know what will happen."

"Back to the slammer, that's all that would happen," Billy said.

He drove to the Best Western and waited in the pickup while Harmony got a room. It was a ground-floor room way at the back of the motel. Crickets were singing in the grass, and the stars overhead were bright. The brightness of the stars reminded Harmony that Billy had once wanted to be an astronomer. He liked looking at the stars, and knew where all the constellations were. When Billy went on the wheat harvest he had used all his money to buy a telescope. He bought it the summer she went away to Las Vegas. In the late summer, just before she left, she remembered that Billy would sit outside until very late, studying the stars through his telescope. He already had a football scholarship to the University of Tulsa, but he wasn't that excited about football. He just intended to stay at the University of Tulsa for two years; then he meant to transfer to the University of Arizona and major in astronomy. At the time, Billy had notions about discovering a new planet; if he managed to discover one he wanted to name it after her. She was close to her brother, that summer. They talked a lot about the planet named Harmony. Billy thought it might be hiding behind one of the other planets. Billy even thought it might be warm enough to welcome life-forms; the fact that it was welcoming was the reason he wanted to name the planet after her.

At that time Harmony expected to finish high school and maybe go to college herself; she had no way of knowing that she was just suddenly going to swing onto a bus and head west.

Of course, it was easy to have big dreams about going to college, or even discovering planets, when you were young. The big dreams got harder to have once life had sort of swept you away.

The night was so nice that she and Billy brought a couple of chairs out of the room and sat in them. Their room hadn't been rented for a while. It smelled musty, like Billy's clothes.

"Remember the telescope you had?" Harmony asked. She was hoping maybe Billy still had it; maybe if she hung around Tarwater another day or two Billy could get out of jail at night and show Eddie some of the constellations. Maybe he would talk to Eddie a little about the planet named Harmony—the planet he never found.

"Oh yeah," Billy said. "That little telescope was my downfall. I stopped watching heavenly bodies and started watching Mildred's body."

Then Harmony remembered that Billy had been a Peeping Tom for a few years, before he became an obscene phone caller, which didn't make the whole thing any easier to understand. Billy had been a star quarterback in a place where quarterbacks were like movie stars. Billy had dated lots and lots of girls—probably he slept with at least a few of them, even though things were a little more strict in those days. What made him switch to the telescope? Of course, she loved her brother, whether he was normal or not. It was just a puzzle she would have liked an answer to; of course there didn't have to be an answer to all of life's puzzles. She would just have liked to know what the deal was with her brother, sexually. But it wasn't easy to ask him questions. After all, he had a right to his privacy.

"What are you going to do next, Sis?" Billy asked. "Surely you aren't going to try and live your life in Tarwater, are you?"

"No," Harmony said. That much she knew. It was nice to sit behind the Best Western with her brother and look at the stars and listen to the crickets. And it was nice that Eddie was getting some time with her father. But if there was one thing she knew about the future, it was that she wouldn't be spending much of it in Tarwater. A day or two would be plenty.

"I guess you lost interest in astronomy," she said; really she was just remembering his promise. Astronomy had just been one aspect of it.

"Nope, I still like to fiddle with it," Billy said. "I subscribe to all the magazines, still. But they took my telescope as evidence in the first trial. It's in the jail. If there's anything interesting happening up there Peewee lets me set it up behind the jail. We had a nice lunar eclipse about a month ago. I took a look at that."

Harmony was trying to come back in memory to the days when Billy had been a sports hero. She was pretty sure she remembered a Mildred somebody—Mildred had been one of Billy's girlfriends, then. As she remembered her, Mildred was a skinny brunette with an overbite. She had a cloudy memory of her mother railing at Billy about Mildred—her mother thought Mildred only wanted to marry Billy in order to get all the money he was going to have. Of course, that was her mother's response to every girl Billy got involved with.

"Billy, didn't you date Mildred, when you were a senior?" she asked. "Wasn't she a brunette?"

"Yeah, the skinny one with the buck teeth," Billy said. "We started to run off to Kansas and get married, but we waited a week too long and Mom chased her off."

"Why?"

"Same reason she ran Neddie's boyfriends off," Billy said. "She didn't want none of us to have sex.

"Mildred and I were pretty crazy about one another," Billy added. He didn't sound wistful, just matter-of-fact.

"But she married somebody else," Harmony pointed out.

"Yep, she married Jack," Billy said. "About all we have left is the phone calls, and Jack don't approve of the phone calls."

The way he said it sounded a little sad.

"Billy, does Mildred *want* you to call her and make suggestions?" Harmony asked—after all, stranger things had happened. She had once had a boyfriend who liked phone sex better than he liked real sex—or as much, at least. His name was Pete; even after he got married he would still call her from time to time and try to have phone sex. Pete had a deep, froggy voice; it was the perfect voice for getting a little phone sex started. More than a few times Pete's froggy voice had cajoled her into doing things.

"Sure, Mildred gets a kick out of it," Billy said. "I make suggestions and then she does whatever I suggest with Jack. We're kind of a threesome, in a way."

"Yeah, but it's not funny that you're in jail," Harmony said. "If Mildred likes it that you call why do you have to be in jail?"

"Because Jack's too dumb to figure out that it works to his advantage, pussywise," Billy said. "Jack don't have no imagination. It ain't dawned on him yet that he wouldn't be getting half as much if it wasn't for me."

"I still don't think you should be in jail," Harmony said. It was a real sore spot with her. Why should her brother, who was kind and gentle, have to be in jail for having phone sex with a woman who enjoyed having phone sex with him? So what if she had a husband who ran an Exxon station?

"Oh well," Billy said, "Mildred's a slave driver. Jack's already had one heart attack. The way she works him it wouldn't surprise me if he dropped dead. I've lived in the jail so long Peewee and me are like a married couple, ourselves. I probably get along with Peewee better than I would with Mildred, anyway. It ain't so bad in the lockup when Momma leaves us alone."

Harmony felt her tiredness coming back, but she didn't want to go in and go to bed. It had been years since she had got to sit outside with her brother at night, in Oklahoma. It would give them a chance to catch up.

"Mildred's one of those people who have to have the lawn mowed and the driveway swept and every sock folded and put in the right drawer before she can relax," Billy said. "I doubt we would have worked out, if we'd married. I ain't the type to mow lawns and fold socks. Half the time, when I'm home, I can't even find two socks, much less make them a mate and get them in the right drawer."

"It's hard to be happy when you get older, isn't it?" Harmony said. She was remembering how easy it had been in earlier years —almost as easy as breathing.

"Sis, I ain't unhappy," Billy said. "I'd like to be able to call Mildred a little more often, but other than that I don't have too much to complain about. I got a roof over my head and I ain't living in Sarajevo—that's a big plus, right there."

"Pepper died of AIDS, I don't know if I told you," Harmony said.

"Well, Pat told me," Billy said. "That's bad, but it's over."

"Billy, did you have a baby with that woman you knew in New Mexico?" Harmony asked. "I've always wondered."

"Stillborn—little girl," Billy said. "She would have been about Pepper's age, if she'd lived.

"You look sleepy, Sis," he added. "Maybe you'd better run me back to the jail, before you fade out."

They didn't say much on the way back. Driving into Tarwater, she sort of woke up. Billy hugged her and went back in the jail— the minute he did Harmony started having a sense of a missed opportunity. She and her brother hadn't really caught up. Maybe they had just started the evening too late.

Or maybe it was just that you could never catch up, once you reached a certain age. She and her brother had started life in the same house, with the same parents and the same two sisters, and the same plains out the window; they rode the same school bus, had the same teachers, listened to the same radio stations; they even went to the same dances, even though Billy was three years older. But Billy had chosen to stay at the original point, and she hadn't. She had had one husband and so many boyfriends that she had long ago lost count. Billy had never married, and he clearly didn't want to talk about the relationship that had produced a stillborn child. The two of them could never catch up, any more than she could ever catch up with Neddie and Pat. The years of different experiences had put a continent between them; the bus that took her away, across America, far from her brothers and sisters, would never be bringing her back.

When she got back to her own room at the motel, there was a Western on TV, with Rory Calhoun in it. There had been a time when Rory Calhoun frequented the casinos a lot. He had even come on to her, once or twice. Even as sleepy as she was, she watched a little of the movie. The truth was, seeing Rory Calhoun in a movie made her feel more at home than actually being at home. She was wondering, as she dozed off, why she hadn't taken Rory up on it—maybe it was just the tan. She had never gone for guys with the real deep tans.

12.

"Mommy, Mommy, open *now!*" Eddie said—Harmony could also hear Iggy, yipping just outside her door. It was early; she was so deeply asleep that she wanted it to be a dream, she didn't want to have to deal with Eddie and Iggy just then. Besides that, if they were there, it meant someone else was with them. But she quickly gave up on it being a dream and stumbled to the door. Sure enough, all her nephews and nieces were there, plus a couple of their wives and husbands, or boyfriends and girlfriends, plus the little children they had produced, plus Laurie and Pat.

"Mom, I met all my cousins and I know their names," Eddie said. "Now we're going to go to breakfast and eat pancakes at the waffle house."

He was a little breathless, from excitement. Definitely it was exciting to Eddie to have a large family all of a sudden, and not a pretend family, either.

"Eddie, can't I meet you there? I haven't even washed my face yet," Harmony asked, but Eddie rejected her plea almost before it was out of her mouth.

"No, we're all going to the waffle house *together*," he said. "I want you to come with me and all my cousins and Laurie and Aunt Pat."

"They kidnapped me," Laurie said. She was looking fresh and rested. "It's just as well, too."

"Right, Ethel was getting mighty nosy," Pat commented. None of the nieces and nephews had gotten out of the pickup; they were all just clumped there. She could see Davie, the one who became Bonzo, peeking over the top of the cab.

"She was nosy from the word go, it was just that she was zeroing in," Laurie said. "She's cranky but she's not dumb."

"I wish you'd brought Dad," Harmony said—now that she had seen him again, she realized how much she missed her Dad.

"Grandpa had to plow, but I went with him to milk this morning," Eddie said. "I milked three times—it was like squirts. Grandpa taught me how, only the cow swished her tail and it had poop on it and a little of the poop got in my hair."

Eddie was very excited; the effort to get all his adventures into one statement was making him breathless.

"We fed the chickens too," Laurie said—it seemed to Harmony that Laurie and Eddie were quickly becoming competent farmhands.

"We fed them and they didn't peck me but a rooster did *look* at me!" Eddie said. "I think he was an evil rooster and I think he would have pecked me if Laurie hadn't made him go away.

"And we went up a ladder into the loft, and I saw a rat," Eddie continued. "It was gray and it went under the hay, when we came."

"Dad's kept him jumping," Pat said. "Dad's the most chipper I've seen him in years. I guess all he needed was for Eddie to show up."

Harmony felt stumbly. Her head was beginning to wake up, but the rest of her was still asleep, especially her legs. They just didn't seem to want to move. She sat on the foot of her bed and tried to hug Eddie, but he was much too keyed up to be in a hugging mood, all he could think of was his cousins and the waffle house.

"We have to hurry because David has to go to work and he needs to eat because he has to work very hard in the oil fields," Eddie said.

Through the open door Harmony could see all her nieces and nephews, waiting to spend a little time with her. It was a big responsibility—she knew she had to make some effort to pull herself together and go with them.

Somehow, she managed it—she got in Pat's pickup. Eddie and Laurie rode with the cousins.

"It's all over town that Peewee's in love with you," Pat said, as they left the motel. "I guess you blitzed him."

"Pat, I didn't, that's silly," Harmony said. "I just went into the jail for a few minutes to see Billy. Peewee didn't even say much."

"Peewee's tongue-tied when he gets the hots," Pat said. "That's always been his problem—no conversation."

Harmony was feeling torn—she was still feeling the need to leave. Even Laurie seemed to fit in Oklahoma better than she did—she seemed perfectly relaxed, standing around the pickup yakking with Eddie's cousins.

"You don't look too happy, Harmony," Pat said. "Maybe you ought to date Peewee a few times. He might be more interesting than he looks."

"I don't want to date Peewee," Harmony said. At least she was sure of that much. Too many times in her life she had taken pity because some guy looked as if he needed to have his expectations raised. The next thing she knew, she would find herself involved with some man she really didn't want.

"After breakfast we're going to go to Neddie's to eat lunch," Pat said. "Dick's even planning to stop plowing long enough to barbecue chicken, just for you and Eddie."

"I wonder how much a car costs?" Harmony said.

"Different prices, why?" Pat asked. "What do you want with a car?"

"Pat, just to drive it," Harmony said. She skipped the fact of having no license.

"You just got here," Pat reminded her. "It's your first visit in years. You have to remember that you're the only celebrity Tarwater's ever produced. A lot of people are going to have their feelings hurt if you don't stay around long enough to have a decent visit."

"They don't know me, though," Harmony reminded her.

"No, but they *think* they know you," Pat said. "You grew up here."

"No, I was a child here," Harmony said. "I grew up in Las Vegas, raising Pepper."

"Harmony, what's the matter with you?" Pat asked—she sounded a little impatient.

Harmony didn't want to answer. They were on the highway, heading toward Tulsa. The wind was blowing her hair. Pat seemed to be driving very fast. Harmony felt no appetite at all. She didn't know how she was going to manage to eat waffles and barbecued chicken, when she wasn't hungry. Even the thought of barbecued chicken made her queasy. Another thing that didn't help with the queasiness was all the dead animals on the highway. First there was a coyote, then two skunks, then a possum, then an armadillo. It made her wonder if maybe animals had a need to commit suicide —either that or they were just careless. Pat was driving ninety. If an animal wandered into the road Pat would probably hit it—it would just be smushed.

"I didn't know you had a pickup, Pat," she said. "You work in a bank. Why do you need a pickup?"

"Because you can put a mattress in the back and fuck pretty comfortably," Pat said. "A pickup's useful if you're a sex addict. It's hard to enjoy yourself in them little Jap cars."

"I didn't know you were a sex addict until Neddie told me," Harmony said. "What's that all about?"

"It's about being addicted to sex, just like it sounds," Pat said. "The term sort of speaks for itself."

"You could have low self-esteem," Harmony said. "After I got fired I slept with a whole lot of guys. In my case it was probably low self-esteem."

"Yeah, but that was *your* case," Pat said. "I don't have low self-esteem. I just like to fuck."

"But it's not safe anymore, Pat," Harmony said. "You could get what Pepper got."

"Nothing's much fun if you can't be reckless," Pat said. "I was born reckless."

The plains mostly consisted of weeds, Harmony decided, looking at them. She had wanted to question Pat about the sex addiction a little bit more, but, thanks to the fast driving, they were already pulling up to the waffle house. The other pickup was already there.

Iggy was jumping up and down in the cab, indignant at having been left in the pickup.

"Celebrities don't like to be locked in pickups," Pat observed. She waved at Iggy as they went in.

"Mom, we ordered my waffles," Eddie said. He sat between Deena and Debbie.

"We love Eddie," Debbie said. "He knows stuff about everything. I think he's a genius."

"Well, I *am* a genius," Eddie agreed. Harmony had some doubt that he knew what the word meant.

"Either that or he watches the Discovery Channel," Pat said.

Harmony only had coffee. Even with the coffee in her she had a hard time connecting with the group. It was as if the part of her brain that had kept her sociable for so many years had broken off or something. Now, instead of feeling sociable, she just felt dull, as if her pores were stopped up with sunblock or some other gooey substance. More and more she had difficulty in getting out of her own insides. It was a little bit like being in the Holland Tunnel; she had claustrophobia even though she was only in a waffle house in Tulsa. She was with her own family, too. It was horrible to be so locked into herself when her own nephews and nieces were sitting there hoping she would tell them anecdotes about her life as a showgirl.

In the light of day her nephews and nieces didn't have the old look they had had last night. What was obvious though was that they weren't really into skin care. None of them had very healthy complexions. The boys' skin was windburned and the girls' skin was rough—maybe it was the water. Some of them had brought their children. One little girl Eddie's age was very withdrawn. Eddie made repeated efforts to engage her in conversation, but for once he was unsuccessful. The little girl refused to say a word.

"Mom, Julie won't talk to me—maybe she's deaf," Eddie said. They had taught him how to sign a little, at his school, so he tried signing, but that didn't work either. The other little children were rowdy and hit one another. Usually Eddie would have criticized such behavior, but this time he kept quiet.

384

Fortunately Laurie was being a wonderful guest. Harmony felt proud that Pepper had chosen such a nice, composed young woman to be her mate. Laurie talked to all the nieces and nephews. She got all their names right straight off, and the names of the little children too. The little children got even more unruly as the meal went on; they yelled and shrieked. One little boy bit his sister on the cheek hard enough to leave teeth marks. Harmony could see that Eddie was shocked by such bad behavior. The other customers didn't seem to mind, though. Most of them were truck drivers who seemed content to eat and smoke.

"Mom, don't they have a no-smoking section?" Eddie asked. "It's not very good for our lungs to be in here."

"Every place doesn't have to be virtuous, Eddie," Laurie said. She was doing her best to wipe all the little children's mouths and keep them cleaned up. All the little girls had hair the color of straw. They kept dropping silverware and pulling food off one another's plates. Harmony began to feel that she might lose her mind if she didn't get to leave soon. Two of the little girls were Pat's granddaughters, but Pat didn't say much to them; she left it to their parents, who left it to Laurie. Due to her claustrophobia, her feeling of being locked inside herself, Harmony didn't take a hand. Mainly she was grateful that Laurie was so poised.

Harmony knew the nephews and nieces were a little disappointed that she wasn't able to be more outgoing. Maybe they had been hoping she would talk about Elvis, or Mr. Sinatra. You couldn't blame them—there couldn't be much glamour to the lives they led.

Finally Donna, the boldest girl, took the lead a little bit.

"We heard you knew Elvis, Aunt Harmony," she said. "Was he nice?"

"We don't never get to hear about nobody famous," Debbie said. "No one famous ever shows up around here."

"He seemed nice," Harmony said. "I just have had my picture taken with him two or three times. He was real busy, you know. He liked to keep his time for himself, as much as possible."

"Who else famous did you know?" Don asked—those were the first words he had spoken.

"We're just dying to have you tell us about every famous person you ever met," Davie said.

"Gosh," Harmony said. "I met a lot, but mostly I was just passing them on stage, on the way to my spot. None of them ever spent any time with me, although Mr. Sinatra sent me flowers once."

"Who?" Debbie asked. It turned out that none of her nieces and nephews had ever really heard of Frank Sinatra. David sort of had an inkling that Frank Sinatra was a famous singer or something, but he was real vague about it. Mr. Sinatra didn't mean nearly as much to them as Elvis—it just went to show how different worlds could be. In Las Vegas Mr. Sinatra was even more of a god than Elvis—of course, Mr. Sinatra was still alive.

Harmony managed to come alive enough to tell a few stories; she reeled off the names of every celebrity she could remember meeting, including President Nixon and President Ford; they were also pretty impressed that she had met Muhammad Ali.

"She actually met a President," Debbie said.

"Well, I'm a celebrity now too, and Iggy's a celebrity and we met *the* President," Eddie chimed in—he was a little tired of listening to his mother reel off stories about celebrities she had met.

"Iggy's the best celebrity," he went on. "He's the best celebrity because he fell all the way off the Statue of Liberty and he did *not* die."

"He better be careful around here, though," Davie said. "Old coyote might get him."

"No, old coyote *won't* get him, because he's in the pickup and he's very safe," Eddie insisted.

Even so, he rushed out to the pickup the moment breakfast was over, to reassure himself.

Despite having listed celebrities and talked about them a little bit, Harmony still had a sense that, where her nephews and nieces were concerned, she was a bit of a disappointment. She hadn't produced the stories of glamour and excitement that they wanted to hear. It was her fault, she knew; her heart hadn't really been in it when she tried to talk about celebrities. The years when she had been a showgirl and was in a position to know celebrities were long past; those events now seemed like events that had happened to someone else. Nothing like that would ever happen to her again. For one thing, since leaving the casinos, she had sort of let herself get heavy. When she happened to catch a glimpse of her own body in the mirror it was always a shock; she didn't have a flat belly anymore. She had kept a perfect figure for so long that it was a little hard to recognize herself, now that she didn't have one. All those years of having the best figure in town, in a town that really appreciated good figures, had failed to prepare her for the aging process.

Her main problem as a showgirl had been dealing with the envy of the other showgirls, all of whom constantly worried about *some* part of themselves—their butts or their bellies or something. But she had never had to worry, she had the perfect body, or at least she had been told that she did, many, many times. Mostly she hadn't done much to deserve it, either; maybe a little exercise now and then, plus keeping to a reasonable diet. For many years a day rarely passed without her getting some compliment on her looks— it didn't always come from a guy who wanted to date her, either. It might just be from someone on the street, or in a drugstore or somewhere.

But those days were just over: now she had a middle-aged body that was definitely too heavy; not too many compliments came her way anymore. Probably one of the reasons she had trouble talking to her nieces and nephews about the old days was that she didn't feel she was still the person who had had the experiences with the celebrities. When she tried to talk about it she felt she was talking about someone she no longer knew well: herself, as she had once been.

All the way down the highway toward Neddie's house, with Pat blazing along at more than ninety, Harmony more and more felt that it had all gotten away from her; she no longer felt at home, either in the past or in the present. She didn't have a clue as to what to do next, but she was afraid—very afraid—that she was going to be a big disappointment, not only to her family in Oklahoma, but also to Laurie and Eddie. More and more she had the fear that she might just stop functioning altogether.

"What if I get so I can't function?" she asked. She had begun to feel very anxious, as if she were tearing inside. This time, though, it wasn't just a tearing grief over Pepper's death. It was as if her whole frame or structure was splintering and collapsing. It was a very bad feeling. What if it collapsed and she let Laurie and Eddie down in a major way?

"Harmony, if you're having a panic attack, take deep breaths," Pat said.

"Deep breaths won't stop it, Pat," Harmony said. "I think I'm cracking up. I'm going to fail Eddie, and everybody else.

"I may just have to give up," she added. That was how she felt.

"We all give up now and then," Pat said. "Life's too heavy a matter. I guess our kids just survive those times, somehow."

"Pat, this is worse, I may need to go away," Harmony said. "I may not be able to be around anyone I know."

"Okay, if you do you do," Pat said, looking at her kindly. "I've often had to resort to strangers myself—my kids kind of took it in stride."

But they didn't, Harmony wanted to say. She didn't believe that Pat's kids, or Neddie's, were particularly bad, but she didn't want Eddie to grow up to be like them, either. She wanted Eddie to have unrestricted opportunity—she wanted him to have an unthreatened childhood, too. It couldn't be said that her sisters' children had had that.

"Harmony, leave him with us if you have to go bonkers," Pat said. "Just leave him and don't worry. Dad loves him. We all love him, and we really haven't got to spend enough time with him. You can come back and get him whenever you're feeling better."

Harmony thought she really was going to break down if she didn't get away from her family immediately. They were just passing the Best Western when the feeling became unbearable.

"Pat, stop," she said. "I forgot something. I have to go to my room for a while."

"But Neddie's waiting," Pat said, a little horrified by the way her sister looked.

"Dick took off from plowing," she added. "It's once every twenty years that Dick takes off from plowing. You can't skip out now."

Nevertheless, she braked and pulled to the side of the road. She looked annoyed for a moment, but when she realized how bad Harmony was shaking she just looked scared. She stopped the pickup, but she caught Harmony's arm, so she wouldn't jump out.

"Now calm down," she said. "Just calm down."

"Pat, shut up!" Harmony said. "I can't calm down—it's like that time I beat you with the stuffed dog, only there's no stuffed dog. You have to let me out."

Pat took a good look at her sister.

"I guess it ain't that big a deal, that Dick stopped plowing," she said. "What's a couple of barbecued chickens?"

"Bye, Pat—tell Neddie and Dick I'm sorry," Harmony said. "I just have to be alone right now."

"Harmony, I'll drive you to your room," Pat said. "In the state you're in you might get run over if you try to cross this highway. Forget about the barbecue. Just don't jump out. I'll drive you right to the door."

"Okay," Harmony said—she was so upset that she knew Pat was probably right. Maybe she would run right in front of a truck, if she tried to cross the four-lane highway on her own.

Pat slowly started the pickup and drove down the road to the exit by the Best Western; then she drove Harmony around to the back of the motel.

"If there's anything I can do to help, I will," she said, as Harmony was getting out.

"No, just tell Eddie his mother will see him later," she said. She knew it sounded formal but it was the best she could do.

"I like Laurie, for what it's worth," Pat said. "I think she's a real nice young lady."

"She is, bye," Harmony said, getting out.

Once she was in the motel, Harmony only sank lower. She felt she was going to die of the tearing and splintering feeling inside. I can't die, she kept telling herself. I can't die, I've got Eddie. Who would he have if I died?

She didn't get an answer to that one. Whether Eddie would be lucky enough to get anyone good to raise him if his mother died was a question there was no one to answer. Little boys all over the world lost their mothers, without having any replacement ready. She knew that. It could be a war that took the mother; or it could be a fire, a flood, an earthquake, a tornado, even just a disease or a divorce. It was a thing that happened constantly, wherever there were mothers and children; then the little boys or girls would just have to get by on whatever guts or strength they had. Probably luck was what they needed most; not too many little children could

389

be expected to be strong enough to deal with the loss of a mother particularly well. Harmony didn't want Eddie to have to try. At least she was in her room; she had managed not to get run over on a four-lane in Oklahoma.

After Harmony had been in the room a minute or two she thought she still heard the pickup, so she looked out. Pat was just sitting there; probably she was concerned. Even so, Harmony checked to be sure the door was locked; she even put the little chain across it. She didn't want Pat or anyone else coming in. She sat on the bed, expecting to cry her eyes out, but no tears came. She just sat there, trying to cope with the terrible sense that she was lost. There was no way back to where she needed to be. She needed to be the self she had once been, but she couldn't. That self had gotten shattered; there were just pieces of it floating around, she didn't think she had much hope of getting the pieces to fit together into a person again. She didn't know what her next step was; she had no clue.

She heard the pickup turn slowly in the motel parking lot; then it left. Probably Pat had just lingered because she dreaded showing up at the barbecue without Harmony. Evidently it was a very big deal that Dick had taken off work in order to cook.

After Harmony sat for a few minutes on the end of the bed, feeling crazy, so crazy that she could not predict her next action, she began to take her clothes off. Her mind was whirling. She began to have the fantasy that a lover was coming to sleep with her, to hold her and help her be a little less upset. Even while she was having the fantasy she knew she had been dislodged from sanity: there was no lover coming, there was no one coming; what sickness or sadness was loose inside her to make her suppose or even imagine that a lover was coming? The fantasy kept flickering, though. She even went to the bathroom and combed her hair.

The fantasy was evidence that she had broken down. No man in Oklahoma even knew she was there, unless you counted Peewee, and Peewee was very unlikely just to show up in the middle of the morning, expecting her to be sitting naked on the bed, with her hair combed, expecting to make love.

Harmony stood up and paced around the room; then she stopped and rubbed some lotion onto her hands. She was trying hard to think of normal activities, such as rubbing the lotion on

390

her hands; anything that might slow her thoughts down long enough to allow her to slip back into the mode of sanity. If she could just get past the crazy whirling feeling maybe she could get enough of a grip to be a little bit helpful to her loved ones again.

Then she heard what sounded like a big lawn mower, which seemed odd. The parking lot was paved, why would they be mowing it? When she peeked out the window she saw that she had been right, it was a lawn mower, only it was the area behind the parking lot, a sort of weedy field, that was being mowed.

In the field the weeds and Johnson grass grew so tall in places that they hid the mower, which was on the backside of the field. When the mower came in sight—it was a big riding mower—she saw that the guy riding it was young, maybe about twenty. He had long hair and was mowing with his shirt off; the mower threw up a lot of grass and chaff that would have got inside his shirt and made him itch, if he'd kept his shirt on. As he mowed around the edge of the parking lot the mower spewed up the remains of several Styrofoam coffee cups that people drinking coffee in the parking lot had been careless with. Little pieces of white Styrofoam and stems of weeds spumed into the parking lot, in the wake of the big mower. The young man was sweaty—mowing was hot work. Still, Harmony thought he looked good. She had not thought about a guy, young or otherwise, in that way in a while; certainly Jimmy Bangor, the last man she had been with, had never on his best day looked half as good as the young man on the mower. Jimmy had some pretty unattractive tattoos—also he had not bothered to watch his weight.

Harmony peeked out the window and watched the young man mow for a while; she liked the confident way he steered the mower, clipping just the patches of weeds he wanted to clip. It was nice to see a young man with smooth muscles doing his work. But, after a while, she closed the curtain and got in bed. In the old days she might have thrown something on and gone out and chatted with the young guy for a bit. She could at least have given him a smile —something might have happened, or maybe not. In those days, with her perfect figure, sex appeal was just something that was always there, available; if it didn't work with one guy it would soon work with another.

In bed, Harmony slowly began to feel a little better—no reason, but the feeling that she had gone haywire was easing a little. She looked at her motel room. Clothes were strewn everywhere, as if she were in the midst of torrid love or something. She felt she had better try to get ahold of someone from her old life—maybe they would assure her that she wasn't crazy. Who would that be but Gary?

"Who is it? I'm asleep," Gary said, picking up after only about six rings. Probably he had had a late night and was not in the best of moods.

"Gary, it's me, I'm in a motel," Harmony said. "I went crazy a minute ago. I think I cracked up."

"Harmony, I was up very very late," Gary said, reproachfully.

"Gary, what else is new?" Harmony said. This was a man who had been up late every night of his life and would undoubtedly be up late the day he died unless he happened to die around nine o'clock in the evening or something.

"All I meant is, don't rush me," Gary said, backing off from the reproachful tone a little. "I'll get in synch with you as soon as I get my eyes open—I tried tanning yesterday and my eyelids are sticky from all the goo."

Harmony held the receiver and waited. Probably Gary had several drugs coursing through his body; she knew she should try to be a little patient.

"Now then, I'm getting awake, how are you?" Gary asked. "Life out here just isn't the same without you."

"Gary, I miss you—I don't know what I'm going to do," Harmony said.

"I'm naked," she added, just to kind of fill him in on the scene. Gary liked details. She looked at the clothes strewn all over the room—she had taken off every last stitch—and tried to remember why she had started taking clothes off in the first place. She had sort of torn them off in the minute or two when she had felt the craziest.

"My God, naked?" Gary said. "I don't think you've been naked since you left the show. I wonder what your boobs look like now."

"Gary, they're bigger," Harmony said—the sound of his voice was really reassuring; it was deeply comforting in fact. The sound of Gary's voice drew her back into his world, which had been her world too, most of her life.

"I wish I could see you," Gary said. "Naked, I mean. I haven't seen you naked since you left the show."

"I don't think you'd want to look at me now," Harmony said. "I let myself go."

"You had the best figure ever seen in Las Vegas," Gary reminded her—probably he was just trying to cheer her up. "It was glory. But nobody gets to keep glory forever, though, sweetie. Why do you have all your clothes off, anyway? I hope you're inside, at least. I read that the ozone layer is very thin in Oklahoma."

"I'm inside a motel, calm down," Harmony said. "I lost it today, Gary. Dick took off work to barbecue chicken for me and I lost it on the way to Neddie's house and didn't go. I came here to be alone and I took off all my clothes."

"Does that mean you're thinking about being a nudist, or are you in love, or what?" Gary asked. "I don't get it about the naked part. You were usually pretty modest for a showgirl."

"I felt like my clothes were strangling me," Harmony said. It was the only explanation she could offer.

"I think you should come right back today and get started with your shrink," Gary said. "You and Eddie can stay with me until you get on your feet."

"Don't you have a boyfriend?" Harmony asked.

"No, the little prick left me for a Salvadoran drug dealer," Gary said. "All those greasy creeps do is corrupt American boys. Got a pencil?"

"No, why?" Harmony said; then she spotted one on the bedside table.

"Because I have Ross's phone number for you," Gary said. "We should just bomb El Salvador and be done with it."

"Gary, I don't think we have to bomb a whole country just because you lost your boyfriend—what's the number?" she asked.

Gary gave it to her, and she scrawled it down. Her handwriting was a little shaky, probably from the period of craziness.

"Ross is right here in Las Vegas—he's working the lights for a burlesque show," Gary said.

Harmony didn't say anything, but it wasn't a big surprise that Ross had sunk to the level of burlesque. There was a lot of technology involved in doing the lights for the big shows now—probably Ross just hadn't kept up.

Gary could never stand it when there was silence on the line; he immediately rushed in with a question.

"What about your love life?" he asked. "Any swinging surprises on your trip? I've had a few lovers from Oklahoma myself."

"Gary, I'm in mourning, I haven't been thinking about sex," Harmony said, though the truth was, when she had seen the young guy with his shirt off, mowing the lawn, she *had* thought about it briefly—maybe if sex could have happened it would have distracted her from the tearing inside. It was a bad thought, though—he was just a young guy mowing a field. He probably had a little girlfriend or a little wife somewhere. Fortunately the worst of her pain had begun to ebb; she was in a state so awful that she would just have offered herself to a stranger—it had only been a moment when she wanted to get her hands on the young guy.

While she was talking she managed to hook her toe under her underpants; she pulled them to her and quickly slipped them on. Her time of being naked was over.

"The thing is, Eddie loves my Dad, and my Dad is old," Harmony said. "Eddie might not get very much time with my Dad—I don't want to cheat him of a chance to know Daddy."

"Who said you had to? Leave him for a few days," Gary said. "You could stay with me and look for an apartment, and then bring all your stuff out."

"Gary, I don't have any stuff, it all fell into a canyon," Harmony said, remembering the accident.

"Then we'll just go to Kmart and buy you some more," Gary said. "I'll borrow some money or something. It would be fun to help you select furniture. That stuff you had deserved to fall into a canyon, if you ask me."

The thought of being without Eddie, even for a few days, caused a panic feeling to set in; she would have to be a lot more stable than she was to be able to be without Eddie.

While she was talking to Gary somebody knocked on the door. Her first thought was that it was the young guy on the mower— maybe he had caught a glimpse of her through the window and had come over to investigate; after all, he was of an age to be adventurous. Maybe he had caught sight of a tit or something.

She got into her clothes real quick; whoever was at the door knocked again. When she opened it there stood her sister Neddie

394

and her brother-in-law Dick. Both had plates in their hands. One plate had barbecued chicken on it; the other had corn on the cob, green beans, and a sliced tomato.

"The tea's in a thermos," Dick said—the first words he had spoken to her in a few years. Dick had a real slow manner of speaking. He sounded sort of gruff even when he was trying to be friendly.

"We wasn't about to let you miss out on all that good grub," he added, handing her the plate of vegetables.

"Dick, I'm so sorry, I know you took off work to make me lunch," Harmony said. "I just got too upset to come. I really am touched that you took off work."

"It's happened twice, since we married," Neddie said, in her dry way. "When it does happen we all have to buck up and take advantage of it, even if we feel like hanging ourselves at the time."

Dick didn't react to Neddie's comment at all—Harmony thought it sounded a little sarcastic. He just walked back to the car and got the thermos of iced tea.

"We brought extra corn on the cob," Dick said. "Neddie said you used to like it."

Harmony felt she should hug Dick—after all, she hadn't seen him in nearly fifteen years. But she still had a few buttons to button; she had dressed hastily. Dick set the thermos down and stood there, with his hands in the pockets of his big overalls. Harmony had forgotten how large he was; his hair was white around the edges of his dozer cap. He still had the large wart on one side of his nose that he had had since he married Neddie. His big arms were brown, from working in the sun; the thick hairs on his arms were silver against his brown skin. He was just standing there, looking at her, planted, like a large tree. Harmony decided the moment for hugging had passed—maybe she would get a good opportunity later.

"Dick's so proud of his barbecuing that we just thought we'd bring you some," Neddie said. "I don't know if you have much appetite, though. I don't, when I'm upset,"

"I know how that grief is," Dick said, looking at Harmony sympathetically. His eyes were as big as the eyes of a cow. "My oldest brother drowned in a creek when he was about Pepper's age."

"Oh, Dick, I'm sorry," Harmony said. "How did it happen?"

"I wish you hadn't asked him," Neddie said. "We try not to get Dick started on that, if we can help it."

"Sorry, forget I asked," Harmony said quickly—Neddie had given her a look that indicated she should backtrack if at all possible. But it was too late. Dick's big face darkened and darkened some more—Harmony had the terrible feeling that he might cry. She felt pretty guilty, just looking at him—no doubt the story of Dick's drowned brother was a family story she should have known already. Dick's face was contorted—he took his hands out of his pockets and clutched them together, as if some terrible memory was buried in his body like a root; now, because of her question, the root was about to tear out through his chest or his back. It was too late to stop the root; it seemed to be boring through Dick like a drill.

"It was my fault," Dick said—his voice came from so deep within him it was almost as if it was the voice of the root.

"We were scuffling in the water," he said. "It was just scuffling, Jim and me—we were always scuffling. Hell, we were brothers. Only I was huskier, I could always get the best of Jim—he was skinny. I threw him in the water and ran like hell, thinking he'd chase me. What happened was, he got his foot caught in a root and drowned. His lungs just happened to fill up, and he drowned before we could get him loose."

"Do you feel like eating, Harmony?" Neddie asked. It was clear she was trying to do her best to ignore Dick's story.

Harmony did feel a little hungry. The corn on the cob looked tempting. But Dick was still standing there—he didn't look as if he would be capable of eating.

"Eating's a safe thing to do," Neddie commented—she was looking at Harmony, not her husband.

Dick took his hands out of his pockets and then put them back *in* his pockets. He sighed a heavy sigh, at the memory of his drowned brother Jim. Harmony decided she couldn't resist the corn on the cob or the green beans either. Once she had eaten the corn and the beans she consumed half of the chicken, in order to be polite to Dick. He was standing in the door of the motel, looking out at the fields. Neddie shrugged, as if to say she had no idea what to do about her husband. Harmony sure didn't know what to do about him; but she was touched that Neddie and Dick had been so concerned about her that they had brought her food, all the way to the Best Western. The food was good, too. The peach cobbler made the perfect dessert. Now that there were people around, and now that she wasn't naked anymore, she felt that she had indeed been briefly crazy. She asked about Laurie and Eddie and discovered they had gone to swim in a pond, with all the cousins—it was good they had gone off to have some fun. It made her feel a lot less guilty; at least her period of insanity had not caused Eddie to miss a swim.

Pretty soon all the food was gone. Neddie sat in a chair smoking while Harmony ate. Harmony thought Neddie must be in a depression as deep as her own, if not deeper. At least hers had a clear source—but what was the source of Neddie's?

Harmony decided it was no good holing up in the Best Western; she might as well go out into the world and be a member of her family. The sun was shining on Oklahoma, why not try to be normal for a little while? She still had her father's pickup, a source of guilt. What if he needed to go somewhere? Not having his vehicle meant that he was trapped with her mother all day. But when she asked about her parents Neddie said they were both over at her farm—of course they hadn't wanted to miss Eddie.

When they started to go to Neddie's, Dick decided he had to hurry back to his plowing—his little vacation to visit his long-lost sister-in-law was over.

"I'll just ride with you, I ain't in a hurry," Neddie said. "How's Gary?"

Harmony had forgotten that she had had to cut Gary off. They hadn't really finished their conversation—the only thing Harmony could remember about it was that Gary had wanted the government to bomb El Salvador, on account of a stolen boyfriend.

"Gary is just the same," Harmony said. "He's always just the same unless he's in love, and then he's crazy."

"You remember asking me about being in love with Dick and I told you I wasn't?" Neddie asked. She was looking out the window of the pickup, while Harmony drove. Obviously being in love was a subject Neddie had some difficulty talking about. She wasn't making eye contact with her sister at all.

"I remember," Harmony said. "Pat thought you were in love with Dick's brother or something—I forget his name."

"His name is Rusty," Neddie said. "He's the brother who didn't get drowned."

Then she lit another cigarette and looked out the window again. Harmony was wondering if Rusty would be as large as Dick—the thought of two men that large was interesting.

"Is he plowing, too?" she asked, wondering if she was going to meet Rusty in a field, or what.

"Oh no, he ain't plowing—he's not a workaholic like Dick," Neddie said. "Rusty likes to spend his afternoons drinking in a beer joint. The beer joint where he's at is right down the road here. Since I have you for cover, maybe we could stay and have a beer or two. You could visit with Rusty and see what you think."

"Neddie, sure," Harmony said. She wanted to try and help Neddie be a little less nervous.

"That's the beer joint," Neddie said, pointing to a little shack they were just about to zoom by. Two battered white pickups sat in front of it. One of them had a large black dog pacing around in the back end.

"Don't even look at that dog, he ain't friendly," Neddie said. "That is, he ain't friendly except to Rusty."

There was a heap of old tires piled by the door of the beer joint. It was a pretty ramshackly building, too—Harmony had to remind herself not to be picky; she wasn't in the big city now.

"I wouldn't never have the nerve to see him here, if you wasn't along," Neddie said. She was nervously watching the cars that passed on the interstate, seeing if they contained familiar faces who might spot her and figure it out.

"I ain't the type to go drinking with my boyfriend in the middle of the afternoon," she added, unnecessarily. Harmony knew her sister wasn't that type, but, even so, anyone could feel the need to break the mold, once in a while.

"It's okay, Neddie, Dick's plowing," Harmony reminded her. "Anyway, nothing's happened, has it?"

"Something's happened," Neddie said, glancing at the highway one more time before pushing open the door.

"Uh-oh," Harmony said. There could only be one thing, namely sex, that had happened.

"It happened because I went away with you and realized when I came back that I can't live with Dick anymore," Neddie said.

"When I realized that, I went over to tell Rusty. Melba—that's Rusty's wife—works in Tulsa and don't never get home much before six. That leaves the whole afternoon wide open for something to happen."

"Well, if it's what I think it was, it's happened before in this world, Neddie," Harmony said.

Neddie still hadn't entered the beer joint. She pushed the door halfway open and then stood in it to talk.

"You know, when you travel it sort of rearranges things inside you," Neddie said. "Then you come back and have to try to put things back where they were before they got rearranged, and sometimes it just don't work. I think that's what happened to me. I went away and it rearranged the furniture inside me and now I can't get it to fit back where it used to be. It's moved and that's that. Now what do I do?"

"Neddie, can't we just go in?—I thought you wanted me to meet Rusty," Harmony said.

"I do and I don't," Neddie said, still blocking the doorway, not shutting the door but not going in either. "What I'm thinking is that this is gonna tear Dick up—the trouble with Davie and the cocaine has got him all torn open anyway. It's gonna tear Dick up so bad I don't know if he'll make it."

She took a cigarette out of her purse—she still had her hand on the door.

"But another thing I'm thinking is, I can't help it," she said. "The furniture got moved and I'm forty-nine and that's that."

Harmony stepped around her and pulled her inside the beer joint, which was so dark she couldn't see a thing. She had to stop immediately and continue her conversation with Neddie, but at least they were inside.

"I'm your sister," she reminded Neddie. "I'm no angel, either. I've had my furniture moved around fifty or sixty times. I don't know how many times."

"Things with me and Dick look smooth on the surface, but underneath . . . well, there ain't no underneath," Neddie went on; she was more interested in talking than in listening.

"Pretty much the whole family's gonna be against me, when this comes out," she said. "If you're against me I don't know if I can stand it."

"I'm not against you, can't we just go meet him?" Harmony said. Her eyes had adjusted a little, enough to let her see that there was almost no one in the bar. At a table by the jukebox there was a lanky man with a dozer cap turned backward on his head. Another man was with him, a small man who seemed to have a flat nose. It was as if someone had banged his nose with a hammer a few times and flattened it against his face.

"Hi, this is Rusty and this is Dill," Neddie said, in a shaky voice. "This is my long-lost sister Harmony that everybody's been wanting to meet."

"Howdy," Rusty said, standing up. He had a nice smile, sort of shy.

"Hi," Dill said. He stood up too. "I wish they'd turn the lights up in here, so I could see you. What's the use of being with two beautiful women if it's so dark you can't even give 'em a thorough looking over.

"All I can see of you two girls is an outline," Dill went on.

"Why do they call you Dill?" Harmony asked.

"They call him Dill because he's such a sour son of a bitch, most of the time," Rusty said. "I work with him every day of my life, I ought to know."

"You don't work with me, because you don't work," Dill said. "Chewing toothpicks ain't work. I've been in your employ twenty years and you've only done about three solid days' work that I can remember."

"He's a liar," Rusty said, smiling his shy smile at Harmony. "I admit I don't work any harder than I have to, though. Why work harder than you have to?

"Harmony, I'm in love with your sister," he added, looking Harmony right in the eye.

"That ain't as big a secret as you think it is, Rusty," Dill said, looking not at all embarrassed by the intimate turn the conversation had taken.

"It may not be no big secret to you, but that don't mean it's been said aloud in public, like Rusty just said it," Neddie pointed out. Though she was still a little nervous, her face lit up when Rusty said that he was in love with her. Even in the dim bar, Harmony could see a look on her sister's face that she had never seen before.

"Well, Neddie, it's been said in public ever since I've been working for Rusty, because *I've* said it in public," Dill said. "Unless you don't consider Rusty the public."

Neddie had no comment on that point.

"The truth will out, they say," Rusty said. "I guess me and Ned are just tired of hiding our feelings—wouldn't you be?"

He looked at Harmony when he asked the question. Harmony got the feeling that Neddie and Rusty were relying on her to help them with their life. They were in a situation and needed her wisdom to help them get through it—only why did they think she had any wisdom? Wise was not a quality she would ever assign herself. But she liked the way her sister looked when Rusty said he was in love with her. Also, she liked Rusty—he was definitely cute, in his lanky way, with his dozer cap turned backward. He had big eyes, direct and a little sad, but now and then they twinkled when he saw the humor in something. On some level it seemed to amuse him that he had fallen in love with his brother's wife.

"Well, if you love Neddie, that's good," Harmony said. She felt they needed to know that they had her approval.

"Good from Ned and Rusty's point of view, maybe," Dill said. "What about Dick's point of view—and what about Melba's?"

"Dill's always been a good one for asking awkward questions," Rusty commented. "He couldn't fix a broken-down tractor if he had a year, but he can ask those awkward questions a mile a minute."

"What's Melba like—she's not from Tarwater, is she?" Harmony asked. She was pretty sure she didn't remember any Melbas from her high school years.

"Oh, Melba's from Ardmore—she's practically a Texan," Dill said.

"I ain't gonna be losing much sleep over Melba," Neddie said. "If she'd ever been halfway good to Rusty I doubt this would ever have happened."

Rusty looked a little pained when Neddie said what she said. "Neddie, it would have happened even if she'd been an angel," he said, with a note of sadness in his voice. "You can't say it's Melba's fault or Dick's fault—hell, I was in love with you even before you and Dick married, and I hadn't even met Melba yet, when that happened."

"If you was in love with me that long ago, I wish you'd spoke up," Neddie said—she sounded a little put out. "If you had maybe I would have married the right person in the first place."

"Honey, I was just a brat when you married Dick," Rusty said. "I was six years younger. You would have laughed in my face if I'd even asked you for a date."

Just then the owner of the bar, a large, red-faced man wearing a Dallas Cowboys T-shirt and a cowboy hat came over, without being asked, and sat down right by Harmony, close enough that she could smell his armpits, which could have used a squirt or two of deodorant. Harmony felt like scooting her chair over about a foot. She had been intent on her sister's situation and didn't want to have to smell some big smelly guy's armpits, just then.

"Neddie, ain't you even gonna introduce me to your famous sister?" he asked, looking at Harmony in a not too nice way.

"Fuck off, Tommy, we're having a private conversation," Rusty said, getting a cold glint in his eye.

"Mind your damn manners," the man said, ignoring Rusty and continuing to look at Harmony in the not too nice way. "This is my bar and there ain't no discussions gonna take place in it too private for me to sit in on."

"Then we'll find another bar—let's go, girls," Rusty said, standing up.

"I just asked to be introduced to Harmony, that's all," Tommy said. "This woman's got the most famous pair of tits ever to come out of Tarwater, why wouldn't I want to sit by them for a while?"

"Don't pay no attention to Tommy," Dill said, looking at Harmony. "Tits are his main interest in life, along with beer."

Tommy was still looking at Harmony.

"Honey, I got a fine bar in Tulsa and you ain't too old to bring your floor show home," he said. "We'll give you an hour or two on stage anytime you want."

"No thank you," Harmony said. "I'm retired."

Before she even finished saying it Rusty grabbed her hand—in a moment all four of them were out in the bright sunlight.

"I told you we ought to find a nicer place," Neddie said, looking at Rusty a little critically.

"How'd I know Tommy would be there—this is usually his day off," Rusty said. "Besides, there ain't no nice places to meet in, in

402

this whole county—you know that. All this would have come to a head years ago if we'd had a halfway decent place to meet."

"Well, you lovebirds can yak all you want to, I'm going to work," Dill said. "Pleased to meet you, Harmony."

He got in one of the battered white pickups and immediately gunned it straight across the highway, right in front of two trucks, both of which honked at him angrily.

"It's a wonder Dill is still alive, he has no instinct for traffic," Rusty said, reaching up to rub the head of the big black dog, who looked at them with his tongue lolled out.

"Do you want to come to the Best Western, so we can talk?" Harmony asked. "It's not very far."

"Okay," Neddie and Rusty said, at once. They were a little over-whelmed by their situation and seemed willing to obey anyone who might make a suggestion or give them a little help.

"You ride with Rusty, it'll give you a chance to get to know him," Neddie said. "I'll drive Rusty's pickup."

"Remember about the clutch slipping," Rusty said, as he got in with Harmony. The big dog jumped from the back of one pickup into the back of the other when he saw Rusty get in with Harmony.

"That's Clyde, he's obsessed with me," Rusty said, grinning. "He's got the notion that the world might end if he lets me out of his sight."

"Rusty, maybe he's just loyal," Harmony said. "Iggy's that way —Eddie's dog. He gets annoyed if we go into the waffle house or someplace and he gets left in the car."

"I hear you saw Dick," Rusty said—maybe he was just trying to get some sense of how Harmony felt about the situation.

"He got upset," Harmony said. "He mentioned the brother who got drowned."

"Dick's been blaming himself for that accident for thirty-five years," Rusty said. "Accidents like that just happen. Dick mainly brings it up when he wants sympathy."

"I guess we all want sympathy once in a while," Harmony said.

Rusty was silent while Harmony steered the pickup carefully across the highway and headed back toward the Best Western. She didn't want to make any trucks honk at her, if she could help it.

"Will you tell Dick for us?" Rusty asked then. "Tell him Neddie wants a divorce? I know it's a big thing to ask, but I got no one else to appeal to. If Neddie has to do it herself she'll put it off till we've lost another five years—we've already lost the better part of twenty.

"I know it's Neddie's place to do it," he went on. "I know it's a lot to put on you, when you just lost your little girl. But I got no one else to appeal to, and this is mine and Ned's last chance."

"Maybe Dick knows it already—I mean, inside maybe he does know," Harmony said. She wasn't sure she believed it, she was just stalling, really. The thought of having to tell that large man she scarcely knew that his wife wanted a divorce so she could marry his brother was a scary thought.

"I used to think that, but Neddie says no," Rusty said. "Ned don't think he has a clue. Dick don't look ahead, unless it has to do with the farming. He thinks about planting and harvesting, when he thinks at all. He don't think about people—that's one big reason this is happening."

Then Rusty stopped talking and looked out the window at the weedy plains.

"No, it would have happened anyway, no matter what Dick thought or didn't think," Rusty said. "Me and Ned, we're just meant to be together. That's how I feel and that's how I always felt."

"I guess I can tell him, if it will help you and my sister," Harmony said. "I'm sure it will be a shock."

Rusty looked out the window some more.

"The thing is, Dick, he's all work," Rusty said. "He can be pretty happy just working that place. He don't need a woman—not like I need Neddie. I need Neddie in the worst way, Harmony."

Harmony was remembering the look on Neddie's face, when Rusty said he loved her. It was the first look of real happiness she could ever remember seeing on her sister's face. She was also trying to remember when a man had said those words to her, with true feeling, as Rusty had said it to Neddie.

But she couldn't pull up a name, a face, or a moment when a man had said that to her. Many men had said they loved her, and some of them must have meant it, but none that she could remember had made it sound as special as Rusty made it sound, when he said it to Neddie. Rusty didn't have too good a complexion, either, but his face lit up when he told Neddie he loved her.

"What about Melba?" she asked, remembering that Rusty did have a wife.

"I think Melba may have figured this out," he said with a sigh. "I guess I'll find out when I break the news."

"Rusty, will she be real upset?" Harmony asked.

Rusty sighed again. "Our family's all Melba cares about," he said. "It will just about kill her, I expect."

"I think I better talk to my friend Gary," Harmony said. "Gary understands things like this."

"He's smarter than me, if he understands this," Rusty said. "I sure don't understand it. I like my brother Dick. I don't know why in hell I had to fall in love with his wife."

"I don't understand it either, Rusty," Harmony said. "I guess things just don't wait for people to understand them. They just happen anyway."

"That's about the size of it," Rusty said.

13.

When they got back to the motel there were complications waiting, in the form of Eddie and Iggy and Laurie and Sty and Ethel, all waiting in the blue Buick that Ethel used for going to church in. Ethel didn't like anyone else to touch her Buick, much less drive it, for any reason.

"Uh-oh," Rusty said, when he saw the Buick. "How are we going to explain this?"

"We'll just say we had lunch," Harmony said. "That's normal, isn't it?"

"It's normal, but it won't fool your mother," Rusty said. "She's going to want to know why you're with me and not Dick."

"Besides that she knows we didn't have lunch, because she was at the barbecue," Harmony remembered. "I don't know what we'll say."

"Where's Dick?" Ethel asked immediately. Fortunately she was so upset about having to use her personal car for a social occasion that she didn't pursue the other complications very thoroughly.

"It makes the oil dirty to drive this car on weekdays," she pointed out at once. "You were supposed to bring the pickup home early, and here it is the afternoon. Sty's been afoot all day and I don't know where Pat is and it's just luck that Eddie didn't drown."

"Why? Was there an accident while he was swimming?" Harmony asked, apprehensively.

"No accident," Eddie and Laurie said, simultaneously. Laurie was still smiling; evidently she hadn't found a whole morning with the family too much of a burden.

"Well, that boy was in the deep water, he could have drowned," Ethel insisted.

"You're cracked," Sty said. He looked a little weary—probably he had been having to cope with a lot of complaints.

"I can swim, Grandma," Eddie said, a little testily. "Why would I drown when I can swim?"

"You could get cramps and sink like a rock," Ethel said. "When people get cramps they drown before anyone even notices."

"She's cracked," Sty said, again.

As soon as Neddie got out of his white pickup, Rusty got in it. The big dog jumped back across, into his master's pickup. As soon as he did, Rusty waved and drove away.

"I'd like to know what that lazy no-good was doing alone with you?" Ethel asked, loudly, looking at Harmony. "Everybody knows he runs around on his wife. You don't need to be stirring him up."

"Everybody does not know any such thing, Momma," Neddie said. "That's just idle gossip and you ought to be ashamed of yourself for repeating it."

"Where there's smoke there's fire," Ethel said. "That's a true saying if there ever was a true saying."

"Don't argue with her," Sty said, getting out of the Buick. "Just leave her alone and maybe she'll drive off down the road and get lost for a month or two—then we could all have some peace."

"This car's got dirty oil in it now," Ethel informed them. "I'm going up to the filling station and see if I can get them to change it—they better not charge me for it, either. It's just oil."

"Why shouldn't they charge you for it, Momma?" Neddie asked —Harmony could tell she was incensed with her mother because of the remark about Rusty running around on his wife.

"Because I'm a good customer, why should they charge just for changing the oil?" Ethel said.

"I have to get Eli out of this blue car," Eddie said. "Grandma's too cranky and she doesn't like Eli anyway."

"Ooops, I think Eli may have crawled under the seat," Laurie said, reaching under one of them. "He's sensitive to argument."

"Get him out before he pees, we'll have to trade this Buick in if an old turtle pees in it," Ethel said. "We won't get much trade-in either, not with the dirty oil."

As soon as Laurie got the turtle out from under the car seat, Ethel began to back up. As everyone watched, she backed all the way across the parking lot and kept on backing until she was way out in the middle of the field that the young man had just mowed, a little earlier in the day.

"She's cracked—she don't even know she's going backward," Sty said. "Let's all get inside before she starts coming forward again. Ethel makes real wide turns. She'll mow us all down if we stand here and give her a target."

Eddie leapt into Harmony's arms and gave her a kiss. "It's fun here, Mom," he said. "My cousins all like me and I like them. Iggy tried to swim but he bogged and got himself muddy and Grandma hates him and she hates Eli too."

Ethel got the Buick into a forward gear and was executing a wide—very wide—turn through the little field. They all stood and watched as she drove across the field, in the general direction of the highway.

"Maybe she'll get lost and drive to Oz, and the Wicked Witch of the West will get her, only the Wicked Witch won't get me and she won't get Iggy and she won't get Eli," Eddie said. As soon as they went inside he began to bounce on the king-sized bed, bouncing as high as he could. Sty sat in a chair, Neddie smoked, and Laurie lay down on the bed despite the fact that Eddie was bouncing on it. She put the turtle on the bed but it soon crawled so close to the edge that she had to put it on the floor.

"I'm tired," she said. "We swam a lot."

Harmony had the sense that Neddie was watching her closely—probably she wanted to know whether Harmony had promised Rusty that she would tell Dick that she wanted a divorce. At times Neddie could be pretty intent on getting her way.

"Riding around with your mother always wears me to a nub,"

her father said. "I can't keep up with Eddie anyway, and I sure can't keep up with him if I have to ride around with Ethel very much."

"Just rest, Grandpa," Eddie said. "She's gone."

He stopped jumping on the bed and climbed up in his grandfather's lap. Sty smiled.

"What a boy," he said.

Harmony had a sort of "What next?" feeling; it was a time when the pieces of life just didn't fit together too well. Maybe they never had—probably they never had, but definitely they weren't at the moment.

Just as she was having the "What next?" feeling the phone rang. Harmony thought it was probably Gary calling back; he hated to have his phone calls interrupted, no matter what the circumstance. Gary always preferred long phone conversations, an hour or two was nothing to him. She was a little nervous about picking up the phone, he was probably going to bawl her out for cutting him off so abruptly. At the very least he was apt to be a little moody —Gary's interpretation would be that he wasn't getting enough attention. Still, the phone was ringing and it was her room. She finally picked it up.

"Harmony, I have a confession to make," Pat said. "I'm a heroin addict. I got on them pain pills after Debbie was born and I'm still on them. I've been embezzling a little bit from the bank, just enough to pay for the drug, but it's beginning to add up. I'm afraid they're going to catch me and put me in jail with Billy. It'll disgrace my whole family. What should I do?"

That's why she wouldn't let me touch her purse during the whole trip, Harmony thought—it had seemed weird at the time but in view of the heroin addiction it made perfect sense.

"Well," Harmony said—she still had her "What next?" feeling and was not in a good position to advise her sister about heroin addiction.

"Harmony, can't you do better than 'Well'?" Pat asked.

"No, everybody's in the room," Harmony said.

"Oh, gotcha, bye," Pat said. "Think about it, though. I think the auditors are zeroing in."

"That was Pat," Harmony said. "She was just checking in."

"I worry about Pat," Sty said. "I don't think she's happy. She looks too pale, to me. Happy people ain't usually that pale, especially not here in Oklahoma, where there's plenty of sunshine."

"The reason Iggy is brown on his stomach is because he bogged in the mud," Eddie explained. He held Iggy up for inspection. Iggy wiggled.

Harmony felt very confused. The sisters who had come to Las Vegas to help her out in her grief now turned out to have massive problems of their own; both of them needed her to help them, though only an hour ago she had been naked and crazy herself. Besides, there was the question of their privacy. Should she tell Pat that Neddie wanted a divorce, so she could marry her brother-in-law? Should she tell Neddie that Pat was a heroin addict and an embezzler? Did they already know these things about one another? Did she dare inquire, or would that just make things worse? She had been stuck in the driver's seat and the car was moving, but she had no map and no idea where she was supposed to go.

As if that wasn't enough, her father was looking at her a little strangely. He looked needy, just as Neddie had, before she made her unusual request. Her father was looking at her with longing and hope—but longing for what? Hope for what?

"Daddy, if you want me to drive you home, I will," she said. "I didn't mean to keep the pickup all day."

"Mom, it's okay," Eddie said. "Grandpa wanted to stay with me today. He wanted to tell me a lot of stories while we were here visiting in Oklahoma."

"We had a good day, too," Sty said. "But maybe you ought to run me on home. Keeping up with Eddie's kinda got me tuckered out."

"You two run along," Laurie said. "Eddie and Iggy and I could use a nap."

"I'll catch a ride too," Neddie said. "Dick's plowing, he'll expect me to milk."

"Where's the remote? I want to see if there's cable," Eddie said to Laurie, as the rest of them went out the door.

Once they got on the highway, Harmony had to ask directions to Neddie's farm—she hadn't been there in so long she didn't know the way.

"I'll talk to you later, Neddie," Harmony said, when she let Neddie out at her back gate. She tried to sound reassuring—of

410

course she would break the bad news to Dick, if that was what her sister needed. She didn't want Neddie worrying while she took her father home.

"Okay," Neddie said—she took a deep breath, as if she were about to dive into deep water.

When they started back down the dirt road toward the home-place, Sty didn't speak for a mile or two. Then he looked at Harmony and smiled.

"Well, what do you think of our big happy family?" he asked.

"It's big but it's not too happy, is it, Daddy?" Harmony said.

"Nope, it's a mess," Sty said. "I guess once things start slipping in a family, they just keep slipping."

"I guess they do," Harmony said.

"When was you planning to go home?" he asked.

"Daddy, I thought I was coming to stay when I came here," Harmony said. "But I don't think I can stay. Las Vegas is the only place where I know how to survive."

"Honey, I know you're grief-stricken," Sty said. "That's normal. But you know something? You're doing better than us. Eddie wouldn't be the wonderful child that he is if you weren't doing a good job being a mother."

"I think I'm just lucky," she said. "He's always been that way."

"It's not just luck," her father said. "I guess Pepper got away from you, but Eddie's a well-brought-up boy."

"He never sees his Dad," Harmony mentioned—she didn't want to gloss that over.

Her father looked at her, started to say something, sighed, and then said it.

"Honey, when you go back to Las Vegas, do you think you could take me with you, for a while?" he asked. "It might give me a new lease on life if I could be with you and Eddie for a month or two."

Harmony was startled—it was the last thing she would have expected her father to ask. At the same time, she wasn't sorry he had asked.

"Sure you can, Daddy," she said. "Eddie would love that. But what's Mom gonna say?"

"She's gonna think I've left her and she's gonna be right," Sty said. "It's that or lay down and die."

411

"Is it that bad, Daddy?" she asked.

"You've been home a day and you haven't heard her say a nice word yet," Sty said. "If you stayed here for the rest of your life you still wouldn't hear her say a nice word. Ethel hasn't said a nice word to me in ten years, and she don't intend to, either."

"She never did say many nice words," Harmony said. "If she did, I can't remember them."

"No, she's always been negative," Sty said. "It can't be a nice enough day for Ethel. It can't be safe enough for her—and I can't work hard enough to please her. And none of her children or grandchildren can please her. I can't go to church often enough, or drive well enough, or garden well enough, or please her at all, no matter what I do."

"Why do you think she's so hard to please?" Harmony asked.

"I used to ask myself that question, when I was young," Sty said, looking out the window. "I asked it when I was middle-aged too. I even asked it when I began to get old. But now I'm old and I'm tired of asking it, because I don't care anymore. Ethel's not hard to please, she's impossible to please. She don't like anything I do and I've stopped caring why—it don't matter to me now. I've spent nearly fifty years of my life trying to please her, but I failed, so I'm giving up. I want to come live with you and Eddie—me and Eddie just hit it off right away. You can't know what a lift it gives an old man, to have a boy like Eddie who wants to know all the stuff his Grandpa knows.

"It's not just a pleasure," he said, looking at her kindly. "For me, it's life."

"You can come, Daddy," Harmony said again, in case he missed it the first time she said it. "You can live with Eddie and me for the rest of your life, if you want to."

"I guess it's a shame," her father said. "Me and Ethel have been husband and wife for nearly fifty years. It's nice to think of us going on to the end together, like an old married couple should. But thinking about it and living it are two different things. The fact is, it's a living death and I've lived it as long as I can."

Then Sty leaned forward, put his head against the dashboard, and began to sob. He didn't make a lot of noise as he cried; he had always been a quiet man. But he was sobbing, nonetheless. Harmony took one hand off the steering wheel and reached over and rubbed her father's neck, a little. She was hoping he wouldn't cry for too long because she was more or less lost. She had taken a left turn at a little crossroads and now she was beginning to feel that the left turn might have been a bad idea. Instead of seeing the farm and the pond and the stump all she saw ahead was empty prairie.

"Dad, is this the way?" she asked; but her father, crying out his sadness, didn't hear her at first. He had probably waited years to let his feelings out, and he couldn't immediately choke them off.

Harmony stopped the pickup. She didn't see any reason to go farther astray, and also she wanted to hug her father, comfort him a little for his sadness.

"Daddy, just leave her," she said. "Just leave her. Come and live with Eddie and me."

Her father sniffed a few times, took out an old cotton handkerchief, and carefully dried his eyes. Then he looked around.

"My Lord, this ain't the road," he said. "We're over here by the Harrises? You're going to have to turn around."

It was a pretty narrow dirt road—Harmony didn't feel confident that she knew how to turn the pickup around; normally she would just have whipped into a parking lot to do it, but there were no parking lots in sight.

"Maybe you should drive me now, Dad," she said. Even though he was red-eyed he seemed calm again.

"Maybe I better," Sty said. They both got out, walked around the pickup, and traded places.

Harmony felt curious about the woman her mother had mentioned, the one in the old folks' home in Bartlesville. It was obvious her father was starved for affection. Harmony decided she couldn't resist asking; he didn't have to tell her if he didn't want to.

"Momma thinks you have a girlfriend," she said.

Sty was carefully turning the pickup around. He was so meticulous about it that he didn't get even one tire in the ditch.

"She thinks what?" he asked.

"She thinks you have a girlfriend," Harmony repeated. "Some woman in an old folks' home in Bartlesville."

"Oh, May," Sty said. "She died seven years ago. That's how cracked Ethel is. She can't keep it in her head who's dead and who's alive."

"Do you miss May, Daddy?" Harmony asked—she was still curious about the woman; also she was curious about her father's life.

"I sure do miss her," Sty said. "She was the wife of our banker —he keeled over in church about fifteen years ago. May and I had been sweethearts, back in the thirties. After Joe died we got in the habit of having coffee, whenever I was in town. Both of us were lonely, you know. Ethel was jealous of May all her life and she's still jealous of her, although May's been dead seven years."

"You better just come on and live with us, Dad," Harmony said —it was terrible that her mother wouldn't even let him enjoy a few memories of his friend May.

Sty looked at his daughter and smiled. "That's a relief," he said. "I'm an old worn-out man. Not every daughter would have me."

"Dad, you might not feel so old and worn out once you leave Mom," Harmony said.

"Well, maybe I won't," Sty said.

14.

After Harmony dropped her father off at the farmhouse he looked at her quizzically.

"Think I ought to tell Ethel what we decided tonight, or should I wait till we're about ready to leave?" he asked.

"I'd put it off until we land in Las Vegas, if I were you," Harmony said. "That's how I left, remember? If I'd told Mom I was getting on that bus she'd have rammed the bus."

"Rammed it, she would have bombed it," Sty said. "She cussed the bus company for five years, after you took off. She's not above killing fifty or sixty innocent people, if that's what it takes to get her way."

"Daddy, she's not that bad," Harmony said.

"That's what I said for the first forty years," Sty said. "That's not what I say now.

"The thing is, I don't think I could stand being without Eddie now," he added. "I just don't want to be without that kid."

"You won't have to, Daddy," Harmony said.

"I know exactly what your father means," Laurie said, an hour later. Harmony had rushed back to the Best Western and told her everything: about Neddie and Rusty, about Pat's addiction and embezzlement, about her father's desire to leave her mother and start a new life in Las Vegas. Laurie was a good listener, too. She didn't even seem surprised, though she did reveal a deep uncertainty about what she herself should do next.

"I don't really have any business tagging along with you and Eddie," she said. "I should have stayed in New York, like Sheba and Otis did."

"But Sheba and Otis didn't know Pepper," Harmony reminded her.

"That's right—they didn't know Pepper, and they weren't in love with her," Laurie said. "I was too lonely to stay. I needed to be with you and Eddie as much as your father does now."

"There's nothing wrong with that, is there?" Harmony asked. With so many lives falling apart, including her own, she felt a little apprehensive. She wasn't sure what point Laurie was trying to make.

"Nothing's wrong with it for now," Laurie said. "But at some point we have to let Pepper go on and be dead. Because she *is* dead, you know. And we're not. At some point I have to go back into the world and make a life—so do you. It's going to be hard. I'll be missing you and I'll be missing Eddie . . . I'll miss you both a whole lot."

Eddie had been in the bathroom, brushing his teeth in the correct manner—the manner he had been shown in a film at his dentist's office. He finished and came back into the room just in time to hear Laurie say she would miss him and his mother very much.

"But why would you miss me?" he asked. "You're *with* me."

"I know, Eddie—I'm with you now," Laurie said. "But the sad fact is that people being together can be temporary."

She made the statement nervously—she had not meant for Eddie to overhear her.

"It *cannot* be temporary," Eddie insisted—his face got instantly red. "You came with me and Iggy and my mother and now I want you to stay with us forever so we can be a family."

Laurie didn't answer. She just got tears in her eyes.

"Mom, please ask her to stay," Eddie said. "We need her."

Laurie just looked at him. Now the tears were on her cheeks.

"Eddie, here's a deal," she said, in a small shaky voice. "From

416

now on, no matter what, I'll come to visit with you four times a year—and if I can't get to Las Vegas because of my job I'll send money and you and your Mom can come see me in New York."

"But are you leaving *right now*?" Eddie asked, bereft. "I wanted you to be a member of my family."

"I *am* a member of your family now, Eddie, and I always will be," Laurie said. "But your Aunt Neddie and your Aunt Pat and all your cousins are members of your family, and they don't live where you live all the time."

Eddie said nothing. His face made it clear that reasoned argument wasn't making him like the fact that Laurie was leaving one bit better.

"Guess what, though, Eddie?" Harmony said.

"I don't want to guess if it's bad news," Eddie said.

"No, it's good news—very good news," Harmony said. "The good news is that Grandpa is going to come to Las Vegas and live with us."

Eddie shrugged. "But Laurie still won't be with us," he said. "I want my Grandpa to come but I want Laurie to be with us too, sometime. If Grandpa can live in Las Vegas Laurie can live there too, and we'd be a family."

"What about your grandmother living there, then?" Laurie asked. Harmony could tell she was mainly trying to put a lighter cast on things.

"No, Grandma has to stay here because she's too gripy," Eddie said. "And she doesn't like Iggy and she hates Eli, so she *cannot* live in Las Vegas."

"But it'll be fun to have Grandpa, won't it?" Harmony asked. "He can meet all your friends. You'll probably be the only person in your school who has your Grandpa living with you."

Eddie still didn't like the fact that Laurie was leaving. He flung himself on her lap and hugged her tightly. Laurie had tears in her eyes as she held him. Iggy climbed up in her lap, too. Eddie yawned a few times, glanced at the TV, and fell asleep.

"Harmony, could you just take me to the airport?" Laurie asked. "I don't think I'm up to parting with Eddie unless I do it right now."

"I wanted you to meet Billy," Harmony said—she was upset that Laurie was leaving so abruptly.

"Maybe we could go by the jail and say hello to him on our way to the airport," Laurie said. "I'm just afraid that if I stick around another day I'll be too chicken to leave—and I know in my gut that it would be better for all of us if I go back for a while."

"I don't know why," Harmony said. "I was hoping we could take care of one another."

"I know," Laurie said. "Maybe we can, in our way. I just think it's too soon for me to totally throw in my lot with you and Eddie. I'm afraid I'll get so far out of my other life that I can never get back, even though I don't really know what I mean when I say my other life. I don't know what life I have that I'm so afraid of getting out of."

She stroked Eddie's hair. Iggy licked her fingers.

"You've got all that stuff with your family to deal with," Laurie reminded her. "And all that stuff came up just in one day."

Harmony thought she knew what Laurie was saying. She was saying that life was going to push them on, past Pepper. There was Eddie and Neddie and Pat and her father to think about. Pepper was quiet in her death, past all pain and hurt. But those who still lived were loud. Their cries were carrying her on, past Pepper's silence. Pepper had stopped, but she and Eddie and Laurie couldn't stop—the only stopping they could have, where Pepper was concerned, was in memory.

"It would be selfish to stay together now," Laurie said. "I have people who need me, too, you know. I kind of have a little set I ran off from. Maybe some of the cousins would come and stay with Eddie while you run me to the airport. I better just make some reservations."

Laurie got a reservation from Tulsa via Chicago to New York; then Harmony got on the phone and called Pat, to see if either of her daughters wanted to come and sit with Eddie. Pat volunteered to come herself.

"I've been sitting here climbing the walls," Pat said. "I was about to head out to the oil rigs."

"Why the oil rigs?" Harmony asked, when Pat showed up at the motel.

"Because there's always pills around an oil rig," Pat said. "Sometimes the roughnecks work two or three days straight—they have to have a little speed to help them stay awake."

418

"Pat, I thought you said heroin," Harmony said. "I didn't know you took speed."

"Harmony, I'm sort of a general drug addict," Pat admitted. "If I can't get one drug I'll take another, particularly when there's no sex on the horizon, and there's no sex on the horizon right now, not in smelling distance anyway."

"What about Rog?" Harmony asked.

"No message from Rog," Pat said. "I expect that means he's found a new love."

Harmony and Laurie didn't go by the jail, after all. They turned off the freeway, toward town, but then they looked at one another and decided they'd rather just spend Laurie's last hour or two together.

"I'm sure your brother's nice, but I don't think I can stand to look at any more sadness, right now," Laurie said. "I suppose there's just as much sadness everyplace as there is here, but somehow it seems more concentrated when you're in a place where there aren't many people. At least in New York there are millions of people—it sort of spreads the sadness out."

Harmony agreed. Lots of times, in the casinos, watching all the little old ladies pulling the handles of the slots and watching the money they had worked for all their lives wash away, Harmony had got a sense of the sadness of things, but at least it was spread out among all the people in the casinos. In Tarwater it was sort of more tightly packaged.

"I miss Eddie already," Laurie said, when they were back on the highway, heading toward Tulsa. "That little boy sure tugs at your heartstrings."

Harmony was trying to imagine how it would be if Laurie changed her mind at the last minute and decided to stay with them —would it work, or would it mean that Laurie had had an odd life, of the sort she herself had lived, a life in which nothing emotional had ever quite worked?

"Laurie, do you think I have to find a man so Eddie can have a male role model?" she asked. They could already see the lights of Tulsa, glowing in the distance. Harmony had no idea where the airport was, although Pat had tried to give good directions. Suddenly Harmony felt she had to hurry up and ask Laurie all the questions she had meant to ask her over the next few years.

"I'd think just having your Dad there would provide enough of a male role model," Laurie said. "Your father is a really fine man.

"I don't know that Eddie even needs a male role model," she added. "Eddie sort of *is* the model—you know what I mean?"

Then they were suddenly at the exit to the airport—Harmony knew that her time with Laurie was slipping away real quickly. The biggest block of time they got that wasn't frantic was in the ticket line. The old woman in the line just ahead of them turned out to be going to Russia, and there were quite a few things wrong with her ticket. All the people behind them in the line began to get huffy. They were incensed that an old fat lady was taking so long to get her ticket changed.

"The truth is, Pepper was only interested in me for a few months, Harmony," Laurie said. "I kept on wanting her but she stopped wanting me."

"Did it make you sad?" Harmony asked. She was taken aback by the comment and felt she had to say something.

"Make me sad—it broke my heart," Laurie said. "I mean, she still liked living with me and everything—she just didn't want to have sex. I didn't get it then, and I'll never get it. She just stopped wanting me."

"Did it make you want to leave?" Harmony asked. She noticed that there were several rodeo cowboys in the ticket line—maybe the rodeo in Tulsa had just ended or something.

"Yeah, I wanted to leave, but I didn't leave—I didn't have the guts," Laurie said. "I pretended it was just a phase. I kept telling myself that one day Pepper would want me again. Maybe it would be a year, maybe it would be two—but one day we would have sex again. I mean, it's not like our whole lives were gloomy—we'd go out and eat and stuff, or go see some comedy. We'd have fun. I spent a lot of time pretending things would change, but they didn't."

When the old woman who was going to Russia finally got her ticket worked out, there was only time to buy Laurie's ticket and rush for the plane.

"This is happening too quickly, but maybe it's better," Laurie said. They only had time for a kiss and a hug and a few tears; then Laurie was on the plane and gone; gone away.

Harmony took a seat by the window where the plane sat. She

420

didn't want to leave the airport until she knew for sure that Laurie's plane was actually taking off. Also, the running and the emotion had left her feeling a little weak in the knees. She felt she could use a little rest before she had to face the task of trying to find her way back to Tarwater. She knew it was north, but that was about all she knew. Fortunately the Best Western was right on the highway—if she could find north, then she probably wouldn't miss it.

While she was resting, waiting for the plane to move off the gate and fly Laurie back to her life in New York, Harmony noticed a young cowboy, sitting a few seats away. The cowboy was short and skinny. When she glanced at him she saw that he was bent over, with his face in his hands, crying. His skinny shoulders were shaking, and his black cowboy hat had fallen off his head and was on the floor, by his boots.

Harmony had never been able to ignore distress, even if what was causing the distress was totally none of her business. Maybe the boy's mother had just died. Maybe his girlfriend had just left him for his best friend. Maybe someone had stolen all his money. All he had with him was a small duffel bag, with a pair of spurs dangling from the handle, and a rope. His boots were dusty and his pants legs were a little too long—he had stepped on the cuffs and left them pretty frayed. Since he had his face in his hands it was difficult to tell exactly how old he was, but he looked to be only in his late teens.

Harmony saw Laurie's plane backing away from the gate. For better or worse, Laurie was gone. She got up and started to walk on past the young cowboy—maybe he would prefer to be sad privately. Then she stopped and went back to him. After all, she was soon going to have to start dealing with all the problems in her family, why not get a little practice in the airport?

"Can I help you, sir?" she asked, sitting down beside him.

The boy, his face wet with tears, looked up at her—his look was blank.

"I just saw that you were upset," Harmony said. "I'm sorry if I intruded."

"Jody's dead," the young man said, simply, as if it should be obvious to any passerby why he was sitting in the Tulsa airport at midnight, crying.

"That old pickup of ours didn't have no seat belts on the driver's side," he went on. "Jody always drove like a bat out of hell even when there wasn't no hurry. She missed a curve and flipped. Got thrown clean out of the window and broke her neck. Kilt instantly. The kids weren't hurt, though."

Then he paused, as if a new fact had just dawned on him.

"Oh, God," he said. "How am I gonna raise them without Jody?"

"Jody was your wife?" Harmony asked.

"Yep, only she ain't no more, she's dead, and I got two kids to raise and not a cent to my name. I sure can't make enough calf roping to support two kids, so I guess that's the end of rodeoing."

"You were in the rodeo?" Harmony asked—mainly she was just trying to absorb the fact that this child with the red, tear-streaked face already had children of his own—children who were now without a mother.

"By the way, I'm Harmony," she said. "I hope you don't mind if I sit with you for a while."

"No, ma'am, I don't," the boy said. "I'm Wesley Straw. I come all the way up here from Lubbock and didn't win a cent. I don't know how we'll even scrape up the money to bury Jody. Her Pa just had his leg amputated—he drunk so much whiskey it shriveled up his leg. Her folks don't have a cent, and my folks don't think I should have married Jody in the first place. I don't know whether they'll help me bury her or not."

He sighed and dropped his head back into his hands. The deep sobs came again. Harmony put her arm around him. She wasn't sure that he would accept it, but he did; he clung to her gratefully. Wesley Straw was so skinny that hugging him was a little like hugging Pepper—every time she had hugged her daughter in her life she felt her bones.

"Oh God, ma'am, I just can't believe she's dead," Wesley said. "All she was doing was driving home. They estimate she was going better than ninety and there wasn't a thing to do once she got home except sit there with the kids and watch cartoons."

"Maybe you can get back to rodeoing a little later, Wesley," Harmony said, still hugging him—she was trying to say something that might make him feel at least a little hopeful.

But Wesley Straw shook his head.

"I should have give it up already," he said. "It was just a dream I had, when I was growing up. I wanted to be a world's champion

422

cowboy so bad—or at least to get to the national finals. But I can't afford my own trailer, so when I enter a rodeo I have to borrow a horse to rope off of. But that's no good. I ain't familiar with the horse, and the horse ain't familiar with me. Sometimes I'll be riding a different roping horse every time I rope. You don't get nowhere that way. All the good ropers got their own trailers and their own horses.

"It don't matter now," he went on. "Jody was getting tired of me going off and never bringing home no money. I would have had to give up and go to work in the oil fields anyway, pretty soon. God, I hate the thought of spending the rest of my life working in the stinking oil fields."

"Wesley, I lost my daughter, recently," Harmony said.

"Aw, ma'am, that's worse," Wesley said, turning his anguished eyes to hers. "Losing Jody is hell, but if I was to lose one of my girls I'd take a shotgun and blow my head off."

On impulse he dug in his pocket and pulled out a sweat-stained wallet and showed Harmony small snapshots of his daughters, aged three and four.

"That's Jilly," he said. "And this is Jane."

Then he pulled out a picture of his wife.

"And this is Jody," he said, offering Harmony a picture of a thin-faced, pretty brunette. The little girls both looked like their mother, except that their hair was in braids.

Just then Wesley Straw's flight was called. He popped up and put his black hat back on his head—it looked much too large for his small head and thin neck. He picked up his duffel bag, which made his spurs jingle a little.

"It'll be late when I get to Lubbock and I'll still have eighty miles to hitch," he said, pausing for a moment. "Jody was planning to get a babysitter and meet me but that plan's gone with the wind."

Harmony reached in her purse and took out some bills—she had an urge to offer the young man something.

"Please take this, Wesley," she said. "Maybe you can get a cab to take you home."

Wesley Straw looked at her strangely.

"A cab? In Lubbock?" he said. "They'd think I was crazy if I showed up at home in a cab."

"But you shouldn't have to hitchhike, Wesley, if it's late at night," Harmony said. "Don't you have a friend who could come and get you?"

"I didn't call none of them—rather hitch," he said. "That way I won't have to deal with it for an hour or two longer. I can try to pretend it didn't happen."

He gave Harmony a little nod, and a grateful glance before getting in line to board the plane. Then he dried his eyes on his shirtsleeve and straightened his black hat on his head. There was something about his look that broke Harmony's heart. He was only nineteen, he had said, and now he was flying off to try his best to be a brave cowboy and raise his little girls, letting go forever his dream of being a world's champion calf roper and getting to compete in the national finals rodeo; all because his wife was driving too fast and failed to make a curve. Probably it had been hard for Wesley to keep up his hopes anyway, since he didn't even have enough money to own a trailer and didn't get to rope off his own horse. But he had still been trying, still flying to rodeos. Now it was over.

Harmony walked out of the airport into the hot night, so devastated by Wesley's tragedy that she couldn't find the pickup. She had to walk back and forth in the parking lot for fifteen minutes before she found it. She wasn't actually looking for it very hard, though—she was thinking of Wesley, his little thin-faced wife dead on the highway at eighteen; maybe she had been a good mother to her little girls even if she did drive too fast.

Harmony stood by the pickup a few minutes; then she went back into the airport and made a reservation for Eddie and her father and herself to fly to Las Vegas on the evening of the next day. She didn't have enough money on her to buy the tickets just then, and she wouldn't have enough tomorrow, either, but she thought she could probably borrow a little money from Billy, enough to get them all home. Billy, despite his problems, had always been good at making money—he owned property in Tulsa and seemed to mostly win when he gambled on sports. She had a great urge just to get her son and father and go right back to the place where she felt most at home.

The fact was, it could all end in a minute, as it had for Wesley Straw. One moment his wife had been alive, the next he was a single parent of two little girls. All around her, even in the small airport in Tulsa, cords that had knitted lives together were being cut. Probably there were several people, sleeping now in Tulsa, who had lost loved ones but hadn't even got the phone call yet, informing them of their loss; they didn't yet know, as they slept, that they would wake to discover that their lives had changed forever, as hers had when she opened Laurie's yellow letter and discovered that Pepper was dead.

She walked back to the pickup and then returned to the airport for a third time; she dug in her purse and found the number Gary had given her—Ross's work number, Gary claimed. She dialed and then realized she didn't have enough change to make a call to Las Vegas, so when the operator came on she billed the call to her parents.

The man who answered the phone definitely wasn't Ross; in fact he sounded a good deal like Denny, an old boyfriend but not one of the better ones. It fit that it would be Denny, since the place she called was a burlesque house. Working in burlesque would certainly suit Denny, if there was one thing he liked it was tits.

"Could I please speak to Ross?" she said, trying to make her voice sound neutral—if it was Denny she was hoping he wouldn't realize it was her on the phone.

"He's on his break, I'll see if he's around," the voice said. Then, bad luck, it turned out that it *was* Denny, and the neutral tone didn't work, he immediately recognized her voice.

"Hey, is this who I think it is?" he said.

"Denny, can I just speak to Ross, it's real important," Harmony said. The last thing she needed was a telephone conversation with Denny. As she was talking she remembered that she had caught a glimpse of Denny on his motorcycle, not long ago. He had put on a lot of weight, which fit with what she had heard from Gary, which was that Denny had become a bouncer in a titty bar somewhere on the outskirts of town. Sure enough, she had called a titty bar and who had picked up the phone but Denny?

"Well, you can speak to Ross if I can find the little wimp, but why would you want to when you can speak to me?" Denny asked. He had always been vain. "Better than that, you can come on out here and suck my dick, it would be like old times, wouldn't it, babe?"

"Denny, my daughter is dead, would you go get Ross?" Harmony said; she was wondering why Denny and Ross had to be working in the same titty bar.

"Oh," Denny said. "Okay. I think he stepped outside for a minute, I'll go see if I can find him."

There was a pause, as if Denny was maybe considering apologizing for his remark about her sucking his dick; but he didn't make the apology, he had never apologized for anything, that she could remember. It was true that he was obsessed with blow jobs; one of the things that flashed through her mind when he made the remark was that he had once asked Pepper to give him a blow job; Pepper had been no more than sixteen at the time. Harmony felt a twinge of guilt for having brought her daughter into contact with such a man; it was one of the many puzzles of her life, that she had had such a big attraction for a man who had so few redeeming qualities. Gary just put it that she liked bad boys; he told her several times that she wouldn't be interested in Denny for five minutes if he reformed and became a decent citizen; of course, it never happened, Denny didn't have the slightest interest in becoming a decent citizen. Whether that had prompted all that sex she didn't know—but she did feel a little wistful for the days when she could get attracted to a guy. It had been a while since anything that compelling had happened to her in the romantic area.

Then she heard footsteps on the other end of the phone; probably Ross was coming. She felt a strong urge to hang up—why should she have to stand in the airport, in the middle of the night, charging a long-distance call to her parents, in order to tell a man who hadn't even been interested enough in Pepper to make her birthday parties that she was dead? When Pepper had been a lead dancer at the Stardust, Ross had never once come from Reno to see her show. It was no big deal to get from Reno to Las Vegas, either—the bottom line was, no interest.

"Harmony?" Ross said—he sounded tentative, probably he had not been expecting to get a phone call while he was on his break. From the way he said her name she could tell that it was not an entirely pleasant surprise, either.

"Ross, Pepper is dead, she died of AIDS in New York, she's already cremated," Harmony said—it seemed best just to get it out.

"You mean our daughter?" Ross asked. "Our little girl?"

"Ross, she was in her twenties," Harmony said. "You should have kept in touch."

"What? I guess I lost her phone number," he said. "Oh my God. You mean our little girl is dead?"

"Ross, she died of AIDS in New York City," Harmony said. Then, to her own surprise, she just hung up. What was the point of telling Ross or any man that he should have kept in touch? Ross had never particularly been in touch. The only touch that mattered to him was the sex act—long forgotten by both parties involved—that produced Pepper in the first place.

This time she got out of the airport and into the pickup as fast as she could go. She didn't like all the memories that were crowding into her head—Denny and the sex and Ross never making it to the birthday parties, and a lot of others, most of them not nice memories. It was even disturbing to her that Ross and Denny were working in the same titty bar now. Ross had always hated Denny. He knew about Harmony's big attraction and was very jealous, since her attraction to him had never been that big—it was more of a chum thing with him.

She didn't have too much trouble getting out of Tulsa—north turned out to be easy to find; she didn't do ninety like Pat, but she kept up a good speed and pretty soon the sign for the Best Western appeared. She didn't go to the Best Western, though; she cruised on into Tarwater and parked at the jail.

Billy and Peewee were right where she had found them the night before, drinking beer and watching old Dick Van Dyke reruns. Harmony felt a little speedy, she was really ready to get home to Las Vegas and get Eddie back in school.

"Hi, Sis, where you been?" Billy asked. "Me and Peewee been hoping you'd show up. We've seen this episode of Dick Van Dyke about twenty times apiece."

"Yep, we've nearly got it memorized," Peewee said. His eyes lit up when he saw her, but Harmony wasn't in the mood to welcome the lighting up. It wasn't Peewee's fault that he reminded her of Ross, but he *did* remind her of Ross; just then it was hard for her to be very welcoming to anyone who reminded her of Ross.

"Billy, could you lend me money for three air tickets?" she asked. "I need to take Eddie home."

"Plenty of money available," Billy said. He seemed cheered a little, to think that he could be of some help to his sister.

"Who's the third ticket for?" he asked. He was pretty alert, for someone who had chosen to live his life in the local jail.

Harmony started to lie and say the third ticket was for Laurie. Her motive for the lie was that the minute she mentioned that her father was leaving her mother it would be all over town. The fact that Sty was leaving Ethel would be all anyone would talk about, in the beauty parlor, in the filling station, or at the grocery store.

"I'm taking Daddy," she said. She didn't want to start concealing family things from her brother.

"You're taking *Dad*?" Billy said. He looked delighted and even sat up straighter on the couch.

"That's the best news I've heard in years," Billy said. "If there was a bottle of champagne in the icebox I'd break it out and we'd drink it. This might give Dad a new lease on life. He's been slipping fast, as things stood."

"I wonder what Ethel will do, without Sty to torment," Peewee said. "That's always been her main occupation, tormenting Sty."

"She'll turn it on you, hoss," Billy said. "She'll probably sue the city, claiming you ain't taking proper care of me—which you ain't, by the way."

"I ain't?—what ain't I doing?" Peewee asked. He seemed startled by the thought that Billy considered him remiss in his duties.

"Well, the vacuum cleaner ain't worth a shit," Billy said. "Also, we could use a VCR. I'm getting tired of memorizing these reruns."

Billy went to his cell, came back with his checkbook, and gave Harmony a check for five thousand dollars.

"Billy, I don't need this much," Harmony said.

"Take it for Dad," Billy said. "I hope he finds a girlfriend and gets a new lease on life, out there in Las Vegas."

"Couldn't you come out to the motel with me, again?" Harmony asked. "I'd like you to meet Eddie."

"Sure, I'd like to meet Eddie," Billy said.

"Take him, Harmony," Peewee said. "Just don't let him near a phone."

When they got to the Best Western Pat was in the parking lot, talking to a man in an older-model Cadillac. The man had the door of the car open, but when he saw them he closed it and drove away.

"There's Pat, meeting her pusher," Billy said. He seemed a little annoyed.

"Billy, I've taken drugs, don't be judgmental," Harmony said. Pat looked a little forlorn, standing there waiting for them.

"Oh, I ain't judgmental," Billy said. "It's the law that will be judgmental, when they finally pull the plug on her embezzling. You could have two siblings in the same jail, if you ain't careful."

"Hi, Billy," Pat said. "Peewee must have lost his mind to let you come out here to a motel full of telephones."

"Peewee's too in love with Harmony to deny me anything," Billy said.

"Eddie woke up about half an hour ago and he's wired," Pat said.

When they went inside Eddie was wearing the long T-shirt that he preferred to sleep in, and he was using the bed as a trampoline again, bouncing as high as he could. Iggy was snarling and trying to catch the end of Eddie's T-shirt—he thought it was a game.

"Eddie, this is your Uncle Billy," Harmony said.

Eddie ceased bouncing at once and smiled at his uncle.

"But I wanted to come meet you in jail," Eddie said. "The reason is that I've never been in a jail before and if I went in one I could tell all my friends about it when I get home."

"That's a good reason, bud," Billy said. "You can come take a look when your Mom runs me back to the slammer."

"Eddie, you should be asleep," Harmony said. "It's the middle of the night."

"Well, I *was* asleep," Eddie pointed out. "Only in my dream Grandpa's black rooster was chasing me and he pecked me very hard and I woke up."

"Are you heading out already, or what?" Pat asked, looking at Harmony a little accusingly. "How can you leave just when we all need you?"

"Pat, I have to get a job and Eddie needs to be in school," Harmony said. "I'm taking Dad with me, too."

"What?" Pat said—she looked disbelieving, as if what Harmony had just said couldn't possibly be true.

"I'm taking Dad with me, he wants to leave Mom," Harmony said.

"He's always wanted to leave her—that don't mean you can just fly in here and take our Dad away," Pat said.

"Pat, he asked if he could go," Harmony said.

"I don't doubt it—he's always favored you," Pat said.

Then she burst into tears and ran out the door.

"Aunt Pat's upset," Eddie remarked. "I hope she remembers to fasten her seat belt."

"I don't think Dad favored me," Harmony said.

"Of course not, he favored Pat," Billy said. "That's why she's so upset that he's going away.

"Maybe we better load up Eddie and toddle on back to the jail," he said, a moment later.

"Billy, we just got here—are you tired?" Harmony asked.

"No, but I'm getting a powerful urge to grab that phone and call Mildred," he said. Harmony noticed that he was sort of eyeing the phone.

"Who's Mildred?" Eddie asked.

"Eddie, let's just go see the jail," Harmony said.

On the ride into Tarwater Eddie was as bright and bouncy as if he'd had a full night's sleep.

"It's not much like Las Vegas, is it, Mom?" he said, looking at the town. "Where do all the cars go at night? I see very few cars."

"They go home to their little dinky garages," Billy said.

Eddie and Peewee hit it off at once—they played two games of checkers and Eddie won both games. Then Peewee let Eddie listen to the police radio, after which he locked Eddie in a cell so he could pretend he was a dangerous criminal.

While Eddie was playing Harmony enjoyed a few more minutes with her brother. They sat on a bunk in one of the empty cells and talked.

"I think you're doing the right thing, taking Dad," Billy said.

"What do you think Mom will do?" Harmony asked. Even though her mother was cranky she was old enough that it was natural to worry about her a little.

"Momma will be fine," Billy said. "She'll play a little more bridge, and drop in on me and Peewee a little more often."

Harmony still had an ache inside her, from thinking about her

430

brother living in the jail. It seemed so sad that he had chosen to live his life that way because he couldn't resist making obscene phone calls to a woman he could have married at one time, a woman who probably would have given him all the sex he wanted.

"I just wish you'd think of a way to change, Billy," she said. "Maybe you could get paroled and come out west with me and Eddie and Dad."

"Harmony, don't be jumping on the bandwagon to save me," Billy said, not unkindly. "I'm all right. Life being what it is, I ain't doing too badly."

Harmony let it go. Billy was right. Who did she think she was, to be giving people advice? She had ignored millions of words of good advice herself, most of it Gary's advice—Gary had ignored just as much of hers. The point was, people had to live their own lives; if Billy chose to live his in the jail in Tarwater, well, she should just mind her own business.

Billy gave her a long hug, though, when it came time to go—he was a little misty-eyed, obviously he loved his sister. Peewee took such a liking to Eddie that he gave him a key ring with a tiny oil rig attached to it, and also a baseball cap that said *Tarwater Tigers*, that being the name of the local ball team. Eddie was pleased with both gifts—he wanted to go immediately to an all-night locksmith and have some keys made to put on his key ring.

"Eddie, I don't think they have all-night locksmiths in Tarwater," Harmony informed him.

"But I need a locksmith and I need one now because there are *no* keys on my key ring," Eddie said.

As they were driving out of Tarwater, back toward the Best Western, Harmony noticed that the sky to the east was tinged with light. The night was ending, and it was probably going to be her last night in her hometown for a very long time. Already there was a yellow band of sunlight on the horizon, across the plains.

Eddie was watching her closely, as bright-eyed as if it were not five o'clock in the morning. He was watching with a special look he had, a look that meant he was gauging how much pressure he would have to apply to get his mother to do what he wanted her to do, in this case get him a few keys for his new key ring. There was no ignoring Eddie when he wanted something. It was a question of saying no and taking the consequences. In this case, seeing that it would soon be sunup, she had what she thought was a good idea.

"Eddie, Grandpa gets up early—he probably has some keys he could give you," Harmony said. "Why don't we go to the farm and see if he's milking the cow or something."

"Okay," Eddie said. "That's a good suggestion."

They found Sty down by the barn. He had finished milking the one milk cow—a foamy pail of milk sat by the water trough. The chickens were gathered around him, and a few guinea hens. Four heifers and two goats stood nearby, as well as the old brown mule. In the pigpen the three pigs had their snouts through the rail, watching. The two turkeys were foraging in the dust, not far away, and the black rooster that had appeared in Eddie's dream was out in the grass trying to catch grasshoppers.

"Hi, Grandpa," Eddie said.

"Morning, Eddie," her father said—when she came closer she saw that he had tears in his eyes.

"What's wrong, Dad?" she asked—she was not used to seeing her father in such an emotional state.

"Oh, I guess I was just thinking how much I'll miss these critters, when you and me and Eddie head out west," Sty said.

"We're going tonight, Dad," she said. She was hoping he wouldn't change his mind—it would be too big a disappointment for Eddie.

"But you could take some chickens, Grandpa," Eddie suggested. "I have Iggy and Eli—why don't you bring some chickens if they're your family?"

"Nope, these chickens need to stay here, where they can peck grasshoppers and bugs," Sty said, wiping his eyes with the same old cotton handkerchief he had used the day before. "There might not be enough grasshoppers for them, out in Las Vegas. I hear it's kind of deserty, out there."

"Well, we don't have grasshoppers but we do have many ants," Eddie reflected. "The chickens could peck the ants."

"Oh, that's okay, Eddie," Sty said. "I'll be so busy talking to you and meeting all your friends that I wouldn't have much time to devote to a chicken, even if I had one with me."

Harmony began to feel some qualms—it was obviously going to

432

be a big change for her father. What if he got to Las Vegas and missed his cows and his mule and his pigs too much? What if he was miserable without them? It was nice in Oklahoma. Birds were chirping, and the sun was shining on the dewy grass. Her father looked so in place there, with the prairie behind him and the deep sky overhead. After all, he had been born on the farm—he had lived his whole life in that very place. Maybe he would miss the breeze and the sunlight and the animals so much that he'd wither up and die. The thought of moving him sort of gave her qualms.

On the other hand, she hadn't come to Oklahoma planning to remove him; he himself had asked to go.

"What will you do with all your animals, Daddy?" she asked. The animals expected him to be there when the sun came up, only the very next time it would be coming up he wouldn't be, to feed and milk and do the chores.

"Dick is going to take them—Dick's reliable," Sty said. "He'll come over and do the chores for a few days, and then he'll move the stock over to his and Neddie's place."

"Daddy, I don't want this move to be a thing that makes you sad," Harmony said. "I worry that you won't be happy without your animals."

Her father picked up the pail of milk and carried it over to the pigpen—he poured it into a wooden trough and the pigs immediately began to slurp it up.

"Oh, I expect I'll miss them a little bit, but Dick will take fine care of these critters," Sty said. "I ain't really farming anymore—I'm just piddling. I'd rather spend the time I have left talking to Eddie. He's got a lot more to say than these critters and this poultry."

Sty suddenly picked Eddie up and sat him on the back of the brown mule. The mule stood by the water trough, occasionally dipping its nose in the water.

The old mule paid no attention to the little boy on its back, but Eddie looked very surprised to find himself on top of a mule. His eyes widened and he gripped the mule's mane with both hands.

"I hope he doesn't run away with me, Grandpa," Eddie said.

"He won't run away with you because he's too lazy to run," Sty said. "This here is a walking mule."

"Dad, do you really want to come?" Harmony asked. The thought that she was taking him away from the place where he had lived his whole life suddenly seemed a big responsibility.

"I'm coming and I'm coming happily," Sty said. "I've gone as far with your mother as I can go—that's what it amounts to. I'll miss the place and the critters but I won't miss the hostility."

"It's going to be a big change, Dad," Harmony said—she was not quite reassured.

"I expect so," Sty said. "But nobody really needs to be a dirt farmer all their life. I'm ready for something different."

"The plane's at eight-thirty tonight," Harmony told him. "Is that enough time?"

"Plenty of time," Sty said.

"What about telling Mom?" she asked.

"Well, we'll just see if it comes up," Sty said. "I may just leave her a note. She won't read it because she can't see, and she ain't interested anyway. It might take Ethel a week or two to notice that I ain't around, if she *ever* notices. We run on separate tracks most of the time anyway."

Harmony thought of all the times she had been left by men— even if it was a boring man who left, someone at the level of Jimmy Bangor, there was still no missing it when a man departed. Her mother wouldn't fail to notice, Harmony was sure of that.

"Okay, Dad," Harmony said. "I have to go talk to Dick about something. Do you want Eddie to stay with you?"

"Why, sure . . . leave Eddie," Sty said. "I want to walk him around the place and tell him a few things nobody but me remembers. I can show him the spring where his great-grandmother drew water, when she and Dad settled here, in the pioneer days. I can show him a skunk den and a badger den and where all the bones are of the livestock that have died on this place in the last fifty or sixty years. There's just a few things about this old place that it would be good for Eddie to have in his head."

"Well, I've milked already but I don't like the pigs," Eddie said, from his perch on the mule. "They look like evil animals to me. And that black rooster is an evil animal too—it pecked me in my dream."

"Yep, that rooster is a little on the mean side," Sty said, looking across the pastures and the fields.

434

"You go on, honey," he added. "Leave me and Eddie to our own devices. Maybe his grandmother will be in a mood to make us lunch, but if she ain't we can get by on cheese and crackers."

"Bye, Mom, Grandpa is going to show me all around the farm now," Eddie said. He had a tendency to be unsentimental when there was something he really wanted to do.

Sty helped Eddie off the mule—they walked off toward a line of trees a few hundred yards from the barn, where the old spring was.

Harmony drove up to the farmhouse, thinking she might go in and have breakfast with her mother. Ethel *was* her mother—when would she get another chance? At least it would allow her to put off telling Dick that Neddie wanted to divorce him and marry his brother.

When she opened the screen door and stepped onto the back porch, her mother was standing in the kitchen, an electric tooth-brush buzzing in her mouth. She was watching Sty and Eddie walk off toward the spring.

"Now why is he taking that boy off in that tall grass?" Ethel asked, taking the toothbrush out of her mouth for a second.

"Mom, he's just showing Eddie the spring," Harmony said. "It's where his mother got water when she was a pioneer."

"That grass is soaking wet and they'll be lucky not to step on a snake down there in those rocks by that spring," Ethel complained.

Then she fixed her eye on Harmony.

"I think it's a disgrace that you're staying in that motel when you could be staying with your parents," she said. "You must have some old man or something—you never were interested in anything except seeing some old man and letting him get in your pants."

"Bye, Mom, I just came in to say good morning," Harmony said.

"That boy of yours has hardly said two words to me the whole time he's been here," Ethel said. "He ought to love his grand-mother more than that. He won't even sit on my lap. I tried to bribe him with an all-day sucker but it didn't work. He just looked at me as if I was a fool, and I'm his own grandmother."

"Momma, suckers are bad for his teeth and sugar isn't too good for him, anyway," Harmony pointed out.

"Well, why won't he sit in my lap when I ask him to?" Ethel

435

asked. "A boy that age ought to want to sit in his grandmother's lap."

"He just met you yesterday, Mom," Harmony reminded her. Her mother's dark views of every aspect of life made her want to be somewhere else. Even telling Dick that Neddie was leaving might be more upbeat.

"You ought to be married, Harmony," Ethel said. "Both my other daughters are married and you ought to be married too."

"Pat isn't married, Pat's divorced," Harmony pointed out.

"If she ain't married right this minute it's a temporary thing, why bring it up?" Ethel asked.

"Billy isn't married," Harmony said—she was annoyed at being singled out for criticism again. It seemed to her that her mother had started singling her out as soon as she had begun to develop and had to get a little bra. She had had to wear a bra before Neddie had to, although Neddie was two years older. At one point her mother had even accused her of taking pills to make her breasts grow.

"Thank God Billy escaped," Ethel said. "Billy don't need to be married—no better judge of women than he is, it would just be a big mistake. He'd get some old gal who couldn't cook half as well as I can, and who wouldn't keep his clothes as clean as I can, either. It'd be someone who wouldn't even nag him about smoking too many cigarettes."

"Mom, he might get someone who would be sweet to him and who would make him feel loved enough that he wouldn't need to make obscene phone calls to his high school girlfriend," Harmony said. She wasn't in the mood to let her mother get away with statements that were completely ridiculous.

"If all you can think of to do is contradict your own mother, then you can just go on back to Titty Town," Ethel said. "You're a bad mother anyway and I still think there was something funny about that girl you brought down here from New York."

"Momma, there wasn't, she's a very nice young woman," Harmony said. She was already missing Laurie and wondering if she had got home safely. Laurie was a lot more rewarding person to be with than her mother, that was for sure.

"I can't see Sty and that boy anymore, they might have fallen into that old cistern," Ethel said. "There's an old cistern down there somewhere—it's full of snakes. If they've fallen into that cistern it would explain why I can't see them anymore."

Harmony shut the screen door and left. She remembered what her father had said about the difficulty of getting a last word with her mother. She felt sorry that she couldn't manage to love her mother as a daughter ought to, but the fact was she couldn't. Maybe it was a failing she had passed along to Pepper, who hadn't seemed to love *her* that much, either—if she had loved her very much, probably she would have wanted to come home at some point during the last six years of her life.

"There's snakes all over that hill, if one of them bites that boy we'll have to rush him to the hospital, it'll dirty up that oil in my car again," Ethel said, just as Harmony got in the pickup and drove away.

15.

The morning was still fresh, though—her mother hadn't been able to keep the sun from shining or the breeze from blowing. It was a pleasure just to drive through it. In the pasture, several cows were going about the business of being cows. Far off she saw three cowboys, loping along a fence line.

Harmony thought it would be a fun experiment to try and find her way to Neddie's house. If she didn't get it right the first time, she could stop and ask. She tried a couple of dirt roads that weren't the right dirt roads. She turned in at a couple of farmhouses that weren't the right farmhouses, either. But finally she *did* find the right farm—she knew it was right because of the name on the mailbox. The mailbox had several bullet holes in it—for some reason it seemed to be the practice to shoot at mailboxes, in that part of the country.

Harmony pulled around to the back of the house and parked beside a kind of miniature tractor, the kind people used to work in their gardens, if they had big gardens. In fact, there was a big garden right beside the house where Neddie and Dick lived. Even without knowing that much about botany Harmony could recognize corn and tomatoes and green beans and watermelons. There

438

was also yellow squash and several other vegetables that were sort of hidden by the foliage.

While she was inspecting the garden—killing time, really; stalling might be an even better word—a large brown dog came racing around the corner of the house. The dog stopped abruptly when it saw her. It didn't bark, or appear to be hostile. It just stood there looking at her, with its tongue hanging out.

Finally Harmony decided to go on in—why put it off? She went in the back door—very few people used their front doors, in Oklahoma; front doors just seemed to be there so people could run out them in case of fires.

The back porch wasn't very neat. It was piled with rakes and hoes and overshoes and buckets for bringing in vegetables from the garden—one bucket was still full of black-eyed peas that hadn't been snapped. There were some cucumbers and a few squash, on a brown table. But the main thing that was on the back porch was Dick himself; large as he was she didn't notice him at first because he was sitting in the shadows, in an old wicker chair. Dick was just sitting there quietly, with several magazines at his feet. When she got a little closer she saw that they were girly magazines; she recognized *Penthouse*. It seemed odd—why was her large brother-in-law sitting on his own porch in the early morning with copies of *Penthouse* on the floor at his feet? She wouldn't have thought a farmer like Dick would be the type to be reading *Penthouse* before he went to work.

More disconcerting than the girly magazines was another thing she didn't notice at first, in this case a shotgun, which Dick held across his lap. Harmony knew the hunting season didn't come in the summertime; there had to be another explanation for the shotgun—it wasn't hunting.

"Hi, Dick," she said. "I didn't see you at first."

"They won't neither," Dick said.

"Well, who won't?" she asked. It was a phony question; she had a pretty good idea who Dick meant.

"My brother and my wife," Dick said. "I expect they'll walk in here after a while—Rusty's probably getting his milking done now. He was always a late milker.

"I left my big tractor down in the west field," he went on. "Once they spot that I expect they'll think the coast is clear. Nine times out of ten when my tractor is in the field I'm down there getting ready to plow.

"On the other hand, I may not shoot them," he said. His large face was anguished, twisted by the need to make a decision.

"Oh, please don't shoot them, Dick," Harmony said. "It would be a horrible tragedy if you shot Rusty and Neddie."

"Why not?—they deserve it," Dick said. "Neddie didn't come home last night—first time in thirty years my wife didn't come home. Rusty didn't go home, neither. It just depends on which house they show up at, who shoots them. Melba's got a shotgun too."

"What if they just had a car breakdown?" Harmony suggested. She wanted to try to think of some explanation for Neddie and Rusty's absence other than the obvious one, although the only reason she was at Dick's house at that hour was to tell Dick that Neddie loved Rusty and vice versa.

"I might do better just to shoot myself," Dick said. "What do you think?"

He looked at Harmony in a trusting way.

"It'd save a shell," he pointed out. "There's two of them and just one of me."

"Dick, couldn't you just put the shotgun away and save both shells for hunting season?" Harmony asked. "Maybe you could just shoot some ducks or something."

Dick shook his head.

"I don't like duck, it's got that gamy taste," he said. "I'd rather shoot Rusty and Neddie."

"Why, Dick?" she asked—she thought a good strategy might be to keep him talking.

"Because they had sex together," Dick said. "Ruint my good name and Rusty's too—it's the same name."

"Dick, what if it was something they just couldn't help?" Harmony asked. She looked out the window and saw two cottontails nibbling the grass not far from the porch.

"Can't help it—why not?" Dick said. "I never had sex with no-body's wife but my own—ain't even had sex with her in six or seven years. Lost count. If I could help it, why couldn't they?"

"Maybe you never ran into the right wife," Harmony suggested.

Dick looked offended by this conjecture. "There wouldn't be no right wife," he said. "I don't go having sex with other men's wives, and even if I did I think I could stay clear of my own brother's wife."

"Dick, people are different," Harmony pointed out. "Not everybody is as strong as you are—look at me, for example."

Dick seemed not too interested in the notion that people were different, but he did look at her, in his trusting way, again.

"What's strong got to do with it?" he asked. "It ain't like lifting a tractor tire or nothing. You don't have to be strong not to have sex with your brother's wife."

"You do if you're in love with her," Harmony said. She thought it was an odd conversation—who was she to be acting like an authority on love? She had been in love with two or three married men, but fortunately never with one of her sisters' husbands. Now her brother-in-law was sitting right in front of her with a shotgun in his lap and a pile of girly magazines at his feet. The girly magazines were a saddening touch—more like a heartbreaking touch, really. Why did this big, nice man, who had been devoted to her sister for thirty years, have to be looking at *Penthouse* at six in the morning? It bespoke a sadness where sex was concerned that was a little too deep to think about. Harmony was afraid that if she let her mind dwell on it, it might incline her to the view that life was hopeless, just hopeless. If it was so hard for a good man like Dick to get a little sex, what did it mean?—after all, he was an appealing man, in his way—a kind of lumbering way.

"Is it that she won't sleep with you, Dick?" Harmony asked, remembering that he had said six or seven years had gone by without that particular thing happening. Dick and Neddie had been married a long time; maybe they had sort of worn it out— then she remembered the remark Neddie had made about wishing Dick would fall in love so maybe he would leave her alone. She tried to put herself in Neddie's place for a few minutes: What if she had a nice husband, a large man who was devoted to her, but, little by little, they stopped making love, he stopped wanting her, she got horny, then she got sad, and years passed; one day he came in and informed her that he was in love with her sister. Maybe by that point she was having to play with herself or something, to get even a little sex—maybe a vibrator or something. Once or twice during periods of no boyfriend she had actually tried a vibrator, but at some point in the process she had just given up, turned it off, left herself alone. If it had to be such a lonely experience then it really wasn't sex, who cared?

Then, after all that despair, her man came in and told her he was in love with her sister, what would she do? Get a shotgun?

But Harmony didn't get very far with her effort to empathize. The main obstacle was that she couldn't imagine one man who would care enough about her to stay around thirty years—thirty months was exceptional in her experience—quite exceptional, in fact; thirty days was closer to the average. The long-term thing was something she had no experience of and really couldn't imagine. Meanwhile Dick was sitting there with the gun in his lap and *Penthouse* at his feet. His big face was gathering as if he might be about to cry—even to yell, or something. Just seeing Dick look like that was frightening—Harmony was thinking that maybe running out the back door wouldn't be such a bad idea. Before she could run, though, Dick suddenly leapt to his feet and fired both barrels of the shotgun through the window and the screen. Evidently he was aiming at the cottontails, because both cottontails sort of disappeared; so did the window and most of the screen. The sound was so loud that Harmony flinched; she really felt like running, but she hadn't delivered the message she had promised to deliver—if she didn't deliver it now, she would be breaking a promise to her sister. She thought she ought to try and keep her promise to her sister while they were all still alive.

Scared as she was, she wasn't as scared as she was sad for Dick, her brother-in-law. Why was it that three decades of loyalty had earned him only defeat and despair?

"I can't kill Neddie and Rusty now, them was the last two shells —I'm relieved," Dick said.

"Dick, they want to get married," Harmony said. "Neddie just told me yesterday. She wants a divorce so she can marry Rusty."

Dick looked at her, in shock.

"They want to get married?" he said. "What about the wife Rusty's already got?"

"I don't know, I haven't met her," Harmony said. "I guess Rusty's hoping she'll give him a divorce if you'll give Neddie one."

Dick carefully propped the empty shotgun against the wall; Harmony could smell the gunpowder and see, out of the corner of her eye, the remains of the dead bunnies.

"Well," Dick said, "that's another relief. If they want to marry and live proper, I got no objections. I was afraid they were just going to sleep around until there was nothing left of our good name.

"I wonder if they've been wanting to marry this whole time?" he asked. "That would explain a lot. It's nearly twenty years that I've been worrying about this. If they've been wanting to marry all this time then it's a shame they didn't tell me. They wasted about half their lives, not to mention half of mine."

"I don't know, Dick," Harmony said. "I don't know how long they've been wanting to marry."

Dick stooped and picked up his dozer cap—it was lying near the girly magazines. He put the cap on and took it off and put it on again, evidently perplexed. He looked at Harmony in a way that suggested deep perplexity.

"Well, I'm older than Rusty but I ain't dead yet," Dick said. "Neddie can't understand that I have to have somebody female and I have to find her quick—I'm eleven years older than Neddie. I gotta find a gal or I'll die. People think you need it most when you're young, but that ain't how it is."

"It's not?" Harmony asked—she didn't know where the conversation was leading.

Dick shook his large head. "Course you need it, young or old," he said. "But old means higher stakes."

He looked out the window he had just blasted away.

"When you're young it's fun or frustration," Dick said. "When you're older it's life or death."

"Oh, Dick, you won't really die," Harmony said.

"Yes, I will," Dick said, with a flash of anger in his eyes. "It ain't hard to die when you feel you've already stopped living. You know what I mean? I could catch a sniffle and die right off, the way I feel today."

In this case Harmony did know what he meant, sort of. It was the way she had been feeling since Pepper's death. It would be easy to die because she had already stopped living—Eddie was the only living factor she had to deal with, really.

"Dick, you could get a girlfriend," Harmony said. "Neddie's not the only woman in the world."

"She's the only one for me," Dick said, but then he had a thought that caused him to blush.

"At least she's the only one who's the right age," he added, speaking in a low tone.

Then, to her surprise, Dick stepped toward her. For a moment she had the fear that he might be about to embrace her. But he stopped a foot away, with a desperate look on his face. He had on old-fashioned blue overalls, with snaps at the shoulders, and as she stood there, amazed, he unsnapped the shoulder snaps and let the heavy overalls fall around his ankles. His long work shirt hung down to the middle of his thighs. For a moment Dick just stood there, large and sad, looking silly—how could he look anything but silly, with his pants around his ankles? She didn't know what to think, really, but so far she didn't feel offended. Why be offended because her own nice brother-in-law was so overcome by need that he couldn't help himself?

"Dick, I'm only two years younger than Neddie," Harmony said —she was thinking he might have *her* in mind when he mentioned the part about no one the right age.

But that wasn't what Dick was talking about, it wasn't that personal; it was just his great need that caused him to drop his overalls.

"Please," Dick said. "Please." He got no further—it wasn't even a clear request, but that he had even said that much caused him to drop his head in embarrassment.

What am I supposed to do? Harmony thought—sleep with my own brother-in-law on my own sister's back porch? Why did I even come here?

"Please," Dick said, again. He sounded like a person who was dying. He had just finished saying how easy it would be to die, in fact.

Oh well, wait till Gary hears about this one, Harmony thought. She reached under Dick's long shirttail and touched him—a touch was all it took, too. He immediately came and came and came, into the back of his shirttail.

"Boy," Dick said, before he had even really stopped coming. "You don't know how obliged I am to you, hon. The reason I don't

444

wear no underwear is because of this fungus. It flat eats me up, in the summertime."

"Dick, couldn't you get a lotion?" Harmony asked. She had reached under the long shirttail to touch him and of course hadn't seen any fungus—or anything else improper, although something at least on the borderline of improper had taken place.

"Takes longer than that to milk a cow, don't it?" Dick said, in a more normal voice—he immediately began to pull his overalls up, without even washing the semen off his legs.

"Dick, I've never milked, how would I know?" Harmony said. She went in the kitchen to wash her hands, a little embarrassed. Of course Dick had really needed help, but it wasn't the kind of help she wanted to get in the habit of providing.

"She's twenty-two," Dick said. He had followed Harmony into the kitchen and stood looking at her like a giant dog who was grateful for a favor.

"Twenty-two?" Harmony said, puzzled. She was busy washing his semen off her hands.

"Sally," Dick said, as if Harmony would know exactly who he was talking about. No one in her family could quite grasp that she hadn't lived in Tarwater for many years and didn't know all the names.

"Sally, down at the feedstore," Dick said. "She's the bookkeeper. I got where I hang out there some, when I ain't plowing.

"Sally's a redhead," he added.

"Does she like you, Dick?" Harmony asked, trying to imagine this large man with a twenty-two-year-old.

"I think so," Dick said, tentatively. "But I ain't courted in a spell. Maybe I'm just fooling myself."

Harmony was feeling a little pressured—her brother-in-law was so distraught and so needy for a little sex that she had sort of accidentally given him a hand job, and now he was seeking her approval to date a twenty-two-year-old. She was beginning to feel angry at her sister; if she didn't want the man why hadn't she just divorced him, years ago? It was a little hard to imagine Dick with a young woman—but then she remembered that Jimmy Bangor had lost his job as head of security at Caesar's for sleeping with a thirteen-year-old. Why shouldn't Dick sleep with a twenty-two-year-old?—at least it wouldn't be statutory rape. It might even lead

445

to a little happiness, down the road somewhere. It seemed like even a little happiness was hard to come by in Tarwater—Dick would be a fool to pass it up.

"Only thing is, she's younger than my daughter," Dick said. "What's Donna going to say?

"I can't do anything about it today, though," he said. "I've got that west field to plow, and then I'll have to fix the window I shot out—I don't know what came over me."

Now that he had enjoyed a little relief, the thought of the damage he had done made Dick feel shy. He managed one more grateful look before pulling his cap firmly on his head—then he went out the door and walked off toward his tractor.

Harmony was remembering that Rusty had said Dick didn't need a woman—it just showed that people managed to believe what they needed to believe when it came to other people.

Once she was sure Dick had gone back to his plowing she went straight to the phone and called Gary.

"Hi, Gary," she said; fortunately he answered on the first ring, which probably meant he hadn't been asleep. If he was asleep it was usually about the fortieth ring before he picked up; he would usually be bitchy for a while, on the forty-ring calls.

"Hi," Gary said—just from that one syllable Harmony knew that he had probably been taking uppers. She had known Gary for so long that even one syllable was enough to give her a clue as to what his drug of the moment might be.

"Gary, I'm coming tonight, and my Dad is coming with me," she said hurriedly. Sometimes when Gary was on uppers he would just hang up if he felt he wasn't going to get much out of the conversation.

"Okay, I'll meet you, I'm dying to see you, what's the flight number?" Gary said. He was definitely in his efficient mode.

"Gary, I don't even have the tickets yet, how would I know the flight number?" Harmony said. "Just remember it's American from Dallas and it comes in about midnight."

"Oh good, I can come get you on my break," Gary said. "I have a wonderful car now, it's a purple Cadillac."

"Gary, how did you get a purple Cadillac?" she asked. Just hearing that he had that car gave her a little lift. It made her feel that she was almost home. Gary in a purple Cadillac was the sort of thing that could only happen in Las Vegas.

"Sweetie, that's my business," Gary said. "I'll only say that it was a wild exchange.

"Actually, not that wild," he added, a moment later. "I just happened to have a good night at the craps tables, and a dope addict I know needed money and sold the Cadillac to me for nine hundred dollars—talk about timing, I had only won the money about seven minutes before I ran into my friend the dope addict. Eddie's gonna love this car. The stereo in it's worth more than I paid for the whole thing. So what's happening to you?"

"Neddie's getting divorced and she's going to marry Rusty, that's Dick's brother," Harmony said.

"Good for her," Gary said. "People need to go with their feelings —I guess Neddie has feelings. It's hard to tell."

"She has feelings for Rusty, but she stopped having them for Dick, that's why I just gave him a hand job on the back porch," Harmony said.

"Well, that's certainly being a good sister-in-law," Gary remarked. "If I had a brother-in-law in dire straits I certainly hope I'd be kind enough to give him a hand job."

"Dick was in dire straits," Harmony said. "I barely touched him."

Just as she said it she had the thought that there might still be come on the floor of the back porch. The reason the thought came to her just at that moment was that she saw Rusty's dirty white pickup coming up the lane. If Rusty was coming, Neddie might be with him. What if she walked in and saw a puddle of semen on her own back porch?

"Gary, I can't talk anymore, Neddie's coming," she said. "I have to go clean up the back porch—there might be a mess."

Gary got a little annoyed. He really did hate having his phone conversations nipped in the bud.

"Harmony, why call me if you don't have more than eight seconds to talk?" he asked.

"Gary, I'll be home tonight," Harmony said. She hung up and grabbed a washrag. Sure enough, there was a puddle where the little sex act happened; she got it wiped up just in time, too. Neddie and Rusty got out of the pickup and stood looking at the two dead rabbits in the yard. Then they came around to the window that had been blown away. They peeped through the empty window frame and saw Harmony standing there, with the dishrag in her hand.

"What kind of weirdness is going on here?" Neddie asked. "Couldn't you have come outside, if you wanted to hunt rabbits?"

"Hunt 'em, obliterate them," Rusty said.

"It was Dick," Harmony said.

"Oh," Neddie said. She looked again at the window and the bunnies.

"Was he waiting for *us*?" she asked.

"Yep," Harmony said. She didn't really want to say any more than she had to.

"Oh," Neddie said. "I guess that means you told him."

"Yep," Harmony said, again—she had settled on the word as being the most useful she could think of, for the moment.

"So, was he upset?" Neddie asked.

"Neddie, he blew the window out," Rusty said. "I've known Dick all my life and he's never done nothing like this before. It's the most violent thing he's done since we had that aggravating black mule. I *reckon* he's upset."

"Well, I hope so," Neddie said. "I would have liked to see it. I've been waiting thirty years to see Dick show some emotion—maybe if he'd managed it sooner I wouldn't be running off with you."

"Neddie, Dick just doesn't know how to show it," Harmony said. "Lots of men don't know how to show it."

"Well, let him learn with somebody else, if he intends to learn," Neddie said. "I don't see why I should have to wait thirty years for a man to blow out a window."

Rusty cocked an eye.

"Better be glad it was just a window," he said.

Harmony was remembering how sad Dick looked; she was thinking of all the years he had been sad—about his wife, about sex, about life. It angered her that her sister had just sort of let it go on. Dick was right—she *had* wasted half his life, and half her own, and half Rusty's.

"Where'd he go?" Rusty asked. "He might buy some more shells for the shotgun and come back and blast us."

"That's a thought," Neddie said. "Maybe it wouldn't be a bad idea to gather up all the guns and take them to Dad's house for a while."

"Dick's plowing—he won't bother you," Harmony said. "It was a relief to him that you plan to marry."

"Of course we plan to marry," Neddie said. "I wonder what old Dick will do?"

"I hope he gets a young girlfriend and fucks his brains out, for a while," Harmony said; she was still angry at Neddie for not having cut Dick loose.

Both of them looked at her as if she'd gone crazy, but Harmony didn't care. After all, Dick was human too.

"I wonder if he will," Neddie said. She sighed.

"He's sure been spending a lot of time at the feedstore lately," Rusty observed.

"Sally?" Neddie asked.

"Sally," Rusty agreed.

16.

Out of here, out of here, Harmony was thinking. Neddie got a broom and she and Rusty began to clean up the remains of the broken window. Rusty found a little spatula and removed the rest of the glass from the window frame. But Neddie did look happier as she worked; she sort of had color in her cheeks, a little bloom; she was a good deal more relaxed in the way she moved. It must be nice to be doing a few little chores with the man she loved, rather than with the man she was finished with. It was unfortunate that Dick had to be sad in order for Neddie to be happy with his brother. Still, it was better that at least one of them was happy— at least that was Harmony's take on it.

While they cleaned up the broken glass Harmony kept rinsing out the washrag; she was still nervous about what had happened on the porch. While she was rinsing the phone rang. Neddie and Rusty were in the yard, cleaning up broken glass. Since they were out of earshot she answered the phone.

"Well, they finally lowered the boom, come get me out," Pat said. "I need a lawyer too, and not one of these bozos around here. I've had romances with both of the lawyers in Tarwater, and they're too resentful that we broke up. I doubt they'd do a good job even if they had the brains."

"Pat, you mean you're in jail?" Harmony asked. "If you are, how's Billy?"

"Snoring, he ain't up yet, he don't even know his sister's joined him in disgrace," Pat said.

"Then how's Peewee?" Harmony asked. She was wondering how Neddie would take the latest news. She happened to glance out the window, as she wondered, and saw Neddie and Rusty kiss. Watching, Harmony felt a little nostalgic. It had been a while since a nice man had turned to her and just spontaneously given her a kiss. Neddie's hair was blowing in the prairie breeze she loved so much. She looked girlish, almost—only a few days before, she looked like an old woman. Love could come and take away your years; maybe it could come and take away grief; shave it away; whittle it away. Neddie was getting some happiness, but Pepper was dead—the thought was like a burn, like a torn blister. She had the impulse to phone Laurie and see if she made it home safely.

"Harmony, are you listening? I'm in *jail*," Pat said. "Get Neddie or somebody to bail me out of here."

"Neddie and Rusty are kissing," Harmony informed her—the kiss was still going on. Harmony couldn't quite keep her eyes off the new lovers, although she knew it was wrong to peek.

"They're kissing?" Pat said. "In broad daylight?"

"Yep," Harmony said. "They're getting married. I told Dick this morning. Dick likes a girl named Sally, at the feedstore."

"Sally, that little slut," Pat said. "I guess he does like her. So do a lot of other men. Sally's a peanut brain. She's about eighty percent tits."

"She could still be sweet," Harmony said. She liked the idea of Dick having a nice romance. The fact that Sally had big tits shouldn't be held against her.

"Harmony, I know you have big tits too, but try to keep your mind on the point," Pat said. "The point is I want out of jail.

"Peewee gives me the creeps," she added.

Rusty and Neddie had broken their kiss and were walking back toward the house, their arms around one another.

"Pat, did they get you for the embezzling?" Harmony asked.

"That, and the fact that I got stopped with a few pills in my car," Pat said. "Seventeen thousand pills, to be exact."

"Seventeen thousand pills?" Harmony said. "Even Gary couldn't take that many pills."

"Well, I just happened to make a real good score," Pat said. "All I meant to do was sell them to some oilman, so I could replace the money I took from the bank. It was just my luck to have a taillight broken out. The damn patrolman only pulled me over because he was bored—it was Sammy Jackson, he's liked me since we were in grade school together. I don't know why he looked in the trunk— I guess he noticed I was a little jumpy. Seventeen thousand pills is hard to miss."

"Pat, I'll tell Neddie, we'll be right down," Harmony said; actually, she had the plane tickets on her mind.

"Okay, but don't let any grass grow, I feel like a caged animal down here in this cell," Pat said.

"Okay, we'll come," Harmony said, wishing it was time to go to the airport. Much as she loved her sisters and brother, their needs were not her needs. It saddened her that she could not get to know their children—in the young ones of the family there lay the best hope.

For herself, she wanted to go. She had to recover her spirit, to try and be herself again, and she knew she couldn't recover it in Oklahoma. The best place to try might be the casinos. Beneath their lights she had spent the happiest years of her life. She thought maybe as soon as she got home she would call Myrtle. Maybe if the other half of the duplex wasn't rented she and Eddie and her father could live in it for a while. They could get a goat or two—her father might like that—or maybe a few peacocks, or even some chickens.

"I wish Dick was interested in Melba instead of Sally," Rusty said. "Then they could have my farm and me and Ned could keep this one. Plus it would solve what to do about Melba."

"Melba don't want Dick and little Sally don't either, so stop dreaming," Neddie said.

"Neddie, Pat's in jail," Harmony said.

"Uh-oh," Neddie said. "So the bank finally figured it out."

"Nope," Harmony said. More and more she was getting to like the short responses.

452

Rusty and Neddie just looked at her.

"Pills," Harmony said. "She had seventeen thousand pills in the trunk of her car and some patrolman stopped her because her taillight was broken."

"Wow," Rusty said. "Seventeen thousand pills."

"She was planning to sell them," Harmony said. "We have to go down and get her out of jail."

"Why can't she just stay in?" Neddie asked. "She'd be good company for Billy."

"Neddie, we can't leave her in jail, even if she has committed a few crimes."

"Pat's got the temperament of a fugitive," Neddie remarked. "If we bail her out she'll just run off."

"That's what *I* think," Rusty said. "Me and you need to save our money for the divorce lawyers. Speaking of which, I need to get over to my place and try to catch Melba before she leaves for work."

"Okay, I'll go get Pat out," Harmony said. She felt sure she had probably been heartless too, during periods when she was in love. Neddie and Rusty should get to enjoy their feelings for a while, without having to worry about Pat's problems.

She left Neddie's with every intention of going straight to the jail and getting Pat out; but when she came to the Tarwater turnoff she didn't take it. Somehow her arms just wouldn't make the wheel turn. She didn't want to go into Tarwater again—so her arms informed her. Despite a desire to be helpful she couldn't make the pickup take her to the jail.

When she drove up the lane toward her parents' house she saw Eddie sitting on the stump by the pond, with her father. There was a fishing pole stuck in the ground nearby. Harmony crawled through the fence again, and picked her way through the grass burrs to where they sat. Eddie was listening raptly, so entranced by what his grandfather was telling him that he scarcely gave his mother a glance. Her father noticed her picking grass burrs out of her socks and smiled a sympathetic smile.

"Some years we get grass and other years we just get grass burrs," he said. "This year it's mostly grass burrs."

"Momma, Grandpa was telling me about an Indian chief who painted himself red when he wanted to fight," Eddie said. "His name was Santana. He was very large and he killed six buffalo right over there on that hill. Grandpa showed me the place and while I was walking around I found an arrowhead."

He dug in his pocket and produced the arrowhead, which was made of dark flint.

"I'm going to keep it forever and forever, to remember the farm by," Eddie said. "I'll show it to my friends though. I think it belonged to Santana and I think it was what he killed the buffalo with.

"It's my greatest treasure," he added, "and my stuffed animals are my other treasures. And Iggy and Eli are treasures, but they're alive."

"Dad, do you still want to go?" Harmony asked—she was nervous on that subject.

"You bet—I could leave now, if I had my shirts packed," Sty said. "Me and Eddie had a pretty good look around the old place. We're going to come back once in a while, just the two of us, so I can fill him in on some stories I might have forgotten this morning."

"Would you keep my arrowhead, Grandpa?" Eddie said, handing it to him. "I don't want to lose it. It's very important because it belonged to an Indian long ago."

When they went in the house her mother was sitting at the kitchen table, painting her fingernails and watching a soap.

"People just let me sit here all day, alone, never give me a thought—I could have drunk lye and be dying and no one would come to check on me," Ethel said.

"Mother, why would you drink lye?" Harmony asked.

"Anybody can make a mistake and drink lye," Ethel said. "I sit here from morning till night and don't see a soul. I might drink lye just to have something to do."

"Momma, can't you be glad about anything, ever?" Harmony asked, curious.

"Sure, my hair and my figure," Ethel said. "I still get compliments on my hair and my figure.

"I called Pat and I called Neddie and I never got either of them," Ethel went on. "I don't see why those girls can't stay home in their own houses. They both have real nice homes—better than this old mess of a place."

454

Harmony decided not to comment—why tell her mother the truth about Pat and Neddie? But, the very next second, some demon prompted her to do just that.

"Mother, Pat's in jail for selling drugs and Neddie's going to divorce Dick and marry his brother," she said, just as her mother was applying a little more polish to the nails of her left hand. Ethel lifted an eyebrow but didn't stop painting her nails.

"Well, Rusty's a loser, Neddie will soon regret that move," Ethel said. "Dick ought to take a gun and shoot Rusty, the lazy skunk."

"Momma, did you hear me say Pat's in jail for selling dope?" Harmony asked.

"I guess she was set up," Ethel said. "She works in a bank and steals all the money she needs, why would she sell dope?"

"Mom, I'm taking Dad to Las Vegas—he wants to live with Eddie and me, for a while," Harmony said.

"Good riddance," her mother said. "I knew he'd run off, one of these days. He ain't been doing much under the quilts for the last few years. I expect he'll find himself some floozy, as soon as he hits the ground. At least he won't be where he can steal my social security checks out of the mailbox. I might just move Billy into that spare bedroom, once Sty's gone. Billy had no business leaving home in the first place."

"Mom, the family's gone to pieces, don't you care?" Harmony asked. But Ethel thought she meant the family on the soap she was watching. The soap interested her more than the fact that her husband was leaving, or that her daughter was in jail.

"I know, but that's because they're all atheists," Ethel said. "When you slight the Lord you pay for it."

Harmony left the kitchen and went upstairs. With the house almost empty the stairs didn't seem so claustrophobic. Her old room was claustrophobic, though. It wasn't much bigger than a closet. On the little dresser there were pictures of Pepper, sitting with pictures of all the other grandchildren. On the wall there was a picture of herself, the year she had been made homecoming queen, with Huggie Rawlins, the captain of the football team that year. He had escorted her to the fifty-yard line and kissed her—it was about then, Harmony remembered, that things began to go wrong for her at home. Neither of her sisters ever forgave her for being made homecoming queen. It was an honor they both dreamed of. About six months after the homecoming game she left Tarwater, more or less for good. Nobody liked it that she had been made homecoming queen but didn't even feel obliged to stick around and live her whole life in the town, as a result.

Harmony wandered into her parents' room, briefly—there was another picture of Pepper, again with all the grandkids. Pepper had had braces at the time.

It was in the dentist's office, about a year later, while they were having an appointment to get the braces removed, that Harmony learned that Pepper wasn't a virgin anymore. Pepper was so happy to be getting the braces off—in her view they marred her perfect appearance—that she blurted out the fact that she had been having sex for nearly six months with a lifeguard at the Trop.

But there was Pepper's picture, on her parents' old brown dresser—there at least she was a grandchild among grandchildren, perfect in the eyes of her grandparents.

"Oh, Pepper," Harmony said, aloud. The burn of grief came again—she rushed right out of the room. She couldn't bear memories of her daughter—couldn't bear them.

To her mother's astonishment she rushed into the kitchen and grabbed the telephone—by good luck she even remembered Laurie's number. Fortunately Laurie answered right away.

"Laurie, when you were upstairs at my parents' did you see the picture of Pepper in braces?" she asked.

"Yes, didn't it break your heart?" Laurie said.

"What will we do, Laurie? I can't bear any more memories," Harmony said.

"I don't know, sweetie," Laurie said.

"Isn't there a part of your brain they can cut away, so you have no memory?" Harmony asked. "I want mine cut away. I don't want to remember anymore—it's too hard. Why did I have all those boyfriends? Why couldn't I have just been a mom?"

"Harmony, you need to ease up on yourself," Laurie said. "We all have plenty we can blame ourselves for. But you need to ease up on yourself, for Eddie's sake."

Harmony couldn't remember the rest of the conversation, all she knew was that Laurie said she wished she hadn't left. Her father came in and went upstairs to pack. Eddie ran up the stairs behind him. He was sticking close to his grandfather, now that he'd found him.

Her mother still sat at the kitchen table, waiting for the polish on her fingernails to dry.

"Yankees have more diseases than we do, I expect that was the cause of the tragedy," Ethel said, when Harmony hung up.

17.

"**W**ell, it's so long to the prairie—I expect I'll miss it," Sty said, when the plane took off.

"But it's not so long to *me*, Grandpa," Eddie reminded him. He had Iggy in a little carrying case, under the seat. Eddie was holding his grandfather's hand, and his mother's hand as well, even though he was a little put out with his mother for her lack of regard for proper goodbyes—they had spent the whole day at her parents' house and hadn't really said goodbye to anyone.

"It will make my cousins very sad, I know it," Eddie told her.

"I'm sorry, I'm sorry, I can't—we'll make phone calls once we get to Las Vegas," Harmony said. Even though Eddie was quite annoyed, she really couldn't face seeing anybody. She didn't get Pat out of jail, or call Neddie, or anything. The only family member they saw on the way to the airport was Dick. They passed him as the sun was setting. He was still in his field plowing, on his tractor, with a big cloud of dust hanging in the rear. He looked so lonely, on his tractor, that Harmony felt a pang. What if Sally, twenty-two years old, just wasn't interested? What would that leave Dick, except the girly magazines?

"I wonder if Dick will remarry?" she asked her father.

458

"Not unless some woman's enterprising enough to go drag him off that tractor," Sty said.

"I hope some woman does," Harmony said—she was remembering his look of gratitude when she made him come.

"At least we said goodbye to Grandma," Eddie said—he was a little bit obsessed with the need for proper goodbyes. "At least she didn't get to turn Eli loose."

Actually, Ethel had thought they were going frog hunting when they left. She was watching *Jeopardy*, and hardly gave them a glance.

"Don't bring none of them old smelly frogs in this house," she said. "People catch TB from handling frogs."

"Ethel, we're not going frog hunting, we're going to Las Vegas," Sty said. "I may be back someday, but, on the other hand, I may not."

"It's not just TB you get, it's polio too, and you get it from handling old smelly frogs or fish heads or anything that lives underwater," Ethel insisted. It was her last comment, as they went out the door.

"She's cracked, always was," Sty said. He meant to leave the pickup at the airport, for one of the grandkids to pick up.

"I spent my life with a crazy woman, that's what it boils down to," Sty said, as they were driving down the lane, past the ponds and the stump and the fields he had tended all his life.

"But *I'm* not cracked, and my mother isn't and Iggy isn't and Gary isn't," Eddie insisted, as they turned onto the highway.

"The northern part of Texas ain't a lot different from Oklahoma," Sty said, as the plane flew westward, over the grasslands. He looked out the window, keenly interested in the dark land below—here and there, on the plains, were sprinkles of lights. Sty mused about what towns the lights might be.

"I like being up in the sky, Grandpa," Eddie said. "We might fly by a goose."

"Or a flying badger," Sty said.

"No, we will *not* fly by a flying badger," Eddie said, with the conviction of one who had spent many hours glued to the Discovery Channel.

Harmony had mixed feelings—really mixed. She was wishing the plane could just fly on forever—just fly on and never land, so she could always be somewhere in the sky, with her father and her son. She didn't want to come down, into the world of memory, not to mention the world of apartment hunting, job interviews, bank accounts with eight dollars in them, men with their greed and their needs. Once she had had the energy to meet all those demands; now she didn't know where she would find the energy to meet any of them.

But she knew she had to find it somehow; an old man and a boy had put their trust in her. She had to let the memories go, and the regrets as well; she had to fold them away, as she had folded away her hopes for a man who would love her and care for her. Such a man wasn't going to come; but the old man and the young boy were there, she had to quit being selfish, she had to be good; even if she didn't think she *could* be good, she had to try.

Then she dozed a little. When she woke the plane was banking over Las Vegas. Eddie and her father were looking out the window at the million lights. They were looking with almost identical expressions—keen expressions. She realized at that moment that they had the same eyes.

"Grandpa, look!" Eddie said, as the plane banked over the Strip. Harmony could make out Caesar's, and also the Stardust.

"It's Las Vegas, Grandpa—that's the Strip!" Eddie said. "It's where I'm growing up. It's my home!"

"Oh, golly, that's a bunch of lights, this town must run up a big electricity bill," Sty said, smiling. He could tell that Eddie was very excited, and he seemed excited too.

"It's a bunch of lights because it's the Strip," Eddie informed him. "It's a very important place—it's where millions come."

Harmony couldn't get over how much Eddie looked like her father—she had been too sad to notice it sooner. It made something lift a little, in her, seeing how excited they both were to be coming down over the lights of the Strip. Seeing how alike they looked gave her a little sense of promise.

"You okay, hon?" her father asked. "You had a pretty good nap."

"I'm okay, Dad," Harmony said—she didn't want him to worry. Going away hadn't worked. Maybe coming back would work a little better. She would just have to soldier on, if that was the phrase—she had never been a soldier, and if there was a war she

460

had lost it. But seeing the lights affected her too—she had always loved them. Eddie was right—those lights lit up a place where millions came. She and her son and her father would be part of the millions soon.

"I just hope Gary's there—otherwise we don't have a ride," she said. "He's got a purple Cadillac, you're going to love it, Eddie."

"A purple Cadillac," Eddie said.

"You have to be a little tolerant of his driving, Dad," Harmony said—she didn't want her father to get too much of a shock on his first night in town.

"Tell Grandpa how Gary drives, Eddie," she said—let him hear it from his grandson.

"Pedal to the metal," Eddie said, grinning his irresistible grin.

"Pedal to the metal—oh boy, here we go," her father said.